Wehmer

THE GUARDIANS *of* GA'HOOLE

Northern Kingdoms

Glauxian Brother's
Retreat

Bitter
Sea

Kiel Bay

Stormfast Island

Bay of Fangs

Everwinter Sea

Ice Talons

Ice
Narrows

Dark Fowl Island

Southern
Kingdoms

GUARDIANS
of GA'HOOLE

Books 1-3

BY KATHRYN LASKY

SCHOLASTIC INC.

New York Toronto London Auckland
Sydney Mexico City New Delhi Hong Kong

Book 1 dedication:

To Ann Reit, Wise Owl, Great Flight Instructor

— K. L.

Book 2 dedication:

To Max, who imagines universes

— K. L.

Guardians of Ga'hoole #1: The Capture
ISBN 978-0-439-40557-7
Text copyright © 2003 by Kathryn Lasky
Illustrations © 2003 by Scholastic Inc.

Guardians of Ga'hoole #2: The Journey
ISBN 978-0-439-40558-4
Text copyright © 2003 by Kathryn Lasky
Illustrations © 2003 by Scholastic Inc.

Guardians of Ga'hoole #3: The Rescue
ISBN 978-0-439-40559-1
Text copyright © 2004 by Kathryn Lasky
Illustrations © 2004 by Scholastic Inc.

Guardians of Ga'hoole #1: The Capture was originally published in paperback by Scholastic Inc. in 2003.
Guardians of Ga'hoole #2: The Journey was originally published in paperback by Scholastic Inc. in 2003.
Guardians of Ga'hoole #3: The Rescue was originally published in paperback by Scholastic Inc. in 2004.

ISBN 978-0-545-26352-8

12 11 10 9 8 7 6 5 4 3 2 1   10 11 12 13 14 15/0

Printed in the U.S.A.   23

First compilation printing, June 2010

GUARDIANS
of GA'HOOLE

BOOK ONE

The Capture

. . . and then the forest of the Kingdom of Tyto seemed to grow smaller and smaller and dimmer and dimmer in the night . . .

Contents

Prologue

The world spiraled, the needles of the old fir tree blurred against the night sky and then there was a sickening sensation as the forest floor raced toward him. Soren madly tried to beat his stubby little wings. Useless! He thought, I am dead. A dead owlet. Three weeks out of the shell and my life ends!

Suddenly, something began to soften his fall — a pocket of breeze? A cushion of wind? A downy fluff of air lacing through his unsightly patches of fuzz? What was it? Time slowed. His short life flowed by him — every second of it from his very first memory. . . .

CHAPTER ONE

A Nest Remembered

Noctus, can you spare a bit more down, darling? I think our third little one is about to arrive. That egg is beginning to crack."

"Not again!" sighed Kludd.

"What do you mean, Kludd, not again? Don't you want another little brother?" his father said. There was an edge to his voice.

"Or sister?" His mother sighed the low soft whistle Barn Owls sometimes used.

"I'd like a sister," Soren peeped up.

"You just hatched out two weeks ago." Kludd turned to Soren, his younger brother. "What do you know about sisters?"

Maybe, Soren thought to himself, *they would be better than brothers.* Kludd seemed to have resented him since the moment he had first hatched.

"You really wouldn't want them arriving just when you're about to begin branching," Kludd said dully. Branch-

1

ing was the first step, literally, toward flight. The young owlets would begin by hopping from branch to branch and flapping their wings.

"Now, now, Kludd!" his father admonished. "Don't be impatient. There'll be time for branching. Remember, you won't have your flight feathers for at least another month or more."

Soren was just about to ask what a month was when he heard a *crack*. The owl family all seemed to freeze. To any other forest creature the sound would have been imperceptible. But Barn Owls were blessed with extraordinary hearing.

"It's coming!" Soren's mother gasped. "I'm so excited." She sighed again and looked rapturously at the pure white egg as it rocked back and forth. A tiny hole appeared and from it protruded a small spur.

"Its egg tooth, by Glaux!" Soren's father exclaimed.

"Mine was bigger wasn't it, Da?" Kludd shoved Soren aside for a better look, but Soren crept back up under his father's wing.

"Oh, I don't know, son. But isn't it a pretty, glistening little point. Always gives me a thrill. Such a tiny little thing pecking its way into the big wide world. Ah! Bless my gizzard, the wonder of it all."

It did indeed seem a wonder. Soren stared at the hole

that now began to split into two or three cracks. The egg shuddered slightly and the cracks grew longer and wider. He had done this himself just two weeks ago. This *was* exciting.

"What happened to my egg tooth, Mum?"

"It dropped off, stupid," Kludd said.

"Oh," Soren said quietly. His parents were so absorbed in the hatching that they didn't reprimand Kludd for his rudeness.

"Where's Mrs. P.? Mrs. P.?" his mother said urgently.

"Right here, ma'am." Mrs. Plithiver, the old blind snake who had been with the owl family for years and years, slithered into the hollow. Blind snakes, born without eyes, served as nest-maids and were kept by many owls to make sure the nests were clean and free of maggots and various insects that found their way into the hollows.

"Mrs. P., no maggots or vermin in that corner where Noctus put in fresh down."

"'Course not, ma'am. Now, how many broods of owlets have I been through with you?"

"Oh, sorry, Mrs. P. How could I have ever doubted you? I'm always nervous at the hatching. Each one is just like the first time. I never get used to it."

"Don't you apologize, ma'am. You think any other birds would care two whits if their nest was clean? The stories

3

I've heard about seagulls! Oh, my goodness! Well, I won't even go into it."

Blind snakes prided themselves on working for owls, whom they considered the noblest of birds. Meticulous, the blind snakes had great disdain for other birds that they felt were less clean due to their unfortunate digestive processes that caused them to eliminate only sloppy wet droppings instead of nice neat bundles — the pellets that owls yarped, or spit up. Although owls did digest the soft parts of their food in a manner similar to other birds, and indeed passed it in a liquid form, for some reason they were never associated with these lesser digestive processes. All the fur and bones and tiny teeth of their prey, like mice, that could not be digested in the ordinary way were pressed into little pellets just the shape and size of the owl's gizzard. Several hours after eating, the owls would yarp them up. "Wet poopers" is how many nest-maid snakes referred to other birds. Of course, Mrs. Plithiver was much too proper to use such coarse language.

"Mum!" Soren gasped. "Look at that." The nest suddenly seemed to reverberate with a huge cracking sound. Again, only huge to the ear slits of Barn Owls. Now the egg split. A pale slimy blob flopped out.

"It's a girl!" A long *shree* call streamed from his mother's throat. It was the shree of pure happiness. "Adorable!" Soren's mother sighed.

"Enchanting!" said Soren's father.

Kludd yawned and Soren stared dumbfounded at the wet naked thing with its huge bulging eyes sealed tightly shut.

"What's wrong with her head, Mum?" Soren asked.

"Nothing, dear. Chicks just have very large heads. It takes a while for their bodies to catch up."

"Not to mention their brains," Kludd muttered.

"So they can't hold their heads up right away," said his mother. "You were the same way."

"What shall we call the little dear?" Soren's father asked.

"Eglantine," Soren's mother replied immediately. "I have always wanted a little Eglantine."

"Oooh! Mum, I love that name," Soren said. He softly repeated the name. Then he tipped toward the little pulsing mass of white. "Eglantine," he whispered softly, and he thought he saw one little sealed eye open just a slit and a tiny voice seemed to say *"hi."* Soren loved his little sister immediately.

One second, Eglantine had been this quivering little wet blob, and then, minutes later, it seemed as if she had turned into a fluffy white ball of down. She grew stronger quickly, or so it appeared to Soren. His parents assured him that he, too, had done exactly the same. That evening it was time for her First Insect ceremony. Her eyes were fully open and she was bawling with hunger. Eglantine could hardly make it through her father's "Welcome to Tyto" speech.

"Little Eglantine, welcome to the Forest of Tyto, forest of the Barn Owls, or Tyto alba, as we are more formally known. Once upon a time, long long ago, we did indeed live in barns. But now, we and other Tyto cousins live in this forest kingdom known as Tyto. We are rare indeed and we are perhaps the smallest of all the owl kingdoms. Although, in truth, it has been a long long time since we had a king. Someday when you grow up, when you enter your second year, you, too, will fly out from this hollow and find one of your own in which to live with a mate."

This was the part of the speech that amazed and disturbed Soren. He simply could not imagine growing up and having a nest of his own. How could he be separated from his parents? And yet there was this urge to fly, even now with his stubby little wings that lacked even the smallest sign of true flight feathers. "And now," Soren's father continued, "it is time for your First Insect ceremony." He turned to Soren's mother. "Marella, my dear, can you bring forward the cricket?"

Soren's mother stepped up. In her beak she held one of the summer's last crickets. "Eat up, young'un! Headfirst. Yes, down the beak. Yes, always headfirst — that's the proper way, be it cricket, mouse, or vole."

"Mmmm," sighed Soren's father as he watched his daughter swallow the cricket. "Dizzy in the gizzy, ain't it so?!"

Kludd blinked and yawned. Sometimes his parents really embarrassed him, especially his da with his stupid jokes. "Wit of the wood!" muttered Kludd.

That dawn, after the owls had settled down, Soren was still so excited by his little sister's arrival that he could not sleep. His parents had retired to the ledge above him where they slept, but he could hear their voices threading through the dim morning light that filtered into the hollow.

"Oh, Noctus, it is very strange — another owlet disappeared?"

"Yes, my dear, I'm afraid so."

"How many is that now in the last few days?"

"Fifteen missing, I believe."

"That is many more than can be accounted for by raccoons."

"Yes," Noctus replied grimly. "And there is something else."

"What?" his wife replied in a lower wavering hoot.

"Eggs."

"Eggs?"

"Eggs have disappeared."

"Eggs from a nest?"

"Yes, I'm afraid so."

"No!" Marella Alba gasped. "I have never heard of such a thing. It's unspeakable."

"I thought I must tell you in case we are blessed with another brood."

"Oh, great Glaux," his mother gasped. Soren's eyes blinked wide. He had never heard his mother swear before. "But we so seldom leave the nest during broody times. Whoever it is must watch us." She paused. "Watch us constantly."

"Whoever it is can fly or climb," Noctus Alba said darkly.

Soren felt a sense of dread seep into the hollow. How thankful he was that Eglantine had not been snatched while just an egg. He vowed he would never leave her alone.

It seemed to Soren that as soon as Eglantine ate her first insect she never stopped eating. His mother and father assured him that he had been the same. "And you still are, Soren! And it's almost time for your first Fur-on-Meat ceremony!"

That was what life was like those first weeks in the

nest — one ceremony after another. Each, it seemed in some way or another, led to the truly biggest, perhaps the most solemn yet joyous moment in a young owl's life: First Flight.

"Fur!" whispered Soren. He couldn't quite imagine what it was like. What it would feel like slipping down his throat. His mother always stripped off all the fur from the meat and then tore out the bones before offering the little tidbits of fresh mouse or squirrel to Soren. Kludd was almost ready for his First Bones ceremony when he would be allowed to eat "the whole bit" as Soren's father said. And it was just before First Bones that a young owl began branching. And just after that, it would begin its first real flight under the watchful eyes of its parents.

"Hop! Hop! That's it, Kludd! Now, up with the wings just as you begin the hop to that next branch. And remember, you are just branching now. No flying. And even after your first flight lessons, no flying by yourself until Mum and I say so."

"Yes, Da!" Kludd said in a bored voice. Then he muttered, "How many times have I heard this lecture!"

Soren had heard it many many times, too, even though he was nowhere near branching. The worst thing a young owl could do was to try to fly before it was ready. And, of course, young owls usually did this when their parents were out hunting. It was so tempting to try one's newly fledged wings, but it would most likely end in a disastrous crash, leaving the little owlet nestless, perhaps badly injured, and on the ground exposed to dangerous predators. The lecture was brief this time, and the branching lesson resumed.

"Crisply! Crisply, boy! Keep the noise down. Owls are silent fliers."

"But I'm not flying yet, Da! As you keep reminding me constantly! What's it matter if I'm noisy now when I'm just branching?"

"Bad habit! Bad habit! Leads to noisy flight. Hard to outgrow noise habits started in branching."

"Oh, bother!"

"Oh, I'll bother you!" Noctus exploded, and gave his son a cuff on the head that nearly tipped him over. Soren had to admit that Kludd didn't even whimper but just picked himself up and gave his da a glaring look and resumed hopping — slightly less noisily than before.

There was a series of soft short hisses from Mrs. Plithiver. "Difficult one, that one! My! My! Glad your mum's not here to see this. Eglantine!" Mrs. Plithiver called out suddenly. Even though she was blind she seemed to know exactly what the young owlets were doing at any given moment. She now heard the crunch of a nest bug in

Eglantine's beak. "Put that nest bug down. Owls do not eat nest bugs. That's what house snakes do. If you keep it up, you'll just grow fat and squishy and won't be prepared for your First Meat ceremony, and then no First Fur, and then no First Bones, and then no, well, you know what. Now your mum is just out looking for a nice chubby vole with soft fur for Soren's First Fur ceremony. And she might even find a nice wriggly little centipede for you."

"Ooh, they're so much fun to eat!" Soren exclaimed. "All their little legs pittering down your gullet."

"Oh, Soren, tell me that story about the first time you ate a centipede," Eglantine begged.

Mrs. Plithiver sighed softly. It was so sweet! Eglantine hung on every word of Soren's. True sisterly love, and Soren loved her right back. She wasn't sure what exactly had happened with their older brother, Kludd. There was always one difficult one in a brood, but Kludd was more than just difficult. *There was something ... something ...* Mrs. Plithiver thought hard. Just something missing with Kludd. Something rather unnatural, un-owlish.

"Sing the centipede song, Soren! Sing it!"

Soren opened his beak wide and began to sing:

> *What gives a wriggle*
> *And makes you giggle*

When you eat 'em?
Whose weensy little feet
Make my heart really beat?
Why, it's those little creepy crawlies
That make me feel so jolly.

For the darling centipede
My favorite buggy feed
I always want some more.
That's the insect I adore
More than beetles, more than crickets,
Which at times give me the hiccups.
I crave only to feed
On a juicy centipede
And I shall be happy forevermore.

Just as Soren finished the song, his mother flew into the hollow and dropped a vole at her feet. "A nice fat one, my dear. Enough for your First Fur ceremony and Kludd's First Bones."

"I want my own!" Kludd said.

"Nonsense, dear, you could never eat a whole vole."

"Whole vole!" squeaked Eglantine. "Oh, Mum, it rhymes. I love rhymes."

"I want one all for myself," Kludd persisted.

"Now, look here, Kludd." Marella fixed her son in a dark steady gaze. "We do not waste food around here. This is a very large vole. There is enough for you to have your First Bones ceremony, Soren to have his First Fur ceremony, and Eglantine to have her First Meat."

"Meat! I get to eat meat!" Eglantine gave a little hop of excitement. She seemed to have forgotten all about the joys of centipedes.

"And so, Kludd, when you want a vole all of your own, you can just go out and hunt it for yourself! I spent most of the night tracking down this one. Food is scarce in Tyto this time of year. I'm exhausted." A huge orange moon sailed in the autumn sky. It seemed to hover just above the great fir tree where Soren and his family lived, and it cast a soft glow in through the opening of the hollow. It was indeed a perfect night for the ceremonies that these owls loved and that marked their growth and the passage of time.

And so that night, just before the dawn, the three little owlets had their First Meat, First Fur, and First Bone ceremonies. And Kludd yarped his first real pellet. It was the exact shape of his gizzard, which had pressed it into the tight little bundle of bones and fur. "Oh, that's a fine pellet, son," Kludd's father said.

"Yes, indeed," his mother agreed. "Quite admirable."

And Kludd, for once, seemed satisfied. And Mrs. Plithiver thought privately to herself how no bird could be really bad that had such a noble digestive system.

That night, from the time the big orange moon began to slip down in the sky until the first gray streaks of the new dawn, Noctus Alba told the stories that owls had loved to hear from the time of Glaux. Glaux was the most ancient order of owls from which all other owls descended.

So his father began:

"Once upon a very long time ago, in the time of Glaux, there was an order of knightly owls, from a kingdom called Ga'Hoole, who would rise each night into the blackness and perform noble deeds. They spoke no words but true ones, their purpose was to right all wrongs, to make strong the weak, mend the broken, vanquish the proud, and make powerless those who abused the frail. With hearts sublime they would take flight —"

Kludd yawned. "Is this a true story or what, Da?"

"It's a legend, Kludd," his father answered.

"But is it true?" Kludd whined. "I only like true stories."

"A legend, Kludd, is a story that you begin to feel in your gizzard and then over time it becomes true in your heart. And perhaps makes you become a better owl."

CHAPTER TWO
A Life Worth Two Pellets

True in your heart! Those words in the deep throaty hoot of his father were perhaps the last thing Soren remembered before he landed with a soft thud on a pile of moss. Shaking himself and feeling a bit dazed, he tried to stand up. Nothing seemed broken. But how had this happened? He certainly had not tried flying while his parents were out hunting. Good Glaux. He hadn't even tried branching yet. He was still far from "flight readiness" as his mum called it. So how had this happened? All he knew was, one moment he was near the edge of the hollow, peering out, looking for his mum and da to come home from hunting, and the next minute he was tumbling through the air.

Soren tipped his head up. The fir tree was so tall, and he knew that their hollow was near the very top. What had his father said — ninety feet, one hundred feet? But numbers had no meaning for Soren. Not only could he not fly, he couldn't count, either. Didn't really know his numbers. But there was one thing that he did know: He was in trouble — deep, frightening, horrifying trouble. The boring lectures that Kludd had complained about came back to him. The weight of the terrible truth now pressed upon him in the darkness of the forest — those grim words, "an owlet that is separated from its parents before it has learned to fly and hunt cannot survive."

And Soren's parents were gone, gone on a long hunting flight. There had not been many since Eglantine had hatched out. But they needed more food, for winter was coming. So right now Soren was completely alone. He could not imagine being more completely alone as he gazed up at the tree that seemed to vanish into the clouds. He sighed and muttered, "So alone, so alone."

And yet, deep inside him something flickered like a tiny smoldering spark of hope. When he had fallen, he must have done something with his nearly bald wings that "had captured the air" as his father would say. He tried now to recall that feeling. For a brief instant, falling had actually felt wonderful. Could he perhaps recapture that air? He tried to lift his wings and flutter them slightly. Nothing. His wings felt cold and bare in the crisp autumn breeze. He looked at the tree again. Could he climb, using his talons and beak? He had to do something fast or he would become some creature's next meal — a rat, a raccoon. Soren felt faint at the very thought of a raccoon. He had seen them from the nest — bushy, masked, horrible creatures with sharp teeth. He must listen carefully. He must turn and tip his head as his parents had taught him. His parents could listen so carefully that, from high above in their tree hollow, they could hear the heartbeat of a mouse on the forest floor below. Surely he should be able to hear a raccoon. He cocked his head and nearly jumped. He did hear a sound. It was a small, raspy, familiar voice from high up in the fir tree. "Soren! Soren!" it called from the hollow where his brother and sister still nestled in the fluffy pure white down that their parents had plucked from beneath their flight feathers. But it was neither Kludd nor Eglantine.

"Mrs. Plithiver!" Soren cried.

"Soren . . . are you . . . are you alive? Oh, dear, of course you are if you can say my name. How stupid of me. Are you well? Did you break anything?"

"I don't think so, but how will I ever get back up there?"

"Oh, dear! Oh, dear," Mrs. Plithiver moaned. She was not much good in a crisis. One could not expect such things of nest-maids, Soren supposed.

"How long until Mum and Da get home?" Soren called up.

"Oh, it could be a long while, dearie."

Soren had hop-stepped to the roots of the tree that ran above the ground like gnarled talons. He could now see Mrs. Plithiver, her small head with its glistening rosy scales hovering over the edge of the hollow. Where Mrs. Plithiver's eyes should have been there were two small indentations. "This is simply beyond me." She sighed.

"Is Kludd awake? Maybe he could help me."

There was a long pause before Mrs. Plithiver answered weakly, "Well, perhaps." She sounded hesitant. Soren could hear her now, nudging Kludd. "Don't be grumpy, Kludd. Your brother has . . . has . . . taken a tumble, as it were."

Soren heard his brother yawn. "Oh, my." Kludd sighed and didn't sound especially upset, Soren thought. Soon the large head of his big brother peered over the edge of the hollow. His white heart-shaped face with the immense dark eyes peered down on Soren. "I say," Kludd drawled. "You've got yourself in a terrible fix."

"I know, Kludd. Can't you help? You know more about flying than I do. Can't you teach me?"

"Me teach you? I wouldn't know where to begin. Have you gone yoicks?" He laughed. "Stark-raving yoicks. Me teach you?" He laughed again. There was a sneer embedded deep within the laugh.

"I'm not yoicks. But you're always telling me how

much you know, Kludd." This was certainly the truth. Kludd had been bragging about his superiority ever since Soren had hatched out. *He* should get the favorite spot in the hollow because *he* was already losing his downy fluff in preparation for his flight feathers and therefore would be colder. *He* deserved the largest hunks of mouse meat because *he*, after all, was on the brink of flying. "You've already had your First Flight ceremony. Tell me how to fly, Kludd."

"One cannot tell another how to fly. It's a feeling, and besides, it is really a job for Mum and Da. It would be very impertinent of me to usurp their position."

Soren had no idea what "usurp" meant. Kludd often used big words to impress him.

"What are you talking about? Usurp?" Sounded like "yarp" to Soren. But what would yarping have to do with teaching him to fly? Time was running out. The light was leaking out of the day's end and the evening shadows were falling. The raccoons would soon be out.

"I can't do it, Soren," Kludd replied in a very serious voice. "It would be extremely improper for a young owlet like myself to assume this role in your life."

"My life isn't going to be worth two pellets if you don't do something. Don't you think it is improper for you to let me die? What will Mum and Da say to that?"

"I think they will understand completely."

Great Glaux! Understand completely! He had to be yoicks. Soren was simply too dumbfounded. He could not say another word.

"I'm going to get help, Soren. I'll go to Hilda's," he heard Mrs. P. rasp. Hilda was another nest-maid snake for an owl family in a tree near the banks of the river.

"I wouldn't if I were you, P." Kludd's voice was ominous. It made Soren's gizzard absolutely quiver.

"Don't call me P. That's so rude."

"That's the last thing you have to worry about P. — me being rude."

Soren blinked.

"I'm going, Kludd. You can't stop me," Mrs. Plithiver said firmly.

"Can't I?"

Soren heard a rustling sound above. *Good Glaux, what was happening?*

"Mrs. Plithiver?" Only silence now. "Mrs. Plithiver?" Soren called again. Maybe she had gone to Hilda's. He could only hope, and wait.

It was nearly dark now and a chill wind rose up. There was no sign of Mrs. Plithiver returning. "First teeth" — isn't that what Da always called these early cold winds? — the first teeth of winter. The very words made poor Soren shudder. When his father had first used this expression, Soren had no idea what "teeth" even were. His father explained that they were something that owls didn't have, but most other animals did. They were for tearing and chewing food.

"Does Mrs. Plithiver have them?" asked Soren. Mrs. Plithiver had gasped in disgust.

His mother said, "Of course not, dear."

"Well, what are they exactly?" Soren had asked.

"Hmm," said his mother as she thought a moment. "Just imagine a mouth full of beaks — yes, very sharp beaks."

"That sounds very scary."

"Yes, it can be," his mother replied. "That is why you do not want to fall out of the hollow or try to fly before you're ready, because raccoons have very sharp teeth."

"You see," his father broke in, "we have no need for such things as teeth. Our gizzards take care of all that chewing business. I find it rather revolting, the notion of actually chewing something in one's mouth."

"They say it adds flavor, darling," his mother added.

"I get flavor, plenty of flavor, in my gizzard. Where do you think that old expression 'I know it in my gizzard' comes from? Or 'I have a feeling in my gizzard,' Marella?"

"Noctus, I'm not sure if that is the same thing as flavor."

"That mouse we had for dinner last night — I can tell

you from my gizzard exactly where he had been of late. He had been feasting on the sweet grass of the meadow mixed with the nooties from that little Ga'Hoole tree that grows down by the stream. Great Glaux! I don't need teeth to taste."

Oh, dear, thought Soren, he might never hear this gentle bickering between his parents again. A centipede pittered by and Soren did not even care. Darkness gathered. The black of the night grew deeper and from down on the ground he could barely see the stars. This perhaps was the worst. He could not see sky through the thickness of the trees. How much he missed the hollow. From their nest, there was always a little piece of the sky to watch. At night, it sparkled with stars or raced with clouds. In the daytime, there was often a lovely patch of blue, and sometimes toward evening, before twilight, the clouds turned bright orange or pink. There was an odd smell down here on the ground — damp and moldy. The wind sighed through the branches above, through the leaves and the needles of the forest trees, but down on the ground . . . well, the wind didn't seem to even touch the ground. There was a terrible stillness. It was the stillness of a windless place. This was no place for an owl to be. Everything was different.

If his feathers had been even half-fledged, he could

have plumped them up and the downy fluff beneath the flight feathers would have kept him warm. He supposed he could try calling for Eglantine. But what use would she be? She was so young. Besides, if he called out, wouldn't that alert other creatures in the forest that he was here? Creatures with teeth!

He guessed his life wasn't worth two pellets. But even worthless, he still missed his parents. He missed them so much that the missing felt sharp. Yes, he did feel something in his gizzard as sharp as a tooth.

CHAPTER THREE
Snatched!

S oren was dreaming of teeth and of the heartbeats of mice when he heard the first soft rustlings overhead. "Mum! Da!" he cried out in his half sleep. He would forever regret calling out those two words, for suddenly, the night was ripped with a shrill screech, and Soren felt talons wrap around him. Now he was being lifted. And they were flying fast, faster than he could think, faster than he could ever imagine. His parents never flew this fast. He had watched them when they took off or came back from the hollow. They glided slowly and rose in beautiful lazy spirals into the night. But now, underneath, the earth raced by. Slivers of air blistered his skin. The moon rolled out from behind thick clouds and bleached the world with an eerie whiteness. He scoured the landscape below for the tree that had been his home. But the trees blurred into clumps, and then the forest of the Kingdom of Tyto seemed to grow smaller and smaller and dimmer and dimmer in the night, until Soren could not stand to look down anymore. So he dared to look up.

There was a great bushiness of feathers on the owl's legs. His eyes continued upward. This was a huge owl — or was it even an owl? Atop this creature's head, over each eye, were two tufts of feathers that looked like an extra set of wings. Just as Soren was thinking this was the strangest owl he had ever seen, the owl blinked and looked down. Yellow eyes! He had never seen such eyes. His own parents and his brother and sister all had dark, almost black eyes. His parents' friends who occasionally flew by had brownish eyes, perhaps some with a tinge of tawny gold. But yellow eyes? This was wrong. Very wrong!

"Surprised!" The owl blinked, but Soren could not speak. So the owl continued. "Yes, you see, that's the problem with the Kingdom of Tyto — you never see any other kind of owl but your own kind — lowly, undistinguished Barn Owls."

"That's not true," said Soren.

"You dare contradict me!" screeched the owl.

"I've seen Grass Owls and Masked Owls. I've seen Bay Owls and Sooty Owls. Some of my parents' very best friends are Grass Owls."

"Stupid! They're all Tytos," the owl barked at him.

Stupid? Grown-ups weren't supposed to speak this way — not to young owls, not to chicks. It was mean. Soren decided he should be quiet. He would stop looking up.

"We might have a haggard here," he heard the owl say. Soren turned his head slightly to see who the owl was speaking to.

"Oh, great Glaux! One wonders if it is worth the effort." This owl's eyes seemed more brown than yellow and his feathers were spattered with splotches of white and gray and brown.

"Oh, I think it is always worth the effort, Grimble. And don't let Spoorn hear you talking that way. You'll get a demerit and then we'll all be forced to attend another one of her interminable lectures on attitude."

This owl looked different as well. Not nearly as big as the other owl and his voice made a soft *tingg-tingg* sound. It was at least a minute before Soren noticed that this owl was also carrying something in his talons. It was a creature of some sort and it looked rather owlish, but it was so small, hardly larger than a mouse. Then it blinked its eyes. Yellow! Soren resisted the urge to yarp. "Don't say a word!" the small owl said in a squeaky whisper. "Wait."

Wait for what? Soren wondered. But soon he felt the night stir with the beating of other wings. More owls fell in beside them. Each one carried an owlet in its talons.

Then there was a low hum from the owl that gripped Soren. Gradually, the other owls flanking them joined in. Soon the air thrummed with a strange music. "It's their hymn," whispered the tiny owl. "It gets louder. That's when we can talk."

Soren listened to the words of the hymn.

> *Hail to St. Aegolius*
> *Our Alma Mater.*
> *Hail, our song we raise in praise of thee*
> *Long in the memory of every loyal owl*
> *Thy splendid banner emblazoned be.*
>
> *Now to thy golden talons*
> *Homage we're bringing.*
> *Guiding symbol of our hopes and fears*
> *Hark to the cries of eternal praises ringing*
> *Long may we triumph in the coming years.*

The tiny owl began to speak as the voices swelled in the black of the night. "My first words of advice are to listen rather than speak. You've already got yourself marked as a wild owl, a haggard."

"Who are you? What are you? Why do you have yellow eyes?"

"You see what I mean! That is the last thing that you should worry about." The tiny owl sighed softly. "But I'll tell you. I am an Elf Owl. My name is Gylfie."

"I've never seen one in Tyto."

"We live in the high desert kingdom of Kuneer."

"Do you ever grow any bigger?"

"No. This is it."

"But you're so small and you've got all of your feathers, or almost."

"Yes, this is the worst part. I was within a week or so of flying when I got snatched."

"But how old are you?"

"Twenty nights."

"Twenty nights!" Soren exclaimed. "How can you fly that young?"

"Elf Owls are able to fly by twenty-seven or thirty nights."

"How much is sixty-six nights?" Soren asked.

"A lot."

"I'm a Barn Owl and we can't fly for sixty-six nights. But what happened to you? How did you get snatched?"

Gylfie did not answer right away. Then slowly, "What is the ONE thing that your parents always tell you not to do?"

"Fly before you're ready?" Soren said.

"I tried and I fell."

"But I don't understand. It would have been only a week, you said." Soren, of course, wasn't sure how long a week was or how long twenty-seven nights were, but it all sounded shorter than sixty-six.

"I was impatient. I was well on my way to growing feathers but had grown no patience." Gylfie paused again. "But what about yourself? You must have tried it, too."

"No. I don't really know what happened. I just fell out of the nest." But the second Soren said those words he felt a weird queasiness. He almost knew. He just couldn't quite remember, but he almost knew how it had happened, and he felt a mixture of dread and shame creep through him. He felt something terrible deep in his gizzard.

CHAPTER FOUR

St. Aegolius Academy for Orphaned Owls

The owls began to bank in steep turns as they circled downward. Soren blinked and looked down. There was not a tree, not a stream, not a meadow. Instead, immense rock needles bristled up, and cutting through them were deep stone ravines and jagged canyons. This could not be Tyto. That was all that Soren could think.

Down, down, down they plunged in tighter and tighter circles, until they alighted on the stony floor of a deep, narrow canyon. And, although Soren could indeed see the sky from which they had just plunged, it seemed farther away than ever. Above, there was the sound of wind, distant yet shrill as it whistled across the upper reaches of this harsh stone world. Then, piercing through the shriek of the wind, came a voice even louder and sharper.

"Welcome, owlets. Welcome to St. Aegolius. This is

your new home. It is here that you will find truth and purpose. Yes, that is our motto. When Truth Is Found, Purpose Is Revealed."

The immense, ragged Great Horned Owl fixed them in her yellow gaze. The tufts above her eyes swooped up. The shoulder feathers on her left wing had separated, revealing an unsightly patch of skin with a jagged white scar. She was perched on a rock outcropping in the granite ravine where they had been brought. "I am Skench, Ablah General of St. Aegolius. My job is to teach you the Truth. We discourage questions here as we feel they often distract from the Truth." Soren found this very confusing. He had always asked questions, ever since he had hatched out.

Skench, the Ablah General, was continuing her speech. "You are orphans now." The words shocked Soren. He was not an orphan! He had a mum and da, perhaps not here, but out there somewhere. Orphan meant your parents were dead. How dare this Skench, the Ablah blah blah blah, or whatever she called herself, say he was an orphan!

"We have rescued you. It is here at St. Aggie's that you shall find everything that you need to become humble, plain servants of a higher good."

This was the most outrageous thing Soren had ever heard. He hadn't been rescued, he had been snatched away. If he had been rescued, these owls would have flown up and dropped him back in his family's nest. And what exactly was a higher good?

"There are many ways in which one can serve the higher good, and it is our job to find out which best suits you and to discover what your special talents are." Skench narrowed her eyes until they were gleaming amber slits in her feathery face. "I am sure that each and every one of you has something special."

At that very moment, there was a chorus of hoots, and many owl voices were raised in song.

> *To find one's special quality*
> *One must lead a life of deep humility.*
> *To serve in this way*
> *Never question but obey*
> *Is the blessing of St. Aggie's charity.*

At the conclusion of the short song, Skench, the Ablah General, swooped down from her stone perch. She fixed them all in the glare of her eyes. "You are embarking on an exciting adventure, little orphans. After I have dismissed you, you shall be led to one of four glaucidiums, where two things shall occur. You shall receive your number designation. And you shall also receive your first lesson in the proper manner in which to sleep and shall be inducted into the march of sleep. These are the first steps toward the Specialness ceremony."

. *What in the world was this owl talking about?* Soren wondered. Number designation? What was a glaucidium, and since when did an owl have to be taught to sleep? And a sleep march? What was that? And it was still night. What owl slept at night? But before he could really ponder these questions, he felt himself being gently shoved into a line, a separate line from the little Elf Owl called Gylfie. He turned his head nearly completely around to search for Gylfie and caught sight of her. He raised a stubby wing to wave but Gylfie did not see him. He saw her marching ahead with her eyes looking straight forward.

The line Soren was in wound its way through a series of deep gorges. It was like a stone maze of tangled trails through the gaps and canyons and notches of this place called St. Aegolius Academy for Orphaned Owls. Soren had the unsettling feeling that he might never see the little Elf Owl again, and even worse, it would be impossible to ever find one's way out of these stone boxes into the forest world of Tyto, with its immense trees and sparkling streams.

They finally came to stop in a circular stone pit. A white owl with very thick feathers waddled toward them and blinked. Her eyes had a soft yellow glow.

"I am Finny, your pit guardian." And then she giggled softly. "Some have been known to call me their pit angel." She gazed sweetly at them. "I would love it if you would all call me Auntie."

Auntie? Soren wondered. *Why would I ever call her Auntie?* But he remembered not to ask.

"I must, of course, call you by your number designation, which you shall shortly be told," said Finny.

"Oh, goody!" A little Spotted Owl standing next to Soren hopped up and down.

This time, Soren remembered too late that questions were discouraged. "Why do you want a number instead of your name?"

"Hortense! You wouldn't like that name, either," the Spotted Owl whispered. "Now, shush. Remember, no questions."

"You shall, of course," Finny continued, "if you are good humble owlets and learn the lessons of humility and obedience, earn your Specialness rank and then receive your true name."

But my true name is Soren. It is the name my parents gave me. The words pounded in Soren's head and even his gizzard seemed to tremble in protest.

"Now, let's line up for our Number ceremony, and I have a tempting little snack here for you."

There were perhaps twenty owls in Soren's group and Soren was toward the middle of the line. He watched as the white owl, Auntie or Finny, whom Hortense had informed him was a Snowy Owl, dropped a piece of fur-stripped mouse meat on the stone before each owl in turn and then said, "Why, you're number 12-6. What a nice number that is, dearie."

Every number was either "nice," or "dear," or "darling." Finny bent her head solicitously and often gave a friendly little pat to the owlet just "numbered." She was full of quips and little jokes. Soren was just beginning to feel that things perhaps could be worse, and he hoped that Gylfie had such a nice owl for a pit guardian, when the huge fierce owl with the tufts over each eye, the very one who had snatched him and called him stupid, alighted down next to Finny. Soren felt a cold dread steal over his gizzard as he saw the owl look directly at him and then dip his head and whisper something into Finny's ear. Finny nodded and looked at him blandly. They were talking about him. Soren was sure. He could barely move his talons forward on the hard stone toward Finny. His turn was coming up soon. Only four more owls before he would be "numbered."

"Hello, sweetness," Finny cooed as Soren stepped forward. "I have a very special number for you!" Soren was silent. Finny continued, "Don't you want to know what it is?" *This is a trick. Questions are discouraged. I'm not supposed to ask.* And that was exactly what Soren said.

"I'm not supposed to ask." The soft yellow glow streamed from Finny's eyes. Soren felt a moment's confusion. Then Finny leaned forward and whispered to him. "You know, dear, I'm not as strict as some. So please, if you really really need to ask a question, just go ahead. But remember to keep your voice down. And here, dear, is a little extra piece of mouse. And your number . . ." She sighed and her entire white face seemed to glow with the yellow light. "My favorite — 12-1. Isn't it sublime! It's a very special number, and I am sure that you will discover your own very special-ness as an owl."

"Thank you," Soren said, still slightly mystified but re-lieved that the fierce owl had apparently not told Finny anything bad about him.

"Thank you, what?" Finny giggled. "See? I get to ask questions, too, sometimes."

"Thank you, Finny?"

Finny inclined her head toward him again. There was a slight glare in the yellow glow. "Again," she whispered softly. "Again . . . now, look me in the eyes." Soren looked into the yellow light.

"Thank you, Auntie."

"Yes, dear. I'm just an old broody. Love being called Auntie."

Soren did not know what a broody was, but he took the mouse meat and followed the owl who had been in front of him into the glaucidium. Two large, ragged brown owls escorted the entire group. The glaucidium was a deep box canyon, the floor of which was covered with sleeping owlets. Moonlight streamed down directly on them, silvering their feathers.

"Fall in, you two!" barked a voice from high up in a rocky crevice.

"You!" A plump owl stepped up to Soren. Indeed, Soren's heart quickened at first, for it was another Barn Owl just like his own family. There was the white heart-shaped face and the familiar dark eyes. And yet, although the color of these eyes was identical to his own and those of his family, he found the owl's gaze frightening.

"Back row, and prepare to assume the sleeping position." These instructions were delivered in the throaty rasp common to Barn Owls, but Soren found nothing comforting in the familiar.

The two owls who had escorted the newly arrived orphans spoke to them next. They were Long Eared Owls and had tufts that poked straight up over their eyes and twitched. Soren found this especially unnerving. They each alternated speaking in short deep *whoos*. The *whoos* were even more disturbing than the barks of Skench earlier, for the sound seemed to coil into Soren's very breast and thrum with a terrible *clang*.

"I am Jatt," said the first owl. "I was once a number. But now I have earned my new name."

"*Whhh* —" Soren snapped off the word.

"I see a question forming on your disgusting beak, number 12-1!" The *whoo* thrummed so deep within Soren's breast that he thought his heart might burst.

"Let me make this perrr-fectly clear." The thrumming of the owl's sound was almost unbearable. "At St. Aggie's such words beginning with the *whh* sound are not to be spoken. Such words are question words, a habit of mental luxury and indulgence. Questions might fatten the imagination, but they starve the owlish instincts of hardiness, patience, humility, and self-denial. We are not here to pamper you by allowing an orgy of *wwwhh* words, question words. They are dirty words, swear words punishable by the most severe means at our disposal." Jatt blinked and cast his gaze on Soren's wings. "We are here to make true owls out of you. And someday you will thank us for it."

Soren thought he was going to faint with fear. These owls were so different from Finny. *Auntie!* He silently corrected himself. Jatt had resumed speaking in his normal *whoo*. "Now my brother shall address you."

It was an identical voice. "I am Jutt. I, too, was once a number but have earned my new name. You are now in the sleeping position. Standing tall, head up, beak tipped to the moon. You see in this glaucidium hundreds of owlets. They have all learned to sleep in this manner. You, too, shall learn."

Soren looked around, desperately searching for Gylfie, but all he saw was Hortense, or number 12-8. She had assumed the perfect sleeping position. He could tell by the stillness of her head that she was sound asleep under the glare of a full moon. Soren spotted a stone arch that connected to what he thought was another glaucidium. A mass of owls seemed to be marching. Their beaks were bobbing open and shut but Soren could not hear what they were saying.

Jatt now spoke again. "It is strictly forbidden to sleep with the head tucked under the wings, dipped toward the breast, or in the manner that many of you young owls are accustomed, which is the semi-twist position in which the head rests on the back." Soren felt at least seven *wh* sounds die mutely in his throat. "Incorrect sleeping posture is also punishable, using our most severe methods."

"Sleep correction monitors patrol the glaucidium, making their rounds at regular intervals," Jutt continued.

Now it was Jatt's turn again. Their timing seemed perfect. Soren felt they had given this speech many times. "Also, at regular intervals, you shall hear the alarm. At the sound, all owlets in the glaucidium are required to begin the sleep march."

"During the sleep march," Jutt resumed, "you march, repeating your old name over and over and over again. When the second alarm sounds, you halt where you are. Repeat your number designation one time, and one time only, and assume the sleep position once more."

Both owls next spoke at once in an awesome thrum. "Now, sleep!"

Soren tried to sleep. He really did try. Maybe Finny, he meant *Auntie*, would believe him. But there was just something in his gizzard, a little twinge, that seemed to make sleep impossible. It was almost as if the shine of the full moon that sprayed its light over half the glaucidium became a sharp silver needle stabbing through his skull and going straight to his gizzard. Perhaps he had a very sensitive gizzard like his da. But in this case he wasn't "tasting" the sweet grass the meadow mouse had feasted on. He was tasting dread.

Soren was not sure how long it was before the alarm sounded but it was soon time for his first sleep march. Repeating his name over and over, he followed the owls in his group and now moved into the shadow of the overhang of the arch. "Ah," Soren sighed. The stabbing feeling in his skull ceased. His gizzard grew still. And Soren became more alert, the proper state for an owl who lived in the night. He looked about him. The little Spotted Owl named Hortense stood next to him. "Hortense?" Soren said. She stared at him blankly and began tapping her feet as if to move.

A sleep monitor swooped down. "Whatcha marching in place for, 12-8? Assume the sleeping position."

Hortense immediately tipped her beak up, her head slightly back, but there was no moon to shine down upon it in the shadow of the rock. Soren, also in the sleep position, slid his eyes toward her. *Curious*, he thought. She responded to her number name but not her old name, except to move her feet. Still unable to sleep in this newfangled position, Soren twisted his head about to survey the stone arch. Through the other side of the arch, he caught sight of Gylfie, but too late. The alarm sounded, a high, piercing shriek. Before he knew it, he was being pushed along as thousands of owls began to move. Within seconds, there was an indescribable babble as each owl repeated its old name over and over again.

It became clear to Soren that they were following the path of the moon around the glaucidium. There were, however, so many owls that they could not all be herded under the full shine of the moon at the same time. Therefore, some were allowed an interval under the overhang of the rock arch. Perhaps he and Gylfie, since they had wound up before at the arch at the same time, could meet there again. He was determined to get close to Gylfie the next time.

But that would take three more times. Three more times of blathering his name into the moonlit night. Three more times of feeling the terrible twinge in his gizzard. "12-1, tip that beak up!" It was a sleep monitor. He felt a thwack to the side of his head. Hortense was still next to him. She mumbled, "12-8, what a lovely name that is. 12-8, perfect name. I love twos and fours and eights. So smooth."

"Hortense," Soren whispered softly. Her talons might have just vaguely begun to stir on the floor, but other than that, nothing. "Hort! Horty!" He tried, but the little Spotted Owl was lost in some dreamless sleep.

Finally, Soren was back under the arch and quickly moved over to the other side, which connected to the neighboring glaucidium. The sleep monitors had just barked out the command, "Now, sleep!"

Suddenly, Gylfie was there. The tiny Elf Owl swung her head toward Soren. "They're moon blinking us," she whispered.

CHAPTER FIVE

Moon Blinking

W hat?" It felt so good to say a *whh* sound that Soren almost missed the answer.

"Didn't your parents tell you about the dangers of sleeping under the full shine?"

"What is 'full shine'?" Soren asked.

"When did you hatch out?"

"Three weeks ago, I think. Or so my parents told me." But again, Soren was not really sure what a week was.

"Ah, that explains it. And in Tyto there are great trees, right?" Gylfie asked.

"Oh, yes. Many, and thick with beautiful fir needles and spruce cones and leaves that turn golden and red." Again, Soren wasn't sure about leaves turning for he had never seen them anything but golden and red. But his parents had told him that once they were green in a time called summer. Kludd had hatched out near the end of the green time.

"Well, you see, I hatched out more than three weeks

ago." They spoke softly, so softly, and managed to maintain the sleep position, but neither one of them was the least bit sleepy. "I was hatched after the time of newing."

"The newing? When is that?" asked Soren.

"You see, the moon comes and the moon goes, and at the time of the newing, when the moon is no thicker than one single thin, downy feather, well, that is the first glint of the new moon. Then, every day it grows thicker and fatter until there is full shine, like now. And it might stay that way for three or four days. Then comes the time of the dwenking. Instead of growing thicker and fatter, the moon dwenks and becomes thinner, until, once more, it is no thicker than the thinnest strand of down. And then it disappears for a while."

"I never saw this. At least, I don't think I have."

"Oh, it was there but you probably didn't *really* see because your family's nest was in the hollow of a great tree in a thick forest. But Elf Owls like myself live in deserts. Not so many trees. And many of them are not very leafy. We can see the whole sky nearly all the time."

"My!" Soren sighed softly.

"And that is why they teach all of us Elf Owls about full shine. Although most owls sleep during the day, sometimes, especially after a hunting expedition, one might be tired and sleep at night. This can be very dangerous if one sleeps out bald in the light of a full moon. It confuses one's head."

"How?" Soren asked.

"I'm not sure. My parents never really explained it but they did say that the old owl Rocmore had gone crazy from too much full shine." Gylfie paused, then hesitating, went on. "They even said that he often did not know which was up and which was down and that finally he died of a broken neck when he thought he was lifting off from the top of a cactus." Gylfie's voice almost broke here. "He thought he was flying toward the stars and he slammed into the earth. That's what moon blinking is all about. You no longer know what is for sure and what is not. What is truth and what are lies. What is real and what is false. That is being moon blinked."

Soren gasped. "This is awful! Is this what is going to happen to us?"

"Not if we can help it, Soren."

"What can we do?"

"I'm not sure. Let me think a while. Meanwhile, try to cock your head just a bit, so the moon does not shine straight down on it. And remember, when flying in full shine there is no problem. But sleeping in it is disastrous."

"I can't fly yet," Soren said softly.

"Well, just be sure you don't sleep."

Soren cocked his head and while doing so tipped his beak down to look upon the little Elf Owl. *How,* he wondered, *was such a tiny creature so smart?* He hoped with all his might that Gylfie would come up with something. Some idea. Just as he was thinking this, there was a sharp bark. "12-1, head straight, beak up!" It was another sleep monitor. He felt a thwack to the side of his head. They did not fall asleep, and as soon as the patrolling owl left, they began whispering again. But then, all too soon, came the inevitable alarm for a sleep march to begin. It would be three more circuits before they could meet again under the arch.

"Remember what I told you. Don't sleep."

"I'm so tired. How can I help it?"

"Think of anything."

"What?"

"Anything —" Gylfie hesitated before a sleep monitor shoved her along. "Think of flying!"

Flying, yes, thinking of flying would keep Soren awake. There was nothing more exciting. But in the meantime, all thoughts of flight were drowned out by the sound of his own voice repeating his own name.

"Soren . . . Soren . . . Soren. . . . Soren . . ." There was also the sound of thousands of talons clicking on the hard stone surface as they marched in lines. Soren was between

47

Hortense and a Horned Owl whose name blended into the drone of other names. Three Snowy Owls were directly in front of him. There were perhaps twenty or more owls to each group, all arranged in loose lines, but they moved in unison as one block of owls, each owl endlessly repeating his or her name. It was impossible to sort out an individual name from the babble, and it was not long when, on the fourth sleep march, his own name began to sound odd to Soren. Within another one hundred or so times of repeating it, it seemed almost as if it was not a name at all. It was merely a noise. And he, too, was becoming a meaningless creature with no real name, no family, but . . . but . . . but maybe a friend?

Finally, they stopped again. And it was in the silence of that moment when they stopped that Soren suddenly realized what was happening. It all made sense, particularly when he thought of what Gylfie had explained to him about moon blinking. This alone would keep him awake until he met up with her again.

"They are moon blinking us with our names, Gylfie," Soren gasped as he edged in close to the little owl under the stone arch. Only the stars twinkled above. Gylfie understood immediately. A name endlessly repeated became a meaningless sound. It completely lost its individuality, its significance. It would dissolve into nothingness. Soren continued, "Just move your beak or say your number, but don't say your name. That way it will stay your name." There would, however, be at least three more nights of full shine and then the fullness would begin to lessen until the moon was completely dwenked.

Gylfie looked at Soren in amazement. This ordinary Barn Owl was in his own way quite extraordinary. This was absolutely brilliant. Gylfie felt more than ever compelled to figure out a solution to sleeping exposed to full shine.

CHAPTER SIX

Separate Pits, One Mind

When Soren and Gylfie parted at the end of that long night, they looked at each other and blinked, trembling with fear. If only they could be together in the same pit, then they could think together, talk, and plan. Gylfie had told Soren a little about her pit. She, too, had a pit guardian who seemed very nice, at least compared to Jatt and Jutt or Skench. Gylfie's pit guardian was called Unk, short for Uncle and, like Auntie, he tried to arrange special treats for Gylfie — a bit of snake sometimes, often even calling Gylfie by her real name and not her number, 25-2. Indeed, when Gylfie had told Soren how her pit guardian had asked her to call him "Unk" it was almost identical to the way in which Aunt Finny had insisted on Soren calling her "Auntie."

"It was all so weird," Gylfie had said. "I called him sir at first, and then he said, 'Sir! All this formality. Really, now! Remember what I asked you to call me? 'Uncle,' I answered. 'Now . . . now . . . I gave you my special name.'"

The special name was Unk and the way in which Gylfie described Unk drawing that name of endearment from her, well, Soren could just imagine the Great Horned Owl dipping low to be on eye level with the little Elf Owl, the huge tufts above his ears nearly scraping the ground.

"The pit guardians go out of their way to be nice to us," Soren had said. "But it's still kind of scary, isn't it?"

"Very!" Gylfie had replied. "It was after I called him Unk that he gave me the bits of snake." She had then sighed. "I remember so well, as if it was yesterday, my First Snake ceremony. Dad had saved the rattles for me and my sisters to play with. And you know what, Soren? It was as if Unk had read my mind because I was thinking about my ceremony and just then he says, 'I might even have some rattles for you to play with.' And then I thanked him. I over-thanked him. It was disgusting, Soren."

And Soren knew just what the little Elf Owl meant.

But now they were separated and Soren hoped desperately that Gylfie would come up with some solution. And Gylfie, once more stuffed with some extra snake bits that Unk had given her, had become very drowsy in her pit. Unk had even allowed her to sneak in some extra sleep — another little treat, or was it a bribe? But Gylfie could not sleep. She would be on the brink of sleep, drowsy with the succulent snake meat she had gorged on — much too much for an owl of her size, but just as she was about to fall asleep something would prick her dim consciousness, some thought. Soren, in the pit next door, was concentrating as hard as he could. *"Think of something, Gylfie! Think of something!"*

Auntie had been so nice. When Soren returned to the stone pit, she had said that she'd never seen a more tired-looking owl. "Didn't sleep a wink, huh?"

"'Fraid not, Auntie," Soren had replied.

"Now, you hear me. Why don't you hop up there in that little stone niche, just your size and out of prying eyes, and take yourself a little blink or two?"

"You mean sleep?" The question just slipped out. "Sorry about the question."

"Of course, dear, I mean sleep and don't apologize about the question. We'll get stricter with that later."

"But it's against the rules. We're suppose to be getting ready for our work assignments."

"Sometimes rules are made to be broken. In my opinion, they should go much easier on you owlets after you first arrive. You're orphans, for Glaux's sake."

It still disturbed Soren deeply to be called an orphan.

He had a mother and a father and a sister and a brother. He wasn't sure why, but there was something shameful about being called an orphan, especially when one wasn't. It was as if you were this disconnected, unloved creature.

"I know," Auntie continued. "I'm just an old broody." *What was a broody?* Soren wondered, but he suppressed the urge to ask. Soren hopped up into the stone niche. *My goodness,* he thought. *I did that rather well. Could have passed my branching test on that one.* And then he became very sad when he thought that he had not even been able to begin his first branching lessons with his father.

Sleep indeed was hard to come by — even a blink or two, because when Soren started to think about branching, he, of course, could not help but think about flying and remembered watching Kludd's attempts and finally his first very small flight. Something pushed at the back of Soren's brain, a memory. Soren was not sure how long he had been sleeping but it was not Auntie who woke him up. It was something else, something unspeakable. Once more he felt that terrible queasiness mixed with dread. It was as if his gizzard might burst. But the terrible truth settled like a stone inside him. Kludd had pushed him! It came to him in a flash. So real that he could still feel the swift kick of Kludd's talons in his side and then pitching over the edge of the hollow.

His legs began to shake. Auntie was at his side. "Need to yarp, dear?"

"Yes," Soren said weakly. He yarped a miserable little pellet. What did he expect? He had never even had his First Bones ceremony, which again made him remember all of Kludd's strutting about when he yarped his first pellet with bones. Would they have such things as First Bones ceremonies here? They did everything so strangely. The Number ceremony, for example. They called that a ceremony! Ceremonies were supposed to make you feel special. The Number ceremony hadn't made him feel anything. Auntie Finny was nice, but the others really weren't so nice at all, and this orphanage business — what was that all about? What was the real purpose of St. Aggie's? Skench, the Ablah General, said, "When Truth Is Found, Purpose Is Revealed." No questions, just be humble. The only truth that Soren knew right now was a deep gizzard-chilling one: His brother had shoved him from the nest. *Think, Gylfie,* thought Soren. *Think of something!*

CHAPTER SEVEN
The Great Scheme

Pretend to march, Soren. That is what we must do!"

It was just after the first rising shriek had been sounded by the brutish Great Horned Owl, who perched on one of the outcroppings. Soren and Gylfie had met at the stone ledge for morning food rations.

"What do you mean, pretend to march?" Soren blinked. Between the horrible truth about his brother and missing his parents, Soren could hardly hear what Gylfie was saying. His head was filled with the thoughts of his parents. It seemed as if every hour he found a new, more painful way to miss them. *One*, he decided, *did not get used to missing parents*. The thought of never seeing his mum or da again was the most unbearable thing he knew. And yet he could not stop thinking of them. He did not want to stop thinking of them. He would never stop thinking of them.

"Listen to me, Soren. It came to me first that the reason for the march is because of the shadows cast from the high cliffs into the glaucidium, and the arch is always in the shadows. Right?"

"Right." Soren nodded.

"We are forced to march so that no one group of owls will spend too much time under these shadowy shields against the moon's light. I remembered what you said, how we must pretend to say our names but instead we actually repeat our numbers. And then it was easy. We have to pretend to march but never move, so we stay under the protection of the shadows. I suddenly remembered how my father, who was a great navigator, one of the best in the entire Desert of Kuneer, had tried to explain to me that stars and even the moon do not move in the way they seem to from our view on Earth. Some stars, my father said, even appear to stand still in the sky, but, in fact, they do move."

"Huh?" Soren grunted.

"Look, I know it's a little weird, but my da explained that this was because of the great distance that disguises in stillness a star's motion. Even the moon, my father said, which is closer than many stars, is so distant that we cannot see the wobbles in its path as it glides through the night. So, don't you see that if the motion of something as big as the moon could be disguised, well, couldn't the motion of something as small as us be disguised?"

A new light began to glimmer in Soren's eyes. Gylfie grew more excited. "We can be like the stars, only in reverse. In other words, what would happen if we just stayed still and pretended to march — if we marched in place?"

"What about the monitors?" Soren asked.

"I've thought about that. The monitors always stand at the edges of the mass of marching owls. They don't really see what is going on in the middle. I saw a Grass Owl stumble last night. No one said, 'Oh, sorry' or 'Move it!' or 'You clumsy bird.' All the owls simply parted and went around the Grass Owl. So what if we pretend to march and stay under the shadow of the arch each time? Get it? We would march in place and give the appearance of motion."

"It's a great scheme, Gylfie!" Soren's voice was filled with awe.

"We'll try it tonight. I can't wait," Gylfie said. "But I'm hungry now."

"This is it?" Soren blinked as a large rusty-colored owl shoved one dead cricket toward him on the stone ledge. "I mean, this is it!" Soren quickly said, correcting what had been a question, as he stared down at what St. Aggie's called breakfast. No mouse meat, no fat worms — oh, for a hummingbird! But one cricket! This was ridiculous. He would starve.

As the owlets stopped to eat, there was only the sound of their beaks crunching the crickets. Soren couldn't believe that no one talked. Owlets always talked when they ate. His little sister, Eglantine, jabbered so much sometimes that his mum had to remind her to eat. "Eat the feet on that bug, Eglantine. Eat the feet. You talk so much you're missing the very best part of the beetle."

So the silence began to bother him and there was indeed a terrible quiet to the stone canyons that made up St. Aggie's. Always, of course, there was the hollow whistle of the wind and the endless clicking of talons on the hard rock surfaces. Other than that, there was not much sound. Instead, there was an overwhelming sense of being cut off, separated from Earth, and even from sky. Soren began to realize that the entire lives of these owls, if one could call it living, were carried out in the deep stone boxes and slots, the canyons and ravines of St. Aggie's. There was very little water — just a trickle here and there into which they could dip their beaks for a drink. There were no leaves, no mosses that he could see, no grasses — none of the soft things that wrapped the world and made it tender and springy. It was a stone forest with its jagged outcroppings, rock needles, and spires and ledges.

They had almost finished eating, so there was not even the clicking, just the sound of crickets being crunched.

An owl next to him muttered, "I'd love a little piece of rat snake."

"Oooh." Soren sighed and thought of Mrs. Plithiver. His family avoided serving snake out of respect for Mrs. Plithiver. Mrs. Plithiver said it was nonsense. "Show me a rat snake or a bull snake that anyone really loved." She would say, "Don't worry about my feelings. I have no feeling toward such snakes." But still his parents avoided such foods. Soren's father called it "species sensitivity." Soren had no idea what that meant, except he didn't want to hurt Mrs. Plithiver's feelings and she had just said she had none. Soren, of course, didn't really believe this. He thought Mrs. Plithiver had plenty of feelings. She was a most lovable creature, and his heart beat a little harder when he remembered her calling down to him from the hollow high in the fir tree. It almost made him cry to remember her voice. What had happened to her that night? Had Kludd done something to her as well? Or had she gotten away to get help? Did she miss him? Did his parents miss him? Once more, there was that sharp pain of missing and Soren nearly staggered with the very idea of never seeing his parents. Then he thought of Kludd and began to tremble all over again.

"You all right?" Gylfie asked. She was so small that she barely reached up to Soren's wing tips.

"No, I'm not all right," Soren gasped. "Nothing is right. Don't you miss your parents? Don't you wonder what they think happened to you?"

"Yes, yes. I just can't think about it," Gylfie replied. "Listen, pull yourself together. We have our Great Scheme, remember?"

"What do you mean pull yourself together? Do you know what I just figured out about my brother?"

"Look, we don't have much time," Gylfie said quickly. "Make sure you get assigned to the pelletorium."

"The pelletorium?" Soren said blankly.

CHAPTER EIGHT
The Pelletorium

Auntie Finny suddenly appeared. "Cricket hunter. You're perfect. You see, here in our lovely stone country the cricket season is much longer. They hide in the nooks and crannies and then come out in the sunshine to bask in the heat of the day."

"Uh..." Soren started to speak. "I'm feeling a little peckish, you know, Auntie. I think maybe the pelletorium would be better for me."

"Oh, the pelletorium!" Auntie Finny looked slightly confused. She had never had an owlet suggest another workstation or training schedule. She looked at the Barn Owl. He didn't look well. And if he failed as a cricket hunter, it would reflect poorly on her. And then again, if she fulfilled this owl's request, it would perhaps put him in her debt. It was always good to have an owlet indebted to you. "Yes, yes. I suppose so." She gazed at the young owl. Soren felt the soft yellow glow of her eyes. "Now, remember, dear, what I've done for you and remember the little" —

she beaked the word — "'nap' I allowed you." The yellow light turned a bit hard like glinting gold. "Then follow that line over there into the pelletorium."

"I am 47-2. I am to be your guide for the pelletorium. Follow me." The owlet spoke in a peculiar manner. Her sounds were clipped and hollow. It was not like the terrible thrum and clang of Jatt and Jutt, but it was like no owl sound Soren had ever heard.

Soren and Gylfie followed number 47-2, who had begun to march. Soon, they heard the *click* of all the owlets' talons as they struck the ground, for they were once more marching in time. Now the strange hollow tone in which 47-2 had spoken seemed to hover over the vast marching assembly of owlets. They were singing!

Every pellet has a story all its own.
Every pellet has a story all its own.
With its fur and teeth and bones
And one or two stones,
Every pellet has a story all its own.

We shall dissect every pellet with glee.
Perhaps we'll find a rodent's knee.
And never shall we tire

In the sacred task that we conspire,
Nor do our work less than perfectly
And those bright flecks at the core,
Which make our hearts soar,
Shall forever remain the deepest mystery.

Nothing could have prepared Soren and Gylfie for the shock of what met their eyes as they entered the pelletorium. They had been led into another box canyon, and on slabs of rock ledges hundreds of owls bobbed their heads up and down over thousands of pellets that had been yarped by owls. If either one of these two little owlets had known the meaning of the word "hell," they would have known that this was certainly the deepest and worst part of it. But neither Soren nor Gylfie in their short lives knew of such things as hell or the words that would describe such a place. Until their snatching, they really had only known what might be called heaven. Life high in a lovely tree hollow or cactus lined with the downy fluff of their parents, plump insects delivered several times a day, and then the first juicy mouse morsels. And besides all the delicious meals, there were stories — stories of flight, of learning to fly, of the feeling that must be deep in their gizzards in order to rise on the wind.

Number 47-2 stepped up to them and, in her weirdly

hollow voice, she began to speak. "I am what is called a third-degree picker. I pick through the pellets for the larger objects — pebbles, bone, and teeth mostly. Second-degree pickers pick for feathers and fur. First-degree pickers pick for flecks. This is a fleck." 47-2 pointed with her talon to the tiniest speck that glinted in an open pellet. "It is a kind of metal." She paused. "Or something," she added vaguely. "You need not know what they are. You need only know that flecks are precious, more precious than gold. To become a fleck picker is the highest level of skill in the pelletorium. Tomorrow I shall be advanced one level. I shall be a second-degree picker. Therefore, as the most advanced third-degree picker, it is my task to instruct you." And then the owlet blinked. She began humming the dreadful song.

"It is best when beginning as a picker to use your beak. Your talons can be used to steady the pellet. Each object you find is to be lined up neatly on the stone ledge — your work area. Failure to line up objects neatly is a most serious offense. Offenders are severely punished, as shall be demonstrated during our laughter therapy sessions."

Soren and Gylfie had no idea what this owlet was talking about. Laughter therapy? "Do your work diligently and you, too, may be advanced someday." The owlet then stepped up to the ledge, which was covered with pellets, and bent over one. "Proceed. It is strictly forbidden to use your own pellets in this work." 47-2 glared at Soren. The owlet bent her speckled head and began to pick.

Soren felt a gagging sensation and yarped another pellet.

Soren and Gylfie had no idea how long they had been working. It seemed endless. It was not entirely quiet, however. At certain intervals, a low soft whistle alarm would be sounded from one of the smaller owls who monitored the work from overhead ledges and the sound of another pellet song would begin to rise. The songs were sung in the same hollow tones in which 47-2 had spoken. But Soren felt that they were sung mostly to provide a rhythm for their work. The words, he supposed, like their own non-number names, had become meaningless. In between the songs it was not completely silent. There were, of course, certain commands that had to be given. "New pellets needed in area 10-B." Or "Area 20-C needs to pick up the pace." And then there was some talk among the owls as they worked, but the more carefully Soren and Gylfie listened, the stranger this talk seemed. And then suddenly an owlet working at the same ledge as Soren began to speak. "12-1. I feel perfect this morning. I have just completed my first set of pellets. I am sure you shall feel perfect, too, when you have completed your first set. It is a feeling of rare contentment to complete a set. I feel this sense of rare contentment every morning at this hour."

Rare? Soren thought. That was a word he knew, for his parents had told them that the family of Barn Owls to which they belonged, the Tyto Alba, had become rare, which meant there were not many of them. So how could this owlet's contentment be rare if it happened every morning at a particular hour?

"I, too, feel perfect." Another owlet now spoke, turning toward Gylfie this time. It was nearly the same speech.

At regular intervals now, the two owls turned alternately to Soren and Gylfie and gave short little reports on their states of contentment. On occasion, these reports became interspersed with comments. "25-2, for an owlet of your exceedingly tiny stature you have a fine posture as you peck."

"Thank you," Gylfie replied, and dipped her head in what she thought was a docile manner.

"You are most welcome, 25-2."

Then the owlet closest to Soren began, "12-1, your beak work is quite advanced. You work with industry and delicacy."

"Thank you," said Soren. And then for some reason he added, "Thank you very much."

"You're welcome. But you need not be excessively polite. It wastes energy. Politeness is its own reward — just like flecks."

"What are flecks?" The question slipped out, but many of the pellet songs referred to flecks and Soren could not understand for the life of him what they were. He understood the feathers and bones and teeth being found in the pellets, but what were these mysterious flecks? The two owlets each gave small piercing shrieks that contrasted sharply with their usual tones. "Question alarm! Question alarm!" Two ferocious, darkly feathered owls, their glaring yellow eyes framed above by dark red eye tufts, swooped down and plucked up Soren.

"How could you, Soren?" Gylfie nearly cried out, but luckily the question died on her beak.

Soren felt as if his gizzard were dropping to his talons as the two owls soared with him dangling between them. They were transporting him in a most painful manner. Each one held a wing in his talons and it was as if he were being torn in half! And as they spiraled upward in the pelletorium, Soren felt beneath him not the cushion of captured air of which his father had often spoken, but instead a surge of noisy vibrations that seem to pummel him from below.

"They are laughing at you, 12-1. They laugh so hard the air is tossed with their chuckles!" said one of the owls.

"You, 12-1," the other owl was speaking now. "You are our first object of the day for laughter therapy." Soren remained mute. No matter how many questions might batter his brain, his imagination, or dance on the tip of his beak, he would never ask them. The two owls had now alighted with him on a very high ledge that was visible to the entire pelletorium below. The laughter of the owlets and the scores of monitors and guards ricocheted off the stone walls. It filled Soren's head with a terrible clatter. He thought he would go yoicks right there and start screaming.

"And now for the best moment of all in laughter therapy!" There was a shrill screech. The air stirred, and Skench, the Ablah General, landed next to Soren. And then Skench's second-in-command, Lieutenant Spoorn, arrived, eyes darting in an amber glee. *Oh, great Glaux!* thought Soren. *What now?*

CHAPTER NINE
Good Nurse Finny

"Oh, 12-1! Oh, my goodness! Look at you." Soren groaned and blinked.

"What happened?" Soren asked. His eyes fluttered open and he felt himself basking in the tender yellow light of Auntie Finny's eyes.

"Now, now, dear. Questions are what got you into trouble in the first place. We'll have to be a little stricter. All you need to know is that you were naughty and now you're back with me in the stone pit and . . ." A soft babble of soothing hoots streamed from Auntie's beak. But one question after the next pounded inside Soren's head. He nearly had to clamp his beak shut not to ask them. He must have fainted at some point during the laughter therapy session. He was trying to reconstruct what had happened in his head. There had been the question alarm, the two ferocious beaks, the laughter — oh, the laughter had been terrible — but why were his wings hurting so much? This time the question simply withered in his mind, not

69

because he was too frightened to ask but because he had turned his head and seen his wings. Bare! "Great Glaux!" he muttered, and promptly fell over once more in a faint.

"Now, now!" Auntie Finny was clicking her beak. "I'm going to take care of that. You'll feel better in no time. You don't need those silly little feathers."

"Don't need my feathers!" It was not a question. Was this owl totally yoicks? "Don't need my feathers," he repeated, and was about to ask how he would ever fly, but he clamped his beak shut tight. Auntie was now crushing something in her beak. She gave a yarp-like hiccup and a pulpy wad of soggy moss flew from her beak directly onto Soren's wings. It felt good and Soren sighed. "Nice feeling, yes it is. Nothing like this stone moss for curing what ails you. Now you can call me Nursey."

"Nursey?" And then Soren corrected himself. "Oh, Nursey!"

"You're learning, dear. You're learning fast. Sometimes we do have to be a little stricter. But I bet you've learned your lesson and you'll never get plucked again."

"Plucked!" Soren gasped. They had actually plucked him? This wasn't an accident?

"I know! I know what you're thinking. I really don't approve. But you know I have very little say. I can only do my best for each and every little owlet in my pit. I try. I try." She almost whimpered.

But Auntie or Nursey didn't know what Soren was thinking, not at all. She looked at him kindly. She asked no questions, of course, but Soren felt compelled to say, "Auntie . . . I mean, Nursey." Names seemed awfully important to this old Snowy Owl. Very carefully, he was going to try to explain his thoughts without asking questions — oh, he had indeed learned his lesson. "I do not understand, Nursey, why you are so nice here in the stone pit and they are so awful, the owls in the glaucidium and the pelletorium. They are mean for no good reason."

"Ah, but there is a reason."

"There is a reason." Soren's words were flat and carried no inflection of a question. This was indeed possible.

"You see," Nursey Finny continued, "it builds character."

"It builds character, " Soren repeated in the same even tone.

"Through carefully meted-out punishment and self-denial, you shall be made hardy." Nursey spoke in a singsong voice as if she had said these same words many times before.

"Destroying wings builds character. I see." Soren tried to sound logical and keep any hint of the incredulous out of his voice.

"Oh, yes, you do see. I am so pleased."

"And to think I always thought flight was a natural part of an owl's character. Silly me." He was getting awfully good at this.

"Oh, you are a bright little thing," Nursey hooted cheerfully. "You're catching on. Yes, flight is to be earned if one is destined for flight at all."

"Yes, yes, of course," Soren said, trying desperately to keep the reasonable tone in his voice. But inside, his gizzard was twitching madly, his heart was beating rapidly, and a dark panic began to fill him.

"Oh, and here comes 12-8. A fine example of a DNF."

Soren stared at her with incomprehension.

"DNF, dear. It means Destined Not to Fly. 12-8 is one. And a nursey in training, too!"

Who was number 12-8? Soren sorted through all the numbers in his mind. The number sounded familiar and then Soren saw the little Spotted Owl named Hortense, who was so happy to receive her number designation because she hated her name. She was hopping about nearby.

"Come here, 12-8. Your first nursing lesson," Auntie trilled.

Hortense, or number 12-8, had an even blanker look than ever in her eyes. "Ooh, a patient! A patient! Show me how to make moss pulp."

Finny began to show the little owl how to beak the moss until it was soft and squishy. Soren had to admit he didn't mind the attention to his wings that indeed were feeling much better. He observed 12-8 carefully as she applied the moss compresses. He wondered why she was not destined for flight. He carefully tried to figure out how to get the answer without asking a question. "I saw you, I think, in the pelletorium this morning."

"Oh, no, no, not me! I'm strictly a broody."

"A broody," Soren repeated. Only silence followed. "A broody," Soren repeated again. Still silence. "It must be nice to be a broody, to work in the *broodorium*." Soren just made up the word.

"It's not called a broodorium." 12-8 spoke in the perfect hollow tones of the truly moon blinked.

"Oh, it isn't," Soren said flatly. "Yes, how stupid of me. It's that other word. Slips my mind right now."

"No, it doesn't slip your mind. You don't know. No one does." 12-8's voice had turned brittle. "Top secret."

"Top secret."

"Top secret. I've got clearance." The little owl swelled up now with pride.

"Flight clearance."

"Absolutely not! That is stupid. I couldn't have top secret clearance if I had flight clearance." *But don't you want to fly?* Soren was ready to scream the question. Just then, Finny returned.

"Ah, 12-8, you are doing a splendid job. What a little nurse you'll make."

"My wings do feel a lot better," Soren said sweetly, and marveled how deceptive he was quickly becoming. Oh, yes, his wings did feel better, but Soren had another idea, another question he wanted to throw out under the guise of a statement. "I'll tell you the thing that really always perks me up and makes me feel just fine in the gizzard."

"Oh, that's what we want, my dear," Finny cooed.

"A story. My favorite stories are the legends of Ga'Hoole. Yes, the Ga'Hoolian cycle, I think they are called."

A strange sound halfway between a yarp and the screech of a Screech Owl issued from Auntie Finny's beak, and she crumpled into a dead faint.

"Oh, my goodness! Oh, my goodness. I don't know what you said, 12-1, but I've got to nurse Nursey now." The little Spotted Owl trotted off to find a remedy.

"I know what I said," Soren whispered to himself. "I said, 'the legends of Ga'Hoole.'"

CHAPTER TEN

Right Side Up in an Upside-down World

The next night, Gylfie and Soren met under the arch of the glaucidium. They were to begin the Great Scheme, but Soren suddenly had doubts.

"I'm really worried, Gylfie. It might not work."

"Soren," Gylfie pleaded, "who knows if it will work or not, but what have we got to lose if we don't try it?"

"Our minds, to start with," Soren replied. Gylfie gave the soft *churrr* sound of a chuckle that is nearly universal for all owls.

There was a swoosh in the air and suddenly the little Elf Owl was flat on her back. "There is no laughing. Laughter may only be practiced under the direction of Lieutenant Spoorn. Don't do it again. Next time you shall be reported immediately, and I shall anticipate eagerly your first lesson in correct laughter."

The monitor then moved away. Soren and Gylfie

looked at each other wordlessly. This had to be the strangest place imaginable. They taught one how to sleep! Lessons in laughter! Laughter therapy! Soren wondered what possibly could be the purpose of a place like St. Aggie's. What were they really learning to do here and why? What were the flecks, more precious than gold? What were Skench and Spoorn trying to turn them into? Not owls, for sure! But there was not time to dwell on that. Soren had another matter that had been bothering him more and more since his own laughter therapy session.

"Gylfie, you can get out, maybe, but not me. But you can."

"What are you talking about, Soren?"

"Gylfie, you are just a short time from being fully fledged — look at you. I think you've budged some more beginning primaries today. You'll be able to leave soon."

"And so will you."

"What are you talking about? I think you have been moon blinked. They just plucked my feathers, Gylfie."

"They plucked your down. Look, your primary shaft points are still there, and I see some secondary ones, too."

Soren lifted one wing and examined it. There were still budging points. Gylfie was right on this. *But*, Soren wondered, *without down what . . . ?*

It was as if Gylfie had read his thoughts. "You don't

need down to fly, Soren. Down just keeps you warm. You can fly without it. It'll just be cold, and who knows? By the time your flight feathers really come in, you'll probably have some more down."

Soren blinked again. For the first time, there was hope in the dark eyes set like polished stones in his white heart-shaped face, and something quickened in Gylfie's own heart. She had to convince Soren that he could do this. She had to make him really believe in the Great Scheme.

Gylfie had watched as her older brothers and sisters had reached that point, when they seemed to mysteriously gather strength and lift into flight after days of endless hopping. She remembered asking her father how they did it. Now her father's words came back to her:

"Gylf, you can practice forever and still never fly if you do not really believe you can. That is what gives you that feeling in the gizzard." Then her father had stopped and, in a musing tone of voice, said, "Funny isn't it, how all our strongest feelings come through our gizzards — even a feeling that is about our wings." He had ruffled a few of his flight feathers as if to demonstrate. "It all comes through our gizzard," he had repeated.

"Listen to me, Soren," Gylfie said. "I found out a lot in the pelletorium after you fainted and they had to carry you out."

Soren blinked and shivered his shoulders in the way young owls do when they are embarrassed or ashamed. "Yes, Gylfie, while I was stupidly asking questions you were listening."

"Quit beating up on yourself," Gylfie said sharply. "They've already done that." Gylfie's directness shocked Soren. He stopped blinking and looked straight at the Elf Owl. "Look. What did I just tell you? Everything here at St. Aggie's is upside down and inside out. It's our job not to get moon blinked and to stand right side up in an upside-down world. If we don't do that we'll never be able to escape. We'll never be able to think. And thinking is the only way we'll be able to plan an escape. So listen to me." Soren nodded and Gylfie continued. "Now first, I have figured out that tonight is the third night of full shine. In fact, the moon has already started to dwenk. Remember, I told you about this. You'll see that in a few days it shall almost disappear and we won't have to worry about being moon blinked. Every night in the glaucidium, it will become darker and darker and easier and easier for us to find the shadows. But in the meantime, we must act as if we are moon blinked."

Soren resisted asking a question even though he knew there was no danger with Gylfie. But still, he simply did not want to break into Gylfie's thoughts. It was clear to

Soren that this Elf Owl might be very small in every way but her ideas. And he could tell that Gylfie was thinking very hard now.

"After one more newing," Gylfie continued, "you shall be very close to having fledged all of your flight feathers, and certainly by the time of full shine, you shall be ready to fly."

"But what about you, Gylfie? You will be ready in a few days."

"I shall wait for you."

"Wait for me!" It was not a question. Soren was simply shocked. Too shocked to even speak. So finally it was Gylfie who asked the question.

"What's wrong, Soren?"

"Gylfie, I cannot believe what you just said. Why would you wait for me when you can get out of here?"

"That's just the point, Soren. I would never leave you behind. You are my friend, first of all. If I escaped without you, my life would not be worth two pellets to me. And second, we need each other."

"I need you more than you need me," Soren said in a small voice.

"Oh, racdrops!" Once more Soren could hardly believe his ears. Racdrops, short for raccoon droppings, was one of the most daring, dirtiest, worst words an owlet could say. Kludd had gotten thumped good and hard by his mother when Mrs. Plithiver had reported that he had said "racdrops" to her when she insisted he stop teasing Eglantine.

"Soren, you were the one who realized that they were trying to moon blink us with our own names by having us repeat them. That was brilliant."

"But you were the one who knew about moon blinking in the first place. I'd never heard of it."

"I just knew something that you didn't. That's not thinking, just happening to know it. You would have known it if you had been hatched a little earlier or lived in the desert. But now I learned something new. You see, Soren," Gylfie continued, "after they took you away, I made a discovery. That owlet 47-2, she sent me on an errand. It was outside the pelletorium and . . ." Gylfie looked about, then continued her tale in a low voice. The first shine of the moon was just beginning to slither over the dark horizon.

CHAPTER ELEVEN

Gylfie's Discovery

I was supposed to go and tell the pellet gatherers that new trays were needed in our area. So 47-2 pointed me in the direction of what she called the Big Crack. It was, in fact, very near our area and ran straight up a rock side of the pelletorium. I was told to go into the crack and I would find a line of other owlets also going to the store-rooms and to follow them and not go off the trail. So I did just that."

Gylfie was telling the story so well that Soren could imagine every little turn on the path through the rock crack. It was as if he were right there with Gylfie. . . .

"There were many cracks leading off the main crack and sometimes voices could be heard. It was interesting that none of the other owlets who I followed seemed to even notice these cracks or hear the voices. Perhaps they had walked this trail so often it was meaningless to them. But I looked about and could see that at one point in the crack the sky cut through. Yes, it was quite beautiful, really, just a little piece of sky like a blue river flowing above, and then at one point the sky seemed very low. You know" — Gylfie stopped and mused for a moment — "ever since we have been here, Soren, I have had the feeling that St. Aegolius Academy is deep, deep in a stone canyon. That its very steepness and depth make it the perfect prison. But at this one point along the trail, I realized we were up higher and not so deep. Close to the sky."

"Close to the sky," Soren repeated softly. Once he, too, had been close to the sky. Once he had lived in a hollow high up in a fir tree lined with the fluffy down from his parent's breasts. Once he had lived close to that blueness. That blueness of the day sky and the blackness of the night had been so near. No wonder a little owlet could almost believe it could fly before it really could. The sky was a part of owls and owls were a part of the sky.

Gylfie continued her story. "I thought that on the way back to the pelletorium I would try and look a little harder around this particular spot. Maybe slow down. Then I thought, maybe I could just pretend to be marching. You know, just like the Great Scheme idea. It would be a good test. Would anyone notice? Maybe not and better yet, there did not seem to be any monitors around." Gylfie's eyes brightened and she paused, hoping this idea would sink in with Soren and convince him that it could all work.

"So, on the way back, that is exactly what I did. No one seemed to notice at all. They just moved around me as if I were a part of the stone wall that jutted out. And then something extraordinary happened. An owlet seemed to stumble near me. This owl, a young Snowy, just blinked at me and I thought, 'Great Glaux, I've been discovered standing here.' So I pointed up toward the sky — as if I were admiring the view. "'Sky,' I said pleasantly. And the owl blinked, not a question blink, but a real moon blink. The same look that is in their eyes when they repeat their names on the sleep march." Gylfie took a deep breath, as if what she was about to say was terribly important. And it was. "I realized then that many words for these owlets, just like their names, have no meaning, no meaning at all. Can you imagine, Soren, an owl not knowing what the sky is?"

Soren thought for a moment. It was indeed unimaginable. Or was it? He remembered what Auntie Finny had said about some birds not destined for flight. But Soren had another question. "Does this owlet just not know the word or does she really not know what the sky is?" Gylfie blinked. Soren truly was a deep thinker. He continued, "Mrs. Plithiver, our nest-maid snake, I told you about her, well, she is blind, but she knows about the sky. She says that all snakes, whether they are blind or not, call the sky 'the Yonder' because it is so far away for snakes. It is about as far as anything can be for a snake and that is why she loved working for our family — because she felt close to the Yonder."

"No, Soren, I think this owlet truly has been completely and perfectly moon blinked. She does not know the word, nor does she have any idea of sky."

"That's so sad," Soren said softly.

"It is sad, but you know it makes our job of escaping easier. Maybe the monitors have been moon blinked about words. But I have to tell you the other thing I discovered when I stopped at this place."

"What's that?"

"Well, down a side crack I saw a place that was guarded by an owl who looked familiar. As a matter of fact, I don't know how I didn't recognize him instantly. It was Grimble, the owl who snatched me. I've thought a lot about him. Do you remember what he said when we were flying here, something about it hardly seeming worth the effort and how the owl who snatched you warned him that he might get a demerit if Spoorn heard him talking that way?"

"Yes," Soren said slowly. He was not sure where Gylfie was going with this.

"Well, I think Grimble has perhaps not been perfectly moon blinked and that could be really good, too."

"Wait! One time you say it will be helpful to us if someone is perfectly moon blinked and the next minute you say someone like Grimble, who might not be, can be helpful, too."

"Grimble might be one of us, don't you see, Soren? He might be pretending to be moon blinked the way we have. As a matter of fact, I am almost sure he is."

"Why?"

"Because I went down that side crack and I found out what he was guarding."

"You did?"

"Yes. And do you know how hard it is to find out information when it's against the rules to ask a question?"

"Oh, yes!" Soren said.

"A couple of times I almost did ask questions, and Grimble seemed to sense it."

"What did you find out?"

"Have you ever heard of books?"

"Of course I have," Soren said indignantly. "Books and Barn Owls go very far back." These were the exact words that his parents often said when they took out their few books to read aloud to the owlets. "Especially since so many of us once lived in churches. My parents had a book of psalms."

"Psalms?" Gylfie was truly impressed. "What are psalms?"

"Like songs, sort of, I think." Soren had not really heard that many. But when his mother read him the psalms it seemed that she sang the words more than spoke them. "But what about books? What did you find out from Grimble?"

"The place he guards is a book place. They call it a library. Have you ever heard of that — a library?"

"Never. How did you find out all this? You certainly didn't ask questions."

"No, of course not. You see, it is off-limits. Only Skench and Spoorn are allowed in. That's how I sensed he might be one of us. He seemed to know the question before I ever had to think of a way of asking it. I want to get in."

"Why? I think we just need to get out of here."

"I want to know about the flecks," Gylfie said.

"Flecks? What flecks?"

"The flecks we're always singing about — the bright flecks at the core, the ones the first-degree pickers pick for."

"Are you yoicks, Gylfie? You want to stay around this place long enough to become a first-degree picker?"

"Soren, something worse than just moon blinking

young owls is going on here. I just sense it. Something very bad. Something that could destroy all the kingdoms of all the owls on all the earth." Gylfie paused. "Something deadly." The word seemed to hang in the air, and Gylfie stared ahead unblinkingly.

"These owlets are the walking dead. I think it would be better to be dead than be like 47-2, but you said all the kingdoms of all the owls on all the earth?"

"Total destruction," Gylfie said. Her voice was like ice. "Look, Soren. I want to get out as much as you do. I think Grimble might be helpful, but we'll have to be very careful, and that library with those books holds secrets, secrets I think that could help us escape and maybe help other owls — other owls in your Kingdom of Tyto and mine in the Desert of Kuneer. Would you want any other owls to go through what we've been through?"

Soren suddenly thought of Eglantine. He loved Eglantine. The thought of her being snatched, of being moon blinked, was almost more than he could bear. There was a world of Eglantines out there. Did he really want them to become empty-eyed, hollow-voiced, destined-not-to-fly owls? A shudder ran through Soren. It was not good enough to just escape. In fact, their task was greater than he had ever imagined.

A shriek split the night in the glaucidium. The moon

had risen and the alarm for the first sleep march sounded. Soren and Gylfie felt the stir as thousands of owls began to move. The strange babble rose up as each owl repeated its old name over and over again. The two little owls looked at each other and moved their beaks, turning the sound of their numbers into something that might pass for a name — any name but their own. And now, tonight, they would try the second part of their strategy for the first time. The one that Gylfie had tested in the Big Crack. They would march in place giving the appearance of motion but never moving from the cast shadows. If it had worked for Gylfie in the Big Crack it should work here.

Almost immediately they felt the press of owls about them. They held their breath, fearful that their ruse would be discovered. But the throngs of owls simply parted, just as the waters of a stream split to flow around a rock. They were jostled a bit and they felt a terrible chill as a sleep correction monitor swept by, but the monitor did not look twice at them as they marched in place. No, the monitor seemed only concerned about a small Snowy Owl ahead who had apparently been caught sleeping last time with its head under its wing. "Wing alert on number 85-2. Monitors in the fourth quadrant, please be advised."

CHAPTER TWELVE

Moon Scalding

There was an odd rhythm to the days and the nights at St. Aggies, where owls were expected to sleep at night and work during the day. The moon dwenked, the world darkened, and then once more it was the time of the newing. It was not all dreadful at St. Aggie's. Both Soren and Gylfie were the recipients of extra-special treats, beyond the usual cricket fare, from their pit guardians, Auntie and Unk. Indeed, the time in the pits began to seem like an oasis, verdant and green in the stone world of St. Aegolius Academy for Orphaned Owls. Gylfie received extra rations of snake, the occasional nap was permitted, and Soren, too, was even taught by Auntie how to eat a vole with bones. One could hardly call it a First Bones ceremony. But, nonetheless, Auntie slipped Soren a nice plump vole, just the right length to be swallowed whole. And even though questions were discouraged, Auntie was able to guide Soren through the consuming of his first creature, bones and all. She complimented him lavishly on his first yarped bone pellet. And Soren, of course, was struck by the bittersweet memory of his father complimenting Kludd after his First Bones ceremony.

But despite all the extras, the favors, the gentle coddling from Auntie, Soren could not forget Gylfie's icy voice: "Total destruction. All the kingdoms of all the owls on all the earth." Why? Soren had asked himself often, but then realized it didn't really matter why, if indeed it this was the purpose of St. Aggie's. Even more disturbing was a newer idea of Soren's. *Perhaps,* he thought, *these owls were not really owls at all but rather some kind of demon spirits in a feathered guise.* This was why when Auntie came to him now with his favorite, a plump centipede, Soren stared deep into her yellow eyes as if trying to see the dark antic shadow of a demon. *Are you really an owl, Auntie?* he wanted to ask. *Are you really a true Snowy Owl descended from Glaux, come from the North Kingdoms — or are you a white demon?*

It was the third night of the second full shine now. The full shines seemed to last forever. Soren and Gylfie emerged from these periods of full shines exhausted, but they had somehow managed to resist moon blinking so far. Their strategy for the sleep marches had worked.

Had worked up until this second night of second full shine.

"Right, left. Right, left." They clicked their talons in the precise beat that filled the two glaucidiums as they stood in the overhang of the shared arch.

"Hey, you two!" A hoot shredded the air around them, splitting right through the march. It wasn't Jatt nor was it Jutt. It was none other than Spoorn, Skench's dreadful second-in-command. "I saw you two here last round, and now this round. Lazy, no-good haggards!" Soren and Gylfie, caught in the fierce yellow glare of the Screech Owl's eyes, began to tremble. "Avoiding the moon, that's what I'd say! Well, we have remedies for that."

Oh, Glaux, Soren thought. *If I get plucked again! And Gylfie. She'll never survive it.* "March, you two, march to the moon blaze!"

"Don't say anything," Gylfie whispered. "We're together, that should count for something." *For what?* Soren wondered. *We'll get plucked together? We'll die together?*

The two youngs owls were marched into a stone chamber off to one side of one of the glaucidiums. The walls of this chamber were made of pure white stone and slanted outward at peculiar angles. Indeed, the moonlight seemed to pour into the white stone cell and blaze off the walls in a fierce brightness. "You shall remain here and be scalded by the moon's light until the moon goes. See how you like that!" Spoorn blasted them with a screech to

91

punctuate her remarks, and the screech, as powerful as a wind, nearly toppled the little Elf Owl.

"And no head ducking. We'll be watching," added Skench.

Gylfie managed to recover her balance and planted her tiny talons firmly on the stone. "Well," she said, "at least we're not plucked."

"Gylfie, are you yoicks?"

"In these situations, Soren, you have to look on the bright side — no pun intended," Gylfie said as she looked around and saw moonlight bouncing off every surface.

"Gylfie, I don't think there is a bright side, pun or not. Plucked or moon scalded? You consider that a choice?"

"We're not going to be either!" A new fierceness had crept into Gylfie's voice.

"Well, how do you think we can avoid it? You can stand in my shadow but it's not exactly as if I can stand in yours — you're a midget."

"That is not fair, Soren, and you know it. Stature jokes are not appropriate. They are considered very bad form where I come from. Indeed, there is a society, the Small Owl Society — SOS — and its charter is to prevent cruel and tasteless remarks concerning size. My grandmother and a Pygmy Owl founded it." Gylfie brimmed with indignation. She seemed far more upset about Soren's use of the word "midget" than being stuck in the white stone chamber for moon scalding.

"I'm sorry. But I still don't see how we're going to avoid the moonlight in here."

"We have to think."

"But that is just what it is impossible to do when one is moon blinked, Gylfie. I think this is it for us." Soren looked down at Gylfie and, even as he said it, he felt a strange numbness stealing over him. And Gylfie's eyes began to blink in an odd manner.

In the blaze of the moon's light, the two young owls felt their essence departing. Soren's brain swam with confusion. His gizzard seemed to grow still. He looked at the moon-blasted walls of the stone cell and they appeared slippery, slippery as ice, and on this ice of the moon's light he felt his memories slip, slip, slipping away. He wanted to grab on to them with his talons, hold them, but he was simply too tired. He was about to fall asleep and when he awoke he knew he would be a changed owl. He would be unrecognizable to himself. He would truly have become 12-1 and Gylfie, too, would no longer be Gylfie but a number, 25-2 — rhymes with Ga'Hoole!

There was a click inside Soren's head. The moment he had thought of the word Ga'Hoole something seemed to clear in his brain. His gizzard stirred. *Ga'Hoole.* The mere mention of the Ga'Hoole legends had made Auntie Finny faint, but the mere thought of the word crashed like thunder and seemed to wake Soren up.

"Gylfie! Gylfie!" He nudged the tiny owl with one of his talons. "Gylfie, have you ever heard of the legends of Ga'Hoole?" Gylfie, whose movements seemed thick and slow, suddenly twitched. Soren could almost see a pulse course through the little owl, jerking her into alertness.

"Ga'Hoole — why, yes. My mother and father would often tell us tales. Tales of Yore we called them."

"We called them legends — the Ga'Hoolian legends." With each mention of the word, the young owls seemed to grow slightly more alert, something within them quickening.

"I think," said Soren, "that we should tell those Tales of Yore until the moon goes down, and maybe these words will thin the full shine and be our shield against this scalding."

Gylfie looked at Soren in wonder. *However did this Barn Owl come upon these ideas?!*

And so Soren began . . .

"Once upon a time, before there were kingdoms of owls, in a time of ever-raging wars, there was an owl born in the country of the Great North Waters and his name was Hoole. Some say there was an enchantment cast upon him at the time of his hatching, that he was given natural gifts of extraordinary power. But what was known of this owl was that he inspired other owls to great and noble deeds and that, although he wore no crown of gold, the owls knew him as a king, for indeed his good grace and conscience anointed him and his spirit was his crown. In a wood of straight tall trees he had hatched, in a glimmering time when the seconds slow between the last minute of the old year and the first of the new, and the forest on this night was sheathed in ice."

Soren's voice was hushed and lovely as he told the tale of the first legend of Ga'Hoole, the "Coming of Hoole." The two little owls' hearts grew strong, their brains cleared, and their gizzards once again quickened.

CHAPTER THIRTEEN

Perfection!

I think it's working," the Screech Owl Spoorn said to the Ablah General, Skench. From their stone perches high above the moon blaze cell, Skench and Spoorn looked down on Soren and Gylfie. They could not hear the hushed tale that Soren was repeating and the two young owls were careful to stand very still. When the moon finally slipped down in the night sky, Skench and Spoorn alighted onto the floor of the moon blaze cell and peered into each of the owl's eyes.

"Perfect!" Spoorn declared.

"We are perfect," Gylfie replied. "We are so pleased to be perfect for our masters. Number 25-2 feels quite perfect and complete."

Soren picked up the cue. "Number 12-1 also feels perfect. We await your commands."

"Come along, little ones. I knew you could do it," Spoorn said. This was the most kindly tone either Soren or Gylfie had ever heard Spoorn use.

"Next thing you know, you'll be having your Specialness ceremony."

Racdrops! thought Gylfie.

"You know, Spoorn," Skench was saying, "these two were marked as haggards from the start, or at least the Barn Owl was, and sometimes I think that a haggard once scalded actually makes a better servant to our cause."

Dream on, you addle-brained idiot bird. The words roared silently in Soren's head.

"I am thinking of the little one for battle claw maintenance and the Barn Owl for the eggorium."

"Or maybe even the hatchery for the little one."

Hatchery! Eggorium! Battle claws! Soren and Gylfie were suddenly very alert. Yet they managed to walk in the dazed manner of the perfectly moon blinked.

"You know," Skench continued, "I think we need to put them in the same stone pit and the same glaucidium — reinforced moon scalding. If they look into each other's eyes, I think it has been proven that it reinforces the effects of the scalding."

Ha! Gylfie nearly laughed out loud.

So the two young owls were returned to Soren's glaucidium, and Jatt and Jutt were duly informed that these two were to be together and periodically made to gaze into each other's eyes.

"All right, you two!" barked Jutt. "Face off!"

And neither Jatt nor Jutt could see the twinkle deep within each of the young owl's eyes, nor did they hear Soren say, as they turned their backs, "We did it, Gylfie. We did it."

So once more the days slipped into the nights, and the nights became dark links in the silver chain of the moon as it cycled through its dwenkings and full shines, sometimes appearing as an immense, throbbing, bright globe, at other times as thin as the finest thread of down filament from an owl's breast. Patiently, they waited for their flight feathers to grow in. Each day, Soren would do a quick inventory of what he had, what showed promise. His flight feathers were definitely advancing, perhaps not fully fledged, but definitely out there. When he flipped his head back, as owls could do, and rotated it, he could get a good view of his tail feathers, and when no one was looking, he would practice rotating and ruddering maneuvers. There would, of course, be no First Flight ceremonies. In fact, Soren lived in perpetual dread of being informed in a most unceremonious way that he was not "destined" for flight as, apparently, the Spotted Owl, 12-8, formerly Hortense, had been. This, she always said, was due to her top secret status that had something to do with being a broody.

"Think of all we've learned, Soren," Gylfie said one day, after having served in the battle claws chamber. She seemed blithely confident that when the time came for them to fly they would, and that it was much more important to survey the entire range of canyons and gulches that composed St. Aggie's, so that when they were ready they could escape, never be caught again, and warn others. "Let me tell you what I've learned today in the battle claws chamber. . . ."

Soren indulged Gylfie and let her run on. "Well," she began, "they have the battle claws that fit over their talons but they don't make them themselves. They can sort of repair them but basically they have to scavenge them from other places, other battlefields."

"But what other battlefields? Look, Gylfie, I didn't live long in Tyto but I never saw or heard my parents talk about any battles. Did you ever hear your parents talk of any?"

Gylfie thought hard. "No. No, I didn't," she said slowly. "And when we were snatched they weren't wearing them."

"They would hardly need them for us. We were nestlings. Our own talons were not even hardened off." Gylfie blinked at Soren as if he had just said something astonishing. She remained silent for a moment.

"That's just it, isn't it, Soren? They didn't need them for

us. No. But they needed us and these battle claws for something bigger . . . much bigger. Remember in the third legend of the Ga'Hoolian cycle when the sea serpents that could walk upon the land and swim in the sea started to form their plan? Remember how they wanted to drag the entire world of owls and birds into the sea, so that they could reign on both land and sea?"

"Yes," Soren said quietly.

"I think they are planning something big like that."

Soren started to say that the story of the serpents was just a legend and not true, that such sea creatures did not exist. But then he realized deep within himself it didn't really matter. These owls did exist and maybe they wanted just what the imaginary creatures of the legends wanted. Soren had a horrible vision of the entire forest kingdom of Tyto and the desert kingdom of Kuneer and all the owl kingdoms being swirled into this stone world of St. Aggie's.

"So," Gylfie continued, "when we do escape, Soren, we must know as much as we can. We must know about flecks and why they are more precious than gold, and what they plan to do to the kingdoms of owls. It is going to be our duty to warn the rest of the owl kingdoms. Don't worry about flying now. Think about how much we are learning. Look, we know the pelletorium inside out, we've been on cricket detail, now battle claws; the last area we have to crack — pardon the pun — is the eggorium and that broody place."

"Top secret. Remember."

"As if 12-8 would ever let us forget. Oh, Glaux, here she comes now. Hang on, Soren, I'm going to try some of my charm." Gylfie winked and then the dull light of a moon-blinked owl stole into her eyes.

Soren watched as Gylfie, in the semblance of the perfectly moon-blinked owl, trotted up to Hortense. "12-8, you appear calm and satisfied from the perfection of performing your duty well. I cannot imagine that your Specialness ceremony is far off."

"I do not need a ceremony to feel special. For you see, 25-2, I am entrusted with the most sacred and vital of tasks for our beloved St. Aggie's community."

"Yes, that must be so. 12-1 and I would feel it an honor to serve in such a manner. But then again we do not have the qualifications, the obvious talents of you, 12-8. Ah, to be the vessel of such trust."

12-8 seemed to swell with pride before their eyes. A pit monitor suddenly swooped down. "Humbleness correction, humility check, dear." It was a smallish, whiskered

Screech Owl. Her amber eyes blinked a warning out of her bristly face. 12-8 seemed to shrink to half her size instantly. "Oh, I beg your pardon. It is pride in my work, not pride in myself. I remain a humble servant to a great cause."

"Yes, a great cause." Gylfie repeated the words, and although it was a statement, Soren really heard a question at the center. *What was this great cause?*

"Yes, that's better, dear." The whiskered Screech Owl nodded and floated off to a higher perch in the stone pit.

Gylfie felt that the moment was right. "You are the last owl in the world that I would ever say lacked humility, 12-8. You are for my friend and myself a perfect example of humility. You are beyond humbleness! You are . . ." Gylfie was madly searching for a word. *What's she going to say next?* Soren couldn't imagine. He had never seen such a demonstration of outrageous fawning. "You are *subglaucious*." 12-8 blinked at the word as did Soren, who had no idea what *subglaucious* meant. "We, my friend and I, only wish that we could serve in the eggorium and thus attain such humbleness as yourself."

"Your words are kind, 25-2. I shall hope that they might encourage me in my continuing quest for humility while in service to a great cause." She wandered off looking a tad more moon blinked than before, if that was possible.

"What in Glaux's name is *subglaucious?*" Soren said as soon as she was out of earshot.

"No idea. I made it up. We've got to get into that eggorium and the hatchery," Gylfie replied, and the twinkle returned to her eyes.

CHAPTER FOURTEEN
The Eggorium

The following day, Soren was back at his post in the pelletorium. Indeed, he had been promoted to a second-degree picker and was now appalled to find himself reciting the exact same words to a new owlet that 47-2 had said to him upon arriving. "I am 12-1. I am to be your guide for the pelletorium. Follow me." He spoke in the same peculiar manner. The hollow, clipped sounds came naturally to him now. So when Gylfie came up with a tray of fresh pellets, he was perhaps more than ready to listen to her suggestions of a possible new worksite.

"The eggorium. I think I found us an entry-level position. Egg sorting. Fellow in the pellet storage area told me about it. Mite blight in the hatchery."

"So what does that mean?" Soren asked.

"I'm not sure. All I know is that they had to take owls off duty in the eggorium and put them in the hatchery."

"I still don't really understand what they do in either one of those places. Not to mention, what are these flecks that the first-degree pickers pick? It's like a puzzle that never seems to quite come together. It's as if we have all these pieces of things, but are we any closer to knowing what this place is about and how to get out of it, or if we'll ever learn to fly?" Soren was getting more and more agitated as he spoke.

"Try to keep calm, Soren. I just have a feeling that we're close to something."

Soren and Gylfie stood in a small antechamber. Above them perched a large Snowy Owl.

"Welcome to the eggorium!" the Snowy hooted deeply. "To work in the eggorium and the hatchery is the highest of honors. You have been given temporary top secret clearance. We are in a bit of a bind these days as we have had an epidemic of mite blight. For this reason you shall not be given a DNF, or Destined Not to Fly ranking, but you shall have to undergo a procedure at the end of your term, which, although not painful, shall make you forget the information that you shall be exposed to here."

"Moon scalding," Gylfie whispered. "But we know how to handle that."

"Right." Soren was still weak with relief over not being a DNF.

"And now into the eggorium. Please follow me." The Snowy hooted softly.

There was a collective gasp from all the owls. For even a perfectly moon-blinked owl could not help but be stunned by the scene before them. Thousands upon thousands of eggs were being sorted, eggs of all sizes and all pure white, glistening now in the moonlight. And as they sorted, they sang a song.

> *By these eggs we set a store*
> *We sort them out and ask for more.*
> *Pygmy, Elf, Spotted, and Snowy*
> *Make our gizzards get all glowie.*
> *Barn Owls, Great Grays, Barred, and Screech*
> *Give our hearts an extra beat.*
>
> *The work's top secret, that is true,*
> *But we are the best — the eggorium crew!*
> *Don't give a hoot that no one flies*
> *For upon these eggs the future relies.*
> *Such is our noble destiny*
> *To guard St. Aggie's through eternity!*

The instructions were simple. For this first phase, each of them was to look for eggs of their own species, as these would be the easiest for them to identify. Thus Soren was to sort out Barn Owl eggs and Gylfie was to sort out Elf Owl eggs. They were to roll the eggs into a designated area. From there, they would be transported by larger and more experienced owls to the hatchery.

Soren was simply aghast. This was exactly what he had overheard his mother and father talking about — egg snatching. "Unspeakable!" That was the word his mother had used. *Unspeakable.* But here it was, right before his very eyes. He began to tremble. There was a sickening feeling in his gizzard.

"Don't go yeep on me," Gylfie hissed.

"How can I go yeep? I don't even know how to fly yet."

Going *yeep,* as every owl and bird knew, was a term for when one's wings seemed to lock, when a bird lost its instincts and could no longer fly and would suddenly plummet to the ground.

As loathsome as the work was, it was pretty easy. However, Soren could not help but wonder with each Barn Owl egg he found where it had come from in Tyto. Did his parents know this owl egg's parents? Luckily, the Barn Owl egg station and the Elf Owl station were not that far apart. So as Soren and Gylfie arrived at their respective stations, rolling their eggs, they would exchange a word or two. "I haven't seen 12-8, Hortense," Soren said.

"She's not here. She's in the hatchery. That's where the broodies are — they sit on the eggs. We've got to get in there."

"How do you plan to do that?" Soren asked.

"I don't know. I'll think of something," Gylfie said.

Just before their shift ended, Gylfie thought of something.

"You!"

"Me what?" Soren asked.

"You're a perfect broody."

"What? Me a broody? Have you gone yoicks? I'm a male owl. Male owls don't sit nests."

"They do occasionally — in very cold climates sometimes."

"Well, this isn't an especially cold climate. Why not you?"

"They don't need an Elf Owl now but they do need a Barn Owl. I heard them talking and, by the way, they have plenty of male owls up there sitting on nests."

"What do you mean by 'up there'? Up where?"

"Up there, Soren. I think it's higher than the library. . . ."

I think it's very close to the sky. I think . . ." Gylfie paused for dramatic effect. "We could fly from up there."

Soren felt his gizzard give a lurch. "I'll go!"

"Good fella!" Gylfie gave Soren a friendly cuff, although she was so short she could hardly reach his wing. But it seemed like a really male owl thing to do and she wanted to assure Soren that, although he was going to be a broody, he was still one tough little owl. "And I myself plan on getting promoted to moss tender."

CHAPTER FIFTEEN
The Hatchery

It was Soren's second night on the job. He actually worked a shift with three other Barn Owls, one of whom was male. When it was a night shift, he did not have to report to the glaucidium. It wasn't quite as humiliating as he had thought. There certainly was a constant stream of food. Broodies were well tended. Someone was always coming by, clucking, "How about a nice fat worm, just flown in from Tyto, a bit of snake, a vole, red squirrel." No, the eating was definitely good in the hatchery. Gylfie did manage to get herself in as a moss tender. And if their shifts coincided, there was plenty of time to talk, as Gylfie made extra trips to tuck moss and bits of fluff into Soren's nest. Soren had four eggs in his nest, which seemed a tad crammed. He thought mostly there were two or three eggs to a Barn Owl's nest. But then again, what did he know? Just as he was beginning to think on this, the second night, that it wasn't so bad, the Barn Owl on the nest next to him spoke in that empty moon-blinked voice, "Crack alert! Crack alert. Egg tooth visible."

Two Barred Owls came hustling over. Soren felt his gizzard twinge with excitement. He leaned out of his nest to take a peek. The egg was giving those familiar shudders — just like Eglantine's egg had, which now seemed so long ago. But no one seemed at all excited. No one was gasping with joy, saying, "It's coming! It's coming!"

The egg was rocking now. Soren could see the little hole and the egg tooth, pale and glistening, poking out.

"All right," said the first Barred Owl in a cool voice. "Enough with that egg tooth. Let's crack it." And with that, the two Barred Owls gave solid thwacks with their talons. The egg split. Then one of the Barred Owls hooked the slimy white blob with its talon and firmly pulled it out while the other one turned the shell up. "Bottoms up!" the owl said crisply, and she dumped out the hatchling.

Soren was so shocked he could barely breathe. No one exclaimed "It's a girl!" No one said "adorable" or "enchanting." No one said anything except "Number 401-2."

The other Barred Owl nodded in response. "So we're into the four hundred sequence with the Barn Owls, now."

"Yes, what an accomplishment," sighed the one who had numbered this little owlet. Soren felt a rage. Accomplishment! This was the most horrid, despicable thing he had ever witnessed. A coldness that began in his gizzard seemed to creep through Soren from his new tail feathers up to his wing tips and down to his talons. He realized that he would rather see this little owl dead than alive in St. Aggie's. They had to get out. He and Gylfie had to get out. They must learn to fly. Where was Gylfie? She was on this shift. He wished she could come by and see this. He craned his head about but there was no sign of the little Elf Owl.

It was the stillest time of the moonless night, and on break Gylfie had stepped into a large crack in the rock, perfect for hiding an Elf Owl. She was watching Hortense. Hortense had proven herself to be such an exceptional broody that she had been given a big nest on a large out-cropping of stone somewhat away from the others, where there was more room. She had become very adept at spreading herself over several eggs at a time. It was a change in shift for moss tenders in Gylfie's area so it would be a while before any came by.

And now the Spotted Owl, who was indeed large for an owl her age, was doing something rather odd. She had actually stepped off her nest, and it appeared to Gylfie as if she were trying to dislodge an egg from the nest. Gylfie blinked and blinked again. Gylfie nearly gasped out loud as she saw 12-8 gently roll the egg to the edge of the stone outcropping. Then, out of the blackness of this moonless night, there appeared a spot of dazzling white — just a spot like a tiny moon floating in the darkness, a tiny feathered moon! Gylfie's eyes widened. It was the head of a bald eagle. She had seen them in the desert. This one was huge and had a wingspan that was immense. It alighted on the ledge and silently picked up the egg in its talons. Not a word was exchanged. Indeed, the only thing that Gylfie heard was a soft sigh in the night as 12-8 climbed back on her nest.

Gylfie and Soren finally met up at dawn when they were both due to go off their shifts. They each were so eager to talk about their experiences that they began to argue as to who would go first. Finally, Gylfie hissed her news. "12-8! She's an infiltrator!"

"What?" Soren was stunned. His beak dropped open. The story of the horrific hatching seemed like nothing compared to this.

"A spy," Gylfie said in a throaty voice.

"Wait. Are we talking about the same owl? Hortense? Number 12-8?"

"She's no more 12-8 than I'm 25-2 or you're — what's your number? I keep forgetting."

"12-1," Soren said dimly. "Hush, here she comes now."

Hortense walked by and then stopped. "I hear, number 12-1, that you are doing an admirable job as a broody. It is the most rewarding work. Each little egg that I bring to hatching makes me feel satisfied in a most humble way."

"Thank you, 12-8," Soren replied numbly. Then the Spotted Owl turned to Gylfie. "And I understand that you are an excellent moss tender. You, too, might advance to become a broody for small eggs. I am sure you shall find complete fulfillment in this task."

Gylfie nodded mutely.

What an actress!

For the next two nights, Soren and Gylfie argued about how they would confront Hortense.

"I think we should just go up to her when she's alone," Gylfie said. "And we say, 'Hortense, it has come to our attention . . .'"

"What do you mean 'come to our attention'? You spied on her, Gylfie. That could make her nervous, 'the come to our attention' bit. She might think a lot of owls have seen her."

"You're right."

"Why do we have to confront her at all?"

"Why? Well, what if she's part of something here?

What if there are twenty Hortenses in St. Aggie's? What if there is some hidden network of . . . of disgruntled un-moon-blinked owls? Maybe they're planning a revolution."

"What's a revolution?" Soren asked, and Gylfie blinked.

"It's kind of like war but the sides aren't exactly equal. It's like the little fellows rising up against the big baddies," Gylfie said.

"Oh," said Soren.

"Look," Gylfie said, "we have to make friends, real friends, with Hortense. Her nest is in the highest place in St. Aggie's. That's where we're going to leave from." Gylfie paused and walked right under Soren's beak. "Look down at me, Soren."

"What?"

"Soren, we've got to learn how to fly. Now!"

CHAPTER SIXTEEN

Hortense's Story

But first, they had to talk to Hortense. It was not, of course, just a question of picking the right moment but the right words. The moment was easy enough. The following evening, Soren and Gylfie managed to synchronize their schedules so that Soren had a break from his broody chores while Gylfie was still on moss-tending duty. Soren requested permission to help his friend deliver moss, which was granted, as there were still shortages in both the hatchery and the eggorium. Together, the two owls made their way up to the distant outcropping where Hortense sat this evening on a large nest with at least eight eggs in it.

"Phew!" Soren sighed. "Some hike up here."

"Nothing to it." Gylfie hopped along. "You get used to it. All right, now, you know the drill. You begin."

It was Soren who had thought of the opening words — or word. The opening word was a name: "Hortense." And the speech was simple.

They were now approaching the top of the outcrop. The wind was strong. Indeed, it was the first time that Soren had felt the wind since he had arrived at St. Aggie's. Silvery dark clouds raced against the sky. This was where owls belonged — up high with the wind and the sky and the stars that swirled in the night. He felt invigorated and confident.

"Welcome 25-2 and 12-1 to my humble abode."

Soren dropped the moss from his beak onto the nest, and Hortense began tucking it into the niches and gaps. "Hortense!"

Hortense looked up and blinked at him. Her yellow eyes thickened with the moon-blink gaze.

"Hortense, this is not humble, this is where owls belong — high, near the wind, near the sky, close to the heartbeat of the night." *Amazing,* Gylfie thought. Soren might not know the word "revolution" but this owl could talk. "Hortense, you are an owl, a Spotted Owl."

"I am number 12-8."

"No you're not, Hortense," Soren said, and this was Gylfie's cue.

"Hortense, cut the pellets. You are Hortense and I saw you acting not as 12-8 but as Hortense, the brave, imaginative Spotted Owl. I saw you deliver an egg from this nest to an eagle."

At that moment, Hortense blinked again and the daze lifted from her eyes, simply evaporated like fog on a sunny day. "You saw?"

"I saw, Hortense," Gylfie said gently. "You are no more moon blinked than we are."

"I had my suspicions about you two," Hortense said softly. Her eyes seemed to lose their brittle stare. Indeed, Soren thought they were the loveliest owl eyes he had ever seen. Deep brown like the still pool in the forest that he had seen from his family's nest in the fir tree. But there was also a kind of flickering light in them. Speckles of white dotted the crown of her head and her entire body seemed dappled in shades of amber and brown, shot through with spots of white like blurry stars.

"We never suspected you," Soren added quickly. "That is, until Gylfie saw you that night."

"Are there any other owls here that are un-moon blinked?" Gylfie asked.

"We're the only three, I think."

"How did you get here? How did you resist moon blinking?"

"It's a long story how I got here. And, as to how I resisted moon blinking, well, I'm not sure. You see, where I come from there is a stream, and the flecks that they pick from pellets run heavily in that stream."

"What are the flecks?" Gylfie asked.

"I'm not sure of that, either. They can be found in rocks and soil and water. They seem to occur everywhere, but in our part of the Kingdom of Ambala there is a large deposit that runs through the creeks and rivers. It is both a blessing and a curse. Some of us have unusual powers because of the flecks, we think, but for others it disrupts their navigational abilities to fly true courses. I had a grandmother who eventually lost her wits entirely, but before that she hatched my father, who could see through rock."

"What? Impossible!"

"No, it's true, yet my brother went blind at an early age. So one never knew how it might affect them. I think in my case it perhaps made me resistant to moon blinking. But that doesn't explain how I got here. It was no accident. I chose to come."

"You chose to come?" Gylfie and Soren both gasped.

"I told you it's a long story."

"I'm on break," Soren said.

"And they're short on monitors. I won't be missed," Gylfie added.

"Well, first of all, I am much older than I appear. I am a fully mature owl."

"What?!" Soren and Gylfie both said with complete disbelief.

"Yes, it's true. I hatched almost four years ago."

"Four years ago!" Soren said.

"Yes, indeed, but perhaps one of the effects of the flecks on me was that I was always small, small as an owlet, and never really grew to be much bigger than owlet size. My feathers were delayed coming in, and, of course, I have further delayed them." At this point, Hortense stuck her beak into the nest and pulled out a lovely brown-and-white Spotted Owl feather.

"Is that from a molt?" Soren asked. He had molted when he had shed his first down. There had been a First Molting ceremony, and his mother had saved those baby feathers in a special place.

"No, not a molt. I pull them out myself."

"You pluck yourself?!" Soren and Gylfie gasped in horror.

"Well," she laughed, and the *churr* sound of a Spotted Owl's laughter was indeed a lovely sound that no moon-blinked owl could ever make. "I am," she said with a twinkle in her eye, "a DNF."

"Destined Not to Fly." Soren said the words softly.

"Yes, because of my top secret work, but also because of my delayed feather development. So I was a natural."

"A natural for what?" Gylfie asked.

"To come here. To find out what was going on. You see,

in the Forest of Ambala, our losses due to St. Aggie's patrols had become increasingly heavy. We had been losing baby owlets and eggs at an astonishing rate. Something had to be done. And this, of course, meant sacrifices. One of our bravest owls had followed a St. Aggie's patrol and discovered this maze of stone canyons in which they lived. That particular owl, Cedric, had sacrificed an egg from his and his mate's nest just so he could follow them.

"I volunteered for service as well. I figured that I probably wouldn't have much of a normal life, what with my delayed feather development, and then when my feathers finally did come in, they just didn't seem to work that well. No power, no lift, shaky drag capabilities. I could hardly manage anything but the shortest of flights. Who would have me as a mate? What kind of mother would I make, not being able to hunt or teach my babies to fly? How should I put it? I was bound to be one of those odd single owls, always dependent on relatives' charity, given the wormy, maggoty, down-the-trunk hollow. I hated the idea of being the pathetic dependent owl, the one the owlets were always forced to visit. I decided that it was contrary to my nature to lead such a life and that if I could not live like a normal owl, I would, in fact, use my disability for some noble purpose. Thus, I chose to go to St. Aggie's and do whatever I could to stop them in their horrible quest for power and control of the kingdoms of owls. For that is what they want to do. You realize this, don't you?"

Soren and Gylfie nodded numbly.

"The eggs are part of it. I do what I can here. Since my arrival I have saved more than twenty eggs. The owls of Ambala work with the big bald eagles. It's safest that way. Eagles can get closest to this place most freely. Rock crevices are the natural nesting places for many eagles. So they know the territory. The eagle is the one bird that really strikes fear into the gizzard of these owls. That scar on Skench's wing — that was the talon work of an eagle."

"But how did you get here if you can't fly long distances?" Soren asked.

"HALO," Hortense replied.

"HALO?" Gylfie and Soren both said at once.

"High Altitude Low Opening situation. You see, you wait for a day with thick cloud cover. I had plucked myself to owlet status." Soren winced. "Two big Snowies who blended in perfectly with the cloud cover flew me to the boulders just before the entrance of the canyons of St. Aggie's. There is a grove of trees there with a lot of moss under them. It's where the moss that is used in these nests comes from. No owls live there anymore but that is where they dropped me on that cloudy day."

"You say you've saved twenty eggs?"

"Yes, indeed. And back in Ambala they now tell stories of me. I, who had no stories, am now the hero of stories," Hortense said with no pretense of humility.

"But Hortense," Soren said, "there must be more to your life than this. You cannot remain here forever."

"The eagles promise to come and get me. But I always say, 'oh, just another dozen more or so.' I have become rather addicted to what I am doing."

"But there are risks," Gylfie said.

"Anything worth doing has risks." Hortense paused. "And believe me, this is worth doing."

"We want to get out of here. Won't you come with us?" Soren said.

"How can I? I can't fly. Nor can you, for that matter."

"But we're going to learn," Soren said fiercely.

"Good," Hortense replied softly, and there was a quaver in her voice that gave both Soren and Gylfie a very creepy feeling. Then, realizing that perhaps she had frightened them, Hortense spoke cheerfully. "Oh, don't worry. I am sure you shall. Where there's a wing there's a way! Now let me see those wings of yours."

Gylfie and Soren both spread their wings for Hortense to examine. "Lovely, lovely," she said softly. "Coverts coming in nicely, Soren. Very nice tip slots developing between the primaries. Essential for drag control, especially during turbulent conditions. Your barbs, both of you, are still soft but they'll stiffen up. And I am sure you will both make splendid fliers."

"Any chance we could see the eagles when they come in?" Soren asked.

"Well . . . they fly in just before first light."

"I'll work a double shift so I can come up here," Gylfie said quickly. "And Soren, try to arrange for a break then for yourself."

CHAPTER SEVENTEEN

Save the Egg!

Number 32-9 reporting for broody duty." An extremely large Barn Owl stood at the edge of the nest. Soren scrambled down and set off to find Gylfie. He met her on the rubbly path leading up to the outcropping where Hortense was.

"You realize, of course," Soren was saying as the winds began to buffet them on their ascent, "that when we learn to fly, the outcropping will make the ideal takeoff spot. Always a breeze to bounce you up. Perfect."

By the time they arrived, Hortense already had the egg out of the nest and was pushing it toward the edge of the rock.

"Can we help?" Soren asked.

"Thank you both, but it is really better if I do it by myself. The fewer birds to touch this egg, the less confused the hatchling will be when it comes out."

"Ah, here she comes. No mate with her tonight again. Must be busy elsewhere," Hortense said. "Gives me such a thrill every time I spot those wings. Magnificent, aren't they?"

Soren saw the white head, brighter than any star, melt from the dim pearly gray of the dawn. The immensity of the eagle wings was incredible. Soren was enraptured. So enraptured that he didn't hear Gylfie's desperate hiss. Finally, a sharp beak poked him in the knees.

"Soren, quick! I hear someone coming up the path." Then Soren heard it, too. Gylfie dived into a narrow slot. The slot was much too skinny for a fat Barn Owl like Soren.

"Come in. Come in. We'll squeeze up. It's wider inside." Gylfie was desperate and Soren was nearly frozen with fear to the rock beneath his talons. When owls are frightened, their feathers lie flat and they do become slimmer. So, with fear pumping through him, Soren indeed seemed to shrink. He pressed himself into the crack that, in fact, did widen as it deepened in the rock. He hoped he was not crushing Gylfie. They both were barely breathing as the horrifying scene began to unfold on the outcropping.

"12-8!" The screech seemed to crack the sky. *Good Glaux, it was Skench and Spoorn and Jatt and Jutt. And Auntie!* Auntie puffed and angry, the yellow light from her eyes no longer soft but a hard metallic glare.

"I suspected her for some time!" Auntie squawked, and

dragged Hortense off the nest that she had just moments before returned to.

The egg, limned by the rising sun, stood fragile and quivering at the edge of the rock. Soren's eyes were riveted on the egg. The egg loomed so large, so fragile against the dawn sky. *It could have been Eglantine. It could have been Eglantine.* The thought began to swell in Soren's brain and fill him with a profound terror. This was the future they were fighting for. This was the evilness of St. Aggie's. The egg teetered on the brink as did the entire world of owls. The eagle hovered above.

Suddenly, there was a deep mournful howl. "Go for the egg! Don't worry about me. Save the egg . . . save the egg!" Hortense shrieked. Then a huge shadow slid across the outcropping and next there was an explosion of feathers. It seemed to Soren that there was nothing but feathers. Feathers and down everywhere swirling in the glimmering rosy light of the new day. The eagle was everyplace at once. And Hortense's voice kept crying, "Save the egg! Save the egg!" Auntie was the fiercest fighter of them all. Her beak open and ready to tear, her yellow eyes flashing madly in her head, her talons extended and trying to rip at the eagle's eyes, she was a white squall of fury. Scalding curses tore from her mouth. "Kill! Kill!" she screamed in a high-pitched deafening voice. Her feathered face hardened until it seemed like stone. Slashed by a dark beak and the savage yellow eyes, it was a blazing white mask of brutality.

Then Gylfie and Soren saw the eagle take a mighty swipe with her wings and send Auntie tumbling flat on her back. In that moment, the eagle reached the egg and rose into the sky with it clutched in her claws.

Yet the voice of Hortense seemed to grow dimmer, as if it was fading away, dwindling as if . . . as if . . . Soren and Gylfie looked at each other. Two big tears leaked from Soren's dark eyes. "She's falling, isn't she, Gylfie?"

"They pushed her." And there was Auntie, standing at the edge of the cliff with Spoorn, looking down into the thousand-foot-deep abyss. "Bye-bye," Auntie cooed, and waved a tattered wing. "Bye-bye, 12-8, you fool!" The coo curled into the ugliest snarl Soren could ever imagine.

"But the eagle got the egg," Gylfie said weakly.

"Yes, I suppose she did," Soren replied.

And now there would be more stories, indeed, legends to tell in Ambala of brave Hortense.

The eggorium was briefly shut down. All temporary eggorium and hatchery owls were to report to the moon-blaze chamber immediately for moon scalding, as indeed there was to be a full shine the following evening. Soren and Gylfie, still crammed in the slot, heard Auntie and Spoorn and Skench talking about how no word of this could get out. Auntie's old voice returned. She fretted in that Auntie way of hers about how she could not imagine that 12-8, the most beautifully moon-blinked owl ever, could have gone so wrong under her guidance.

Once again, Gylfie and Soren survived the moon scalding in the moon-blaze chamber. They told the Tales of Yore, as Gylfie called the Ga'Hoolian legends. And Soren, who had a remarkable gift for storytelling, began to compose a new one that first night that he told in bits through the glare of the moon's hot light.

"She was an owl like none other..." Soren began, thinking of Hortense. "Her face both beautiful and kindly, her deep brown eyes warm and with a glimmer like tiny suns. Her wings, however, for one reason or another were crippled, and it was from this, her weakness, that she drew her great strength. For this was an owl who wanted only to do good, who clung to dreams of freedom while giving up her own and, from a stony perch high in a lawless place, she did find a way to wage her own war."

Soren finished the legend as the scalding moon began to slip down in the sky.

CHAPTER EIGHTEEN
One Bloody Night

It was the last night of the dwenking. The moon this night appeared like a fragile dim thread in the sky. The last full shine in which they had been moon scalded after their work in the eggorium had seemed the longest. But Soren and Gylfie had survived. Soren poked his beak into the feathers, the very feathers that Hortense had said were coming along so nicely. They seemed even thicker now.

"Look at those primaries, Soren, and your plummels! How I do envy your plummels," Gylfie said.

Soren ran his beak lightly through the plummels that hovered like a fine mist over his flight feathers. He remembered his mother saying how one must preen their plummels every day, for, indeed, plummels were unique to owls. Of all birds, only owls, and only certain owls at that, had plummels. Elf Owls did not have these fine, soft feathers that fringed the leading edges of wings. It was these feathers that allowed Barn Owls like Soren to fly in almost complete silence.

"Plummels," his mother had said, "are every bit as important as a sharp beak or sharp talons." These words, of course, were directed mostly to Kludd. Kludd's plummels had just begun to sprout shortly before Soren had been snatched, but all Kludd cared about was his beak and talons."

"So, Gylfie, you think, then, by the time of the next dwenking we shall be able to leave?"

"Yes."

Soren looked at this little owl who had become his friend and felt a twinge. She could leave now, for Gylfie was a fully fledged owl. With her dappled plumage of reddish browns and grays and the striking white feathers that curved over her eyes in lovely sweeping arcs, Gylfie looked so grown up, so ready to fly. "Gylfie," Soren sighed, "you could leave now. Look at you."

Gylfie had, indeed, turned into a very lovely Elf Owl. "We have had this talk before, Soren. I told you. I am waiting."

"I know. I know. I just want you to be sure." Soren bobbed his head up and down twice and then cocked it to the side in a questioning manner.

"We still haven't gotten into the library and I feel —"

Soren began to interrupt. For the life of him, he could not figure out why Gylfie was so set on getting into the library. The flecks were interesting but he didn't see how this was connected with anything that had to do with their escaping. The library, of course, was located in a higher part of the canyon, one closer to the sky. Their chances of getting into the hatchery since the Hortense disaster, which would have afforded them the best take-off spot, were absolute zero. And now that was just what Gylfie was saying. "I just feel it in my gizzard, Soren. If we can get into the library, that might be our way out. But until Grimble comes back, I don't think there's a chance."

"Why didn't we think of asking Hortense about Grimble being imperfectly moon blinked?" Soren wondered aloud.

"I doubt if she would have known anything. All she ever saw of this place was the hatchery, really."

"I suppose you're right," Soren replied. "But Gylfie, what's the sense of us getting into the library, even if the library is the second-best escape route, if we can't fly? You said we have to learn and we'd better start quickly. Do we know the first thing about flying except what we remember our parents saying? How can we practice branching here? Start hopping around and trying to do any of the usual things owl chicks have been doing by the time they are our age to be flight-ready, and you'll see the monitors on us faster than if we had asked a question."

"You're right, Soren. We're not ready. We have to figure out a way to practice."

"I'm not sure that we can. I mean, it just seems too risky."

But Gylfie saw that, in fact, Soren was practicing in a very subtle way as they munched their evening ration of crickets in the glaucidium. The Barn Owl had spread his wings and fluffed them up and, although not hopping, Soren had certainly assumed what was known as a flight-prime position. He turned now to 47-2, their pelletorium guide from the first day, and in Gylfie's mind the most perfectly moon-blinked creature of St. Aggie's.

"Just getting the feel of it," Soren said to 47-2. Naturally, he did not wait for 47-2 to ask, "The feel of what?" He merely went ahead and answered his own question in hopes of provoking 47-2 to offer some information. "It must feel wonderful when you finally lift off." He raised his wings slightly as he spoke. "It is almost as if I know exactly where the air will pouch beneath my wings."

"Oh, yes." 47-2 blinked. "That feeling will pass." 47-2's wings hung limply at her sides. "I remember when I had it as well. You won't be bothered much longer with such feelings." She stared straight ahead, her eyes vacant.

Bothered? Why would such feelings ever be a bother? Soren

dared not ask. He could see that Gylfie had heard this as well and was equally disturbed. A dread began to creep up from their gizzards and seep into their hollow bones. They had thought that DNFs, owls Destined Not to Fly, were only those owls who worked in the hatchery and the eggorium. Were there DNFs in the pelletorium as well?

"Yes, yes," 47-2 spoke in her odd flat tones, "it will pass, not much longer, and it is a lovely feeling that comes as they relieve you of those stirrings of flight."

Soren could hardly steady his voice to form the next statement. "Yes, stirrings of flight. I very much like these stirrings of flight. They feel so lovely under my wings."

"No, no. They become more bothersome, trust me. You will welcome the bats when they come."

Bats? *Bats?* Soren and Gylfie desperately needed to know about the bats. How could he wheedle this information out? "I have not seen any bats around here," Soren said, trying to keep the anxiousness out of his voice.

"Oh, they only come just before every other newing or so. To relieve us of flight urges. You are still not ready, I'm afraid. You will have to wait until the next newing."

A hundred questions battered Soren's brain. But 47-2 continued. "They come tonight, I hear. I am very happy in anticipation. It is so lovely. We always sleep our best after the bats quank."

Just at that moment, Jatt and Jutt screeched a call for attention. "All 40's through 48's shall report on the third sleep march to area three." They spoke in unison.

"Hooray!" The cheer welled up in the glaucidium. "Hooray, hooray!" 47-2 danced a strange little jig.

Two marches had gone by. The silver thread of a moon was drawn down to the edge where the sky meets the earth. A last feeble blink of silver and it was gone. The sky grew blacker and blacker. A third sleep march would seem meaningless, for all was engulfed in shadows, and yet the shriek came. Soren and Gylfie moved, following 47-2, but stopped at the edge of area three.

"Look!" Gylfie said. "Look at what they are doing." Soren and Gylfie both stared in disbelief as hundreds of owls flung themselves flat onto their backs with their breasts exposed to the sky and their wings spread out.

"Never," Soren said, "have I seen an owl perch that way. It looks as if it might hurt."

"I don't think it's called perching," Gylfie said. "I think its called lying down."

"Lying down? Animals do that, not birds, and never owls." Soren hesitated. "Not unless they're dead."

But these owls were not dead.

"Listen!" Soren said.

The sky high above the glaucidium seemed suddenly

to pulse with a throbbing sound. It was the sound of wing beats but not the soft, almost silent, wing beats of owls. Instead, there was a tough leathery *snap*. A strange song began to rise in the glaucidium. Then, blacker than the blackness of the night, printed against the sky, ten thousand bats flew overhead as the owls called to them in an odd wailing lament.

> *Come to us and quackle and quank.*
> *Relieve us of our stirrings*
> *With your fangs so sharp and bright*
> *Take this blood that's always purring.*
> *Through our hollow bones it flows*
> *To each feather and downy fluff.*
> *Quell the terrible, horrid urge that so often prinkles us,*
> *Still our dreams, make slow our thoughts*
> *Let tranquillity flood our veins.*
> *Come to us and drink your fill*
> *So we might end our pains.*

Soren and Gylfie watched in unblinking wonder as the vampire bats fluttered down. Using their tiny wing-thumbs and feet, they began to crawl up onto the owls' breasts. They seemed to forage for a few seconds, seeking out a bare spot on the owls' breasts. With gleaming sharp teeth they made a quick tiny cut. The bats' tongues, narrow and grooved, slipped into the nicks. The owls did not even flinch but seemed merely to sigh into the night. Soren and Gylfie were transfixed and could not move. 47-2 turned her head toward them, her eyes half shut, a mild, contented expression on her face.

"That must hurt terribly," Soren spoke softly.

"No, lovely, lovely. The stirrings go. No more . . ." Her voice dwindled into the darkness of the night.

Soren and Gylfie were not sure how long the vampire bats were there, but, indeed, they seemed to swell before their eyes. And then they appeared so gorged, it was as if they staggered rather than lifted into flight. The moon had vanished now for days. The grayness of a new dawn began to filter through the black and, in drunken spirals, the bats wheeled through the remnants of the night.

CHAPTER NINETEEN

To Believe

Ever since that bloody night, Soren and Gylfie had thought of nothing but flying. It had become abundantly clear to them why none of the owlets of St. Aggie's had the sleek glossy feathers or any of the fluffy down of normal owls who had grown beyond the chick stage. Growing flight feathers for an owl was normally not a complicated business, but deprived of the blood supply, these feathers from the primaries to the plummels would wither and die. With that, stirrings, dreams of flight, notions of skyful joy and freedom shriveled and died as well.

Soren and Gylfie's mission was unmistakable: They must learn how to fly despite lacking any opportunity to ever branch, or hop, or practice for flight in any way. They must keep the dream of flight alive in their minds. They must feel it in their gizzards and in that way they would learn to fly. Gylfie repeated the words of her father to Soren: "He said, Soren, that 'you can practice forever and still never fly if you don't believe.' So it's not just practice,

Soren. We must believe, and we can because we are not moon blinked."

"But moon blinked or not, we have to have feathers. And I am still short of flight feathers," Soren replied.

"You are going to have them. You will have enough by the next newing."

"Well, that's just the problem. That's when the vampire bats come back."

Gylfie looked at Soren gravely. "That is why we must learn how to fly before the next newing."

"But I won't be ready. I won't have enough feathers," Soren said.

"Almost, though."

"Almost? There's a difference, Gylfie, between almost and enough."

"Yes. The difference is belief, Soren. Belief." The little Elf Owl said the last word so fiercely that Soren took a step back. "You have a large and generous gizzard, Soren. You feel. I know this. You feel strongly. If any owl can do this, you can."

Soren blinked in dismay. How could he not believe it if this owl, who weighed no more than a wad of leaves, believed so much. It was Gylfie who had the enormous gizzard, not himself.

So the two little owls began to think constantly about

flying. They discussed it whenever they could. They shared memories of their parents lifting out of their nests into the sky. They argued about wing angles and drift and updrafts and a dozen other things they had seen and almost felt as they had watched other owls. They pondered endlessly the stony maze of the canyons and ravines that made up St. Aggie's. They knew that the only way out was straight up, requiring the most difficult of flight maneuvers, especially now that they had no access to Hortense's stone outcropping high in the hatchery. There could be no gradual glide for a takeoff.

Still, they knew that when they escaped, it was essential to find the highest point possible, the point closest to the sky. And Gylfie continued to feel deep in her gizzard that the library would offer such a place, and that within the library they would discover the secret of the flecks, and in some way this secret would become vital to their escape.

One unseasonably warm day, Gylfie had returned to their station in the pelletorium from a run for new pellets. She was barely able to conceal her excitement. "He's back," she whispered to Soren. "Grimble's back! Get on the next shift with me for new pellets."

That would be easy. It was a snack shift, and if you were

on a new pellet run you missed the snack. So no one ever really wanted to go.

Just as the sun reached its high point, Soren and Gylfie stopped walking forward in the Big Crack. They, of course, continued to move their feet as if they were still marching, and the stream of owlets parted around them and moved on as they remained in the same place. Soren blinked. He did not have to look up to feel the piece of blue sky flowing above them. He had passed this point on the trail many times now, and each time he felt refreshed by the very thought of this small wedge of sky so close. He would close his eyes and feel it. When all the owlets had passed, Gylfie gave the signal and they turned down the smaller crack toward the library.

Gylfie marched ahead. Soren was trembling with fear. What if Gylfie's suspicions about Grimble being imperfectly moon blinked were wrong? What if Grimble sounded an alarm? What if they were both seized for the next laughter therapy session? Soren winced and felt a twinge flicker from his down fluff to his brand-new primaries.

Grimble stood in front of the opening to the library. There seemed to be no other owls about. Soren, however, felt the air stir and suddenly realized that it was a breeze. A wonderful thrill coursed through him as it had when he was on the stone outcropping of Hortense's nest. Grimble now turned and blinked at them. Then commenced one of the strangest conversations Soren had ever heard.

"So you are here," Grimble said.

"So we are," replied Gylfie.

"You are conducting yourselves in a dangerous manner," the Boreal Owl said carefully.

"Our lives are not worth two pellets here. We have nothing to lose," Gylfie replied.

"Brave words."

"Not so brave. Wait until you hear my questions. Then you'll know I am brave."

Soren nearly fainted. How could Gylfie even say the word!

Grimble began to shake almost uncontrollably. "You dare say the Q."

"Yes, and I am going to say the *what*, the *when*, and the *why*, and every other word of a free and un-moon-blinked owl. For we are like you, Grimble."

Grimble began to gag. "Whhh-what?"

"What am I talking about? Is that what you wanted to ask? Say it, Grimble. Ask how I know this. Ask anything you want and I'll tell you with one answer: I feel it in my gizzard."

"Gizzard?" Grimble's face grew dreamy with memory.

"Yes. Gizzard, Grimble. Ours still work. And we know, we sense it — that you are not moon blinked. You're faking it just as we are."

"Not completely." The owl blinked. A thin transparent eyelid swept across his eye. Soren knew about these winking eyelids. His parents had told him that when he began to fly, he would find them useful, for they would keep his eyes clear in flight and protect them from any airborne bits of debris. But Grimble was not in flight. No, Grimble was hardly moving. So why was his wink lid flickering madly? Then Soren noticed huge tears gathering at the far corners of his large yellow eyes. "Oh, if only I were perfectly moon blinked. If only I were —"

"Why, Grimble?" Soren asked softly. "Why?"

"I cannot tell you right now. I shall come to you tonight in the glaucidium. I shall arrange for a pass for you. They won't mind as it is now the time of the newing. But let me tell you right now, what you are doing is terribly dangerous. What you are doing could invite a fate much worse than death."

"Worse than death?" Gylfie asked. "What could be worse than death? We would rather die."

"The life I live is worse than death, I assure you."

CHAPTER TWENTY

Grimble's Story

I thought I was being so smart," Grimble said. He had led them into another crack in the canyon wall that was off the large one that led from the pelletorium. "You see, the snatching patrols had just snatched one of my young ones as I was returning with my mate from hunting. It was little Bess. She was my favorite, I have to admit. I swooped in and attacked ferociously. It was actually a cousin of Jatt and Jutt who had Bess in his talons. His name was Ork. He was considered very dangerous and, well, I killed him. The other owls were stunned. They shrank back from me, but then Spoorn and Skench flew in. They saw what had happened. Oddly enough, they were thrilled that Ork was dead. You see, the previous leader of St. Aegolius had died the year before and since then a bitter power struggle had gone on between Ork and his forces and those of Spoorn and Skench. Skench and Spoorn were so happy that they said they would spare my family, never come by our nest again, if I would agree to return to St. Aegolius and join them. They wanted me for my fighting skills. I had killed Ork with no battle claws at all, just my bare talons and beak. They needed me.

"Well, it seemed that there was no choice. I looked at my dear mate. There were three other young ones in the nest. I had to do it. I had to go. My mate begged me not to. She swore that we could go elsewhere, far away. But Skench and Spoorn laughed and said they would find us no matter where we went. So I joined them. My mate and our owlets promised they would never forget me. Spoorn and Skench promised that I could visit them thrice yearly, which, at the time, seemed very generous. I should have suspected something right away. But I didn't know about moon blinking then, either. The visits would become meaningless if I were successfully moon blinked. My family would not recognize me nor would I have any feeling for them. This is because moon-blinked owls have no real feelings, and without our feelings we become unrecognizable over time to those who do have feelings. That is the evil genius of moon blinking.

"So I was determined, like you, to resist and to pretend. I was fairly successful. Skench and Spoorn had valued my fighting skills so much that they allowed me to earn a name. I had been number 28-5. But I became Grimble." And now . . ." Grimble began to shake again. "Something has changed."

"What do you mean? You resisted," Soren said.

"Yes, to a point."

"To a point? You either are or you're not moon blinked," Gylfie said.

"After every few newings, we are required even as mature owls to be reblinked. I think something has begun to change. It seems that although I resisted, now I am losing something. The faces of my dear mate, my little Bess, have begun to fade. When I used to visit them, my old voice came back. The call of Boreal Owls is like a song, some say like the bells that used to toll in the churches, but now it has become flat. Eight or so newings ago, when I made one of my visits home, I called out as usual as I approached, but no one recognized my call. Then two newings ago, when I arrived, neither my mate nor Bess recognized me."

"Unbelievable," Gylfie whispered.

"And now they are gone," Grimble said.

"Gone?" said Soren. "You mean they left?"

"They left, or perhaps they were killed by Skench and Spoorn or perhaps . . ." Grimble's voice dwindled off.

"Perhaps what?" Gylfie pressed.

"Perhaps they are there and I simply cannot see them

at all, nor do they recognize me. I think I have become like air — transparent, like nothingness. Is that not the ultimate savagery of being moon blinked? I would say that in another few newings I shall be the perfectly moon-blinked elderly owl."

"But why? Why do they do this? What is the purpose of St. Aggie's?" Soren asked.

"And the flecks, what are they about?" Gylfie looked straight up at the Boreal Owl, who towered over her.

"Ah! One simple question, one not quite so simple. The purpose of St. Aggie's is to take control of every owl kingdom on Earth."

"And to destroy it?" asked Soren.

"You can be sure the kingdoms shall be destroyed, but control is really what they want. And for the kind of control they want they must moon blink. That is their main tool, for moon blinking destroys will, erases individuality, makes everyone the same. The flecks, however, are another kind of tool, a weapon for war."

"What can flecks do?" Gylfie asked.

"No one really knows. I am not entirely sure. The flecks do have powers if certain things are done to them."

"What kind of powers?"

"Again, I am not certain. They seem to be able to pull things toward them, sometimes. When I am working in the fleck storage area of the library, sometimes I think I can feel their force."

Soren and Gylfie were mystified. "How strange," Gylfie said.

"Teach us to fly, Grimble! Teach us to fly." It was Soren who blurted out the words. The idea half formed seemed to explode at once in his head, sending tremors all the way down to his gizzard. There was a stunned silence. Gylfie and Grimble both looked at Soren and blinked but remained wordless.

"But you know, Soren, and you know, Gylfie, I can tell you what to do, and I can help you practice, but I cannot do everything. It's very strange with flying. A young owl can do everything just perfectly but if you don't believe . . ."

Gylfie and Soren both blinked at Grimble and together said, "If you don't believe, then you'll never fly."

"Yes, yes. I see you understand. And, of course, that is why none of the owlets in the glaucidium will ever fly. It is not only that the vampire bats quiet their stirrings and cause their feathers to turn brittle, but if an owl is moon blinked it, of course, has no notion of what it means to believe."

"But we aren't moon blinked," Gylfie said. "And I don't believe you are either, Grimble."

"You give me hope, you two young ones. I thought all of my hope had been destroyed, but you give me hope. Yes, I shall try. Here is what we must do."

So Grimble explained to them that he was in charge of organizing the products of the pellets — the teeth, the fur, and the flecks — after each day's work. "I store them in the library and keep lists, inventories. I can get you a pass to help in the listings. I work mostly in a small area off the library and then take them in when I get enough. When I don't do that, I am on day guard of the library. You will never be permitted in the library, but I can try to teach you how to fly in that small space. It isn't ideal but it is the only place we have. It connects to the library, which is larger, but you can't go in there because when I am in the inventory area someone else is guarding the library."

"I thought the library had books," Gylfie said.

"It does. But we store these materials there, too. Near the books that supposedly explain them."

"Gylfie feels somehow deep in her gizzard that the flecks might help us escape."

"Don't depend on such things," Grimble said sharply. "Your own belief in yourself will help you much more than any fleck ever will."

And so it was arranged. Gylfie and Soren would be

given passes to help in the inventory area, the inventorium, each night during the newing and on various nights until the moon was full again and all owlets were required in the glaucidium for moon blinking. Their first lesson would begin that very evening.

CHAPTER TWENTY-ONE

To Fly

"M ore flap, deeper flap. Your wings must almost meet on the upstroke of the flap . . ." Grimble directed. Soren and Gylfie were exhausted. This was much harder than anything either one of them had ever seen their parents or older siblings try to do.

"I know you're tired, but the only way out of here is straight up. You have to build your muscles. That's why I am not even having you practice hopping or branching. You do not have the luxury of gliding gently down from a nest. You have to develop your power-flight skills. So try it again."

"But once we're out," Soren asked, "how will we know what to do?"

"You'll know. What did I tell you? The still air has no shape. In the sky you will feel the mass of air as it moves around your wings. You will sense its speed, if it is bumpy or smooth, hot or cold. And you will know how to shape it and use it. Wind always has shape but there is no wind in

St. Aggie's. It is too deep for the wind to reach. And in these small spaces it is hard to even feel the air. It is dead, unmoving air in here. So you must work extra hard to give it a shape with your power strokes, your flapping. Your downstroke is your most powerful. On your upstroke, you want the air to flow through easily. That is why both of you have those feathers with slots, tip slots at the end of your wings. They separate and let you go up easily."

Grimble demonstrated. He pressed forward just a bit, extended his head, and lifted his wings. And that was it — he was suddenly airborne. Twice Soren's size or more, yet Grimble seemed to float up effortlessly. Would they ever learn? Had they even improved?

Grimble almost seemed to read their minds. "This is just your third lesson. You've grown stronger. I can see that. But you must believe it."

And then, by their fourth lesson, it did seem easier and that was the first time they began to perhaps feel the belief in their gizzards. They could feel the air parting above them. They had each flown higher in the deep stone box of the inventorium than they ever had before. They tried to imagine bursting out of it into the welcoming blackness of the moonless night. They could begin to sense the contours of the bubble of air that formed beneath each wing and buoyed them up into the darkness. The newing would last for another two nights and then their learning sessions would begin to dwindle as the moon swelled, and they would be required to stay in the glaucidium for longer and longer exposures to its light for moon blinking. Finally, after the moon had grown fat and full and the first phase of the dwenking began, they would leave. They must leave at that time, for the vampire bats would be returning. It would be their time, as fully fledged owls, to submit to the bats and then there would be no hope of escape.

Although they had not yet been in the library, they would go there on the night of their escape, for, indeed, it was located higher and closer to the sky than any other region aside from the hatchery. Grimble planned to tell the library guard on duty for that night that he would relieve him for a few minutes as a disturbance had been reported in the pelletorium, in the very area that this guard supervised during the day. Grimble promised them that flying would seem easy after all their practice in the deep hole of the inventorium. They were curious about the library. Grimble had tried to explain what it looked like and how the books and the feathers and the teeth, the bones, the flecks, and all the bits that they picked out of the pellets during the day were arranged and stored. It was also in the library that some of the best battle claws were kept. Gylfie and Soren were very curious about them.

"They don't make them here, do they?" Gylfie had asked.

"No. They don't know how. Oh, how they wish they did. I hear Spoorn and Skench talking about it all the time. It requires a deep knowledge of metals, I think. They steal them. They go on raids to various kingdoms where owl chiefs keep fighting owls. They go into fields after battles and collect them from dead warriors. But they don't know how to make them. You see, you think these owls are smart here at St. Aegolius, but Skench and Spoorn are so frightened of any owl being smarter than they are ... well, that is why they moon blink everyone. No one else really knows how to read here. No questions allowed. So how can anything be learned, be invented? It's impossible. They've been trying to figure out flecks for years, but I doubt they ever will. They never let anyone else study them and maybe find something out. Why, look at you, Gylfie. You, just through wondering and having feelings in your gizzard about flecks, probably know almost as much as they do — because you're curious. But enough talk. Come on you two, time to practice. I want you each to go for that highest chink in the stone wall tonight. Soren, you get five wing beats to do it. Gylfie, since you're smaller, I'll give you eight."

"You have to be kidding," Soren gasped.

"I am not kidding. You're first, Soren. Make every downstroke count. If you believe, you won't ever go yeep."

Soren closed his eyes as he stood on a low stone perch that jutted from the wall. He lifted his wings then, with all his might, powered down. *I can do this! I can do this!* He felt his body lift. He felt the air gather under his wings on the next upstroke. It was a big cushion of air.

"Good!" whispered Grimble. "Again. More powerful." Soren was halfway up the wall to the chink and he had used only two downstrokes.

I can do it, I can do it! I feel the air. I feel the force of my strokes. I am going up. I am going up. I shall fly. . . .

CHAPTER TWENTY-TWO
The Shape of the Wind

"Tonight? Grimble, you must be yoicks. It's not any-where near the dwenking. It's too soon!" Gylfie cried.

"We're not ready," protested Soren.

"You are ready. Soren, I gave you five strokes to get to the chink in the inventorium and you got there in four. Gylfie, I gave you eight and you got there in seven. Tonight is the night."

"Why?" they both said at once.

Grimble sighed. He was going to miss these two. He might miss their questions most of all. It felt so luxurious to be able to ask and answer questions. He had once thought the sweetest taste in the world was that of a freshly killed vole, but now he knew differently. The sweetest thing was a question on the tongue. A word beginning with that wonderful rush of air that w's made. Oh, how he would miss these two young owls. They were lovely to look at, too, in their coats of newly fledged feathers untouched by vampire bats. "The thermals are coming this evening. This is why you must go."

"Thermals? What are thermals?" Soren asked.

"Warm drafts of air. They've arrived earlier than usual. They'll make flying very easy for you once you get out of here. You should meet up with them within a short distance from here. You'll be able to soar."

"We don't know how to soar," Gylfie said. "All we know how to do is flap."

"Don't worry. You'll know exactly what to do when you meet the thermals. The shape of the wind will tell you."

"Who is on guard tonight?"

"It's Jatt."

"Jatt!" Soren gasped. "That's terrible. How will you get him to go to the pelletorium?"

"I'll think of something. Don't worry. I'll get him out of there. I've already got you a pass for tonight between the third and fourth sleep march."

The third sleep march had just finished. Soren and Gylfie sought out the sleep correction monitor in their area and showed them their passes. He blinked and told them to be off. They made their way silently through the stone corridors of St. Aegolius, alone with their thoughts.

Yet those thoughts were the same, for they were deep in concentration as they tried as hard as they ever had to believe in their own ability to fly. They tried not to let themselves be distracted by the fact that the sum total of their flight experience had covered only a very small range of the usual maneuvers a young and newly fledged owl practices. They had no real knowledge of gliding, soaring, or hovering.

"Words, words, words," Grimble would mutter if they ever brought up these notions that they had heard their parents discussing with older siblings. It was Gylfie who mostly asked such questions. And Grimble would always admonish her. "You're thinking too much. You don't need to know anything about hovering and soaring. All you need to know is rapid takeoff straight up — THRUST! POWER FLAPPING!" He poked his head forward as he said each word and fixed Soren and Gylfie in the fierce, uncompromising glare of his yellow eyes. "That's it! That is all you need to get out of here."

So that is what Soren and Gylfie thought of. It filled their minds. The power downstroke. The bunching together of the slots on the leading edge of their primaries. The upstroke, the spacing of those same feathers so the air could pass through with no drag. They had become very muscular from all their practice. They were probably the most muscular young owls in the entire academy of St. Aegolius. This alone should make them believe. Had there ever been an Elf Owl as young as Gylfie who could power flap so strongly?

They arrived at last at the inventorium. Grimble could immediately tell that both owlets were concentrating fiercely. This was good. Now he just hoped that his ruse to get Jatt out would work. Luckily, Grimble had detected that things were not perfect between the two brothers Jutt and Jatt. Perhaps it was jealousy. It seemed as if Skench was paying more attention to Jutt than his brother, particularly on battle flights. There was always a bit of contention after a battle as to the dividing up of the battle claws left on a field from the defeated owls. Skench and Spoorn got first choice and then, when they returned to St. Aggie's, the rest of the claws were sorted and handed out according to rank or battle performance. There was an elderly owl, Tumak, who was the director of the main battle claw repository. But now Grimble was going to tell a bold lie that he hoped would get Jatt out of the library he was guarding. He began talking quite loudly. Soren and Gylfie couldn't imagine what he was doing, for he seemed to be speaking not to them but to some invisible owl.

"You don't say! My word. Trouble in the claw repository. Oh, Jatt's not going to like that at all. I think I better tell him." By the time Grimble, and it was only a matter of seconds, got to the guardhouse of the library, Jatt's feathers were puffed and quivering with agitation. He seemed twice his size and was in obvious pain. If any creature could be swollen with questions it was Jatt. And that, of course, was Grimble's advantage that he planned to work to the fullest.

"Don't worry, Jatt. I shall tell you everything. At least all that I know. Now calm yourself. I had heard Jutt talking with Spoorn earlier, regarding those new battle claws and how he felt Tumak was not handling them correctly. Spoorn had said that she would take it up with Skench."

"Oh, no!" Jatt gasped. "Jutt's been wanting to be the director of the repository forever. And we all know what that means. He'll be the most powerful owl around here next to Skench and Spoorn."

"Well, it is my understanding that they are allowing Tumak and Jutt to fight it out. There's a duel about to begin and Jutt has his forces assembled. Go get your troops, Jatt. Quick — there's still time. I'll stand guard."

"Thank you, Grimble. Thank you. And don't worry. When I am head of the repository, you shall get first choice for battle claws."

"I'm not worried, Jatt. Now, just go while there is still time."

As soon as Jatt turned the corner and disappeared down the long stone crack, Grimble called to Soren and Gylfie. "Come on, you two. There's not a minute to waste." The two owlets raced into the library. They gasped when they entered the room. It was not the books they noticed or the small array of polished battle claws hanging off one wall. It was the sky, black, chinked with stars, stars that seemed so close that an owl could have reached out with a talon and plucked one. Memories rushed back. Memories of sky and breezes — yes, indeed, they did feel a wind, even here. Oh, they were so close. Yes, they believed! Yes, they could do this and, then, just as Soren and Gylfie swung their wings up into their first stroke, Skench burst in. She was ferocious looking in full war regalia. Immense battle claws made her talons twice their size. A metallic needle extended from the tip of her beak and glimmered in the slice of the new moon that hung like a blade over the library.

"Flap!" screeched Grimble. "Flap. You will do it! You will do it! Believe! Power stroke! Power! Two wing beats and you're up." But the two little owls seemed frozen in their fear. Their wings hung like stones at their sides. They were doomed.

Soren and Gylfie watched transfixed as Skench advanced toward them, and then something very peculiar happened. Skench, moved by a power unseen, suddenly slammed into the wall, the wall that had the notches that Grimble had described in which the flecks were stored.

"Go! This is your chance!" Grimble shouted.

An indeed it was. Skench seemed to have been immobilized, paralyzed.

Soren and Gylfie began to pump their wings. They felt themselves rise.

"You can do it! You believe! Feel it in your gizzard. You are a creature of flight. Fly, my children. Fly!" And then there was a terrible shriek and the night was splattered with blood.

"Don't look back! Don't look back, Soren! Believe!" But this time it was not Grimble calling. It was Gylfie. Just as they reached the stone rim, they felt a curl of warm air. And it was as if vast and gentle wings had reached out of the night, and swept them up into the sky. They did not look back. They did not see the torn owl on the library floor. They did not hear Grimble, as he lay dying, chant in the true voice of the Boreal Owl, in tones like chimes in the night, an ancient owl prayer: *"I have redeemed myself by giving belief to the wings of the young. Blessed are those who believe, for indeed they shall fly."*

CHAPTER TWENTY-THREE

Flying Free

In the dark soul of that night, Soren and Gylfie only saw the stars and the moon on its silvery path into the infinite blackness of this new heaven through which they wheeled in flight. So once more the world spiraled. But this time there was a difference. It was Soren who was carving these spirals and loops. With his wings he scooped air, shaped it. There was not the desperate need for flapping and pumping now. Instinctively, he stilled his wings and rode the thermal updrafts, rising higher without even stirring a feather. He looked down at Gylfie, who was a few feet below him, catching the lower layer of the same updraft. Grimble was right. They knew exactly what to do. Instinct and belief flowed through the hollow bones of the two owls as they flew into the night.

It had seemed that after being locked in the still air of the windless canyons and ravines of St. Aegolius, the two owls were encountering every kind of wind and draft imaginable. Soren had not known how long they had flown when he heard Gylfie call out, "Hey, Soren, any idea how we land?"

Land? Landing had been the furthest thing from Soren's mind. He felt as if he could fly forever. But he supposed that the little Elf Owl might be getting tired. For every one stroke of Soren's wings, Gylfie had to make three. "No idea, Gylfie. But maybe we should look for a nice treetop and then . . ." He paused. "Well, I'm sure we'll figure it out."

And they did. Tipping slightly downward at a gentle angle, they began a long glide toward a cluster of trees. Once more, instinct took over as both owls in their descent began to inscribe tighter and tighter circles around the trees below. Each owl angled its wings slightly to increase the drag and then, as they approached the tree, they extended their talons.

"I did it!" Soren gasped as he lighted down on a branch.

"Aiyee!" squeaked Gylfie.

"Gylfie, where are you? What's wrong?"

"Well, except for being upside down, I think I am fine."

"Great Glaux!" Soren exclaimed as he saw the little Elf Owl hanging by her talons with her head pointing toward the ground. "How did that happen?"

"Well, if I knew how, it wouldn't have happened," Gylfie replied testily.

"Oh, dear! What are you going to do?"

"Well, I'm going to think about it."

"Can you do that hanging upside down?"

"Of course I can. What do you think? My brains are going to fall out of my head? Really, Soren!"

Gylfie looked a bit ridiculous hanging upside down, but Soren certainly wasn't going to say anything. He wished he could be of more help.

"If I were you, gal . . ." A voice came from another branch higher up in the tree.

"Who's that?" Soren was suddenly frightened.

"What does it matter who I am? Been in the same spot as your friend there once or twice myself." Soren felt the branch he was perched on shake. The most enormous owl he had ever seen alighted, then swaggered out toward the end. The owl, a silvery gray color, seemed to simply melt out of the moonlight, but he towered over Soren. His head alone, with his enormous facial disk, was almost twice the size of Gylfie. It was very difficult for Soren to imagine that this huge owl had ever been in the same situation as Gylfie.

"Here's what you have to do," he called down to Gylfie in a deep voice. "You have to let go, just let go! Then quickly flap your wings up, an upstroke, hold it for a count of three. You'll come out right side up and then just glide down. Let me demonstrate."

"But you're so big and Gylfie's so small," Soren said.

"I am big — right you are! But I am delicate and beautiful. I can float! I can skim." The enormous owl had lifted off the branch and was flying through the air, performing every imaginable flourish of flight — plunges, twists, swoops, and loops.

He began a hooting song:

> *"Flutter like a hummingbird,*
> *Dive like an eagle,*
> *Ain't no bird that's my equal."*

"Good Glaux!" Soren muttered. "What a show-off."

"Hey, when you got it you show it. When you don't, you usually don't know it." The huge owl lit down, obviously pleased with his wit and flying.

"All right," Gylfie said.

"Letting go is the hardest part, but you got to believe it will work."

Belief again, thought Soren. That seemed to be the word that struck Gylfie as well, because in just that instant Gylfie let go. There was a little blur in the night — like a small leaf caught in a sudden gust — and then Gylfie was flying right side up.

"Beautiful!" exclaimed Soren. In another second, Gylfie had alighted on the branch next to Soren.

"See? Nothing to it," said the huge silvery owl. "'Course I didn't have anyone to coach me. Had to figure it out on my own."

Soren studied the big owl. He seemed young despite his size. He didn't want to be rude but he was genuinely curious about this owl. "Are you from these parts?" Soren asked.

"Here, there, everywhere," the owl replied. "You name it, I've been there." He had a rough manner of speaking that was slightly intimidating.

Gylfie hopped out toward the end of the branch. "I want to thank you for your kindness in advising me on my predicament." Soren blinked. He had never heard Gylfie speak this way. She sounded so much older than she was, and extremely courteous. "We don't mean to be rude but we have never seen an owl of your size. May we be so bold as to inquire as to your species?"

Species! Soren thought. *Where in the name of Glaux did Gylfie come up with these words?*

"Species? What the Glaux is that? Very fancy word for a Great Gray Owl like myself."

"Oh, so you are a Great Gray. I've heard of them, though there were none in Kuneer," Gylfie said.

"Ah, Kuneer! Been there. No, not a good place for Great Grays. As a matter of fact, I can't really tell you where I'm from. See, I was orphaned at a very young age. Plucked up by a St. Aggie's patrol but managed to drop right into an abandoned nest."

"You escaped from a St. Aggie's patrol?"

"You bet. There was no way those idiots were going to take me. Not alive. I bided my time, then bit my snatcher's second talon clean off. He dropped me like a hot coal. They never messed with me again. Word went out, I s'pose." He swaggered a bit, then strutted toward the end of the branch.

Now even Gylfie was speechless. Finally, Soren spoke. "We were snatched as well and only now escaped. I, myself, am from the Kingdom of Tyto, and both Gylfie and I want to find our families again. But we have no idea where we are right now. I mean, that is why I asked who you were. I've never seen your kind in Tyto, but here we are, perched in a Ga'Hoole tree, which are Tyto trees."

"Not necessarily. Ga'Hoole trees follow the River Hoole and the River Hoole runs through many kingdoms."

"Not Kuneer," Gylfie said.

"No, there's not a drop of water in Kuneer, let alone a river."

"Oh, there's water if you know where to look," Gylfie said.

"Hmm." The owl blinked.

Soren could tell right away that this owl was not pleased when someone knew something that he might not.

"So are we in Tyto or not?" Soren asked.

"You're on a border here between Tyto and the Kingdom of Ambala."

"Ambala!" Soren and Gylfie both gasped. Hortense!

"To my way of thinking, it's a second-rate kingdom."

"Second rate!" Soren and Gylfie both said at once.

"Not if you knew Hortense." Soren said.

"Who in the name of Glaux is Hortense?"

"Was," said Gylfie softly.

"A very fine owl," Soren spoke in a tight voice. "A very fine owl indeed."

The huge owl blinked in wonder at these young owls. They seemed to know nothing. And yet . . . He let the thought trail off. Certainly their survival skills must be pretty good if they got out of St. Aggie's. Still, there was no education like the one he had received. The education of an orphan. The orphan school of tough learning. He had to learn it all himself. How to fly, where to hunt, what creatures to stalk and which to avoid at all costs. No, nothing could compare to figuring out on one's own the hard rules and schemes of a forest world — a world with uncountable riches and endless perils. It took a tough owl to figure it all out. And that was exactly how Twilight thought of himself. Tough.

Gylfie seemed to have recovered. "Well, permit us to introduce ourselves. I am Gylfie, Elf Owl, more formally know as Micrathene whitneyi, common to desert regions, migratory, cavity nester."

"I know, I know. Spent some time in a hollowed-out cactus with some of you fellows. Hunting skills . . . uh, how should I put it? Well, if all you eat is snake, let's just say desert smarts are different from forest smarts."

"We eat more than snake. My goodness. We eat voles and mice, but not rats — they're a bit large for us."

"Well, never mind." The big owl turned and blinked at Soren. "So what's your story, kid?" Soren had the feeling he should be briefer than Gylfie and not go into so much detail.

"Soren of Tyto, Barn Owl." Soren sensed that going into the rareness of their breed, Tyto alba, would not interest this owl. As a matter of fact, not much impressed this owl. "Lived in an old fir tree with my parents until . . ." His voice dwindled off.

"Until that horrible day." The big owl blinked and tapped Soren lightly with his beak in a gentle preening gesture. This small movement more than anything surprised Soren and Gylfie. The two owls had not seen nor felt the soothing preening gestures since they had fallen from their nests. But preening had been a large part of their lives. Gently prinking with their beaks, the parents would pick out bits and plump up the feathers of their mates and their children as well, or whatever patchy down a baby owl might have sprouted. It was so soothing and lovely. Preening and being preened by one's family and closest of kin and friends was the essence of being a true owl. Soren was overcome by the kindness of the gesture. The big owl turned to Gylfie and spoke. "You, too, little one with the big words, come over here. Bet it's been a while since anyone prinked your down." And so Gylfie hopped over closer to the owl, and while he preened one and then the other in turn, the Great Gray began to tell some of his story.

"My name is Twilight. I don't know how I got the name. It's just my name."

"It fits you," Soren said softly. "Because you are all silvery and gray."

"Yes, not black or white. It fits, and blast my gizzard if I didn't hatch on the edges of time, for that is one of my first memories. Twilight! That silvery border of time between day and night. Most owls have pride in their night vision. We see things that other birds cannot see from high up in the pitch of the night — a mouse, a vole, a tiny squirrel scuttling through the forest. I can see all that, too, but I can also see at a harder time — twilight — when the boundaries become dim and the shapes begin to melt away. I live on the edges and I like it."

"What are you doing here near the edge of Tyto?"

"I have heard that there is a place and that the best way to find it is by following the River Hoole. This stream that flows beneath this Ga'Hoole tree I figure must flow into the River Hoole, or else why would a Ga'Hoole tree grow here?"

Soren and Gylfie both nodded. This seemed to them to be a sensible conclusion. "Is this place," Gylfie asked, "on the edge of something?"

"Actually, it is, I think, more like the middle of something. But I am interested."

"Middle of what?" Soren asked.

"The River Hoole flows into a huge lake. Some call it a sea, Hoolemere, and in the middle of it there is an island. And on the island is a tree. A great tree. It is called the Great Ga'Hoole Tree. It is the greatest of all the Ga'Hoole trees. The most enormous tree that ever grew, some say, and it is the center of a Kingdom called Ga'Hoole."

Soren felt his breath catch in his throat. His eyes widened. He felt Gylfie grow still.

"You mean it's real?" Soren asked.

"It's not just a legend?" Gylfie said, her voice soft with wonder.

"Well, I believe in legends," Twilight said simply. And for the first time all the boastfulness left his voice.

"And what is there, in this great tree that grows on an island in the middle of a sea called Hoolemere?" asked Soren.

"A band of owls, very strong, very brave." Twilight seemed to swell up even bigger before their very eyes as he spoke.

"And," Soren continued, "do these owls rise each night into the blackness and perform noble deeds?" The words of his father flowed through him. "And speak no words but true ones, and their purpose is to right all wrongs, to make strong the weak, mend the broken, vanquish the proud, and make powerless those who abuse the frail? And with hearts sublime, they do take flight. . . . Is this the place of which you speak?"

"Indeed it is," Twilight replied. "All these owls work and fight together, for the good of all kingdoms."

"Do you really believe this place exists?" Soren asked.

"Do you believe you can fly?" Twilight shot back.

Soren and Gylfie both blinked. What a strange answer. It was not an answer at all. It was a question. How far they had come from St. Aegolius Academy for Orphaned Owls!

CHAPTER TWENTY-FOUR
Empty Hollows

You two are going to have to learn how to hunt. Whatever did they feed you in that place?" Twilight asked.

Soren's and Gylfie's beaks were bloody from tearing at the tender flesh of a vole that Twilight had brought. They had never tasted anything so good. There was an acorn fragrance to this vole, mixed with the withered berries that had dropped from the Ga'Hoole tree in which they still perched. Finally, Gylfie answered, "Mostly crickets, unless you worked in the hatchery."

"That's all?"

"Crickets — day in, day out, every meal."

"Great Glaux, how can an owl live on that — no meat?"

Soren and Gylfie shook their heads, not wanting to miss a bite.

Twilight realized that it would be useless to talk to these two half-starved owls until they were well fed. So when Soren and Gylfie had finished with the vole, he fixed them in the hard glare of his yellow eyes. "So, I want to know — are you two interested in finding the Great Ga'Hoole Tree?"

Soren and Gylfie exchanged nervous glances.

"Well, yes . . ." said Soren.

"And no," said Gylfie.

"Well, which is it? Yes or no?"

"Both," Gylfie said. "Soren and I talked about it when you were off hunting. We would like to go there, of course, but first . . ." Gylfie hesitated.

"But first you want to see if your families are still there."

"Yes," both owls answered meekly. They knew that for Twilight, who had been an orphan almost from the moment he had hatched, it must be hard to understand. He had no memories of nest or family. He had flitted from one place to another, one kingdom to another. He had even lived with creatures not of his own kind — there was a family of woodpeckers in Ambala that had taken him in, an elderly eagle in Tyto, and, most extraordinary of all, a family of desert foxes in Kuneer, which was why Twilight never, ever hunted fox. To eat a fox was unthinkable to Twilight.

"All right. From what you tell me we would not have to go too far out of the way. Our main route follows the river and, Soren, you said your family lived within sight of the river and, well, Gylfie, I know Kuneer very well. I think from what you've told me that your family must have lived by the big gulch."

"Yes, yes! We did."

"That gulch is a dry riverbed that was made by the River Hoole a long, long time ago. So we don't have to go that far off our route."

"Oh, and we promise we'll learn how to hunt. We really will," Soren said.

"Is hunting like flying and . . ." Gylfie offered tentatively, "finding the Great Ga'Hoole Tree — one must believe?"

"Oh, for Glaux's sake, it's only food!" Twilight said with mild disdain.

The three owls left at first black. It had turned quite cold. No thermals to ride, and both Soren and Gylfie realized how lucky they had been — or rather how smart Grimble had been to insist on their leaving at the time of the unseasonable drafts of warm air. It was a lot easier flying on those rising thermals. There were none on this bright winter night but still it was lovely to be free, and the world below, keen with frost, sparkled fiercely. Oh, how Soren wished his parents could see him fly. He flapped his wings, increased his forward thrust, and sailed higher into the sky. "The Yonder! The Yonder!" as Mrs. Plithiver called the sky. Dear Mrs. P. He missed her, too. Oh, he could tell her about the Yonder now. He could tell that dear old blind snake all about the Yonder himself.

By the next day, it had begun to snow very hard. At times, the snow was a blinding fury. Soren's transparent eyelids swept back and forth almost constantly to clear off the snowy crystals. Sometimes the snow was so thick that the sky and the earth below seemed to blend into one mass of grayness. There were no edges. The horizon had melted into nothingness and it was through this blurry world that Twilight navigated with unbelievable skill and grace. They followed him closely, Soren flying on his up-wind or weather wing, with Gylfie on the other side in the lee of Twilight's downwind wing.

"You see, you two, the world is not always black and white — what did I tell you?" Twilight spoke as he expertly guided them through the thickening snow flurries.

"How do you do it?" Soren asked.

"I learned the hard edges of things in the daylight and the night, but then I learned how this is not the only way of seeing. That, in fact, other things might be hidden when it seems the clearest. So I unlearned some things."

"How do you unlearn something?" Soren asked.

"You decide not to trust only in what you can see. You

look for a new way and clear your mind of the old way. You try to feel new things in your gizzard."

"Sounds hard," Gylfie said.

"It is. Oh! All right, enough talk. Prepare to glide. Remember, Gylfie, what I told you about sticking out your talons. We don't want you upside down again."

"Yes, Twilight, I'll remember. Talon extension is vitally important."

"Little owl, big words," Twilight muttered to himself.

"Well, maybe I was wrong. Maybe it wasn't so close to the river. Maybe it wasn't a fir tree after all."

Twilight and Gylfie looked at each other. This was the third tree that they had visited. There was not a sign of an owl family living in any of the trees, but in two of the three, this last one included, there were hollows and definite signs of owls having once nested in them. "You know my memory isn't really perfect," Soren said weakly. "I . . . I . . . could have —"

Gylfie interrupted. "Soren, I think they've gone."

Soren turned on the little Elf Owl. "How can you say that, Gylfie? How can you ever say that?" Soren was trembling with rage. "You don't know them. I know them. My parents wouldn't have left — ever."

"They didn't leave you, Soren," Gylfie said in a very

small voice. "They thought that you were gone forever, snatched."

"No! No! They would believe! They would believe like the way we were taught to believe in flying. They would believe, and my mother would never agree to leave this place. She would always hope that I would come back."

And it was when Soren said the word "hope" that something deep inside him collapsed. It almost felt as if his gizzard was shriveling up. He began to weep with the unthinkable notion of his parents giving up hope for him. Shudders racked his entire body. His feathers, stiff with frost, quivered.

Then Twilight spoke, "Soren, they're gone. Maybe something happened to them. You shouldn't take it personally. Buck up now, old buddy."

"Personally? What do you know, Twilight, that is personal about any family? You've never had a family. Remember, you're always telling us about how much you learned in your own orphan school of tough learning. You don't know the feel of a mother's down. You don't know what it's like to hear stories from a father, or to hear him sing. Do you know what a psalm is, Twilight? I bet you don't. Well, we Barn Owls know about psalms and books and the feeling of down."

Twilight's feathers had ruffled up, spiky with ice crystals. He looked fearsome. "I'll tell you what I know, you miserable little owl. The whole world is my family. I know the softness of a fox's fur, and the strange green light that comes into their eyes during the spring moons. I know how to fish because I learned from an eagle. And when meat is scarce I know how to find the ripest part of a rotten tree and peck the juiciest bugs from it. I know plenty."

"STOP FIGHTING!" Gylfie screamed. "Soren, you're broken, you're sad. I will be the same way."

Soren looked up, startled. "What do you mean 'will be'?"

"What do you think the chances are of my family being found?" She didn't wait for Soren to answer the question. "I'll tell you. None."

"Why?" Soren said. Even Twilight seemed surprised. "We were snatched, Soren. Do you think any owl parents would stay in the same place? Those St. Aggie's patrols know where to find owls. They'd come back. They'd look for young owl chicks. Any family with any sense would move on. They wouldn't want to lose all their chicks. And I think I know where mine would go."

"Where?" Soren asked.

"The Great Ga'Hoole Tree," Gylfie spoke quietly.

"Why?" Soren blinked. "You're not even sure it's a real place. What did you call it?"

"Tales of Yore."

"Yes, Tales of Yore. Why, in the name of Glaux, would your family take off for a Yore place, not proven, not real?"

"Because maybe they were desperate," Gylfie said.

"That's no reason."

Then Gylfie answered in a stronger voice, "Because they felt it in their gizzards."

"How do you feel a legend in your gizzard? You're talking racdrops, Gylfie." It made Soren feel good to use a bad word. But at the same time he felt he was betraying his own father. For hadn't his father said that one began to feel a legend in one's gizzard and over time it could become true in one's heart? "Racdrops!" he repeated. "Complete nonsense, Gylfie, and you know it." As angry as Soren was, what he had just uttered made him feel worse.

"Since when has anything made sense? Does St. Aggie's make sense? Do Skench and Spoorn make sense?"

"Grimble made sense," Soren said in barely a whisper.

"Yes," Gylfie replied, and reached out with the tip of her wings to touch Soren.

Twilight had remained quiet. Finally, he spoke. "I am going to search for the Great Ga'Hoole Tree. You two are welcome to join me. Gylfie, it is not far out of our way to go by the Desert of Kuneer. Even though I think you're right about your parents, maybe for your own peace of mind you should make sure. We can start for there tonight."

"Yes, I suppose you're right."

"You'll never be at peace if you don't know for sure," Twilight added.

At peace? Soren thought. *Am I at peace now?* And it was as if a tiny sliver of ice had burrowed into his gizzard, for Soren knew only one thing for sure, which was that the two owls who had loved him most in all the world were gone, gone far away, and he was far from feeling peaceful.

They would sleep for the rest of this day and begin their desert flight at night. Nights were the best for desert flights, Twilight said, especially in the time of the dwenking. Soren was too tired to ask why. Too tired to hear some long explanation of Twilight's. Twilight seemed to know an awful lot and liked talking about it, always weaving in some story of a narrow escape or something that pointed up his extreme cleverness. But Soren was simply too tired to listen this morning. "Good light," he said in a small voice.

"Good light, Soren," Gylfie said.

"Good light, Soren and Gylfie," Twilight said.

"Good light, Twilight," Soren and Gylfie both said together.

Soren was soon asleep in the hollow. It felt good to sleep in a hollow, even if it was an empty one, with his head tucked under his wing in a normal sleeping position.

Then a voice, a familiar voice, pierced his sleep. He felt himself frozen and unable to move. It was as if he had gone yeep, his wings locked. Was he dreaming or sleeping? It was Grimble's voice. They were back in the library of St. Aggie's. Soren was madly pumping his wings. "Go! This is your chance," the voice cried. And then a terrible shriek. "Don't look back. Don't look back." But they did.

"Wake up, wake up! You two are both having terrible dreams. Wake up." It was Twilight shaking them. Soren and Gylfie awoke together with the same terrible image of a torn owl, bleeding and mortally wounded.

"It's Grimble," Gylfie said. "He's dead."

"I know. We both dreamed the same dream but . . . but . . . but, Gylfie, it was just a dream. Grimble might be fine."

"No," Gylfie said slowly. "No. I tried not to look but I caught a glimpse. The torn wings, his head at a weird angle." Gylfie's voice dwindled into the first dim gray of the coming night.

"Why didn't you say anything?"

"Because," she hesitated. It sounded so stupid, but it

was the truth. "Because I was flying. I had just felt that first soft cushion of air beneath my wings. I was about to soar and I forgot everything. I was just wings . . . and . . ."

Soren understood. It was not stupid. It was just the way they were. In the moment Grimble had died, they had become what they were always intended to be. Their destiny had been rendered. Flight was theirs.

"Well, buck up, you two," Twilight said gruffly. "I want to leave at first black. That will be in minutes. So it should be a perfect night for flying to Kuneer. And let me tell you, there is nothing, simply nothing, like desert flying. And you two can get in some hunting practice. Nice juicy snakes they have in Kuneer."

"I don't eat snakes," Soren said tersely.

"Oh, racdrops!" Twilight muttered under his breath. This owl was finicky. He mustered all the patience he could. "You don't eat snakes? Kindly explain."

"Well," said Gylfie. "You don't eat foxes."

Twilight blinked. "It's an entirely different situation. Few owls do eat foxes anyway. But snakes — snakes are a basic owl food. Look, I can't handle this kind of stuff. Are you stark-raving yoicks? Don't eat snakes. When I was your age I ate anything. Anything to keep me alive and flying. What do you mean you don't eat snakes? What owl doesn't eat snakes?"

"He doesn't," Gylfie said calmly. "It's a family thing. They had an old nest-maid who was a snake, a kind of nursemaid, as well, for the young ones, so it's out of respect for her, Mrs. Plithiver." Soren was touched that Gylfie remembered Mrs. Plithiver's name.

"And as much as I would love to see Mrs. Plithiver, I surely hope she does not hear our conversation," Soren added.

Twilight blinked and shook his head in an exaggerated manner and muttered something about coddled owls and the orphan school of tough learning. "Nest-maids? Nurse-maids?" His head seemed to spin around entirely on his neck as he walked out to the end of the branch, muttering to himself and punching the air with his talons in frustration. "Unbelievable! Bless my sweet gizzard. Next thing they'll be telling me is that they had another owl to do the family flying for them and hunt as well. I tell you, I wouldn't give a pile of racdrops for such a life."

CHAPTER TWENTY-FIVE

Mrs. P.!

They were on a border of scrub between the forest they had left behind and the desert that glimmered ahead in the distance. Twilight said they should take a rest and Soren, still irritated with Twilight's muttering about his and Gylfie's "coddled" upbringing, was determined now to prove himself as a hunter. So while Twilight and Gylfie tucked their heads under their wings for a quick nap, Soren flew off to find a vole or a mouse or perhaps even a rat.

It was not, however, the heartbeat of a mouse that Soren heard, for it was much too slow, but it was a heart-beat. And between two beats did he hear something else as well? A soft whispering sound full of strange agony. Very few creatures have ever heard a snake weep. There are no tears but they weep nonetheless, and that is how Soren found Mrs. Plithiver. He alighted on an old moss-covered stump. There, nestled at the bottom of the stump where two roots poked up, he saw a pale coil glimmering in the light of the nearly full moon. He tipped his head over the edge.

"Mrs. P.?" Soren blinked. He was incredulous.

A tiny head lifted out of the coiled body. There were the two dents where eyes might have been. "Mrs. P.," Soren said again.

"Mercy! It can't be."

"Mrs. P. It's me, Soren."

"Of course it is! Dear boy! Even an old blind snake like me would know that."

This was incredible. She recognized him. All his worst waking dreams vanished. Mrs. P. uncoiled and began to crawl up the stump.

Oh, it was a joyous reunion. They touched each others' faces gently, and had Mrs. P. possessed eyes, they would have shed tears of joy, but she insisted on slipping, slithering, and slinking her way across and over and under Soren's wings. "Be patient, dear. I want to get a sense of your plumage. Oh, my, you have fledged out beautifully. I bet you fly magnificently."

"But Mrs. P., where are Mum and Da and Eglantine and Kludd?"

"Don't mention that owl's name."

"My brother?"

"Yes, dear. He's the one who shoved you from the nest. I knew he was no good from the minute he hatched."

"But you couldn't see him shove me. How did you know?"

"I sensed it. We blind snakes can sense a lot. I knew you weren't on the rim of the hollow. You would have to be right on the rim to really fall out. You were just looking over the edge. You see, when he shoved you, I had been taking a snooze very close to Kludd's talons. I felt him stir. I felt the talons raise up and, well, sort of lurch. And then, of course, did he want me to go get help? No. He tried to stop me, blocked up my exit hole, but I found another all the same. Still, by the time I got back you had been snatched."

Soren closed his eyes and remembered. It all came back. The awful moment. "You're right," Soren said quietly. "You're absolutely right. I was shoved."

"Yes, and I sensed he might do the same to Eglantine. Your parents came back, of course, and they were devastated to find you gone. They gave Kludd strict instructions to mind Eglantine the next time they went hunting. But I knew what was coming. I was frantic when they went on another hunting expedition. I thought I'd have to get help. My friend Hilda worked for some Grass Owls in a tree in another part of the forest. They're a lovely family. I thought maybe they would give me some help. So I sneaked off when Kludd was asleep. Sound asleep, I thought. Well, do you know that by the time I came back Eglantine was gone as well."

"Gone? Where? What did he say?"

"Oh, it makes me tremble to even think of it. He said, 'You breathe a word of this, P., and you'll get what's coming to you.' Well, I couldn't imagine what he thought that was. So I said, 'Young fellow, that is no way to talk to your elders even though I am a servant.' And then . . . oh, this is the hardest . . . he screeched, 'You know, P., I've suddenly developed a taste for snake,' and he swooped down on me."

"Good Glaux!"

"Oh, don't swear, dear boy. It doesn't become one of your station."

"Mrs. P., what did you do?"

"I went down a hole. I waited as long as I could for your parents to return, but I didn't hear anything except that awful Kludd. Well, there was a back way out of this hole and I thought if I wanted to survive I'd better leave. Imagine — I couldn't even give notice to your parents. After all these years, not even to give notice. It really is not a proper way to depart."

"I don't think you had much choice, Mrs. P."

"No, I suppose I didn't."

"Come with me. I've made some friends. We are on our way to Hoolemere."

"Hoolemere!" There was a hiss of excitement in Mrs. Plithiver's small voice.

"You've heard of it and the Great Ga'Hoole Tree?"

"Oh, yes, my dear. It is just this side of Yonder!"

Soren blinked. He felt a wonderful quiver in his gizzard.

"She is NOT for dinner!" Soren glared at Twilight. He had just lit down on the branch that led into the hollow. Mrs. Plithiver was nestled in the feathers just behind his head and between his shoulders. "I want to make that perfectly clear. This is my dear friend, Mrs. Plithiver."

"Mrs. Plithiver!" Gylfie hopped forward on a branch. "*The* Mrs. Plithiver? I am honored. Permit me to introduce myself. I am Gylfie."

"Oh, a little Elf Owl, I believe." Mrs. Plithiver coiled up and raised her head in a greeting. It wavered slightly above Gylfie's head and she could sense her diminutive size. "I am enchanted. Oh, my goodness, you're almost as small as me." Mrs. Plithiver giggled a bit. Laughter in snakes has a slight hiccuppy sound.

"And this is Twilight," Soren said.

"Charmed," Mrs. Plithiver said.

"Likewise," replied Twilight. "Not used to servants, ma'am. Grew up on my own, more or less. Orphan school of tough learning. Not as polished as these two."

"Oh, good manners cannot really be learned, young'un. They are bred."

Twilight looked confused and stepped back a bit.

"Mrs. P., don't worry," Soren said. "I have explained to everyone how I come from a non-snake-eating family, and I expect this rule to be followed." Twilight and Gylfie nodded solemnly.

"Oh, good. I am sure we shall all get along fine."

"Mrs. P. wants to go with us. She can ride between my shoulders."

"I don't know what I'll do for references, of course, if I can find another position," Mrs. P. worried.

"What about me?" Soren said.

"Well, yes, I suppose they'll take the word of a youngster, even though I was actually with your family for much longer than you were. Alas!" She sighed deeply.

"Don't go getting emotional on us, ma'am. We got flying to do." Twilight spoke firmly but not unkindly.

"Of course, I'm so sorry." Mrs. P. gave a little shiver that coursed up her body as if she were trying to shake all such bleak thoughts away. It was almost as if she were shedding her skin.

Then Twilight, perhaps feeling he had been too abrupt with her, added, "I can take you for a spell myself, Mrs. P. I'm bigger than you, Soren. She won't add much weight."

"Oh, aren't you both dear," Mrs. P. said.

"I'm afraid I can't offer any such service," said Gylfie. "I don't think I weigh much more than Mrs. Plithiver. Although I would welcome her charming conversation."

"Oh, how sweet. And I have heard that Elf Owls are wonderful conversationalists." Twilight blinked and muttered something about little owls and big words. "But quite frankly, dear, serving snakes are not encouraged to engage in idle conversation with owls of your station."

"Mrs. P.," Soren said, stepping forward. "Please stop all that."

"All what, dear boy?"

"All this stuff about serving and stations. We are all the same now. There are no stations, no nests, no hollows. We're all orphans. We've all seen horrible things. The world is different now. And part of that difference is that there is no difference between any of us."

"Oh, no, dear boy. There shall always be servants. Don't say that. I come from a long tradition of service. It is nothing to be ashamed of. It is a most noble calling." Soren realized it would be useless to argue with her.

And so the little band of owls, with the blind snake

perched between Soren's shoulders, lifted into flight. The moon still rode high, although a halo of mist seemed to surround it.

"Oh, this is glorious, Soren. I am in the Yonder. Who would have believed it? Oh, my goodness, you are a magnificent flier." Mrs. Plithiver's small voice rang out in sheer ecstasy.

"Hang on, Mrs. P., I have to make a banking turn." Soren really didn't need to make such a turn, but he wanted to show Mrs. P. how gently he could carve the night sky with his wing and angle himself in a new direction. He soon made another one so that he could fall back in with the group.

"Oh, Yonder! Yonder!" Mrs. P. exclaimed again and again. "I am in the Yonder!" Her joy whipped out through the night with a singing hiss that to Soren made the stars shimmer even brighter.

Twilight was right. There was nothing like desert flying. The night was not really black but a deep, dark blue. The sky, moonless, tingled with stars. And although the air was chilly, from time to time heat from the desert sands below rolled up in great waves into the night, turning rough air smooth. The three owls would soar for endless minutes on the soft desert drafts, angling their tail feathers and primaries, carving great arcs in the darkness of the blue, inscribing imaginary figures with their wing tips or perhaps tracing the starry pictures of the constellations.

Twilight did know a lot. He told them the names of the constellations — the Great Glaux, whose one wing pointed toward a star that never moved. There was another one called the Little Raccoon, and then on summer nights, he said, the Big Raccoon rose in the sky and appeared to be dancing, so some called it the Dancing Raccoon. Still another was called the Great Crow because it spread its wings in the early autumn skies. But on this night, they flew under the bright and starry wings of the Great Glaux.

For the first time, Soren realized that his body had really changed. He was a fully fledged owl. It was the utter quiet with which he flew that first made him aware of this change. The last of his plummels had finally sprouted. These soft, fine feathers lay over the surface of his flight feathers, silencing them as he flew.

"I think we're getting near," Gylfie said.

The three owls began a long glide downward. They were now skimming above the sand, just a bit higher than the prickly cactuses. "Don't worry," Gylfie said. "The needles don't hurt. We're too light."

Gylfie had landed and so had Twilight. But just before landing, Soren heard something — a rapid beating sound.

It was a heartbeat. And not that of a snake. In his gizzard Soren knew what it was, a mouse, and his mouth began to water. "Hang on, Mrs. P.! Going in for mouse!"

"Oh, goody!" she cried, and coiled herself tighter into the deep ruff of feathers between his shoulders.

Soren quickly flapped his wings in a series of powerful upstrokes and gained some height. He cocked his head one way, then the other. The heartbeat seemed to pulse across his face. He knew where this creature was and, without even thinking, began a rapid downward spiral.

Within a second, he had the mouse in his talons and had sunk his beak in, just as he had seen his father do when he killed a mouse at the base of their fir tree.

"Good work." Twilight drifted down beside him. "No one can beat you Barn Owls for picking up a mouse's heartbeat." This was the first compliment that Twilight had ever given him.

"Even for one not brought up in the orphan school of tough learning?"

"Not very gracious, Soren!" Mrs. P. hissed softly in his ear. Soren immediately regretted what he had said. "Manners, child!"

"Sorry, Twilight, that wasn't very gracious of me. Thank you for the compliment."

"Gracious!" a voice squeaked. "You call that gracious?

And I'll thank you to take your disgusting talons out of my home."

Soren stepped back and pulled his talons, which were now clutching the mouse, from the sand. From a hole near the base of the cactus from which he had just stepped back, a small face emerged. It was a face not unlike Gylfie's but larger, with brownish feathers and big yellow eyes with a swag of short white feathers above them.

"What in the name of Glaux . . . ?" Soren began to whisper.

"This is wrong. ALL wrong . . ." Twilight gasped.

"Speotyto cunicularia!" Gylfie whispered, then added, "very rare."

"Oh, for Glaux's sake, you and your big words," rasped Twilight.

But at that same moment, there was a terrible shriek and the owl-like thing that had emerged from the hole shrunk back. Then they heard a soft exhalation of air. Twilight stepped up to the hole and peered down. "I think it's fainted."

"What is IT?" Soren asked, completely forgetting the succulent mouse he still clasped in his talons.

"A Burrowing Owl," Gylfie said. "Very rare. But I remember my parents talking about it. It nests in the old burrows of ground animals."

"Oh, Glaux!" both Twilight and Soren said at once, and made gagging noises.

"They don't!" Twilight said, his voice drenched in disbelief. "Well, learn something new every day, even me . . . well, more like every other day. Met an owl who won't eat snakes — oh, pardon me, Mrs. Plithiver."

"No need to apologize," she said quickly. "Soren's family was exceptional in that way. Such elegance they had!" she said wistfully.

"Anyhow, as I was saying," Twilight continued, "then another who lives in holes — not trees. What's the world coming to?"

"I don't think not eating snakes and living in holes of ground animals are quite the same thing. Besides, you said you lived with foxes," Soren said huffily.

"Above foxes, not in their den. Lived in an old cactus hollow. Their den was beneath it."

A rustling noise came from the hole. The three owls stepped a bit closer. A beak poked out. "Is he still there?"

"Who?" asked Gylfie. "We're all still here."

"The one with the white face. The ghost owl."

Twilight and Gylfie spun their heads toward Soren.

"Me?"

That was when Soren realized that he had not only fledged the rest of his flight feathers but his face feathers as well. Like all Barn Owls, his face had turned pure white and was rimmed with tan feathers. His belly and the underneath parts of his wings were the same pure white, while the top of his wings, his back, and his head were a mixture of tans and browns delicately speckled with darker feathers. And unlike almost any other owls, his eyes had not turned yellow but were deepest black, which made his face seem even whiter.

"I'm not a ghost," Soren spoke. "I'm a Barn Owl. We all have white faces." Soren felt a strange mixture of pride and terrible sadness. He wished his parents could see him now. He must look a lot like his father. And Eglantine — what would she look like? If she resembled her mother, her face would be white but with a more distinct and darker rim, particularly on the lower part. She might have a few more speckles and they would be darker. She would almost be ready to fly.

"Are you sure?" The owl was creeping a bit farther out of the hole.

"Am I sure what?"

"Are you sure you're not a ghost?"

"Why would I want to pretend to be a ghost? Are you sure you live in that hole?" Soren replied.

"Of course I do. We've always lived in holes. My parents, my grandparents, my great-grandparents, my great-

great-grandparents. And what's with the snake on your head and all this talk about not eating snakes?"

"This is Mrs. Plithiver. She has been with my family a very long time. And," Soren paused dramatically, "we don't eat snake. We not only find it unappetizing but wrong, and my friends here have agreed — not to touch snake. I want to make that perfectly clear. Or you'll be a ghost before you know it!" Soren said, raising his voice.

"Perfectly clear," the Burrowing Owl answered in a quavery voice, and dipped his head toward Mrs. Plithiver. "Pleased to eat ya. I mean, meet ya."

Soren gave a long rasping sound.

"I'm sure it was just a slip of the tongue, Soren," Mrs. P. said diplomatically.

"So what happened to your parents?" Twilight asked abruptly.

The Burrowing Owl hesitated and then sighed. "I don't like to speak about it."

"Were you snatched?"

Again there was a long silence. And then finally the story spilled out in jagged chunks between gasps and sobs. Soren listened. At one point he heard Twilight mutter, "This is one hysterical owl." Gylfie told him to shut up.

The Burrowing Owl was named Digger and he had not been snatched, but his two brothers had been. From the description of the owls who did the snatching, it must have been Jatt and Jutt. The most horrific part of the story, however, was the fight that Jatt and Jutt had over the youngest, Digger's brother Flick. "He was plump, a chubby little fellow, and they . . . they . . . they ate him!"

Digger crumpled into the sand in a swoon. "Come on, now," Twilight said briskly, and nudged the poor owl. "You can't keep passing out. Buck up."

Gylfie and Soren looked at each other in disbelief. Soren thought if he heard Twilight say "buck up" one more time, he might just attack. But it was Gylfie who bristled up and suddenly seemed twice her normal size. "His brother's been eaten by another owl and you say 'buck up'? Twilight, for Glaux's sake, show some sensitivity."

"Sensitivity gets you nowhere in the desert. If he keeps passing out like this, why, if the moon was full, he'd get moon blinked in no time."

A shudder passed through Gylfie and Soren at the mere mention of those words. Digger began to stir. He dragged himself to his feet.

"How did you get away?" Soren asked.

"I ran."

"Ran?" Soren and Twilight both spoke at once. This, indeed, was a very strange owl.

"Well, I hadn't really learned how to fly yet, but we

Burrowing Owls are good at running." Soren looked at Digger's legs. Unlike most owls, Digger's legs barely had any feathers and were exceedingly long. "I ran as far and as fast as I could. You see, our parents were out hunting when all this happened, and these two owls were in such a tussle over Flick. Cunny, the next oldest brother, had already been snatched, and this other owl had flown off with him, although he kept yelling back to the other two not to eat Flick. His voice was odd, softer than the other two owls, a kind of *tingg-tingg* sound. I never heard anything like it."

"Grimble," Soren and Gylfie said at once.

"So what happened?" Twilight asked. "Did your parents come back and find you?"

"Well, the problem is that I'm lost. I ran farther and faster than I ever thought I could and I have been trying to find my way back ever since. Once I came to a burrow that looked just like the one that I had lived in with my parents, but there was no sign of them. So it must have been the wrong burrow." Digger said this in a quavering voice and then added, "Mustn't it?"

Soren, Gylfie, and Twilight remained silent.

"I mean," Digger continued, "they would never just leave. They would think something had happened and they would go out and search for us. One of them would search and the other would stay behind. You know, in case we returned or . . ." His voice died away and was swallowed in the cool breeze of the desert night.

Deep in his gizzard, Soren felt the Burrowing Owl's anguish. "Digger," he said, "they might have come back and seen the . . . the" — he took a deep breath — "the blood and the feathers of your brother on the ground. They might have thought that you had all been murdered. They didn't really leave you, Digger. They probably thought you were all dead."

"Oh," Digger said quietly. And then, "How awful. My parents think I am dead! We all are dead! How terrible. I must find them, then. I must show them that I am alive. I am their son. Why, I can even fly now." But instead of flying he began to stride off with great purpose into the desert.

"Well, why aren't you flying?" Twilight called after him.

Digger spun his head around. "Oh, there's a burrow right over here. I just want to take a look."

"Oh, great Glaux," sighed Gylfie. "He's going to walk all the way across this desert, poking into every burrow."

CHAPTER TWENTY-SIX
Desert Battle

They flew for another night, skirting the edges of the Desert of Kuneer. Nowhere had they found any signs of Gylfie's family, not even in the old cactus where they had all lived together before the snatching.

As they flew, Soren began to think deeply about St. Aggie's and the absolute evilness of the owls there. The evil seemed to have touched almost every kingdom — egg snatching in Ambala, chick snatching in Tyto, and now the worst horror of all, cannabalism in Kuneer. Hortense had told them that a few of the owls in Ambala had somehow figured out that the source of the evil was St. Aggie's, but his own parents had just thought it was something random, perhaps a small gang of renegade owls — nothing as large and powerful as St. Aggie's. They never could have imagined such a place, and Soren felt that few owls in any of the kingdoms could have, either. Was it possible that Soren, Gylfie, and Twilight were the only ones who were aware of the scope and power of St. Aggie's? Were they the only ones who had all the pieces to this horrible puzzle of violence and destruction that was touching every single owl kingdom? If this was true, they must stick together. There was strength in numbers even if the number was only three. They were the three who knew the terrible truth of St. Aggie's. This knowledge alone could help them save other owls.

Soren remembered when he was still a prisoner of St. Aggie's and first realized that it was not simply enough to escape. How awful it had been to imagine his beloved sister, Eglantine, a victim of the brutality of St. Aggie's. He remembered thinking that there was a world of Eglantines out there. So now they had escaped, and now he knew for certain that their task was greater than he and Gylfie and Twilight had ever imagined. Soren knew he must think carefully about how he could explain all this to Twilight and Gylfie.

Every now and then, the three owls would look down and spot Digger trudging through the desert sand. Occasionally, Digger would lift into flight but always skimmed low, combing the desert for any burrow that might shelter his parents. Mostly, however, he would run, his long, nearly featherless legs striking out across the sand, his short stubby tail lifted to catch any wind from behind that would give a boost to his speed. Or if there was a head wind, as now, he would lean into it, tucking his wings close to his body, and ram ahead.

"That fool owl has the strongest legs I've ever seen," Twilight muttered as the first slice of the moon rose in the sky.

"Strongest legs and the stubbornest head," Gylfie added.

But deep within Soren there was a flicker of bright admiration for this odd owl. One had to marvel at Digger's determination. Just as Soren was pondering this, he heard something. He cocked his head one way, then the other.

As in all Barn Owls, Soren's ear openings on either side of his face were not evenly placed — the left one being higher than the right. His uneven set of ears actually helped him to capture sound better. And now he instinctively worked certain muscles in his facial disk to expand its surface and help guide the sounds to his ear. The noise was coming from his windward side, his right ear, because it was that ear that was picking it up before his left ear. Now the sound was arriving almost at the same time in both ears, perhaps with one-millionth of a second difference.

"Triangulating, are you?" Twilight asked.

"What?" Soren said.

"Fancy word for what you Barn Owls do best. Figure out exactly where a sound is coming from. Something tasty down there? I could use a bite."

"Well, there's something below but it's not on the ground. It's off to windward. You can line it up with that bright star on my wing tip."

Then, suddenly, Soren and Gylfie saw them. "Great Glaux, it's Jatt and Jutt!" Soren exclaimed.

"Look!" said Gylfie. "They're closing in on Digger. I hope there's a burrow nearby."

"47-2 is with them," Soren said. "Look at that stupid owl. It's huge now."

"It's a Screech Owl," whispered Twilight. It certainly was, and 47-2 now resembled that other terrible Screech Owl — Spoorn.

"They must have let her grow flight feathers and taught her to fly," Gylfie said weakly.

"Sheer off to downwind," Twilight ordered. "We don't want them to hear us."

"Right, but hush!" said Soren. "I'm picking up something. Let me listen."

The words that Soren picked up from the three owls that flew below them were chilling, even though the conversation broke up on the rising wind currents.

"47-2, once you taste a Burrowing Owl — well . . . nothing . . . like it . . . run fast . . . no burrows here . . . no place . . . hide . . ."

"We've got to do something," Soren said.

"The three of them against the two and a half of us." Twilight sighed as he turned his head toward Gylfie.

"I can be a diversion," said Gylfie quickly. And giving the other two owls no time to reply, she plunged into a quick downward spiral.

"What's she doing?" Soren asked. Gylfie was already on the ground and she was doing the best imitation imaginable of a burrowing owl, kicking out her feet as she tried to run across the desert sand.

"Look, it's working!" cried Twilight. And sure enough, 47-2 was turning toward Gylfie.

"Charge!" roared Twilight.

"Hang on Mrs. P.," Soren gasped.

Jatt and Jutt were just lighting down on the sand when Twilight and Soren struck. Soren, his feet forward, spread his talons and thrust his legs straight out. He shut his eyes but felt his talons sink into the feathers between Jatt's ear tufts and then one talon hit something not like feathers at all. It was flesh, then bone. A terrible cry ripped through the night. But now Soren was tumbling in the sand. There was a whirlwind of feathers and dust. Something slithered nearby. He hoped it was Mrs. P. finding herself a safe hole.

Then there was a deep hoot that reverberated across the vastness of the desert. It was Twilight beginning his battle cry. Jatt and Jutt, however, had their own fierce thrum that seemed to shake Soren to his gizzard. Twilight was hooting as only Twilight could.

> *You ugly rat-faced birds.*
> *You call yourself a bird?*
> *You call yourself an owl?*
> *You ain't no decent kind of fowl!*
> *They call you Jatt?*
> *They call you Jutt?*
> *I'm gonna toss you in a rut!*
> *Then I'm gonna punch you in the gut!*
> *Then you're gonna wind up on your butt!*
> *Think you're all gizzard!*
> *I seen better lizards.*
> *One-two-three-four,*
> *You're goin' down, won't ask for more.*
> *Five-six-seven-eight,*
> *You ain't better than fish bait . . .*
> *Nine-ten-eleven-twelve,*
> *I'm gonna send you straight to hell.*

The air was laced with Twilight's taunts. From the corner of his eye, Soren saw Jutt trying to jab at Twilight. But Twilight was as fast as his smart-talking beak. He dodged, he feinted with his jabs, seeming to aim for one place, then stabbing at another, and all the while yammering away in his hooting singsong taunts. First at Jatt, then Jutt. He would lure them in close for a strike and then strike back faster. His talons became a blur. Soren had never seen anything as fast and as light as the immense Great Gray Owl.

Soren tried to keep his focus on closing in on 47-2 before, indeed, she caught up with Gylfie. Suddenly, however, Soren felt something strike him from behind. He flipped in the air and came down on his back. Jatt, much bigger, loomed like a monster owl above him. One ear tuft had been torn off completely. The owl was in a mad frenzy. "I'll kill you! Kill you! I'll rip out your eyes!"

Just as the sharp beak began to come toward him, Soren felt the air stir and a shadow slide across them. Then, miraculously, the huge weight that had pinned him down lifted. Still lying on his back, he blinked in utter amazement as he saw the owl rise above him — not in free flight but in the talons of the most immense bird he had ever seen. Its white head glistened in the light cast from the crescent moon that was now directly overhead.

On the ground to the left, another bird, also with a white head, stalked about the lifeless forms of Jutt and 47-2.

Then Gylfie and Digger walked up. "I've never seen anything like it," Digger said. "Who are they? Who are these white-headed birds?"

"Eagles," Twilight spoke softly with great reverence. "Bald eagles."

"Hortense's eagles!" Soren and Gylfie both said at once.

"Hortense?" said Mrs. Plithiver as she crawled out of her hole. "Who's Hortense?"

CHAPTER TWENTY-SEVEN
Hortense's Eagles

My name is Streak," said the smaller eagle, "and this is my mate, Zan. She is mute and cannot speak." Zan nodded to the four owls and dipped her beak almost to the desert floor. "Her tongue," Streak continued, "was torn out by the evil ones."

"The evil ones?" Soren said. "Jatt and Jutt?"

"And Spoorn and Skench, and the wicked creatures of St. Aggie's. I dare not call them birds!"

"Was Zan the one who tried to rescue Hortense's egg?"

Zan bobbed her head excitedly.

"Yes, indeed, and she did rescue it but it was on that mission that she lost her tongue," Streak explained.

Soren turned to Zan. "We saw you that terrible day. We saw what happened. You are both so brave to have helped Hortense."

"Hortense was the brave one. There was never an owl quite like Hortense. Do you know that in Ambala nearly every other newly hatched owl chick is being named Hortense, even if it's male?"

"Oh, my goodness!" Gylfie sighed. "And she hated the name so much. At least, that's what she told us."

"Well, a hero is known by one name now in the Kingdom of Ambala and that name is Hortense."

"What are you doing here in Kuneer?" Twilight asked.

"We fly patrol over Kuneer," Streak said, nodding at Digger. "We have a great liking for these desert creatures. While we were out hunting once, one of our little ones tried to fly before she was really ready. You know young ones. It's the one thing we always tell them not to do — don't try to fly too soon, never leave the nest when Da and Mum are away, and, bless my beak, don't a few always go and try it? She got a far piece but didn't know how to land and broke a small wing bone. One of these strange little owls, the ones that burrow in the sand, found our little Fiona and tucked her into their hole, fed her, coddled her, took the best care of her till her bone mended and she could fly. They found out where she came from and brought her back to us. Zan and I have always believed that there is more goodness than evil in the world. But you know, you still got to work at it. So that's what Zan and I do, now that all the little ones are gone. We work at it — doing good, that is."

Soren, Gylfie, Digger, and Twilight looked at the two large birds in wonder.

"I don't know how to thank you," Digger said.

Zan made a few nodding movements with her head that Streak observed carefully. "My dear mate says — you see, I can understand her even though she does not speak — Zan says that you must quit that foolish walking about in the desert all day and night. Too dangerous. What are you looking for so hard, my dear?"

"My family," Digger said. He then told Streak and Zan the story of what Jatt and Jutt had done to his brother Flick and how he had run off and was now lost.

Streak and Zan exchanged a long look. In that instant, Digger sensed that the two eagles knew his parents' fate. Zan stepped up to Digger and began preening his feathers with her beak in a soothing gesture. Streak took a deep breath. "Well, my son, I am afraid that we know what happened to your parents. You see, the feathers of the little brother you described were still there by the burrow and we saw your mum and da weeping mightily. So we asked what happened, and they told us how this had been their son Flick and they didn't know where in the world their two other young ones might be. Zan thought that this surely was the worst thing she'd ever heard. And though she can speak nary a sliver of a sound, she came back each day to preen your mother — to simply say in her own way 'I've been a mother, too, and though I have not lost a young one in this way I can feel how terrible it must be.'

"Then one day we got there a mite too late. The same two owls that nearly killed you just now came back for another run at the burrows and this time they came with reinforcements. There must have been fifty of them and they were wearing the most ferocious battle claws we'd ever seen. Well, we can take 'em on if there are only two or three in a war party, even with the claws, but fifty — no, no, that's no match."

"D-d-d-did . . ." Digger began to stutter. "Did they eat them?"

"No, just killed them. Said they were too tough and gristly."

There was a long silence now. No one knew what to say. Finally, Gylfie turned to Digger and spoke, "Come with us, Digger."

"But where is it you're going?" he asked.

"To the Great Ga'Hoole Tree."

"What?" said Digger, but before Twilight could answer, Streak broke in. "I've heard of that place, but isn't it just a story, a legend?"

"To some it might be," Twilight said, and blinked at the eagle.

But not to owls, thought Soren. *To owls,* he thought, *it is a real place.*

The dwenking moon had begun to slide down the bowl of the night. It hung like the curve of a talon low in the desert sky, spilling a river of silver across the land that seemed to flow directly to the four owls, lapping at the edges of their own talons. This light, flooding low and cool, seemed so different from the moon's scaldings and blinkings. It was a light that seemed to clear the mind and make bold the spirit. And something strange began to happen. Soren, with Mrs. P. on his shoulder, and Twilight and Gylfie stepped close to one another until their feathers were touching, and even Digger tucked in on the other side of Twilight. Where a short time before, Soren had wondered how he would explain his thoughts to the other owls, now he knew that no explanation was needed, that they had within the slivers of time and the silver of moonlight become a band. They were four owls who had lost their parents. But the time had come for them to become something else. They were not simply orphans. Together they were much more. Hadn't the Great Ga'Hoole Tree of the Ga'Hoollian Legends been the source of their greatest inspiration when they had been at St. Aggie's? Hadn't the Tales of Yore and the nobility of the knights of the Great Ga'Hoole Tree saved them from moon scalding? Could the legend become real? Could they, in fact, become part of the legend?

Soren's dream of Grimble was the worst sleeping dream he had ever had, but there was another dream, a waking dream that haunted the borders of Soren's mind and made his gizzard quiver. It was a dream that filled him with despair. In it, Soren was flying and spotted his parents perched in a tree. They had found a new hollow, and there was a brand-new nest lined with the fluffiest down. In the nest, there were new little owlets. Soren alighted on a limb. "Mum? Da? It's me, Soren." And his parents blinked, not in amazement but in true disbelief. "You're not our son," said his da. "Oh, no," said his mum. "Our son wouldn't look like you even grown up and fully fledged." "No," said his da, and both owls turned and ducked into the hollow. This, Soren realized in the deepest part of his gizzard, was why they had to go to the Great Ga'Hoole Tree. For when the world one knew began to crumble away bit by bit, when not only your memories but the memories that others might have of you grew dim with time and distance, when, indeed, you began to fade into a nothingness in the minds of the owls that you loved best, well, perhaps that was when legends could become real.

But at the heart of this nightmare was another deeper

truth. Soren had become something else. He turned slowly to look at the three other owls in the cool moonlight. Their eyes burned with a new intelligence, a new understanding. *Yes*, thought Soren, *and so had Gylfie and Twilight and Digger become something else.* No words were spoken. No words were needed. But a silent oath was sworn in that desert river of moonlight and the four owls all nodded. In that instant they knew that they were a band forevermore, bound by a loyalty stronger than blood. It was as a band they must go to Hoolemere and find its great tree that loomed now as the heart of wisdom and nobility in a world that was becoming insane and ignoble. They must warn of the evil that threatened. They must become part of this ancient kingdom of knights on silent wings who rose in the blackness to perform deeds of greatness.

And, indeed, Soren knew still another truth: Legends were not only for the desperate. Legends were for the brave.

"Let's go," said Soren.

"To Ga'Hoole!" cried Twilight.

"To Ga'Hoole!" echoed the others.

"All for owls and owls for all!" shouted Soren.

And in the still, deepest part of the night, four owls lifted into flight, their shadows printed on the hard desert sand below by the last spray of the moon's light. A Great

Gray flew in the lead, to windward a handsome Barn Owl, downwind flew a minute Elf Owl, in extremely quiet flight for such a talkative owl with no fringe on her feathers. Flying in the tail position, grappling with his talons across the windy wake of Twilight, flew Digger. All flew toward the River Hoole, which would empty into the great sea of Hoolemere, and an island where the Great Tree of Ga'Hoole grew and where, once upon a very long time ago, in the time of Glaux, there was an order of knightly owls who would rise each night into the blackness and perform noble deeds.

And Soren knew in his heart that now was the time for the legend to be true.

THE OWLS
and others
from

GUARDIANS *of* GA'HOOLE
The Capture

SOREN: Barn Owl, *Tyto alba*, from the kingdom of the Forest of Tyto; snatched when he was three weeks old by St. Aegolius patrols

> His family:
> KLUDD: Barn Owl, *Tyto alba*, older brother
> EGLANTINE: Barn Owl, *Tyto alba*, younger sister
> NOCTUS: Barn Owl, *Tyto alba*, father
> MARELLA: Barn Owl, *Tyto alba*, mother

> His family's nest-maid:
> MRS. PLITHIVER: blind snake

GYLFIE: Elf Owl, *Micrathene whitneyi*, from the desert kingdom of Kuneer; snatched when she was three weeks old by St. Aegolius patrols

TWILIGHT: Great Gray Owl, *Strix nebulosa*, free flyer, orphaned within hours of hatching

DIGGER: Burrowing Owl, *Speotyto cunicularius*, from the desert kingdom of Kuneer; lost in desert after attack in which his brother was killed by Jatt and Jutt

/3   /3   /3

SKENCH: Great Horned Owl, *Bubo virginianus*, the Ablah General of St. Aegolius Academy for Orphaned Owls

SPOORN: Western Screech Owl, *Otus kennicottii*, first lieutenant to Skench

JATT: Long-eared Owl, *Asio otus*, a St. Aegolius sublieutenant, warrior, and enforcer

JUTT: Long-eared Owl, *Asio otus*, a St. Aegolius sublieutenant, warrior, and enforcer; cousin of Jatt

AUNT FINNY: Snowy Owl, *Nyctea scandiaca*, pit guardian at St. Aegolius

UNK: Great Horned Owl, *Bubo virginianus*, pit guardian at St. Aegolius

GRIMBLE: Boreal Owl, *Aegolius funerus*, captured as an adult by St. Aegolius patrols and held as a hostage with the promise that his family would be spared

47-2: Western Screech Owl, *Otus kennicottii*, picker in the pelletorium of St. Aegolius

HORTENSE: Spotted Owl, *Strix occidentalis*, originally from the forest kingdom of Ambala, snatched at an indeterminate age by St. Aegolius patrols; trained as a broody owl in the eggorium of St. Aegolius

STREAK: Bald eagle, free flyer

ZAN: Bald eagle, mate of Streak

GUARDIANS
of GA'HOOLE

BOOK TWO

The Journey

. . . the four owls looked below and saw the vast sea glinting with
silver spangles from the moon's light and then, directly ahead,
spreading into the night, were the twisting branches of the largest
tree they had ever seen, the Great Ga'Hoole Tree.

Contents

CHAPTER ONE

A Mobbing of Crows

Soren felt the blind snake shift in the deep feathers between his shoulders as he and the three other owls flew through the buffeting winds. They had been flying for hours now and it seemed as if in the last minutes the darkness had begun to dissolve drop by drop, and they were now passing from the full black of the night into the first light of the morning. Beneath them a river slid like a dark ribbon over the earth.

"Let's keep flying even though it's getting light," said Twilight, the immense Great Gray Owl that flew downwind of Soren. "We're getting nearer. I just feel it."

It was to the Sea of Hoolemere they flew, and in the middle of that sea was an island and on that island there was a tree called the Great Ga'Hoole Tree and in this tree there was an order of owls. It was said that these owls would rise each night into the blackness and perform noble deeds. The universe of owls was desperately in need of such deeds. For with its many kingdoms it was about to be destroyed by a terrible evil.

Hidden away in a maze of stone canyons and ravines there was indeed a violent nation of deadly owls known as St. Aegolius. The evil of St. Aggie's, as it was often called, had touched almost every owl kingdom in some way or another. Soren and his best friend, Gylfie, the tiny Elf Owl, had both been captured by St. Aggie's patrols when they were young nestlings unable to fly. Twilight, too, had been snatched but, unlike Soren and Gylfie, he had managed to escape before being imprisoned. Digger's youngest brother had been eaten by a St. Aggie's patrol and his parents later killed. Soren and Gylfie had met Twilight and Digger, a Burrowing Owl, shortly after their own daring escape from the stone canyons of St. Aggie's.

Although the four owls had met as orphans, they had become so much more. In a desert still stained with the blood of two of the fiercest of St. Aggie's elite warrior owls, whom they had defeated, they had discovered a knowledge, along with a feeling deep in their gizzards, where all owls felt their strongest emotions. And this knowledge was that they were a band forevermore, one for all and all for one, bound by the deepest loyalty and dedicated to the survival of the kingdoms of all owls. They had sworn an oath in that desert drenched with blood and tinged with the silver light of the moon. They would go to Hoolemere. It was as a band that they knew they must go and find its great tree, which loomed now as the heart of wisdom and nobility in a world that was becoming insane and ignoble. They must warn of the evil that threatened. They must become part of this ancient kingdom of guardian knights on silent wings.

They hoped they were drawing near even though the river they now followed was not the River Hoole, the one that led to Hoolemere. Still, Twilight said he was sure that this river would lead to the Hoole and on to Hoolemere, and the very thought of this legendary island in the sea made the four owls stroke even harder against the confusing winds. But Soren felt Mrs. Plithiver stir again in his feathers. Mrs. P., as he called her, had been the old nestmaid in the hollow where Soren's parents had made their home. These blind snakes had been born without eyes, and where their eyes should have been there were only two slight indentations. The rosy-scaled reptiles were kept by many owls to tend the nests and make sure they were clean and free of maggots and various vermin that found their way into the hollows. Soren had thought that he would never see Mrs. P. again, and yet they had found each other just days after his escape from St. Aggie's. She had told him what Soren had long suspected — that it was his older brother, Kludd, who had pushed him from the nest when his parents were out hunting. Although he had survived the fall, still being flightless he was prey to any ground animal. Ground animal! Who would have ever thought another owl would be the greatest danger? Until that moment when he was snatched and felt himself being carried into the night sky by a pair of talons, Soren had thought that the worst predator in the forest, from an owl's point of view, was a raccoon. And then Mrs. P. told him that she had suspected that Kludd had done the same thing to Eglantine, his baby sister. When Mrs. P. had protested, Kludd had threatened to eat her. So the poor old snake had no choice but to leave — very quickly.

Now Mrs. P. slithered toward Soren's left ear, the higher ear and the easiest for her to reach. "Soren," she whispered, "I'm not sure if it is a good idea to keep flying with all this light. We don't want to get mobbed."

"Mobbed?" Soren asked.

"You know, crows."

Soren felt a chill run through his gizzard.

Perhaps if Mrs. Plithiver had not been whispering her warning in his ear he might have heard the chuffing sound of wings, and not owl wings, overhead.

"Crow to windward!" Gylfie cried. And then suddenly the rosy dawn sky turned black.

"We're being mobbed!" shrieked Twilight.

Oh, Glaux! thought Soren. This was the worst thing that could befall any owl flying in the daytime. But it was still very early. Crows at night were fine. Owls were crows' worst enemies at night. They could attack them as they slept, but crows during the day were something else. Crows in daylight were terrible. If a crow discovered an owl during the daytime, even if it was just one crow, that bird had a way of signaling others and soon an entire flock would arrive and mob the owls, diving at their heads with their sharp beaks, trying to tear out their eyes.

"Scatter!" Gylfie cried out. "Scatter and loop."

Suddenly, Gylfie seemed to be everywhere at once. She was like a crazed insect, zipping through the air. Soren, Digger, and Twilight began to follow her lead. Soren quickly noticed that Gylfie would swoop up from her loops and spiraling dives to just beneath the crows, stabbing them on the underside of their wings. This made the crows drop their wings down close to their bodies and lose altitude.

"I feel one coming up behind," hissed Mrs. P. "Off your windward tail feathers."

Mrs. P. carefully began to crawl backward on Soren. He adjusted his wings. For even with her light weight, as she moved he could feel his balance shift. Mrs. P. could smell the crow's stinky breath as it closed in. Soren began to dive. Mrs. P. continued to make her way toward the tail feathers that were stiffer and coarser. A great whiff of crow stench engulfed her. Mrs. Plithiver raised her head in the direction of the foul odor and began screaming, "Scum of the sky, curse of the earth, riffraff of the Yonder. Scurrilous crowilous," she ranted.

The Yonder was what all blind snakes called the sky because it was so far away, about as far away as anything could be for a snake. But Mrs. P. saved her most poisonous insult for last — "Wet pooper!" Blind snakes were especially impressed by owls' digestive systems, which allowed them to compress certain parts of waste into neat pellets that they yarped up through their mouths, as opposed to other disgusting birds whom they referred to as "wet poopers." The crow seemed to brake mid-flight. His beak fell open, his wings folded.

Crows are simple birds. And what this crow had just seen and heard — a snake hissing curses and rising from the back feathers of an owl — stunned him. He went "yeep," which meant that he simply froze in flight and began to plummet to earth.

The crows by this time had begun to disappear. Twilight flew up to Soren's windward side. "Digger's hurt."

Indeed, when Soren looked in the direction of Digger,

he saw the Burrowing Owl tipping dangerously to one side. "We've got to find a place to land."

Gylfie flew up breathlessly. "I don't know how much longer Digger can last. He's not flying straight at all."

"Which way is he tipping?" Mrs. P. asked.

"Downwind," said Twilight.

"Quick!" she ordered. "Let's get over there. I might be able to help."

"You?" Twilight asked somewhat incredulously.

"Remember, dear, how Digger had been asking me to ride on his back in the desert? This might just be the time."

A few seconds later they were coming in on Digger's upwind wing.

"Digger," Soren said, "we know you're hurt."

"I don't know if I can make it," the Burrowing Owl groaned. "Oh, if I could only walk."

"There's a stand of trees really close," Soren said. "Mrs. P. has an idea that might help you."

"What's that?"

"She's going to get on your good wing. That will tip your injured wing up again, lighten the drag on it. Gylfie meanwhile will fly under your bad wing and create a little updraft for it. It might work."

"I don't know," Digger moaned miserably.

"Faith, boy! Faith!" exhorted Mrs. Plithiver. "Now let's get on with it."

"I really don't think I can make it," Digger gasped.

"You can, boy! You can!" said Mrs. P. Her voice grew amazingly strong. "You shall go on to the finish. You shall fly to the forests, to the trees, to Hoolemere. You have defended yourself against these crows. You have strode across deserts. You shall defend yourself now by flying. You shall fly into the wind, into the light, into this new day. Whatever the cost, you shall fly on. You shall not fail or falter. You shall not weaken. You shall finish the flight." Mrs. P.'s voice swelled in the growing light of the morning and somehow it filled them all with new courage.

Now Soren flew in so close to Digger that his wing was touching the tip of Digger's good wing. They were ready for the transfer. "Now, Mrs. P.! Go!"

The old nest snake began to slither out onto Soren's wing. Soren felt the pressure of air around his body and the cushions of wind under his wings shift. The air surrounding him seemed to fray. He had to concentrate hard not to go into a roll. But if he was frightened, he could not imagine what Mrs. P. was feeling as she blindly slithered out to the tip of his wing and began the precarious transfer to Digger.

"Almost there, dear, almost there. Steady now. Steady."

Suddenly, she was gone. His wing felt light. Soren turned his head. She had made it. She was now crawling up toward the base of Digger's wing. It was working. Digger's flight grew even.

"We're bringin' him in! We're bringing him in!" Twilight shouted triumphantly. Creating direct updrafts that supported Digger's flight, Twilight flew below, along with Gylfie who, under the injured wing, was doing the same.

Finally, they landed in a large spruce tree. There was a perfect hollow for them to spend the day in, and Mrs. Plithiver immediately launched into a frenzy of action. "I need worms! Big fat ones, and leeches. Quick — all of you! Go out and get me what I need. I'll stay here with Digger."

Mrs. Plithiver crawled onto Digger's back. "Now, this won't hurt, dear, but I just want to feel what those awful crows did to you." Gently, she began flicking her forked tongue over his wound. "It's not deep. The best thing I can do is to curl up right on the wound until they come back. A snake's skin can be very healing in many cases. We're a little too dry for the long run, however. That's why I want the worms."

Soon the owls were back with the worms and leeches that Mrs. P. had ordered. She directed Soren to place two leeches on the wound. "That will cleanse it. I can't tell you how filthy crows are!"

After the leeches had done their work, Mrs. Plithiver pulled them off and gently replaced them with two fat worms.

Digger sighed. "That feels so good."

"Yes, there's nothing like a fat slimy worm for relief of a wound. You'll be fit to fly by tomorrow night."

"Thank you, Mrs. P. Thank you so much." Digger blinked at Mrs. P., and there was a look in his large yellow eyes of seeming disbelief that he could have ever considered such a snake a meal, which, as a desert owl, Digger often did.

Within the spruce tree where they perched, there was another hollow that housed a family of Masked Owls.

"They look almost exactly like you, Soren," Gylfie said. "And they're coming to visit."

"Masked Owls look nothing like me," Soren replied. Everyone was always saying this. He had heard his parents complain about it. Yes, they had white faces and buff-colored wings, but they had many more spots on their breasts and head.

"They're coming here to visit?" Mrs. P. said. "Oh, dear,

the place is a mess. We can't receive company now. I'm nursing this poor owl."

"They heard about the mobbing," Gylfie said. "We're even a little bit famous."

"Why's that?" asked Soren.

"I guess that gang of crows is really bad. They couldn't believe we battled back and survived," Gylfie replied.

Soon, they heard the Masked Owls arriving. One poked her head in. "Mind if we visit?" It was the female owl. And although Masked Owls belonged to the same species of owls as Soren's family, which were Barn Owls, and they were all known as Tytos, they were hardly identical.

"See what I mean?" Soren whispered to Gylfie. "They are completely different. Look at how much bigger and darker they are." The point was lost on Gylfie.

"We wanted to meet the brave owls who battled the crows," said the owl's mate.

"Yeah, how'd you ever do that?" a very young owlet who had barely fledged peeped up.

"Oh, it wasn't all that hard," Twilight said and dipped his head almost modestly.

"Not that hard!" Mrs. Plithiver piped up. "Hardest thing I've ever done!"

"You!" the male Masked Owl exclaimed.

"She certainly had nothing to do with the defeat of the crows. She's a nest-maid," his mate said in a haughty voice.

Mrs. Plithiver seemed to fade a bit. She nudged one of the worms that had begun to crawl off Digger's wing.

"She had everything to do with it!" Soren bristled up and suddenly seemed almost as big as the Masked Owls. "If it hadn't been for Mrs. P., I would have been dive-bombed from the rear and poor Digger would have never made it back."

The Masked Owls blinked. "Well, well." The large female chuffed and stepped nervously from one talon to another. "We just aren't used to such aggressive behavior from our nest-maids. Ours are rather meek, I guess, compared to this . . . What do you call her?"

"Her name is Mrs. Plithiver," Soren said slowly and distinctly with the contempt in his voice poorly concealed.

"Yes, yes," the female replied nervously. "Well, we discourage our nest-maids from socially mingling with us at any time, really."

"That was hardly a party, what happened up there in the sky, ma'am," Twilight said hotly.

"Well, now tell me, young'uns," said the male as if he was desperately trying to change the subject. "Where are you heading? What are your plans?"

"We're going to Hoolemere and the Great Ga'Hoole Tree," Soren said.

"Oh, how interesting," the female replied in a voice that had a sneer embedded in it.

"Oh, Mummy," said the young owlet. "That's the place I was telling you about. Can't we go?"

"Nonsense. You know how we feel about make-believe."

The little owlet dipped his head in embarrassment.

"It's not make-believe," said Gylfie.

"Oh, you can't be serious, young'un," said the male. "It's just a story, an old legend."

"Let me tell you something," said the female, who Soren disliked more and more by the second. "It does not do any good to believe in things you cannot see, touch, or feel. It is a waste of time. From the look of your flight feathers' development, not to mention your talons, it is apparent that you are either fly-aways or orphans. Why else would you be out cavorting about the skies at such dangerous hours of the morning? I think your parents would be ashamed of you. I can tell you have good breeding." She looked directly at Soren and blinked.

Soren thought he might explode with anger. How did this owl know what his parents might think? How dare she suggest that she knew them so well that she knew they would be ashamed of him?

And then there was a small soft, hissing voice. "I am ashamed of anyone who has eyes and still cannot see." It was Mrs. Plithiver. She slithered from the corner in the hollow. "But, of course, to see with two eyes is a very common thing."

"What is she talking about?" said the male.

"What happened to the old days when servants served and were quiet? Imagine a nest-maid going on like this," said the female.

"Oh, yes," said Mrs. Plithiver. "And I shall go on a bit more, if you permit me." She proceeded to arrange herself in a lovely coil and swung her head toward Soren.

"Of course, Mrs. Plithiver. Please go on," Soren said.

"I am a blind snake, but who says I cannot see as much as you?" And then she swung her head sharply toward the female Masked Owl, who seemed startled, and it did appear indeed as if Mrs. Plithiver was looking directly at her with her two small eye dents. "Who says I cannot see? To see with eyes is so ordinary. I see with my whole body — my skin, my bones, the coiling of my spine. And between the slow beats of my very slow heart, I sense the world here and beyond. I know the Yonder. Oh, yes. I have known it even before I ever flew in it. But before that day did I say it did not exist? What a fool you would have called me, milady, had I said your sky does not exist because I cannot see it nor can I fly. And what a fool you are to believe that Hoolemere does not exist."

"Well, I never!" gasped the Masked Owl. She looked at her mate in astonishment. "She called me a fool!"

But Mrs. Plithiver continued. "Sky does not exist merely in the wings of birds, an impulse in their feathers and blood and bone. Sky becomes the Yonder for all creatures if, indeed, they free their hearts and their brains to feel, to know in the deepest ways. And when the Yonder calls, it speaks to all of us, be it sky, be it Hoolemere, be it heaven or glaumora." Glaumora was the special heaven where the souls of owls went. "So perhaps," Mrs. Plithiver continued, "there are some who need to lose their eyes to discover their sight." Mrs. P. nodded her head gracefully and slithered back into the corner. A stunned silence fell upon the hollow.

The four young owls waited until First Black to leave. "No more flying during light," Mrs. Plithiver said as she coiled into Soren's neck feathers. "Agreed?"

"Agreed," the owls replied at once.

They were now skirting the edges of the Kingdom of Tyto, the kingdom from which Soren's family came. Although he was as alert as ever and flying most skillfully, Mrs. Plithiver could sense a quietness in him. He did not join in the others' flight chatter. She knew he must have been thinking of his parents, his lost family, and, in particular, his sister, Eglantine, whom he loved most dearly. The chances of finding any of them were almost zero, and she knew that Soren knew this, but still she could feel his pain. Yet he had not exactly described it as pain. He had once said to Mrs. P. shortly after they had been reunited that he had felt as if there were a hole in his gizzard, and that when he and Mrs. P. had found each other again, it was as if a little bit of the hole had been mended. But Mrs. P. knew that despite the patch she had provided there was still a hole.

When the first stars began to fade, they looked for a place to land and settle in before morning. It was Gylfie who spotted an old sycamore, silvery in this moonless night. The full moon had begun its dwenking many nights before, growing slimmer and slimmer until it dwenked and disappeared entirely, and there would not be a trace of it for another night or so until the newing began.

CHAPTER TWO

In the Company of Sooty Owls

Oh, yes, dear. I've heard of it, but you know they say it's just a story, a legend."

"Well, it's not exactly that, Sweetums," said the Sooty Owl's mate.

The four owls had been warmly welcomed into the large and spacious hollow in the sycamore by a family of Sooty Owls. These two owls were much nicer than the Masked Owls. Indeed very, very nice and, Soren thought, very, very boring. They called each other by nicknames — Sweetums and Swatums. They never said a cross word. Everything was just perfect. The children had all grown up.

"Left the nest a year ago. Still nearby," said Swatums, the male. "But who knows, Sweetums might come up with another clutch of eggs in the new breeding season. And if she doesn't, well, we two are enough company for each other." Then they began preening each other.

It seemed to Soren and Gylfie that they preened incessantly. They always had their beaks in each other's feathers, except, of course, when they were hunting. And when they were hunting they were exceptional killers. It was as predators that these Sooty Owls became the most interesting. Sweetums and Swatums were simply deadly, and Soren had to admit he had never eaten so well. Twilight had told them to watch carefully, for Sooty Owls were among the rare owls that went after tree prey and not just ground prey.

So tonight they were all feasting on three of a type of opossum that they called sugar gliders. They were the sweetest things that any of the young band of owls had ever tasted. Maybe that was why the two Sooties called each other Sweetums and Swatums. They had simply eaten too many sweet things. Perhaps eating a steady diet of sugar gliders made an owl ooze with gooiness. Soren thought he was going to go stark raving yoicks if he had to listen to their gooey talk a moment longer, but luckily they were now, in their own boring way, discussing the Great Ga'Hoole Tree.

Sweetums was questioning her mate. "Well, what do you mean, Swatums, by 'not exactly.' Isn't it either a legend or not? I mean, it's not really real."

"Well, Sweetums, some say it's simply invisible."

"What's simple about being invisible?" Gylfie asked.

"Ohh, hooo-hooo." The two Sooty Owls were convulsed in laughter. "Doesn't she remind you of Tibby, Swa-tums?" Then there was more cooing and giggling and dis-gusting preening. Soren felt that Gylfie's question was a perfectly sensible one. What, indeed, was simple about in-visibleness?

"Well, young'uns," Swatums answered, "there is noth-ing simple. It's just that it has been said that the Great Ga'Hoole Tree is invisible. That it grows on the island in the middle of a vast sea, a sea called Hoolemere that is nearly as wide as an ocean. A sea that is always wrapped in fog, an island feathered in blizzards, and a tree veiled in mist."

"So," said Twilight, "it's not really invisible, it's just bad weather."

"Not exactly," replied Swatums. Twilight cocked his head. "It seems that for some the fog lifts, the blizzards stop, and the mist blows away."

"For some?" asked Gylfie.

"For those who believe." Swatums paused and then sniffed in disdain. "But do they say what? Believe in what? No. You see, that is the problem. Owls with fancy ideas — ridiculous! That's how you get into trouble. Sweetums and I don't believe in fancy ideas. Fancy ideas don't keep the belly full and the gizzard grinding. Sugar gliders, plump rats, voles — that's what counts." Sweetums nodded and

Swatums went over and began preening her for the millionth time that day.

Soren knew in that moment that even if he were starving to death, he would still find Sweetums and Swatums the most boring owls on Earth.

That late afternoon as they nestled in the hollow, waiting for First Black, Gylfie stirred sleepily. "You awake, Soren?"

"Yeah. I can't wait to get to Hoolemere."

"Me, neither. But I was wondering," Gylfie said.

"Wondering what?"

"Do you think that Streak and Zan love each other as much as Sweetums and Swatums?" Streak and Zan were two Bald Eagles who had helped them in the desert when Digger had been attacked by the lieutenants from St. Aggie's — the very ones who had earlier eaten Digger's brother, Flick. The two eagles had seemed deeply devoted to each other. Yet Zan could not utter a sound. Her tongue had been torn out in battle.

What an interesting question, Soren thought. His own parents never preened each other as constantly as Sweetums and Swatums, and they hadn't called each other gooey names, but he had never doubted their love for each other. "I don't know," he replied. "It's hard thinking about mates.

I mean, can you imagine ever having a mate or what he might be like?"

There was a long pause. "Honestly, no," replied Gylfie.

They heard Twilight stir in his sleep.

"If I never taste another sugar glider it will be too soon." Digger belched softly. "They keep repeating on me."

The four owls had left at First Black and bid their farewells to the Sooties. They had now alighted on a tree limb with a good view down the valley. They were looking for a creek — any creek that could feed into a river that hopefully would be the River Hoole, which they could follow to the Sea of Hoolemere.

"What do you mean 'keep repeating on you'?" Soren said, imagining little possums gliding in and out of Digger's beak.

"Just an expression. My dad used to say that after he ate centipedes." Digger sighed. "And then Ma would say, 'Well, of course they keep repeating on you, dear. You eat something that has all those legs, they're probably still running around inside you.'"

Gylfie, Twilight, and Soren burst out laughing.

Digger sighed again. "My mom was really funny. I miss her jokes."

"Come on," said Gylfie. "You'll be okay."

"But everything is so different here. I don't live in trees. Never have in my life. I'm a Burrowing Owl. I lived in desert burrows. I don't hunt these silly creatures that glide and fly about through the limbs. I miss the taste of snake and crawly things that pick up the dirt. Whoops, sorry, Mrs. P."

"Don't apologize, Digger. Most owls do eat snakes, not usually blind snakes, since we tend their nests, but other snakes. Soren's parents were particularly sensitive and, out of respect for me, would not eat any snake."

Twilight had hopped to a higher limb to see if he could see any trace of a creek that might lead to a river.

"He's not going to be able to see anything in this light. I don't care how good his eyes are. A black trickle of a creek in a dark forest — forget it," Gylfie said.

Suddenly, Soren cocked his head, first one way, then the other.

"What is it, Soren?" Digger asked.

"You hear something?" Twilight flew down and landed on a thin branch that creaked under his weight.

"Hush!" Soren said.

They all fell silent and watched as the Barn Owl tipped, cocked, and pivoted his head in a series of small movements. And, finally, Soren heard something. "There is a trickle. I hear it. It's not a lot of water, but I can hear that it begins in reeds and then it starts to slide over stones."

Barn Owls were known for their extremely sensitive hearing. They could contract and expand the muscles of their facial disks to funnel the sound source to their unevenly placed earholes. The other owls were in awe of their friend's abilities.

"Let's go. I'll lead," Soren said.

It was one of the few times anyone except Twilight had flown in the point position.

As Soren flew, he kept angling his head so that his two ears, one lower and one higher, could precisely locate the source of the water. Within a few minutes, they had found a trickle and that trickle turned into a stream, a stream full of the music of gently tumbling water. Then by dawn that stream had become a river — the River Hoole.

"A masterful job of triangulation," Gylfie cried. "Simply masterful, Soren. You are a premiere navigator."

"What's she saying?" Digger asked.

"She's saying that Soren got us here. Big words, little owl." But it was evident that Twilight was clearly impressed.

"So now what do we do?" Digger asked.

"Follow the river to the Sea of Hoolemere," Twilight said. "Come on. We still have a few hours until First Light."

"More flying?" Digger asked.

"What? You want to walk?" Twilight replied.

"I wouldn't mind. My wings are tired. And it's not just my wound. It's healed."

The three other owls stared at Digger in dismay. Gylfie hopped out on the tree branch they had landed on and peered intently at Digger. "Wings don't get tired. That's impossible."

"Well, mine do. Can't we rest up a bit?" Burrowing Owls, like Digger, were in fact known for their running abilities. Blessed with long, featherless legs, they could stride across the deserts as well as fly over them. But their flight skills were not as strong as other owls.

"I'm hungry, anyhow," said Soren. "Let me see if I can catch us something."

"Please, no sugar gliders," Digger added.

CHAPTER THREE
Twilight Shows Off

They had settled into the hollow of a fir tree and were eating some voles that Soren had brought back from his hunting expedition.

"Refreshing, isn't it, after sugar gliders?" Gylfie said.

"Hmmm!" Digger smacked his beak and made a satisfied sound.

"What do you think the Great Ga'Hoole Tree will be like?" Soren said dreamily, as a little bit of vole tail hung from his beak.

"Different from St. Aggie's, that's for sure," Gylfie offered.

"Do you think they know about St. Aggie's — the raids, the egg snatching, the . . . the . . ." Soren hesitated.

"The cannibalism," Digger said. "You might as well say it, Soren. Don't try to protect me. I've seen the worst and I know it."

They had all seen the worst.

Twilight, who was huge to start with, was beginning to

swell up in fury. Soren knew what was coming. Twilight was not thinking about the owls of Ga'Hoole, those noble guardian knights of the sky. He was thinking about those ignoble, contemptible, basest of the base, monstrous owls of St. Aggie's. Twilight had been orphaned so young that he had not the slightest scrap of memory of his parents. For a long time, he had led a kind of vagabond, orphan life. Indeed, Twilight had lived with all sorts of odd animals, even a fox at one point, which was why he never hunted fox. Like all Great Grays, he was considered a powerful and ruthless predator, but Twilight prided himself on being, as he called it, an owl from the Orphan School of Tough Learning. He was completely self-taught. He had lived in burrows with foxes, flown with eagles. He was strong and a real fighter. And there was not a modest hollow bone in Twilight's body. He was powerful, a brilliant flier, and he was fast. As fast with his talons as with his beak. In a minute they all knew that the air would become shrill as he sung himself praises and jabbed and stabbed at an imaginary foe. Twilight's shadow began to flicker in the dim light of the hollow of the fir tree, as his voice, deep and thrumming, started to chant.

> We're going to bash them birds,
> Them rat-feathered birds.

Them bad-butt owls ain't never heard
'Bout Gylfie, Soren, Dig, and Twilight.
Just let them get to feel my bite
Their li'l ole gizzards gonna turn to pus
And our feathers hardly mussed.
Oh, me. Oh, my. They gonna cry.
One look at Twilight,
They know they're gonna die.
I see fear in their eyes
And that ain't all.
They know that Twilight's got the gall.
Gizzard with gall that makes him great
And every bad owl gonna turn to bait.

Jab, jab — then a swipe and hook with the right talon. Twilight danced around the hollow. The air churned with his shadow fight, and Gylfie, the tiniest of them all, had to hang on tight. It was like a small hurricane in the hollow. Then, finally, his movements slowed and he pranced off into a corner.

"Got that out of your system, Twilight?" Gylfie asked.

"What do you mean 'out of my system'?"

"Your aggression."

Twilight made a slightly contemptuous sound that came from the back of his throat. "Big words, little owl."

This was something Twilight often said to Gylfie. Gylfie did have a tendency to use big words.

"Well now, young'uns," Mrs. P. was speaking up. "Let's not get into it. I think, Gylfie, that in the face of cannibalism, aggression or going stark raving yoicks and absolutely annihilating the cannibals is appropriate."

"More big words but I like them. I like them, Mrs. P.," Twilight hooted his delight.

Soren, however, remained quiet. He was thinking. He was still wondering what the Great Ga'Hoole Tree would be like. What would those noble owls think of an owl like Twilight — so unrefined, yet powerful. So sassy, but loyal — so angry, but true?

CHAPTER FOUR

Get Out! Get Out!

They had left the hollow of the fir tree at First Black. The night was racing with ragged clouds. The forest covering was thick beneath them so they flew low to keep the River Hoole in sight, which sometimes narrowed and only appeared as the smallest glimmer of a thread of water. The trees thinned and Twilight said that he thought the region below was known as The Beaks. For a while, they seemed to lose the strand of the river, and there appeared to be many other smaller threadlike creeks or tributaries. They were, of course, worried they might have lost the Hoole, but if they had their doubts they dared not even think about them for a sliver of a second. For doubts, each one feared in the deepest parts of their quivering gizzards, might be like an owl sickness — like grayscale or beak rot — contagious and able to spread from owl to owl.

How many false creeks, streams, and even rivers had they followed so far, only to be disappointed? But now

Digger called out, "I see something!" All of their gizzards quickened. "It's, it's . . . whitish. . . . Well, grayish."

"Ish? What in Glaux's name is 'ish'?" Twilight hooted.

"It means," Gylfie said in her clear voice, "that it's not exactly white, and it's not exactly gray."

"I'll have a look. Hold your flight pattern until I get back."

The huge Great Gray Owl began a power dive. He was not gone long before he returned. "And you know why it's not exactly gray and not exactly white?" Twilight did not wait for an answer. "Because it's smoke."

"Smoke?" The other three seemed dumbfounded.

"You do know what smoke is?" Twilight asked. He tried to remember to be patient with these owls who had seen and experienced so much less than he had.

"Sort of," Soren replied. "You mean there's a forest fire down there? I've heard of those."

"Oh, no. Nothing that big. Maybe once it was. But, really, the forests of The Beaks are minor ones. Second-rate. Few and far between and not much to catch fire."

"Spontaneous combustion — no doubt," Gylfie said. Twilight gave the little Elf Owl a withering look. Always trying to steal his show with the big words. He had no idea what spontaneous combustion was and he doubted if Gylfie did, either. But he let it go for the moment. "Come on, let's go explore."

They alighted on the forest floor at the edge of where the smoke was the thickest. It seemed to be coming out of a cave that was beneath a stone outcropping. There was a scattering of a few glowing coals on the ground and charred pieces of wood. "Digger," Twilight said. "Can you dig as well as you can walk with those naked legs of yours?"

"You bet. How do you think we fix up our burrows or make them bigger? We just don't settle for what we happen upon."

"Well, start digging and show the rest of us how. We've got to bury these coals before a wind comes up and carries them off and really gets a fire going."

It was hard work burying the coals, especially for Gylfie, who was the tiniest and had the shortest legs of all. "I wonder what happened here?" Gylfie said as she paused to look around. Her eyes settled on what she thought was a charred piece of wood, but something glinted through the blackness of the moonless night. Gylfie blinked. Glinted and curved into a familiar shape. Gylfie's gizzard gave a little twitch and as if in a trance she walked over toward the object.

"Battle claws!" she gasped. From inside the cave came a terrible moan. "Get out! Get out!"

But they couldn't get out! They couldn't move. Between them and the mouth of the cave, gleaming eyes, redder than any of the live coals, glowered and there was a horrible rank smell. Two curved white fangs sliced the darkness.

"Bobcat!" Twilight roared.

The four owls simultaneously lifted their eight wings in powerful upstrokes. The bobcat shrieked below, a terrible sky-shattering shriek. Soren had never heard anything like it. It had all happened so suddenly that Soren had even forgotten to drop the coal that he had in his beak.

"Good Glaux, Soren!" Gylfie said as she saw her dear friend's face bathed in the red light of the radiant coal.

Soren dropped it immediately.

There was another shriek. A shadow blacker than the night seemed to leap into the air, then plummet to the ground, writhing and yowling in pain.

"Well, bust my gizzard!" Twilight shouted. "Soren, you dropped that coal right on the cat! What a shot!"

"I — what?"

"Come on, we're going in for him — for the kill."

"The kill?" Soren said blankly.

"Follow me. Aim for his eyes. Gylfie, stay clear of his tail. I'll go for the throat. Digger, take a flank."

The four owls flew down in a deadly wedge. Soren

aimed for the eyes, but one was already useless, as the coal had done its work and a still sizzling socket wept small embers. Digger sunk his talons into an exposed flank as the bobcat writhed on the ground, and Gylfie stuck one of her talons down the largest nostril that Soren had ever seen. Twilight made a quick slice at the throat and blood spattered the night. The cat was no longer howling. It lay in a heap on the forest floor, its face smoldering from the coal. The smell of singed fur filled the night as the bobcat's pulse grew weaker and the blood poured out from the deep gash in its throat.

"Was he after the battle claws — a bobcat?" Soren turned to Gylfie.

When the two owls had been at St. Aggie's, Grimble, the old Boreal Owl who had died helping them escape, had told them how the warriors of St. Aggie's could not make their own battle claws so they scavenged them from battlefields. But a bobcat? Why would a bobcat need battle claws? They stared at the long sharp claws that extended from the paws of the cat and looked deadlier than any battle claws.

"No," Twilight said quietly. He had flown over to the cave and now stood in its opening. "The cat was after what was in here."

"What's that?" the three other owls asked at once.

"A dying owl," Mrs. Plithiver said as she slithered out from the cave where she had taken refuge. "Come in. I think he wants to speak, if he has any more breath in him."

The owls moved into the cave opening. There was a mass of brown feathers collapsed by a shallow pit that still glowed with embers. It was a Barred Owl. Although that was hard to tell, for the white bars of his plumage were bloodstained and his beak seemed to jut out at a peculiar angle. "Don't blame the cat." The Barred Owl moaned. "Only here after . . . after . . . they —"

"After they what, sir?" Gylfie stepped closer to the skewed beak and bent her head to better hear the weak voice.

"They wanted the battle claws, didn't they?" Soren bobbed his head down toward the dying owl. Did he move his head slightly as if to nod? But the Barred Owl's breath was going, was growing shallower.

"Was it St. Aggie's?" Glyfie spoke softly.

"I wish it had been St. Aggie's. It was something far worse. Believe me — if St. Aggie's — Oh! You only wish!" The owl sighed and was dead.

The four owls blinked at one another and were silent for several moments. "You only wish!" Digger repeated. "Does he mean there's something worse than St. Aggie's?"

"How could there be?" Soren said.

"What is this place?" Gylfie said. "Why are there battle claws here but it isn't a battlefield? If it had been, we would have seen other owls, wounded or dead."

They turned toward the Great Gray. "Twilight?" Soren asked.

But for once, Twilight seemed stumped. "I'm not sure. I've heard tell of owls — very clever owls that live apart, never mate, not really belonging to any kingdom. Do for themselves for the most part. Sometimes hire out for battles. Hireclaws, I think they call them. Maybe this was one. And the The Beaks is a funny place, you know. Not many forests. Mostly ridges like the ones we've been flying over the last day or so. A few woods in between. So not a lot of places for owls to fetch up. No really big trees with big hollows. Probably a real loner, this fellow."

They looked down at the dead Barred Owl.

"What should we do with him?" Soren asked. "I hate to leave him here for the next bobcat to come along. He tried to warn us, after all. He said, 'Get out! Get out!'"

It was Digger who spoke next in a quavery voice. "And, you know, I don't think he was warning us about the bobcat."

"You think," Gylfie said in a quiet steady voice, "that it was about these others, the ones worse than St. Aggie's?"

Digger nodded.

"But we can't just leave him. This was a brave owl. . . . A noble owl." Soren spoke vehemently, "He was noble even if he didn't live at the Great Tree as a knightly owl."

Twilight stepped forward. "Soren's right. He was a brave owl. I don't want to leave him for dirty old scavengers. If it's not the bobcats, it'll be the crows; if not crows, vultures."

"But what can we do with him?" Digger said.

"I've heard of burial hollows, high up in trees," Twilight said. "When I was with a Whiskered Screech family in Ambala that's what they did when their grandmother died."

"It's going to take too long to find a hollow in The Beaks," Gylfie now spoke. "You said it yourself, Twilight — it's a second-rate forest, no big trees."

Soren was looking around. "This owl lived in this cave. Look, you can tell. There's some fresh pellets just outside, and there's a stash of nuts and over there, a vole killed not long ago — probably his next dinner. . . . I think we should —"

"We can't leave him in the cave," Gylfie interrupted. "Even if it is his home. Another bobcat can come along and find him."

"But Soren is right," Digger said. "His spirit is here." Digger was a very odd owl. Whereas most owls were consumed with the practical world of hunting, flying, and nesting, Digger — with his legs better for running than his wings were for flying, with his inclination for burrows rather than hollows — was undeniably an impractical owl. But perhaps because he was not focused on the commonplace, the ordinary drudgeries and small joys of owl life, his mind was freer to range. And range it did into the sphere of the spiritual, of the meaning of life, of the possibilities of an afterlife. And it was the afterlife of the brave Barred Owl that seemed to concern him now. "His spirit is in this cave. I feel it."

"So what do we do?" Twilight asked.

Soren looked around at the cave slowly. His dark eyes, like polished stones, studied the walls. "He had many fires in this cave. Look at the walls — as sooty as a Sooty Owl's wings. I think he made things with fires in this pit right here. I think . . ." Soren spoke very slowly. "I think we should burn him."

"Burn him?" the other three owls repeated quietly.

"Yes. Right here in this pit. The embers are still burning. It will be enough." The owls nodded to one another in silent agreement. It seemed right.

So the four owls, as gently as they could, rolled the dead Barred Owl onto the coals with their talons.

"Do we have to stay and watch?" Gylfie asked as the first feathers began to ignite.

"No!" Soren said, and they all followed him out the cave entrance and flew into the night.

They rose on a series of updrafts and then circled the clearing where the cave had been. Three times they circled as they watched the smoke curl out from the mouth of the cave. Mrs. Plithiver moved forward through the thick feathers of Soren's shoulders and leaned out toward one of his ears. "I am proud of you, Soren. You have protected a brave owl against the indignities of scavengers." Soren wasn't sure what the word "indignities" meant, but he hoped what they had done was right for an owl he believed to be noble. But would they ever find the Great Ga'Hoole Tree, where other noble owls lived? And now it was not doubt that began to prick at his gizzard, but the ominous words of the Barred Owl — *You only wish!*

CHAPTER FIVE

The Mirror Lakes

M rs. Plithiver was worried. Yes, it was understandable that the owls had been unnerved by the Barred Owl's ominous words. The very notion of something worse than St. Aggie's was indeed a horrifying thought. They needed some time to rest, unwind. Twilight said that he had heard about this place that was so lovely, endless plump voles scampering about, no crows at all, tree hollows in which moss as soft as down grew. Why, it sounded irresistible. And it was! And now Mrs. Plithiver was nearly frantic in this resplendent place. It was perfectly clear to her that the owls would be content to stay here forever.

But life was too easy in this region on the edge of The Beaks, which was called the Mirror Lakes. She knew it wasn't good for them and beneath the gleaming surfaces of the lakes, within the quiet verdant beauty of this crowless place, she sensed something dangerous. She could have just swatted Twilight and his darned big mouth. The four owls seemed to have forgotten their ordeal in the forest with the bobcat and the dying Barred Owl entirely. Shortly after they had turned to fly in the direction of the Mirror Lakes, they began to encounter the wonderful rolling drafts of air that curled up from the rippled landscape below and provided them with matchless flying. The sensation was sublime as they gently floated over the sculpted air currents without having to waggle a wing. The rhythm was mesmerizing and then, shortly before dawn, sparkling below between the ripples of the land, were several still lakes, so clear, so glistening that they reflected every single star and cloud in the sky.

The Mirror Lakes were like an oasis in the otherwise barren landscape of The Beaks. The owls had chosen trees near the lake that had perfect-sized hollows, all cushioned with the loveliest of mosses.

"It's simply dreamy here," Gylfie said for perhaps the hundredth time. And that, precisely, was the problem. It was dreamy. Not just dreamy — but a dream. It didn't seem real with its plentiful game so easy to hunt, and the rolling drafts of warm air so tempting that, against Mrs. P.'s orders, the owls had begun to take playful flights in broad daylight. But perhaps worst of all were the tranquil gleaming lakes themselves. These owls had never been around such clear water. There was no silt, no mud, no muck and bits swirling about in it. So they could see their reflections perfectly. Not one of these owls, except for Twilight, had ever seen its reflection. And even Twilight had never seen his so clearly.

It had all started with Soren, actually, when Gylfie pointed out to him that he had a smudge on his beak from the coal that he had picked up and dropped on the bobcat. Soren had flown a short distance from the tree where they had found a hollow, to the edge of the lake, to clean up. Until that time, Soren had thought that water was only for drinking and occasionally — very occasionally — for washing. But when he peered into the lake he nearly fainted.

"Da!" he gasped.

"It's not your da. It's you, dear," Mrs. Plithiver said. For although she was blind, Mrs. P. knew about reflections in much the same way she knew so many other things that she could not see. "You've probably never seen your face fully fledged."

"It's all white, just like Da's. I'm so, so —"

"Handsome?" Mrs. Plithiver said.

"Well, yeah." Soren muffled a nervous churr, slightly embarrassed to admit it.

Slightly it had been, but no more! That was, indeed, the end of Soren's embarrassment as well as his modesty, and the end of the other owls' as well. They were soon all nodding over the mirror of the lake, admiring themselves. And when they weren't gazing at their reflections from the edge, they were flying above the lakes, marveling at their fabulous flight maneuvers and pitching "wingies," as they called it when they rolled off rising drafts of air. Twilight was, of course, the worst of all because he was so boastful to begin with. Mrs. Plithiver could hear him out there now, hooting about his beauty, his muscular physique, the fluffiness of his feathers, while he tumbled over and under a roll of air.

"Look at me bounce off this cloud!" And then for the tenth time that day, Twilight sang his "I Am More Beautiful Than a Cloud" song.

> *What is as fleecy as a cloud,*
> *As majestic and shimmering as the breaking dawn,*
> *As gorgeous as the sun is strong?*
> *Why, it's ME!*
> *Twilight, the Great Gray,*
> *Tiger of the sky —*
> *Light of the Night,*
> *Most beautiful,*
> *An avian delight.*
> *I beam —*

I gleam —
I'm a livin' flying dream.
Watch me roll off this cloud and pop on back.
This is flying,
I ain't no hack.

"But," Mrs. Plithiver said with a hiss that sizzled, "you *ain't*, as you say, 'rolling off clouds'!" Because, as Mrs. Plithiver could sense, the clouds were too high that day, and Twilight was flying too low to reach them as he admired himself in the Mirror Lakes. In actuality, Twilight was flying off the reflections of clouds that quivered on the glasslike surface of the lake. And that, Mrs. Plithiver concluded, was the heart of the problem with all the owls. They were mistaking the world of image and reflection for the real world. The Mirror Lakes had transfixed them. And in their transfixed state they had forgotten all they had fought for and fought against. Had they once spoken of the Great Ga'Hoole Tree or its noble owls since they had arrived at this cursed place? Had they ever mentioned St. Aggie's and its terrors? Had Soren even once thought of his dear family except the first time he caught his reflection in the lake? And what about Eglantine? Did he ever think of her and what might have happened to his poor sister?

This was a very strange place. It was not just the Mirror

Lakes and the thick soft moss and the perfect tree hollows and the plentiful game. Suddenly, Mrs. Plithiver realized that in the rest of the kingdoms they had flown through it was becoming early winter, but here it was still summer, full summer. She could smell it. The leaves were still green, the grasses supple, the earth warm. But it was poisonous! They had to get out of here. This place was as dangerous as St. Aggie's.

"Come here this instant! All of you!" It was the closest a hissing snake ever got to a snarl.

Soren jerked his head up from admiring his beak in the surface of the pond. He rather liked the smudge on it. He thought it added "character" to his face, as Gylfie said.

"Mrs. P., what in Glaux's name?"

"I'll Glaux you!" she hissed.

Soren nearly fainted. He never had heard Mrs. P. swear, and at him, no less. It was like venom curling out into the air. The other owls alighted next to Soren.

"Hey," Twilight said, "did you catch that curled wingie I just did?"

"Racdrops on your curled wingie."

Now a deep hush fell upon the owls. *Had Mrs. Plithiver lost her mind? Racdrops. She had actually said racdrops!*

"What's wrong, Mrs. P.?" Soren asked in a trembling voice.

"What's wrong? Look at me. Stop looking at yourselves in the lake this instant. I'll tell you what's wrong. You are a disgrace to your families."

"I have no family if you'll recall, Mrs. P." Twilight yawned.

"Worse then! You are a disgrace to your species. The Great Gray Owls."

This really took Twilight aback. "My species?"

"Yes, indeed. All of you are, for that matter. You have all grown fat, lazy, and vain, the lot of you. Why . . . why," Mrs. Plithiver stammered.

Soren felt something really bad was coming.

"You're no better than a bunch of wet poopers!" With that, there was a raucous outburst from a branch overhanging where they stood at the lake's edge, on which a dozen or more seagulls had alighted. The harsh gull laughter ricocheted off the lake and the reflections of the owls on its surface quivered and then seemed to shatter.

"We're getting out of here NOW!" Mrs. Plithiver said in a near roar for a snake.

"What about crows? It's not dark yet."

"Tough!" she spat.

"Are you going to sacrifice us to crows?" Gylfie said in a very small voice.

"You're sacrificing yourself right here on the shores of

this lake." And something sharper than the fiercest gaze of eyes bore into Gylfie's gizzard. Indeed, all the owls felt their gizzards twist and lurch.

"Get ready to fly! And Twilight —"

"Yes, ma'am."

"I'll fly point with you."

"Yes, ma'am." The Great Gray stooped down so that Mrs. Plithiver could slither onto his broad shoulders.

Of all the owls, Twilight had been the most transfixed by Mrs. P.'s outburst. And if Twilight was to fly point, as he usually did, Mrs. P. felt she was going to have to be there to keep him on course. He was a "special needs" case if there ever was one. *What, indeed, had the world come to if an old blind nest-maid snake had to navigate for a Great Gray Owl? Some sky tiger!*

But she had to navigate as Twilight began to circle the lake a second time and dip his downwind wing, no doubt for a better look at himself, and, yes, singing under his breath his next favorite tune —

> *Oh, wings of silver spread on high,*
> *Fierce eyes of golden light,*
> *Across the clouds of purple hue*
> *In sheer majestic flight —*
> *Oh, Twilight!*

Oh, Twilight, most beautiful of owls,
Who sculpts the air
Beyond compare.
With feathers so sublime,
An owl for now —
An owl for then —
An owl for all of time.

Mrs. Plithiver had coiled up and was waving her head as a signal to a gull she sensed overhead. Suddenly, there was a big white splat that landed on the silver wings sublime.

"What in Glaux's name?" Twilight said.

"They like you, Twilight. Blessed, I dare say!"

Twilight flew straight out across the lake and never looked back.

CHAPTER SIX

The Ice Narrows

It seemed as if winter had been waiting for them as soon as the Mirror Lakes dropped behind them. Blasts of frigid air, swirling with ice, sleet, and often hail, smacked into them. The rolling ridges of The Beaks had become sharper and steeper, sending up confusing currents. Ice began to form on their own beaks and, in a few minutes, Soren saw Gylfie spin out of control. Luckily, Twilight accelerated and managed to help her.

"Fly in my wake, Gylfie," he shouted over the roar of the wind. And then he swiveled his head back to the others. "Her wings have started to ice. Ours will, too — soon. It's too dangerous to continue. We have to look for a place to land."

Almost as soon as Twilight had spoken of iced wings, Soren felt his own suddenly grow heavy. He turned his head and nearly gasped when he saw his plummels, the silkiest of all his feathers, that fringed the outer edges of his primaries. They were stiff with frost and the wind was whistling through them. *Great Glaux, I'm flying like a gull!*

It was not long before they found a tree. The hollow was a rather miserable little one. They could barely cram into it, and it was crawling with vermin.

"This is appalling!" Mrs. Plithiver said. "I've never seen such an infestation."

"Isn't there some moss someplace?" Twilight asked, remembering the extraordinarily soft, thick moss of the Mirror Lakes.

"Well, if someone wants to go out and look, they can," Mrs. P. said. "In the meantime, I'll try and eat as many of these maggotty little critters as possible."

Soren peeked out the hollow. "The wind's picked up. You can't even see out there. Snow's so thick on the ground, I doubt if we could find any moss if we did look."

"We can always pulp some of the pine needles," Gylfie said. "First, you beak them hard enough, then let them slide down to your first stomach — the one before the gizzard. Hold it there for just a while, and then yarp it all back up. The pine needles come out all mushy and when they dry they're almost as soft as moss. Actually, technically speaking, it is not called yarping. It's burping when its wet and not a pellet."

"Who cares — as long as it's soft?" Twilight muttered.

"I suppose it's worth a try," Digger said. "The thought of going out there into that blizzard is not appealing in the least."

So the owls leaned out from the protection of the hollow only far enough to snatch a beakful of pine needles. They all began beaking, then swallowing the wads down to their first stomachs and then burping. All the while, Mrs. Plithiver busied herself with sucking up maggots and pinch beetles, and one or two small worms known as feather raiders — all of which were most unhygienic to the health of owls.

"I don't think I could eat another pinch beetle if my life depended on it," Mrs. P. groaned after more than an hour.

There was a huge watery gurgle that rippled through the hollow.

"What was that?" Digger said.

"Yours truly, burping here," Twilight said and opened his beak and let go with another hollow-shaking burp.

"Oh, I've got to try that!" Digger said. In no time the four owls were having a burping contest. They were laughing and hooting and having a grand old time as the blizzard outside raged. They had figured out prizes as well. There was a prize, of course, for the loudest, but then one for the most watery sound, and the one for the most disgusting, and one for the prettiest and most refined. Although everyone expected Gylfie to win with the prettiest, Soren did, and Gylfie won for the most disgusting.

"Absolutely vulgar," muttered Mrs. P.

But soon they became bored with that and they began to wonder when the blizzard would let up. And although not one of them would admit it, secretly their thoughts turned to the Mirror Lakes and they grew quieter and quieter as they tried to remember their lazy beautiful days, flying in spectacular arcs over the lakes' gleaming surface. And the food, the food was so good!

"Oh, what I wouldn't give for a nice vole." Soren sighed.

"You know, young'un, I think the wind is lessening. I think maybe we should take off." Mrs. Plithiver sensed the four owls' thoughts turning to the Mirror Lakes. She simply couldn't allow that. So even though she truly did not believe that the wind was lessening, it was essential to get them flying again.

"You call this less?" Digger hooted from his downwind position.

"A bit, and believe me, dear, sitting there burping pine needles isn't going to get you any closer to the Great Ga'Hoole Tree."

But what would? thought Soren. They could barely see

ahead, behind was thick with swirling snow, below was dense fog that not even a treetop could poke through, and, off to windward, sheets of frigid air seemed to tumble from somewhere.

"There are cliffs to windward." Twilight drifted back from his point position. "I think that if we could get under the lee of them we might be protected and able to fly better."

"Sounds like it's worth a try. We'd better get Gylfie between us," Soren said.

The owls had become adept at creating a still place for Gylfie in the center of their flying wedge formation when the winds became too tumultuous for the Elf Owl. Gylfie moved into that spot now. "All right, let's crab upwind," Twilight hooted over the fury of the blizzard.

Crabbing was a flight maneuver in which the owls flew slightly sideways into the wind at an oblique angle so as not to hit it head-on. The owls scuttled across the wind in much the same way a crab moves — not directly forward but in this case taking the best advantage of a wind that was determined to smack them back. But now, by stealing a bit off the wind's edges, the owls could move forward, although slowly. They had been doing a lot of crabbing since they had left the last hollow and something they thought never could happen had. Their windward wings had actually grown tired and even sore. But at least their wings weren't icing up.

Suddenly, there was a terrible roar. The owls felt themselves sucked sideways as if an icy claw had reached out to drag them. There was another roar and they felt themselves smash into a wall of ice. Soren began sliding down a cold, slick surface. "Hang on, Mrs. Plithiver," he called, but he had no sense of her nestling in her usual place. It was impossible to grab anything with his talons. His wings simply would not work. He felt himself going faster than he had ever flown. But something huge and gray and faster whizzed by him. Was it Twilight? No time to think. No time to feel. It was as if his gizzard had been sucked right out of him along with every hollow bone. But then he finally stopped. He was dazed, breathless, but mercifully not moving, on the slightly curved glistening white ledge on which he had landed.

"Lucky for you and you and you and what?" came a low gurgling sound from above.

"Who? Who's that talking?" Soren asked.

"Oh, great Glaux!" Gylfie whispered as she slid next to Soren. "What in the . . ."

Then Soren saw what she was looking at. The four

owls and, luckily, Mrs. Plithiver had survived. They were all flat on their backs looking up a sheer white wall of ice and, poking their noses out of a hole in the ice above, were the faces of three of the most preposterous creatures any of them had ever seen.

Gylfie whispered, "What are they? Not birds."

"No, never," Twilight said.

"Do you think they're part of the animal kingdom?" Gylfie asked.

"What other kingdoms are there?" Twilight said.

"Plant kingdom — I heard my father speak of the plant kingdom," Gylfie said.

"They do look kind of planty. Don't they?" said Digger.

"What do you mean? Planty?" asked Soren.

"I know what Digger's talking about. That bright orange thing growing from the middle of its, I guess, face?"

"What do you mean — you guess, face?" the creature hollered. "I mean, we're pretty dumb, but you must be dumber if you can't tell a face from a plant."

"Well, you look a bit like a cactus in bloom — the kind we have in the desert," Digger said.

"That's my beak, idiot. I can assure you that neither I nor anyone in my family is a cactus in bloom — whatever a cactus is and whatever a desert is."

"Well, what are you?" Mrs. Plithiver finally spoke up.

"Well, what in the name of ice are you?" the creature retorted.

"I'm a snake . . . a nest-maid snake. I serve these most noble of birds, owls."

"Well," said the creature who was not a cactus, "we're just a bunch of puffins."

"Puffins!" Twilight hooted. "Puffins are northern birds, far northern birds."

"Duh!" said one of the little ones. "Gee, Pop, I'm feeling smarter all the time."

"But if you're puffins," Gylfie continued, "we must be in the North."

"Ta-da!" said one of the puffins. "Gee, you owls are getting smarter every minute!"

"Does she get a prize, Mummy, for answering the question right?" Another little chick, with an immense beak almost as long as it was tall, poked its head out of the hole.

"Oh, we're just having fun with them, Dumpy."

"But how did we get so far north?" Soren asked.

"Must have gotten blown off course," said the female. "Where you come from?"

"The Beaks," Twilight said.

"Where you headed?"

"The island in the Sea of Hoolemere."

"Great Ice! You've passed it by. Overshot it by five hundred leagues."

"What! We flew over it and didn't even see it?" Digger said, his voice barely audible.

"Where are we exactly?" Gylfie asked.

"You're in the Ice Narrows, far side of Hoolemere, edge of the Northern Kingdoms."

"What!" All four owls gasped.

"Don't feel too dumb," the male said. "Bad weather conditions."

"When do we ever have good ones, dear?" his mate mused.

"Well, true. But with the wind coming from that direction, they just got sucked up into the Narrows and then that williwaw came."

"What's a williwaw?" Soren asked.

"You get a big tumble, like an avalanche. Suppose you don't know what that is — an avalanche."

"No, what's an avalanche?" Digger said.

"You know, a big snow slide, but it's not snow in a williwaw. Just cold icy air comes over the wall and crashes down. That's what sucked you up into the Narrows and slammed you into our wall — our home."

"This is home?" Twilight asked.

"Yes, sir. Only one we've ever known," the male said.

"But where do you live?"

"In the ice cracks and some rocky holes. The wall is not all ice. Plenty of boulders. There are places if you know how to find them," he said and then looked at his mate. "Another storm is coming in from the south. We'd better get you owls inside. Follow us."

The ice nest was roomy, but it reeked something horrible. "What's that smell?" Gylfie whispered.

"What smell?" asked the little puffin they called Dumpy.

"That smell!" Digger snorted.

"Probably fish," the male said.

"Fish! You eat fish?"

"Not much else. Better get used to it."

"And I'm going fishing before that storm comes," the female said.

As she waddled toward the nest opening, Soren began to appreciate how truly preposterous this bird was. It was not only her face, with its large bulbous orange beak and the dark eyes ringed in red and set in slightly skewed ovals of white feathers, but also her body was the strangest shape. Chubby, with not one slim or graceful line and, with her chest thrust out, she appeared as if she might topple forward at any second. How this thing flew was a mystery. Indeed, now, tottering on the edge of the nest, it appeared as if she hesitated to take off, but finally she did by windmilling her wings awkwardly until, at last, she seemed to organize them for a direct plunge into the sea. And that was something to behold. She suddenly grew sleek. Her broad head and thick beak split the icy turbulent waters, which then closed over her tail feathers. She completely disappeared beneath the surface. Soren had been joined by Twilight, Digger, and Gylfie at the edge of the nest. They waited and waited, then looked at one another.

"Sir," Gylfie began, "I think something might have happened to your mate . . . uh . . . er. . . . She dove into the sea and no sign of her yet."

"Oh, she'll be a while. Lot of mouths to feed."

It seemed like forever, but then they saw her break through the surface. Several small fish hung neatly from her beak. "There she is! There she is!" Gylfie said.

"Good old Ma," Dumpy sighed. "Hope she brought some capelin. I just love capelin. If you don't like it, will you give me yours? Please, please, please?"

"Sure," Soren said. Every minute that he stayed in this smelly hollow he was getting less hungry.

"Look at that," Twilight said. "How's she going to get off?" The others now crowded to the edge of the ice hollow. Down below, it appeared that the female was trying to run across the surface of the water while madly flapping her wings.

"Water takeoff — not easy for any of us. We're not the best fliers, but, as you can see, we can dive. Got these little air pockets so we can go really deep for a long, long time. Getting back to the nest is the hardest part for us."

The male stepped out of the ice hollow and called down. "Dearest, try that patch over there under the lee, the water is smoother."

She gave her mate a withering glance, and somehow through the mouthful of fish yelled back, "You want me to fly directly into the wall, Puff Head! There's a tailwind. I'll slam beak-first into it. Then where will your dinner be? If you're so smart you come down and go fishing yourself."

"Oh, sorry, dear, silly me." Then he turned to the owls. "We're really not that bright. I mean we dive well, know how to fish, and deal with ice, but that's about it."

But, in fact, the puffins knew more and were not that dumb at all. "Just low self-esteem," Gylfie said. The puffins, in addition to knowing how to dive and fish, knew weather. And just now they were telling them that there would be a small pocket of time when the wind would turn, and they could leave before the next storm came in.

"You see, young'uns," said the male puffin, "nine days out of ten, the wind slams full force up these Ice Narrows. That's how you got sucked into here in the first place. But on the tenth day, it can turn around and suck you right back out. Nice high stream coming through that could pull you right back to The Beaks, if you want to go that far." He paused and each of the owls stole a glance at one another. The Beaks sounded lovely. This place was so harsh and cold and there was the terrible stench of the fish and the awful oiliness that seemed to make their gizzards greasy. How could they help but think of the Mirror Lakes, where it was always summer and the voles were fat and the flying spectacular? They would be liars if they said they weren't tempted.

"So when should we leave?" Soren asked.

"I think since you owls like night flying you should go tonight. Just when it's getting dark is when the wind will begin to turn. It'll be easy flying out of here, and then when the wind finally gets behind your tail feathers, you'll really go, straight out to Hoolemere."

"But the blizzard?" Gylfie said. "When will that start up again?"

"Not before tomorrow, I think, at the earliest."

"We should all get some rest now," Soren said. "If we're going to fly tonight."

"Good idea," Mrs. Plithiver nodded.

"Better go to the back of the hollow," the female puffin called. "Sun's coming out and it reflects so brightly off the ice you won't be able to shut your eyes against it." It was dimmer in the back, but still rather bright as streams of sunlight bouncing off the ice-sheathed rocks pried into the shadows of the hollow.

Soren could hear the steady drip as some of the ice began to melt. But finally he fell asleep. Perhaps it was the melting ice that made him think of that warmer place with the pools of crystal-clear water, his lovely white face shimmering on the surface. Why couldn't they go back there? Where were they supposed to be going instead? Soren kept forgetting. All he could remember were the rolls of warm wind to play on, the still, glasslike lake, the everlasting summer. No ice, no blizzard. Why not live there happily ever after? The dream tugged on him. In his sleep, he felt his gizzard turn and something begin to dim, while the longing for The Beaks and the Mirror Lakes grew stronger and stronger.

"Time to get up, young'uns." It was the male puffin, nudging Soren with one of his large, orange, webbed feet.

"Wind died down. You can fly out of here now. The wall's weeping."

"Huh?" Soren asked. "What do you mean the wall's weeping?"

"The ice is melting. Means warm air, the thermals have come. Easy flying."

The other owls were already up and standing at the rim of the hollow. The wall certainly was weeping. Glistening with wetness, it appeared shimmering, almost fiery as the setting sun turned its ice into liquid flames of pink, then orange and red.

"Dumpy," his father called. "Come over here, son. I want you to step up here and watch the young'uns fly. They are the masters of silent flight. Never going to hear a wing flap with these owls!"

Just before they took off, Soren looked at each of the owls. He wasn't the only one who had dreamed of the Mirror Lakes. They all wanted to go back. Could it be that wrong if they all wanted to do it? Twilight slid in close to him. "Soren, the three of us have been thinking."

"Yes?"

"Thinking about The Beaks and the Mirror Lakes. We've been thinking, why not go back there for just a little while? You know, just to kind of rest up, get this fish out of our system. Eat us some nice fat voles, then go on to the Great Ga'Hoole Tree."

It was so tempting, so tempting. Soren felt Mrs. Plithiver shift in the feathers between his shoulders.

"I . . . I . . ." Soren stammered. "I think there's a problem."

"What's the problem?" Twilight pressed.

"I think that if we go there, we won't go on — ever — to the Great Ga'Hoole Tree," Soren replied.

Twilight paused. "Well, what if some of us think — you know, kind of differently? Would that be wrong of us to go? I mean, you'd be free to go on."

After they took off, Soren could feel Gylfie flying nervously beside him. He turned and looked directly at Gylfie. Together, they had survived moon blinking and moon scalding. Together, they had escaped St. Aggie's. He spun his head toward Twilight and Digger. They had fought with him and Gylfie in the desert and, together, killed the murderers of Digger's brother and parents. It was in that desert stained with blood that the four of them had, within the slivers of time and the silver of moonlight, sworn an oath and become a band. And it was as a band they had sworn to go to Hoolemere and find its Great Ga'Hoole Tree. That was no dream. That was real. But it was a dream that now threatened them, a dream of the Mirror Lakes and endless summer that could, in fact, destroy their reason for living.

Twilight continued, "I mean, Soren, as I said, you could go on if you wanted. What would be wrong with each of us doing what we want to do?"

Soren looked hard at Twilight. "Because we are a band," he said simply. And he sheered off toward an inlet near the end of the Ice Narrows that streamed into the Sea of Hoolemere.

CHAPTER SEVEN

This Side of Yonder

The puffins had told them that there was a current of darker green water that swirled out from the Ice Narrows, then curved into the Sea of Hoolemere and, if they followed it, it would lead to the island. Soren was very thankful that they had found the current quickly. For, although the other three owls seemed to understand what he had said about being a band, he did not know what he would have done if they hadn't found the current. At least for now he could assure them that they were on course. One more navigational error, one more time getting blown off in some wild direction — well, Soren wasn't sure if he could hold the band together. The draw of The Mirror Lakes was powerful. It was odd, but he often thought of the night that he and Gylfie escaped from St. Aggie's. When Skench, in her full battle regalia with claws and helmet, had burst in on them in the library, something had drawn her into the wall where the flecks were stored. She had actually slammed into the wall and become completely immobilized for a few brief seconds. But it had provided them with the time to escape. Somehow The Beaks and the Mirror Lakes had a similarly powerful draw for them. But it was just a dream and that is what Soren didn't understand. How could a dream do this? However, this current of dark green water beneath them was real. All they had to do was follow it.

They had been flying hard and fast for a while now. With each stroke of their wings, they felt surer of their course, and their gizzards began to tremble with excitement. And with each stroke that drew Soren closer to the island with the Great Ga'Hoole Tree, he knew he was flying somehow farther away from St. Aegolius Academy for Orphaned Owls. How dare they call that place an academy? For nothing was learned there. Indeed, one of the worst rules that an owl could break was that of asking a question. The most severe and the bloodiest punishments were reserved for questioners. The foulest words one could utter at St. Aggie's were the cursed *wh* words: *what, when, why.* Soren at one point had all of his just-budging flight feathers ripped out and his wings left with a slick of blood because he had asked a question. Knowledge was forbidden.

Soon it began to snow, rubbing the pinpoints of starlight into smears, feathering the edges of the moon into a blurry softness, and smudging the dark green line of the current. *I can't lose the current!* Soren thought.

"I don't know how we'll ever see this Island of Hoole," Digger said. "Look down. Everything is turning white."

"Where's the current?" asked Gylfie anxiously.

Soren felt Mrs. Plithiver shift nervously in his neck feathers. *So near but so far!* They couldn't lose the current now. Soren thought that the Island of Hoole and the Great Ga'Hoole Tree seemed almost like the sky did to Mrs. Plithiver, the Yonder. And right now it felt as if they were just this side of the Yonder.

The conditions became increasingly confusing for the owls to fly in. Accustomed in night flying to opening up their pupils so wide that they nearly filled the entire size of their eyes, on this snowy night the owls had to do the reverse and yet it was not like day flying. There was too much light and it was all the same color, a shadowy gray. Water would appear no different from the surrounding land. Were they still over water? Or could they be over the Island of Hoole? Or maybe they had been blown off course again! Soren remembered what Mrs. Plithiver had said, that one had to see with one's entire body. Mrs. P.'s words came back to him. The four owls were bunched together in a tight V–shaped formation with Twilight at the point. Soren realized that flying on one side of the V or the other was not the best place to take advantage of the uneven placement of his ears and his good hearing.

"Let me fly point, Twilight. I'll be able to hear better."

Twilight slowed his speed and Soren stroked past him. "Hang on, Mrs. P., I'm going to have to do some head rolls."

An owl's neck is a strange thing. Unlike most birds, owls have extra bones in their necks that allow them to swivel their heads far to each side, in an arc much wider than any other living creature. Indeed, an owl can flip its head back so that its crown touches its shoulders, or turn its face almost upside down as Soren was doing just now. "Hello!" said Soren to Mrs. P., who nestled now directly beneath his beak as he flipped his face about. "Just scanning."

After several minutes of this, Soren noticed a change in the night. He was not sure exactly what it was but something seemed different. "Digger, remember that coyote song you were singing?"

"Yes."

"Sing it again and tip your head down."

"Hard to tell which way is down tonight."

Indeed it was, for the entire world, thick with snow, had suddenly turned completely white. But Digger began to sing in the thin grainy voice of a desert owl. Soren meanwhile was moving his head in small, minute movements. Finally, he said, "I think we're still over water." The sound of Digger's song that was reflected back was different from when he had sung it when they were over land and his sound had disappeared into the softness of an earth clad with trees. Now the song came back sharp and crisp.

And then there came a moment when the wind died and the snowflakes seemed to stand still. Twilight spoke. "It's time for me to fly point again, Soren."

Soren knew he was right. The snowflakes had evaporated into a thick dense fog. The world, the water below, was shrouded in mist. It was time for the vision of Twilight — that time that Twilight had spoken about when Soren and Gylfie had first met him, that time that had given Twilight his name, when boundaries become dim and shapes begin to melt away. It was the time for the Great Gray Owl, who lived on the edges and saw invisible connections, the joinings in a world that had turned foggy and confusing. Maybe Twilight could find the current again.

Soren drifted back as the big owl stroked by him to the point position.

It seemed as if they had flown for hours since they had last seen the current. Gylfie was getting very tired and Digger's wing, the one injured by the crows, had begun to hurt. The wind was kicking up again and not in a favorable direction.

"I can't believe that a current can just disappear. The puffins said it would lead us right to the island," Soren muttered.

"What do they know?" Twilight hooted. "They even admit they're dumb."

"I don't think they're all that dumb," Soren said. "We've got to be able to find it."

"And there's no place to even fetch up out here and rest," Gylfie sighed.

"We got to go back," Twilight said.

"Go back where? Not to The Beaks," Soren spoke sharply.

"To any dry land. If The Beaks is the closest, then The Beaks it is," Twilight replied.

"No!" Soren said more fiercely. "Look, I'm going to fly down close to the water."

"That could be dangerous," Digger said. "Soren, that wind is kicking up big waves. You could be caught by one, and believe me, I don't think that you're the swimmer that the puffin was. You could be dragged right under."

"I'll be careful. Mrs. P., if you want to slither onto Twilight, you can."

"No, dear, I'll stick with you. I'm not frightened."

"Good."

Soren began a banking turn down toward the water.

Now, amid the blizzarding snow, the spume from the crests of waves spun up. How would he ever see a current in this mess? He flew lower. Still nothing. What if the others had flown off? Just given up. Could he truly blame them? He had the most dreadful feeling in his gizzard. What if he was left alone out here — just him and Mrs. P.?

Suddenly, Soren felt something stir in his gizzard. He said nothing but contracted and expanded his pupils. The world was absolutely white now. Oh, this was when he needed Twilight!

"Right here, Soren."

"Twilight! You followed me down."

"Call me a fool." Twilight peered into the whiteness, stretched, then shortened his actual eye tubes so that one second he was focusing near and the next far. Within the depths of the impenetrable white, Twilight saw two even whiter patches.

"Come, young'uns. You're right over the current. Can't tell it on a night like this, though. So, welcome to the Island of Hoole."

Two giant Snowy Owls had melted out from the night and they were so white that by comparison the mist seemed gray.

"I am Boron and this is my mate, Barran."

"You are the king and the queen of Hoole." Twilight whispered.

Digger and Gylfie, exhausted, plummeted down near them.

"Yes, my dears. But we prefer to be called teachers, or rybs. The word ryb means teacher and deep knowledge," said Barran.

"We're not keen on titles," chuckled Boron.

"But you came out to meet us?" said Soren.

"Of course," replied Boron. "You've done the hard part. Now let us guide you the rest of the way. It's not far."

The blizzard had been swallowed by the mist and the mist now seemed to melt away against the whiteness of Boron and Barran. The night turned black again and the stars broke out. As a half moon rose, the four young owls looked below and saw the vast sea glinting with silver spangles from the moonlight and then, directly ahead, spreading into the night, were the twisting branches of the largest tree they had ever seen, the Great Ga'Hoole Tree.

"We are here, Mrs. Plithiver. We are here!" Soren whispered.

"I know, dear. I feel it. I feel it!"

The four young owls, led by Boron and Barran, threaded their way through the branches toward the center of the tree where the opening of a hollow was revealed. Two Great Horned Owls held the moss curtains apart using their beaks as the young ones flew through. They alighted down inside. Soren thought that this hollow was not only huge but different from any other tree hollow he had ever seen, for it was light even though it was night. On the inside were strange flickering things.

Boron came up to Soren and the other three owls. "I see you have noticed our candles. You see, here in Hoole we have discovered how to capture fire and tame it for our own uses. You shall learn all about this, young ones. And who knows? One of you might even become a collier."

"A what?" asked Soren.

"A collier — a carrier of coals. It is a very special skill. But there are many skills you shall be able to learn here in the Great Ga'Hoole Tree, and we are all here to teach you. These shall be your rybs."

With those words, Boron swept his wings toward the walls of the hollow. There were ledges that hung like galleries above. Soren, Twilight, Gylfie, and Digger gasped as they saw a great gathering of owls — all kinds of owls from Burrowing ones to Barn Owls, from Pygmy Owls to Elf Owls, from Screech Owls to Sooty Owls, from Great

Horned Owls to Snowy Owls. Every kind of owl imaginable was here within the hollow of the great tree, their yellow, black, and amber eyes blinking and winking in the most friendly and inquisitive manner at the five new arrivals.

Barran continued, "Welcome, young ones. Welcome to the Great Ga'Hoole Tree. One journey has ended . . ."

Just one? thought Soren.

But just then a series of deep, rolling gongs began to shake the entire tree. Barran stopped mid-speech.

"Chaws — back up to your positions!" This hoot came from a Great Gray Owl in the gallery. Then, it seemed as if the entire hollow suddenly brightened as owls began donning battle claws and helmets, and the flames of the candles flickered off the bright polished surfaces of the armored owls.

"Great Glaux — a battle! Quick, let's get our claws!" Twilight began to hop up and down, pumping his wings.

"Not so fast, young'un." A plump, Short-eared Owl waddled up to them.

"But where's the battle?" Twilight said.

"Beyond the Beyond." The Short-eared Owl fixed him in the glow of her amber gaze. "And it's not for you or you," she said, turning to Gylfie, "or you or you." She nodded to each one of the band. "And who are you?" She blinked at Mrs. P.

"Mrs. Horace Plithiver, nest-maid. I do have references."

"I see. Come along, all of you."

"But what about the battle?" Twilight sputtered.

"What about it? Not much really, just a skirmish on the borderlands between Silverveil and Beyond the Beyond."

CHAPTER EIGHT

First Night to First Light

They had begun by following the Short-eared Owl, known as Matron, through the enormous trunk of the Great Ga'Hoole Tree, which was honeycombed with passages of varying widths, all quite twisty and none that seemed to go in a straight line. Off the passageways there were hollows of different sizes. Some, it seemed, were for sleeping, others for study of some sort, some for stores and supplies. Soren peeked into one and saw stacks and stacks of the strange flickering things that Boron said were called candles. Sometimes Matron led them through a passage to the very end, where there might be a hole from which they would fly to another level of the tree, then reenter through another opening and resume their interior trail through the trunk of the tree. As best as Soren could figure out, the sleeping quarters were closer to the top of the tree, meeting hollows for large and smaller congregations of owls seemed to be below, along with a hollow that was called a kitchen, from which very good smells issued. There were places along the way where small groups of owls gathered to socialize. These seemed to be near the points where some of the larger branches of the tree joined the trunk. There were good-sized openings at these points so that owls could either sit inside on specially constructed perches or outside on the branches themselves.

"Now, I want you young'uns to stay out of the way. We've got some wounded owls coming in and I have to arrange for their care." They were flying up through the branches, following the Short-eared Owl to the hollow that would be theirs.

"Matron, we're going to need moss and down. Search-and-rescue's coming in with two more little ones. Nest decimation." Another Short-eared Owl flew by with a wad of something fluffy in her talons.

"Oh, no! Poor little things."

"Nest decimation. What's that?" Soren asked.

"Accidental destruction of nests." A young Spotted Owl flew up as they landed on a branch midway up the tree.

"Otulissa, thank goodness. Can you show these new arrivals to that hollow we cleaned out yesterday?"

"Certainly, Matron."

"And see if Cook has any tea or cakes left over. They look half starved."

"Certainly."

The Spotted Owl named Otulissa showed them to their hollow. "What is going on here?" Twilight asked her.

"Oh, there've been some skirmishes up in the border-lands, nothing too serious."

"Is it St. Aggie's?" Soren asked. "We know all about St. Aggie's. Gylfie and I escaped." Otulissa blinked.

"And we killed their top two lieutenants when they came after Digger here. So we're ready to fight," Twilight added. The Spotted Owl blinked again. "I mean, we're in the right place, aren't we? The Great Ga'Hoole Tree?" Twilight had stepped closer to the owl to ask his question.

"Where each night the order of knightly owls rises to perform noble deeds," Soren offered in a softer voice. An uncertain feeling that was not quite a doubt, yet not a real belief, began to stir in Soren's gizzard. "This is the place?" his voice quavered.

"Of course it's the place," the Spotted Owl replied.

"Then get us some battle claws — we're ready!" Twilight stomped one talon impatiently.

"You're ready!" Otulissa gasped. "You think just because you escaped and killed two rattlebrained owls, you're ready?"

"And the bobcat," Soren said.

"And the crows," Digger piped up. "Well, not exactly killed them, but drove them off."

Gylfie was very still, however. She had said nothing. But now the Elf Owl stepped forward. "Are you trying to tell us we are not ready . . . that . . . that it takes more?"

"Indeed. There is nothing that noble about slaughtering two bad owls in the desert." The Spotted Owl rose up to her full height and looked down her beak at Gylfie. In a very haughty voice she said, "You have not been tempered by battle yet. Nor do you know the first thing about strategy. You probably don't even know how to fly with battle claws. I have been here much longer than you and still have not yet become a member of a chaw."

"What's a chaw?" Soren said.

"You are selected to join a chaw — a small team of owls — and you will learn a skill that is helpful."

"In battle?" Twilight asked.

"Not just battle — in life. There is more to life than just battles. Each chaw has its own, oh, how should I put it? Personality. Navigation chaw tends to have a kind of elegance, they are all superb flyers, as are the members of search-and-rescue, but they, of course, are less refined. Weather interpretation and colliering are decidely rough and uncouth. But," and the Spotted Owl fixed a very intense gaze on Twilight, "they are all fiercely brave and can fight or fly to the death!"

Twilight seemed to swell in anticipation, but Soren almost shrank with fear. Would he be up to it? He had to be. With his friends, he could. Look what they had accomplished so far! "Do we all get to be in the same chaw?" Soren asked.

"Probably not."

"But we're a band." Soren hoped that he did not sound as if he were pleading.

"That doesn't matter now. You're part of a larger band. I have to go."

"Duty calls, I suppose," Gylfie said with a slight edge in her voice.

"I suppose it does." Otulissa again looked down at the Elf Owl, then she left the hollow. Soren thought Gylfie was going to spit at her.

"I don't like her one bit," Twilight said.

"Me, neither. Did you see how she looked at me? She might think she's all hoity-toity and very refined, but I bet she makes tasteless stature jokes all the time." Gylfie was very sensitive, like many Elf Owls, about remarks concerning size and shortness. Her grandmother had been a founder of SOS — the Small Owl Society — whose purpose was to prevent cruel and tasteless remarks about size.

"Make way! Make way!" Just outside their hollow, they saw two burly Great Horned Owls flying by, carrying a hammock with another owl collapsed on it. The wounded owl's helmet was askew and one wing drooped off the edge of the hammock at an odd angle.

Then, through the walls of the hollow, Soren thought he heard the mewling sound of a young crying owl and another voice saying, "There, there." Soren crept out of an opening leading into an inner passageway that wound through the trunk. There were many of these passageways and it seemed to Soren that one might get hopelessly lost. But he began to follow the sound. Soon, he came to another hollow. Like most, this hollow had both an inside and an outside entrance so that one could either fly in or walk in from one of the many inner pathways through the trunk of the tree. He peeked in. He saw the Short-eared Owl called Matron who had led them to their own hollow. She was bustling about, plucking down from her own breast and tucking it in around an owl. "Now, now, dear, we know you did your best."

"But what will Mum and Da think?" For a moment Soren's gizzard gave a lurch. *Could this little owl be Eglantine?*

"They will think that you were a brave little Pygmy Owl," Matron replied.

Soren sighed.

"What are you doing out there? Just don't stand around, come in and make yourself useful," Matron called. Soren came slowly into the hollow. The little owl was nearly as small as Gylfie; she was very fluffy, although she smelled of soot and some of her feathers were singed. "Now what did you say your name was, dear?" Matron bent over the Pygmy Owl.

"Primrose."

"Yes. Primrose here lost her nest."

"The whole tree," gulped the little owl.

"Yes, indeed. See, her parents had gone off to fight in the borderlands skirmishes, and they had left her all safe and sound."

"I was supposed to be sitting the two new eggs. Mum was really only off hunting, not fighting. She was going to be right back."

"What happened?" Soren asked.

"A fire — forest fire. I didn't think it would reach our tree and when it did, well, I tried to save one of the eggs. But you know, I haven't been flying that long and, well, I just . . ." Here, she began to sob uncontrollably.

A bunchy Barred Owl poked her head in. "Any tea here?"

"Oh, yes, I think a cup of milkberry tea would be lovely."

"I dropped the egg. I don't deserve to live." Primrose emitted a long sound halfway between a whistle and a wail.

"Don't say that!" Soren exclaimed. "Of course you deserve to live. Every owl deserves to live. That's why we came here."

Matron stopped what she was doing and cocked her head and regarded the young Barn Owl. *Perhaps he was learning; just perhaps he was beginning to catch a glimmer of the true meaning of a noble deed.* She would leave him to comfort this little Pygmy Owl and send in an extra cup of tea and some milkberry tart.

Soren stayed with Primrose for the rest of the evening. She was sometimes a bit feverish and would begin to mumble about the little brother she was sure she had killed. She had wanted to call him Osgood. Other times, she was quite lucid and would blink and say to Soren, "But what about Mum? What about Da? What will they think when they come home and find our forest burned, our tree gone? Will they look for me?"

And Soren simply did not know how to answer her, for, indeed, he had asked himself the same question so many times. Near daybreak, Primrose was sound asleep and Soren decided to make his way back to his own hollow. He meandered through the central hollow of the tree and more than once took a wrong turn that led down another passageway. While wandering down a particularly twisty one, he met up with an elderly Spotted Owl.

"Ah, one of the new arrivals, part of that band that flew in from the Ice Narrows," she hooted softly.

"Yes, well, we don't come from the Narrows. We were blown off course. We'd left from The Beaks but somehow . . ."

"Oh, dear . . . Yes, The Beaks, only for the strongest gizzards."

Soren blinked. *Now what did she mean by that?*

"I'm Strix Struma, here. Perhaps you need to sharpen your navigational skills. I am the navigation ryb. It's getting to be First Light, so I suggest you hasten to your hollow. And if you are very quiet, you shall hear the music of Madame Plonk's harp. It is lovely to go to sleep to and she has a fine voice."

"What's a harp? What's music?" Soren asked. He remembered the awful songs of St. Aggie's. Surely this must be different.

"Oh, dear. It's hard to explain. Listen and you'll begin to know."

When he got back to his hollow, they were all having cups of milkberry tea. "It's amazing, Soren," Gylfie said. "Nest-maid snakes brought the tea around on their backs."

"Yes, I really think there will be a place for me here, Soren. I think I can serve." Mrs. P. almost glowed as she said the word.

Everyone seemed quite content except for Twilight. "I didn't kill those two fiends of St. Aggie's, I didn't battle crows and tear out the throat of a bobcat to sit on my tail feathers and be served tea." Twilight seemed to swell to twice his size.

"Well, what can you do, Twilight?" Gylfie said.

"I think we have to have a word with the head owls — Boron and Barran. I don't think they know what real evil is. This border skirmish up there that they are talking about — it has nothing to do with St. Aggie's. You heard what little Miss Stuck-up Spotted Owl said. I don't think they know what they're in for. But we do!" He slid his yellow eyes about the hollow. "Right?"

"You mean the 'You only wish'?" Digger whispered the words of the dying Barred Owl. They had never really spoken about the meaning of those words, but they knew that the Barred Owl had meant, in no uncertain terms, that there was something out there that was far worse than St. Aggie's.

"Yes," Soren said hesitantly. "Maybe we should go talk to the king and queen. But not now. It's daylight. Time to sleep."

The hollow was lined with the finest mosses and the fluffiest down. Soren made his way to a corner near the opening to watch the breaking dawn. The very last of the evening stars was just winking out and a lovely pinkness began to spread in the sky. The immense gnarled limbs of the Great Ga'Hoole Tree stretched out and seemed to embrace the new day.

"This down," Soren whispered to Mrs. Plithiver, "reminds me of Mum."

"Oh, doesn't it, dear!" said Mrs. Plithiver, arranging herself into a neat coil in the same corner. Then, as the owls nestled down, the loveliest, most unearthly sounds began to *pling* softly through the Great Ga'Hoole Tree, and a voice began to sing.

> *Night is done, gone the moon, gone the stars*
> *From the skies.*
> *Fades the black of the night*
> *Comes the morn with rosy light.*
> *Fold your wings, go to sleep,*
> *Rest your gizzards,*
> *Safe you'll be for the day.*

Glaux is nigh.
Far away is First Black,
But it shall seep back
Over field
Over flower
In the twilight hour.
We are home in our tree.
We are owls, we are free.
As we go, this we know
Glaux is nigh.

Soren never remembered feeling so peaceful.

"Digger, Soren, Gylf, you asleep?" Twilight called.

"Almost, Twi," Digger and Soren replied.

"How soon do you think until we get our battle claws?"

"I have no idea, Twilight. But don't worry, good light," Soren replied sleepily.

"Good light, Twi," Digger said.

"Good light, Soren," Gylfie said.

"Good light, Gylf," Soren replied. And then added. "Good light, Mrs. Plithiver."

But Mrs. Plithiver was already sound asleep.

CHAPTER NINE
A Parliament of Owls

The four owls were in the antechamber of another hollow called the parliament. They were waiting to be admitted for their meeting with Boron and Barran.

"Very important business inside, young'uns," an owl on guard spoke in the soft *tings* of a Boreal Owl.

"We won't take long," Gylfie said.

I hope not, thought Soren. He was frightened. The other three had decided that he should be the one to speak.

Another owl stuck her head out. "You can come in now. But be quiet and wait your turn."

She indicated a branch where they should perch. Soren looked about. It was not an especially large hollow, not nearly as big as the one in which they had first been welcomed by Boron and Barran. There were candles, of course, and there was one long white branch from a tree that Soren thought was called a birch that had been bent into a half circle. It was on this white branch that the owls of the parliament, no more than a dozen, perched. He recognized the elderly Strix Struma, the Spotted Owl he had met the night before. She perched next to a Great Horned Owl of an unusual ruddy color with even more unusual very black talons. Then there was an ancient and decrepit Whiskered Screech, who appeared to have the worst case of feather fletch Soren had ever seen. Not that he had seen all that many. The Whiskered Screech had a long bristly beard. One of his eyes seemed stuck in a perpetual squint, and his beak had a notch in it.

"I've never seen a more disreputable-looking owl," Gylfie whispered. "Great Glaux, look at his foot! His talons!" She paused. "Or lack of!" The Whiskered Screech, indeed, had only three talons on one foot. And just as Soren was blinking in a mixture of astonishment and horror, the old owl swung his head about and fixed Soren in his squinted gaze. Soren thought his gizzard was going to drop right out of him.

"So, Elvanryb," Boron turned and addressed another owl, a Great Gray. "It is your notion that we need to have a search-and-rescue attachment chaw on the colliering missions?"

"Not all, Boron. I think they are only necessary when we are in areas near battle zones. So often the parents are off fighting. In normal circumstances, the parents are there if a fire breaks out, but tonight, for instance, we had to pick up that little Pygmy and a Northern Saw-whet. We got them back, but it taxed our chaw, believe me — carrying coals and injured owlets. Can't exactly drop them in the coal bucket. And I don't even like to think of the ones we might have missed and left behind."

The old Whiskered Screech raised his deformed foot.

"Yes, Ezylryb?" Boron nodded to the owl.

"Question for Bubo." the Whiskered Screech's voice was a low growl. "You think this fire was natural or more trouble with the rogue raids?"

"No telling, sir. The rogues make good targets, and it wouldn't be the first time raiding one caused a fire."

"Hmmm," the Whiskered Screech replied, and then scratched his head with the second of the three remaining talons of one foot.

"Next order of business," Boron said. "Something about starvation in Ambala?"

Ambala! Soren and Gylfie looked at each other. Ambala was where their friend the great Hortense came from. When they first had met Hortense at St. Aggie's, they thought she was the most perfectly moon-blinked creature ever. Moon blinking was perhaps the cruelest thing that St. Aggie's did to young owls. By forcing them to sleep during the full shines of the moon, directly exposing their heads to the moon's light, they destroyed the will, the very personalities of individual owls and made them perfectly obedient with no thoughts of their own. Soren and Gylfie had devised a plan for fooling the sleep monitors and escaping the full shine. It turned out so had Hortense. She, in fact, was an infiltrator and had been sneaking out the eggs that St. Aggie's patrols had been snatching. Unfortunately, however, she was caught and killed. Still, they had heard that Hortense had become a legend in Ambala because of her heroic deeds.

"Yes," another owl was speaking now. "The egg production is down, and it is thought to be caused by a blight on the rodent population. Simply not enough food." Soren and Gylfie exchanged looks. It was not just the rodent population. It was the St. Aggie's egg snatchers. This was information they could offer. This might convince Boron and Barran that they really knew something.

"We'll look into it," Boron said. "And now, I believe some of our new arrivals have requested to speak with us." He turned and blinked at the four young owls.

Speak with us! What was he talking about? Soren was not prepared to talk in front of all these owls.

"Now who wants to go first?"

Twilight, Digger, and Gylfie all looked at Soren.

"Up here, young'un." There was a perch in the middle of the half circle to which Boron nodded.

Oh, my Glaux. I have to fly up and stand there all by myself.
Soren was so much more comfortable sharing this lower perch with his friends. Great Glaux, he would be close enough to that weird owl Ezylryb to reach out and touch his three-taloned foot. Soren got a terrible queasy feeling, not in his gizzard but in his first stomach, the one before the gizzard. How embarrassing if something just came up out of his gullet and went *splat.*

"Uh . . . my name is Soren. I am from the Forest of Tyto. I er . . ." He and Gylfie had discussed how he should explain the events leading up to his snatching by St. Aggie's. Gylfie felt it was not good to go into too much detail about Kludd actually shoving him from the nest. "Tales of attempted fratricide might not be the right way to start," Gylfie had said.

Of course, Soren hadn't known what fratricide was until Gylfie explained it meant killing your brother. Then he agreed with her. He certainly didn't want the owls of the Great Ga'Hoole Tree to think he came from such a murderous family. Kludd was the only one, after all. "I was snatched by a St. Aggie's patrol. It was at St. Aggie's that I met Gylfie."

It was difficult at first to speak and not look at Ezylryb's mangled foot, but as he spoke, Soren became more relaxed. The owls seemed attentive but not particularly impressed, not even when he told them about Hortense and that it was not simply starvation that was accounting for the low egg counts in Ambala.

"And so?" Barran said when Soren appeared to have concluded.

"And so what?" Soren asked.

"What is it you want, dear?"

"The four of us are a band. We have flown together, fought together, and escaped many dangers — as a band. We know from our experience that there is great evil that threatens every owl in every owl kingdom on earth. We want only to fight this evil, to become guardian knights of this order." He saw Ezylryb stifle a yawn and pick up what appeared to be a dried caterpillar to munch. "We feel that we have special knowledge. We have much to offer," Soren concluded.

"I am sure you do," said Boron. "Every owl here has special knowledge and, during your training, you will find out what your talents are. You will, after proper instruction, be chosen for a chaw and then your learning will, indeed, advance to a higher level, become more specialized." He explained why they probably would not be put into the same chaws, even though they were a band. "We do not all need to learn the same things. Each of you will make your band better in the end if you learn different skills. And this all takes time."

Soren felt Twilight rustle behind him. He knew it was Twilight without even flipping his head for a look. He also felt that the old owl, Ezylryb, despite his yawning and munching, was looking at him sharply. Indeed, he felt locked in that old owl's sights. He might as well be a mouse scuttling across a forest floor about to be pounced on by a bird of prey. It was as if that little scrap of amber that glimmered through the squinty eye had trapped him. He had never felt such a penetrating, piercing look and yet to the other owls of the parliament it did not appear as if Ezylryb was regarding him at all. Rather, it seemed as if he was bored silly with the young Barn Owl.

Boron continued to speak, "It takes time, of which I think you have an abundance. It takes patience — and that, I am not sure how much you have and, most important, it takes dedication and that, young'un, is found both in the heart and the gizzard. The nobility of the owls you see here in the parliament has not simply been given, nor has it been earned through courageous acts. Indeed, nobility is not always found in the flash of battle claws or flying through the embered wakes of firestorms, or even in making strong the weak, mending the broken, vanquishing the proud, or making powerless those who abuse the frail."

Soren's gizzard grew quiet as Boron spoke. "It is also found in the resolute heart, the gizzard that can withstand the temptations of false dreams, the mind that has the imagination to comprehend another's pain, as I think one young owl did tonight when he sat by the little Pygmy Owl with quiet understanding of her loss of tree, nest, family, and egg. It is all of this that ultimately confers nobility and makes the Guardians of Ga'Hoole rise in the night with hearts sublime." Boron paused and looked at the other three owls. "And so as I said when you arrived, one journey has ended and now another starts. On the night of the morrow your training shall begin."

CHAPTER TEN

Twilight on the Brink

Dawn is the thief of night, and the night is when owls stir and become alive, when they fly. So the day that follows that dawn is only for sleeping, to prepare for the night. For some, however, the day feels like an eternity. And for the four young owls the night to come, the morrow night of their training, was still hours away.

Perhaps it had been a mild twinge in Soren's gizzard or a faint stirring in his heart, but sometime near midday, while the hollow was thick with sleep, the young Barn Owl sensed that something was slightly amiss, perhaps incomplete. It was not the feeling of dreadful cold fear that could steal into one's gizzard and make one's wings go yeep. No, not that at all, but something was not right. Soren's eyes blinked open, and in the dim milky light of the day that filtered into the hollow he saw only two other owls. Twilight was gone!

Soren blinked again. Was he really gone? In the flick of a wing, Soren had lofted onto the rim of the hollow. Every limb of the Great Ga'Hoole Tree stood out keen and black against the dull winter sky. Shadows were cast with sharp edges. There was, however, one long shadow stretched between the thick, gnarled branches of the tree, swelling like a dark cloud dropped down from above. That shadow was Twilight's. The Great Gray was perched on one of the less public takeoff branches. Soren flew up.

"What are you doing, Twilight?" Soren spoke softly.

"Thinking."

That was a good sign. Twilight was a creature of action, of instinct. Not to say that the Great Gray Owl was stupid. He just acted out of an incredibly honed instinct and rarely meditated. "Thinking of leaving," Twilight added in a flat, dull voice.

"Leaving?" Soren was stunned. "But we're a band, Twilight."

"We're not a band, Soren. Boron and Barran said as much."

"They didn't exactly say we're not a band, Twilight."

"I think that is exactly what they meant. They said it was highly unlikely that any of us would be chosen for the same chaw. They said it was not the Ga'Hoolian way. In other words, they are separating us."

"They are separating us only for the chaws and that's because they want us all to learn different things. That doesn't mean we're not a band. A band isn't just perching side by side, or even flying side by side all the time."

Twilight blinked. "Well, what is it, then?"

Soren paused. This was hard. Maybe he wasn't quite sure what a band was. But no, that wasn't right. In his gizzard he knew they were a band. "We are a band despite what any owl says or does. In our gizzards, we are a band and we feel that. It cannot be undone. We are what we are and I know it and you know it and we all know it — even they know it."

Twilight dropped his eyelids so that they were only glinting slits of gold.

He's going to tell me about the Orphan School of Tough Learning. I just know it, Soren thought.

But Twilight didn't. "I am an owl of low birth in the eyes of the world because I have had no proper upbringing." All the bluster was gone from Twilight's voice; even his feathers seemed to sag a bit and he appeared slightly smaller. "I have had no First Ceremonies, no First Insect, no First Fur-on-Meat ceremony. There is much I don't know."

Soren was stunned. Twilight never admitted to not knowing anything.

"But there is much I do know. I know light and shadow and everything in between. I know the life pulse in the throat of a bobcat and where to slash to break the blood pump that is the cat's heart. I know mountains and deserts and the creatures who fly and those who don't, but slither or crawl or leap. I know of all sorts of claws, as well as fangs and poisons that lock the talons and freeze the wings. I know the false horizon that comes in the heat of the summer when the air is thick with dew and confuses old owls so that they go yeep and fall. And I know all this, not because I was reared in a hollow lined with the down of my mother's breast, but because I was not. I was alone within minutes of my hatching. I can be alone. It is a special talent. And I can be alone again."

Soren's gizzard twisted in slow dread. Twilight turned his head slowly and blinked. "But I also know that I am a better owl with you and with Gylfie and Digger. I know now that I am part of a band. And I know this because of you, Soren — you alone." The Great Gray paused and mused. The gold in his eyes seemed to grow softer, like that pale haze of yellow just above the horizon as the sun begins to set.

"Perhaps, Soren, you are the blood pump of the band, and I would not want to slash such a life pulse." Soren blinked. "You are right, Soren. We are a band. And nothing can or will undo it. We are our own guardians."

"And maybe someday we shall become the Guardians of Ga'Hoole," Soren said quietly.

So the two owls returned to the hollow for sleep and the day grew brighter and brighter. And finally, the light began to seep away as the dull blue of the winter sky darkened. The clouds became tinged with purple and the last blaze of the sinking sun turned the horizon as red as the bobcat's blood. Then, at last, the stars broke out and it was time for the owls of Ga'Hoole to rise.

CHAPTER ELEVEN
The Golden Talons

It was the deep, black part of the night. The moon had passed through its last moment of the dwenking and now it was gone completely. Gone for two nights at least, until its first silvery thread would reappear at the newing. Soren had been at the Great Ga'Hoole Tree for almost a month, which meant thirty nights and one complete moon cycle from dwenking to newing. Yes, Soren knew how to count now. To count and much more, really. But counting was special. He remembered thinking that his father had said that the fir tree in which his family had their hollow was nearly ninety feet tall. But Soren had no idea what the number meant, just as he had no idea how long sixty-six days were, which was the length of time it took a Barn Owl, such as himself, to fledge flight feathers. Numbers had been meaningless and he had promised himself, once he had escaped from the awful St. Aggie's, that he would learn how to count.

But there was so much more to learn than simply

counting. For a month now, he had had many lessons — flying lessons, even work with battle claws. They had practiced with almost every chaw except for the navigation chaw and the colliering and weather interpretation chaws. For the last chaw, weather, Soren had felt spared because it was led by the grizzled old Screech, Ezylryb. The members were considered among the fiercest and the bravest of the entire Great Ga'Hoole Tree, for they had to fly through all sorts of storms, blizzards, and even hurricanes to gather important information for troops going into battle or on missions of search-and-rescue. And they brought back coals from burning forest fires, which fed the forge that made so many vital things for the Great Ga'Hoole Tree, from battle claws to pots and pans, and, of course, gave light to the candles.

And now on this blackest of nights, he was learning to navigate from Strix Struma.

"We shall begin with a few simple tracing exercises," Strix Struma had announced when they were poised on the main takeoff branch of the Great Ga'Hoole Tree. "The Great Glaux will soon rise," she continued. "The time of the Little Raccoon has, of course, passed by this season but a new beauty shall appear for the first time tonight. The Golden Talons. It is an unusual constellation, for in this part of the world it shall be with us through summer." She raised her foot from the branch. "And just like our talons, there are four — long, curved, and sharp ones formed by the stars."

"But not gold," piped up Primrose, the Pygmy Owl that Soren had befriended on the night she had been brought in from the borderlands, singed and orphaned.

"The gold is an illusion, my dear," Strix Struma said. "It is caused by atmospheric wobble that you shall learn more about."

With a sudden blur and a slicing sound through the air, Strix Struma's talons shot out and caught a fruit bat on the wing. "A little snack before we fly," she said and quickly de-winged it, then served up tasty morsels to the class. "We don't want to overeat before our lesson. That is never good, but a bit of bat gives a boost, I always find. Now, ready!"

"Yes, Strix Struma," they all replied.

Strix Struma preferred to dispense with the title of ryb and instead be called by her family name. She was a Spotted Owl who came from a very ancient ancestry of which she was intensely proud. "Good, then. Primrose, I would like you flying directly behind me. Otulissa, seeing as you have had navigation class before, I think I shall put you on my windward flank. Gylfie, you shall fly in the downwind flanking position. And Soren, you fly tail. Any questions?"

Soren blinked in amazement. Although he had been at the Tree a month, those two simple words "Any questions" were still like magic to him after St. Aggie's.

Strix Struma always used the battle terminology, such as "flanks." For not only did Strix Struma have a proud and ancient lineage, but she had been trained for combat as a windward flanking sub-commander and had seen action at the Battle of Little Hoole. "Off we go, then!" And the large Spotted Owl rose in flight with the four young owls quickly maneuvering into their positions.

Soren flew several lengths behind Strix Struma so as not to be affected by the eddies curling off her very broad tail. He wished Twilight and Digger were flying with them but Twilight was in a more advanced navigation class. And Digger was still in power-flight school due to his weak flying skills.

Twilight's orphan school of tough learning had apparently taught him a lot because he had been placed in many advanced classes.

"All right, class." Strix Struma spoke in the broad hooting tones that were indeed the voice of a mature Spotted Owl. These hoots now rolled back toward Soren. "Two points off to windward. Please note the first star of the Golden Talons rising."

"Ooooh, this is sooooo exciting." It was Otulissa trying

her best to sound exactly like Strix Struma, which she would someday, for she, too, was a Spotted Owl. But right now, she just sounded like what she was — a beak-polishing, feather-fluffing idiotic owl always trying to impress the rybs. "And it's such an honor to be flying windward flank, Strix Struma, in the grand tradition of your noble family."

Soren blinked and winced. If Twilight had been here he would have yarped a pellet mid-flight right in her face. Soren saw Glyfie spin her head back and blink as she moved her beak silently. But Soren could understand perfectly what she was saying: "Do you believe her?"

Primrose spoke up. "Do you have a cold, Otulissa? You sound clogged up."

Oh, great Glaux. Soren thought he might die laughing. Leave it to Primrose! And the best part of it was that she was sincere. Primrose never suspected anyone of anything. "Guileless," Gylfie called her. "Charmingly guileless." Often Soren didn't understand the words that Gylfie used, but in this case he began to. He knew what Gylfie meant. Primrose didn't have a fake hollow bone in her body. She was utterly truthful and always believed that owls were motivated by the best of reasons. She had, needless to say, never spent any time at St. Aggie's.

The navigation class flew on. It was not long after the first star in the Talons rose that several more broke out of the blackness, and it did seem as if four great golden talons clawed at the night.

"We shall trace each talon from its toe base to its sharp tip," hooted Strix Struma.

Soren was now flying directly behind Primrose, and he was becoming slightly confused as she constantly swiveled her head. An oddity about Pygmy Owls was that they had two dark spots on the back of the head that indeed looked like eyes. Soren was finding this disorienting.

"Confusing, isn't it, dear?" Strix Struma had dropped back. "You're in a difficult position behind Primrose, but it's good training."

"Oh, Soren." Primrose swiveled her head. "It's my darned spots, isn't it? I'm so embarrassed."

"Nonsense, child!" Strix Struma hooted. "Don't you ever belittle those spots. You'll see, they'll come in handy someday. We must learn to use our Glaux-given gifts and in that way they truly become not just gifts but treasures. Now you fly on. You're doing a nice job and I shall teach Soren some tricks to reduce his disorientation.

"I had to fly behind a Pygmy for years. Made me a terrific navigator. Now, what you do, Soren, is you focus just below the spots. That will help you."

And it did. In no time the spots seemed to entirely vanish.

They flew on through the night, practicing mostly by tracing the Golden Talons. But now, one by one, the stars of the constellations slipped away over some distant horizon and into another world, and Strix Struma led her class home to the Great Ga'Hoole Tree in the middle of the Sea of Hoolemere, which, in its own way, was another world as well.

CHAPTER TWELVE
Hukla, Hukla and Hope

There was the noisy chattering of young owls, which was known as gazooling. Soren remembered it from his brief few weeks with his own family in the old fir tree. His sister, Eglantine, his brother, Kludd, and he all would try out their unformed voices in a range of hoots and shreeings. Barn Owls were more screamers than hooters. It was a raucous time of the day before getting ready to rest. Here at the Great Ga'Hoole Tree it was even rowdier. But for Soren, as the black of night thinned to gray and the gray became a cool purple that eventually warmed to rose, it could be a melancholy time.

Soren could not figure out why he felt so sad. He had a lot to gazool about, as much as anyone else. Of course, Twilight came up to him first, and Soren could barely squeeze in a word. "I did a fantastic power dive tonight. A tight spiral and I was down on the ground before you could flick a blink. Soren, I think Barran was really impressed. So you think there's a chance that she might recommend me for search-and-rescue?"

"But, Twilight, if you were in the advanced navigation class with Barran why were you practicing search-and-rescue moves?"

"Because Barran also teaches search-and-rescue. She is the one who taps for the search-and-rescue chaw."

That was all anyone ever talked about — being tapped for the various chaws. Next, Otulissa came up. "Oh, I don't know, Twilight, about you getting tapped for search-and-rescue chaw. Don't get your hopes up. They tend to take owls with very old family lines. Those ranks are almost always reserved for Strix, just like navigation."

"Oh, racdrops!" boomed Bubo. "Make way! Make way! Let the nest snakes serve tea. We all be starving and don't need to listen to none of this nonsense about old family lines. It's what you do here and now on this earth that counts."

Bubo was the ruddy-colored owl with the very black talons whom Soren had first seen in the parliament. A high-shouldered, enormous Great Horned Owl, his ear tufts alone stood as tall as Gylfie. His plumage was of an unusual coloring for a Great Horned, most of whom tended toward the brownish-gray tones. Bubo's feathers were actually almost flame-colored, which seemed appropriate, as he headed up the forge and was the blacksmith. So, despite what was said about Bubo's lowly origins and rough-and-tumble manner — a constant stream of curses issued from his beak — he was treated with great respect in the community of the Great Ga'Hoole Tree because he was an expert blacksmith. The discovery and the taming of fire was the single thing that most impressed Soren about the owls of the Great Ga'Hoole Tree.

"Line up! Line up! Now, please don't rush the dear snakes. Don't crowd the snakes by cramming in too many of you around one snake. Please proceed in an orderly fashion." It was Matron speaking, the Short-eared Owl. The nest-maid snakes began to slither into the dining hollow. These snakes were all blind like Mrs. Plithiver. Gylfie, Soren, Twilight, and Digger always lined up at Mrs. Plithiver's table for, indeed, she had been invited to join the staff and was thrilled to be in service once more.

The melancholy feelings that had filled Soren a few minutes before disappeared as he and his friends stepped up to Mrs. P.'s back.

"Hello, dearies," Mrs. P. hissed in her soft voice. "Good night in the Yonder? Classes went well?"

"Look!" Digger said. "Primrose over there doesn't have a place to sit."

"Sorry, Primrose," Otulissa was saying, "but this snake is all filled up." Otulissa was with four other young Spotted Owls.

"Over here, Primrose." Gylfie waved a wing. "We have a place."

"Always room, dearie," Mrs. P. said as Primrose came over. "I can always stretch myself a little longer and fit in another young one."

"Oh, thank you. Thank you so much," Primrose spoke in a shaky voice.

"You all right, Primrose?" Digger asked kindly.

"I'm fine. Just fine." She didn't sound all that fine. "Well, not so fine," she admitted. "All this talk of tapping is really making me nervous."

"Now, I believe there is entirely too much talk about this tapping business," Mrs. P. said. "I think you young ones should just drink your tea while it is still nice and warm. Cook made a special effort with the milkberries. I think she added a few extra as the season shall be coming again soon and perhaps she can spare more for tea without worrying."

"It's hard not to think about tapping, Mrs. P.," Soren said. "It's all anyone talks about."

"They say most Burrowing Owls like myself are tapped for tracking, since we have such strong legs and really know the countryside so well. I think I'd like that," Digger said quietly.

"I want search-and-rescue myself. You get to wear battle claws," Twilight spoke up.

"You want to fight?" Primrose said with a note of alarm in her voice.

"I'd like to fight any owl from St. Aggie's. Let me tell you, we gave those two a run for it that time in the desert. Didn't we?" He blinked toward Soren and Gylfie. Soren and Gylfie both prayed that Twilight would not break into one of his dancing chants and shadow fights with an imaginary opponent in the dining hall. As much as they loved him, he could be really embarrassing.

"Thank goodness," sighed Digger. "If it hadn't been for them and, of course, the eagles, I would be dead." Digger paused. "Not just dead . . . eaten."

"You're joking?" Primrose gasped.

"I'm not joking," Digger said.

"Oh, come on, tell me the story," Primrose urged.

"Young ones, I don't think this is tea-table talk and since I am the tea table I would prefer not."

But it was too late. Digger had already launched into his story, and Primrose was spellbound. Mrs. Plithiver just sighed and muttered, "Hukla, hukla," which, in the special language of blind snakes, meant "Young owls will be young owls."

Mrs. Plithiver dozed off as the owls continued to talk and sip their cups of tea.

"So here's how the joke goes. You got a bunch of crows and other wet poopers like hummingbirds and seagulls." Twilight had begun telling a joke.

"Oh, yes. Seagulls are disgusting," Primrose offered.

"Definitely," Soren joined in. "They are disgusting."

"We should have a contest to see who can tell the slimiest wet poop joke," Digger said.

Suddenly, their little nut cups of tea trembled. "Enough is enough!" Mrs. Plithiver screeched a hiss that curled through the air. "I shall not have this talk at the table. This is inappropriate on every level." Then her rosy scales seemed to shimmer with a new radiance and with one quick writhing motion all the teacups clattered off her back.

This was not the first time a nest-maid snake had shaken off teacups. There were not many rules at the Great Ga'Hoole Tree but, as Matron instructed the young owls, there were to be no wet poop jokes anywhere, and especially not in the dining hollow. Therefore, the nest snakes were under orders, if it was teatime and they were serving, to immediately dismiss the culprits, and this was accomplished in just the manner Mrs. P. had done when she shook herself.

They were ordered to go see Boron and Barran. As could be expected, Barran scolded them and told them that their behavior was shocking. "Poor form," she called it. Boron kept muttering, "Don't be too hard on them, dear. They're just youngsters. Young males do that kind of thing."

"Boron, I would like to point out that Primrose and Gylfie are not males."

"Oh, but I still know a lot of wet poop jokes," Primrose tooted up.

The air was laced with the soft churr sounds that owls make when they laugh. They were all churring except for Barran. Boron was churring the hardest. His big white fluffy body was shaking so hard that he shook loose a few wisps of down.

"Really! Boron! It's not a laughing matter," his mate said in dismay.

"But it is, my dear. That's the point." And he began to laugh even harder.

The owls had already settled down for the day. It had been several hours since Madame Plonk had sung her lovely "Night Is Done" song and all had wished one another good light until the next night. But Soren had trouble falling asleep, and then he woke up in that slow time of the day for owls, when silence seems to press down over everything and the air is thick with sunlight and the minutes drag by. Time seemed to crawl and one wondered if there would ever be blackness again. Once more, Soren felt that melancholy feeling. He was not sure exactly what was causing it. He should be so happy here. He did feel bad about their misbehavior at tea. Good manners meant a lot to Mrs. P. He hated disappointing her. *Maybe,* he thought, *I should go and apologize.* Mrs. Plithiver was often up at this time of the day. Perhaps he would make his way down to her hollow. She lived there with two other nestmaids.

The three snakes shared a mossy pocket in the tree nearly one hundred feet below where Soren slept. It smelled of damp shredded bark, moss, and warm stones. The nestmaid snakes enjoyed sleeping with warm stones. So, these stones were part of the furnishings of any hollow in which they slept. Bubo always heated up several so they could have them in their quarters. Soren rather liked the smell. The heat from the stones released the fragrance of the moss, and the moss that grew on the Great Ga'Hoole Tree was especially sweet. It was used in a soup that was made by Cook. There was barely a part of the Great Ga'Hoole Tree that was not used for something. It was for this reason that the owls so carefully nurtured and cared for their home — never overpicking the milkberries, and burying their pellets around the roots of the tree where their rich, nourishing contents would be most directly absorbed.

The fragrance of the moss and warm stones drifted up to Soren as he made his way down. He stopped at the opening of the pocket and peered in. But before he could even speak, Mrs. P. must have sensed his presence.

"Soren, dear boy, what are you doing up this time of day? Come on in, young one."

"Aren't the other nest-maids asleep?"

"Oh, no. They're all out doing guild business."

There were several guilds: the harp guild, the lacemakers', weavers', and others to which the nest snakes belonged. One had to be chosen. It was rather like the tapping ceremony for the chaws. Mrs. Plithiver had not been chosen yet for any guild.

"Mrs. P., I came to apologize for my disgusting behavior at tea. I am truly sorry. I know that . . ."

Mrs. P. coiled up and cocked her head in that particularly sympathetic way she had. "Soren," she spoke softly and there was something in the very softness of her voice that brought tears to his eyes. "Soren, dear boy, I know you are sorry, but I don't think that is why you are here."

"It's not?" Soren was dumbfounded. But she was right. That really wasn't why he was here. He knew it as soon as she had said it. Yet he was still confused. "Why . . . why," he stammered, "am I here?"

"I think it has to do with your sister, Eglantine."

As soon as she said it, Soren knew that she was right. He missed his parents terribly but he did not worry about his parents. Eglantine, however, was another story. Mrs. P. had her suspicions about Kludd. These suspicions deepened when Kludd threatened to eat her. Still, she was not sure if Eglantine had been snatched or not. Eglantine had simply disappeared.

"It's the not knowing, isn't it, that's so hard. Not knowing if Eglantine is dead or alive . . ."

"Or imprisoned," Soren said.

"Yes, dear. I know."

"And if she is dead, it doesn't help me one bit to think of her being in glaumora if I am here and she is there."

"No, of course not. She's too young to be in glaumora."

"Mrs. P., I know that St. Aegolius Academy for Orphan Owls is the most terrible place. But remember what the dying Barred Owl said about," Soren dropped his voice, "the 'you only wish' . . ."

"Hush now, dear."

Soren simply couldn't stop himself. "Have you heard anything else about the 'you only wish'?"

Mrs. Plithiver waved her head about in a small figure eight, which was the manner in which blind snakes often moved when they could not quite decide what to say or do. Soren peered at her closely. Was something leaking out of the small dents where her eyes would have been? Soren suddenly felt terrible. "I'm sorry, Mrs. P. I won't speak of this again."

"No, dear. Come to me whenever you want to talk about Eglantine. I think it will help you, but let's not get carried away about rumors of terrible places. I have a feeling deep within me that Eglantine is not dead. Now, I cannot tell you more than that, but I think, together, we can hope. Hope is never a foolish thing — although others will tell you it is. But I don't need to tell you that, Soren — look at yourself. You were snatched and you taught yourself to fly and you escaped from that awful St. Aggie's. You flew straight out of those deep stone canyons and right into the Yonder. Anyone who flies out of a stone hole into the Yonder knows about hope."

It was always this way when Soren spoke with Mrs. P. She always made him feel so much better. It was just as if a clean rain had washed away all of the worry and the sadness. Yes, he still missed his parents. He would always miss his parents, and he would never get used to it, but Mrs. P. had given him hope about Eglantine, and this alone made him feel so much better. He decided to take the outside route back to his hollow. The day guard on this side of the tree was very nice and wouldn't mind that he had gone down to see his old nest-maid. And there weren't any real rules at the Great Ga'Hoole Tree about having to stay in your hollow asleep all day until the wake-up calls of good night. So he stepped out on a branch and lifted into flight, swooping through the spreading limbs of the old tree. Yes, Mrs. P. was right. He could see the beginnings of the new milkberries forming on the long glistening threads they called silver rain at this time of the year.

These slim vines cascaded down from branches of the Great Ga'Hoole Tree and swayed like sheer curtains in the afternoon sun. In winter, they were white and then in spring they turned silvery, by summer they would be golden, and by fall they would turn a deep coppery rose. Thus, in Ga'Hoole, the seasons were not simply called winter, summer, spring, and fall, but the times of the white rain, the silver rain, the golden rain, and the rain of the copper rose. For the young owls, there was nothing more fun than to fly amid the glistening curtains. Therefore they had developed all sorts of games to be played. But on this bright afternoon, everyone was asleep so Soren found himself alone. Rain must have just fallen for the vines sparkled with beads of water and behind one curtain he caught the shimmering colors of a rainbow.

"Lovely, isn't it?" A voice melted like a chime out of the silver rain. It was Madame Plonk, the harp singer, who sang them to sleep each morning. She was a Snowy Owl and, as she sailed through the silver rain, Soren blinked in amazement, for he had never seen such a beautiful sight. She was no longer snowy white but indeed had become a living, flying rainbow. All colors seemed to radiate from her plumage.

Soren wished that one of the chaws of the Great Ga'Hoole Tree could be learning the harp and singing from Madame Plonk. But the pluckers of the harp were never owls, only blind snakes. And the only ones trained to sing were direct descendants of the Plonk line of Snowy Owls.

They flew, weaving themselves through the vines and the hues of the rainbow for a few more minutes. Then Madame Plonk said, "Time for me to go, dear. Wake-up time. Evensong must be sung. I see the snakes coming out now, making their way toward the harp. Can't be late. But I've so enjoyed our afternoon flight. We'll do it again sometime. Or drop by for a cup of milkberry tea."

Soren wondered if he would ever have the nerve to just "drop by" Madame Plonk's for a cup of tea. What would he ever have to say to such a beautiful and elegant owl? Flying was one thing, but sitting and talking was another. Soren saw dozens of rosy-scaled blind snakes crawling up to the hollow where the harp was kept. Soon the Great Ga'Hoole Tree would begin to awake and stir to the lovely harmonies of Evensong. For twilight was upon them.

CHAPTER THIRTEEN
Books of the Yonder

Now, young ones, please follow me as we explore the wondrous root structure of our dear tree. You see where the roots bump up from the ground." It was the Ga'Hoolology ryb, a boring old Burrowing Owl.

"Here's one."

"Oh, yes, Otulissa. A perfect example."

"Here's one," Gylfie mimicked Otulissa. "She has the most annoying voice."

"Now if we can find a pellet or if someone would care to yarp one, I shall demonstrate the proper burying technique. Pellets properly buried nourish the tree," the ryb continued.

"Oh, I'll find you one," Otulissa quickly volunteered and bustled off.

"This is the most borrring class," sighed Soren. They had been stomping around the base of the Great Ga'Hoole Tree all during twilight.

"I don't think it's that bad," said Digger. Digger, of course, being a Burrowing Owl, preferred ground activities.

"I don't know what I'll do if I am tapped for Ga'Hoolology," Twilight muttered.

"You? Never," Soren said, but he was secretly worried that he might be. He realized that knowing about the tree was important. The Ga'Hoolology ryb constantly drummed this into them just as she was doing now. "The Great Ga'Hoole Tree has thrived and flourished for these thousands of years because the owls have been such excellent stewards of this little piece of earth that the Great Glaux gave them." Twilight began to mouth the words as she said them.

"That is so rude," Otulissa hissed.

"Oh, go yarp a pellet!" Twilight barked back.

"What's that? Someone has a pellet to yarp? Twilight dear, come up here. I believe I heard you say you had a little gift to bestow on our Great Ga'Hoole Tree."

Class finally ended an hour before First Black. There was still time to go to the library. This was Soren and Gylfie's favorite place in the old tree. The two young owls had a special fondness for libraries that went beyond the wonderful books that they were now learning how to read. At St. Aegolius Academy, the library had been strictly off-limits to everyone except for Skench and Spoorn, the two brutal owls who ran the orphanage. No one knew how to read at St. Aggie's except for Skench and Spoorn, but here everyone knew how to read and they read constantly. But the reason why libraries were so special to Gylfie and Soren was that it was from the library at St. Aggie's that they had escaped.

For the two young owls libraries meant freedom in every way. Sometimes, Soren thought that libraries for him were a kind of Yonder, in the sense that Mrs. Plithiver and other snakes spoke of the sky. The sky so far away for snakes, as far as anything could be, was a world unseen. But as Soren and Gylfie learned to read they began to get glimmerings of worlds unseen.

The only problem with the library was the old Whiskered Screech, Ezylryb. He was always there, and he was still as frightening as he had been that day when Soren first saw him in the parliament and felt his squinted eye burning into him. The old bird rarely spoke and when he did it was in a low, growlish hoot. He had a fondness for caterpillars and kept a store of dried ones for when they were out of season. These he put in a little pile by his desk in the library. It was not what Ezylryb did say that Soren and Gylfie found unnerving, it was what he didn't. He seemed to quietly observe everything even as he read with his one and a half eyes. Every once in a while he emitted a low growl of what they could only feel was disapproval. But worst of all was his deformed foot. And although Soren and Gylfie knew it was impolite to stare, their eyes just seemed drawn to that foot. Soren admitted to Gylfie that he couldn't help it, and Gylfie said that she herself was fearful of making a terrible slip.

"Remember when Matron came in the other day to serve tea and she asked me to take the cup to him and to ask if he wanted his usual with it — whatever that was. I was so afraid I was going to say something like, 'Ezylryb, Matron would like to know if you'd like your tea with your usual fourth talon.'" Soren laughed but he knew exactly what Gylfie meant.

There were, however, too many compelling reasons to go to the library. So they went and learned to ignore his occasional growlish hoots, trying not to stare at his foot and trying to avoid the amber squint of his eye. The library was quite high in the great tree in a roomy hollow that was lined with books, and the floor was spread with lovely carpets woven of mosses, grasses, and occasional strands of down. When Soren and Gylfie entered, they spotted Ezylryb in his usual spot. There was the pile of caterpillars. Every now and then he would pluck one and munch it.

His beak was now poked into a book titled *Magnetic Properties as They Occur Naturally and Unnaturally in Nature.*

Soren made his way toward a shelf that had books about barns and churches for, indeed, once upon a time Barn Owls like himself had actually lived in such places and Soren enjoyed looking at the pictures and reading about them. Some of the churches were magnificent, with windows stained the colors of rainbows and stone spires that soared high into the sky. But Soren actually preferred the simpler little wooden churches, neatly painted, with something called steeples for their bells. Gylfie liked books with poems, funny riddles, and jokes. She went to see if a book she had discovered yesterday was still there, called *Hooties, Cooties, and Nooties: A Book of Owl Humor with Recipes, Jokes, and Practical Advice.* It was written by Philomena Bagwhistle, a well-known nest-maid snake who had spent many years in service.

But just as Gylfie was about to pull the book from the shelf there was a low growl. "You can do better than that, young one. One day with that Philomena Bagwhistle slop is quite 'nuff, I'd say. Whyn't try something a little weightier?"

"Like what?" Gylfie said in a small voice.

"Try that one over there." Ezylryb raised his foot, the one with three talons, and pointed.

Soren froze. He could not take his eyes off the talons. Was it a deformity that he had been born with, as some said, or had it been snapped off in a mobbing by crows? The three talons raked the air as he pointed, and Soren and Gylfie's feathers automatically drooped as owl feathers do when they find themselves in conditions of fear. The old owl now got up from his desk, lurched toward the shelf, and pulled the book off using only one talon. Gylfie's and Soren's eyes were riveted on the talon. "Look at the book, idiots, not my talons. Or, here, take a good look at the talons so you can get used to it." And he shook the deformed foot in their faces. The two owls nearly fainted on the spot.

"We're used to it," Soren gasped.

"Good. Now read the book," Ezylryb said.

Gylfie began sounding out the words, *"Tempers of the Gizzard: An Interpretative Physiology of This Vital Organ in Strigiformes."*

"What are Strigiformes?" whispered Soren.

"Us," Gylfie said softly. "That's the fancy name for all owls, whether we're Elf Owls or Barn Owls or . . ." Gylfie hesitated, "a Whiskered Screech."

"Right-o. Now go on, the both of you. Try something harder. Read it together." He fixed them in his amber squint. "And you can now quit wasting time thinking about my three talons. If you want to see it again you can." He gave a little wave, and then with his odd gait made his way back to his desk, stopping on the way to poke the small fire in the grate.

Soren and Gylfie opened the book. Thank goodness there were lots of pictures but they had a go at the first paragraph.

The gizzard is a most marvelous organ. Considered the second stomach in owls and often called the muscular stomach, it filters out indigestible items such as bone, fur, hair, feathers, and teeth. The gizzard compresses the indigestible parts into a pellet. The pellets are yarped through the beak. [See footnote pertaining to identification of owl species through pellet analysis.]

"I think we can skip the footnotes," Soren whispered, hoping that Ezylryb wouldn't hear. "This is boring enough as it is."

"Oh, I always skip the footnotes," Gylfie said.

"How many books with footnotes have you read, Gylfie?" Soren blinked in surprise.

"One. It was about feather maintenance. But look." Gylfie pointed with her talon to the next paragraph.

Volumes have been written about the physical processes of the gizzard. But rarely do we find much in the literature concerning the temper of this marvelous organ. This seems like a gross oversight. For do we not attribute all of our most profound feelings to the sensitivity of this muscular organ? How many times a day does an owl think, "Oh, I feel it in my gizzard?" When we feel a strong passion, or perhaps trust, or even distrust, this is our first reaction.

"Well, that's the truth," Soren said. "There's not much new in that. Hardly original."

"Hold on, Soren. Look what he says here."

We do use our gizzards as our guide. Our gizzards, indeed, do often navigate us over treacherous emotional terrain. However, it is my considered opinion that the immature owl does not always know for certain his gizzardly instincts. Why do so many break the one rule their parents tell them never to break and try to fly too young, thus falling out of nests? Stubbornness. They have blocked out certain subtle signals their gizzards might be sending them. . . .

Soren looked up and saw Ezylryb staring at them. "Why do you suppose he's having us read this, Gylfie?"

"I think he's trying to send us a message," Gylfie replied.

"What? Don't be stubborn? Open up your gizzard?"

"I don't know, but it's almost time for night flight exercises."

They closed the book and then backed out of the library, making short little bobbing gestures to Ezylryb. "Very interesting," Gylfie said. "Thank you for the suggestion."

"Yes, thank you," Soren said.

Ezylryb said nothing. He only coughed a ragged hoot and plucked another caterpillar from the pile.

"Great Glaux, I'll just die if I get tapped for the weather interpretation chaw. I mean, can you imagine having Ezylryb as your chaw leader? It's just too creepy to even think about," Soren said.

"You know if you get tapped for colliering, you automatically have to take weather interpretation and fly with that chaw as well," Gylfie said.

"Well, who wants to get tapped for colliering and get their beaked singed, anyway?" Soren replied dejectedly.

"You didn't get it singed when you picked up the coal that you dropped on that bobcat."

"We were all picking them up when we were burying them."

"Yeah, but you flew with yours!"

"That was pure dumb luck."

"Maybe, but if you do it properly you never get singed, and that's what Bubo helps teach. It would be great to have Bubo as a chaw leader."

"Yeah, but if you get Ezylryb with him, I would hardly call that a bargain. I think Bubo only helps. It's that other old owl, Elvan, who is the leader of colliering. I still don't see why you have to do weather with colliering."

"Well, you have to fly into forest fires and pick up burning embers. And forest fires, they say, are like a weather system all by themselves. You have to know about the drafts and winds that the heat can cause. I heard Bubo talking about it the other day."

Soren decided not to worry about it.

Just at that moment Digger came up. "Ready for night flight, Digger?" Soren asked.

"Yes. And I've really improved. Much stronger, that's what Boron says. Wait until you see me."

CHAPTER FOURTEEN
Night Flight

The night flight was always fun. There was never any special purpose to it. It really was mostly recreational. Boron liked to get all the newly arrived owls together with some of the other young owls in the blackness of the sky so they could, as he put it, "Buddy up, tell a few jokes, yarp a few pellets, and hoot at the moon."

"So, Twilight," Boron began. "I've got one that you'll like. Did you hear the story of the wet pooper who was flying over Hoolemere and hit a fish?"

Otulissa dropped back to where Soren was flying. "He's just too much," she muttered.

"Who's too much?" Soren asked.

"Our king, Boron. He's telling a wet poop joke. I think it's undignified for one of his position."

Soren sighed. "Give it a blow, Otulissa." This was not the most polite way for an owl to say, "A little less serious, please."

"Well, I sure hope he doesn't head a chaw. I would find it most unpleasant. You know, tonight the tappings begin?"

"They do?"

"Yes, and I just have a feeling in my gizzard that I'm going to find ten nooties in my bedding down."

Each chaw had symbolic objects that the leader left in a young owl's bedding. Find ten nooties arranged in the pattern of the Great Glaux constellation when you went to sleep at First Light, and that meant you were in the navigation chaw of Strix Struma. A pellet was for the tracking chaw, a milkberry for the Ga'Hoology chaw. A molted feather was the symbol for the search-and-rescue chaw. A dried caterpillar was naturally for Ezylryb's weather chaw. A piece of coal and a caterpillar meant that you had been picked for colliering and were by necessity in for double duty and required to fly with the weather chaw as well.

"Don't you have any feelings, Soren?" Otulissa asked.

"I prefer not to discuss my gizzardly feelings," he replied almost primly.

"Why not?"

"I don't know. I'm just not comfortable doing it. You know I don't mean to be rude, Otulissa, but for someone so well bred you push awfully hard."

"Well, honestly." Otulissa turned to Primrose, who was

flying rather noisily due to her lack of plummels, the fringes at the edge of the flight feathers that helped owls fly in silence. Neither Pygmy nor Elf owls had such fringes. "What about you, Primrose? Any little twinges in the old gizzard?"

"Oh, I don't know, Otulissa. One minute I think I'm a sure bet for search-and-rescue, which I'd love, and then the next, I think they'll tap me for tracking, which I guess I wouldn't mind. You know, I just don't know. I mean, I think that's part of the problem."

"What do you mean — what problem?"

"My gizzard — it's just so here, there, everywhere. I mean, when you said 'old gizzard,' I realized my gizzard isn't so old, nor is yours for that matter, but you seem to know it better."

"Oh, I know my gizzard." Otulissa nodded smugly.

"Lucky you," Primrose sighed.

Soren had been listening and blinked in wonderment at Primrose's words. They were exactly what the author of the book had been talking about — the immature gizzard of an immature owl.

Soren cut behind Otulissa and came up on the windward side of Primrose. "Primrose, were you in the library reading that book about the physiology and the temper of owl gizzards?"

"Oh, great Glaux, no. I only read joke books and romances, for the most part, and never anything with any 'ology' in the title. Do you know that Madame Plonk has written a memoir about her love life? She's had a lot of mates who died. The book is called *My Fabulous Life and Times: An Anecdotal History of a Life Devoted to Love and Song.* There's a lot about music in it. I love Madame Plonk."

"Who wants to read about that?" Twilight flew up. "Enough to make a person yarp, all that romantic stuff. I like reading about weapons, battle claws, war hammers."

"Well," said Otulissa, "I don't especially like reading about weapons but I find Madame Plonk coarse and unrefined, and they say she's got a touch of the magpie in her. Have you ever been to her 'apartments,' as she calls them?"

"Oh, yes," Primrose made a rapturous little low hooting noise. "Aren't they beautiful?"

"Oh, yes, beautiful with other creatures' things — bits of crockery and teacups made out of something she calls porcelain. Now where would she get that stuff? Well, I think under all those snowy white feathers is a magpie in disguise — that's what I think. And frankly, I find the apartment vulgar — rather like its occupant."

Great Glaux, she's obnoxious, Soren thought. Simply to change the subject, Soren decided to ask Otulissa how she came to the Great Ga'Hoole Tree.

"When did you come here, Otulissa?"

"It was during the time of the copper rose rain. I came from Ambala. You might have heard that Ambala suffered a great many egg snatchings because of St. Aggie's patrols. My mother and father had lost two eggs this way and had gone out to see if they could find them, somehow. I was left in the nest under the care of a very distracted aunt of mine. Well, she decided to go visit a friend, and I became worried. I couldn't fly yet, and don't for a minute think I was trying to. I was a very obedient owlet. I was only looking over the edge for Auntie, and I just fell. It's the honest truth."

Racdrops it is, Soren thought. She was doing what many other owlets had tried to do, like Gylfie and dozens of others, trying to fly. Except Gylfie had admitted it. Otulissa wasn't all that different. If she just wasn't so smug about everything.

"Luckily," Otulissa continued, "some search-and-rescue patrols from the Great Ga'Hoole Tree came by and found me. They put me back into my nest and we waited and waited for my aunt and for my parents, but none of them ever returned. So, I must assume that they met with disaster trying to recover the eggs. Of course, my aunt, well, I'm not sure what really happened to her. As I said, she was a very scatterbrained owl — for a Spotted one. In any case, the patrols took me back here to the Great Ga'Hoole Tree." She paused for a second, then blinked. "I'm an orphan like you."

Soren was taken aback. It was perhaps the nicest thing that Otulissa had ever said. Otulissa seldom thought of herself being like anyone else or sharing any traits, except with the most elegant and distinguished of her *Strix* ancestors.

Boron had just clacked his beak loudly, announcing that night flight was finished, and he had spotted Strix Struma making her way upwind to take over for navigation class.

"It will be a short class tonight, young ones," she announced upon arriving. "For as you know, this is a special night, and we want to be sure to get back before First Light."

So, indeed, they returned to the Great Ga'Hoole Tree at that border of darkness that owls call the Deep Gray, when the black has faded but the sun has not yet spilled even the first sliver of a ray over the horizon. Nobody really wanted tea. It all took too long and the nest snakes seemed unbearably slow as they slithered in with the cups on their backs. It was an unusually silent teatime. It was as if everyone was too worried to speak, and there was absolutely no talk about feelings in one's gizzard. Even Otulissa had shut up.

"No seconds, anyone?" Mrs. P. said. "I'd be happy to go back and get some, and there are more nice little nootie cakes."

Soren saw Otulissa blink her eyes shut for the longest time. He knew exactly what she was thinking about: nooties, and not the ones that had been baked in a cake. No, she was thinking of ten nooties arranged in the figure of the Great Glaux constellation. He almost felt sorry for her.

Finally, the time came for good light. Madame Plonk would, of course, sing the beautiful good light song, and then they were allowed to look into the down fluff and discover their destinies. Usually, after Madame Plonk's song there was total silence, but there would not be tonight. Instead, there would be raucous shrieks mixed with some groans, and owls saying, "I told you so. I knew you'd get into that chaw." While others would be quietly thinking, *How shall I survive Ga'Hoolology with that old bore of a Burrowing Owl?*

Soren, Digger, Twilight, and Gylfie went to their hollow.

"Well, good luck, everybody," Digger said. "Twilight, I really hope you get what you want. I know how much it means to you."

Suddenly, Soren realized that was his problem. He didn't know what he wanted. He only knew what he didn't want. He truly was an immature owl with an immature gizzard.

They each tucked into their corners. The first chords from the great harp were plucked and then came the soft *plings* of Madame Plonk's eerily beautiful voice. All too quickly, the last verses of the song came up. Soren felt his heart quicken and a stirring in his gizzard.

Far away is First Black,
But it shall seep back
Over field
Over flower
In the twilight hour.
We are home in our tree.
We are owls, we are free.
As we go, this we know
Glaux is nigh.

Then there were the sounds of owls burrowing into the downy fluff of their beds and then the first gasps. "A pellet!" Digger exclaimed. "I got tracking chaw. I can't believe it!"

Next, a whoop from Twilight. "Hooray! I'm search-and-rescue."

From other hollows came more cries:

"This iron tree is beautiful — great Glaux, I did get metals!"

"A milkberry — oh, no!"

"Ten nooties!!!!" But the voice was not Otulissa's. It was Gylfie's. "Soren, I can't believe it. I didn't think Strix Struma liked me that much," Gylfie whispered as if she couldn't believe her great luck. And then there was silence as six pairs of yellow eyes turned to Soren. "Soren," Digger said, "what did you get?"

"I . . . I . . . I'm not sure."

"Not sure?" Gylfie said. They were all puzzled. How could one not be sure?

"I haven't looked yet. I'm scared."

"Soren," Twilight said, "just look. Get it over with. Come on. It can't be so bad."

Can't be so bad? Soren thought. *No, of course, not for all of you who got exactly what you wanted.*

"Come on, Soren," Gylfie said in a softer voice. She had walked over to the pile of down where Soren slept. "Come on. I'll stand right here beside you." Gylfie was half Soren's size but she stretched up and began preening Soren's feathers in a soothing gesture.

Soren sighed and, carefully, with one talon, plucked away the down fluff so as not to disturb anything. A dark lump poked through and beside it the shriveled body of a dried caterpillar.

"Colliering!" the wail peeled out into the morning. But the voice was not that of Soren, who simply stared in disbelief at the piece of coal and the caterpillar. "I can't believe it. I'm on colliering and weather chaws. Disaster!" The voice was that of Otulissa. *Great Glaux*, Soren thought. As if things weren't bad enough — he was now double chawed with Otulissa!

CHAPTER FIFTEEN
A Visit to Bubo

O
ne — two — one — two. That's it, Ruby. Tuck the beak . . . one — two — one — two . . ." This was their second chaw practice for colliering and Soren had never been more depressed, not since his horrible time at St. Aggie's. The colliering ryb, a Great Gray named Elvan, stood in the center of a circle that had been inscribed on the ground at the base of the tree. It was near the forge where Bubo worked, keeping them supplied with red-hot coals. Elvan barked commands at them and insisted that they march in time as he kept count. Soren had a deep aversion to marching. They had been forced to march all the time at St. Aggie's. Elvan said this marching was necessary to establish the proper rhythm that helped in holding a live coal in their beaks. And it seemed as if his previous experience with live coals in the woods of The Beaks had deserted him. He could hardly believe that he had actually picked up live coals, buried them, and flown with them! Soren had spent the first minutes of class being scared and

the remainder being bored. If anyone had told him that it was possible to be both in the same practice, he would have said they were yoicks. It was odd that he hardly felt the heat. He remembered thinking this before when he was in the woods of The Beaks. He did notice, however, that Elvan's fringe of light feathers below his beak seemed to be a permanently sooty gray.

Soren thought of his own face, covered in pure white feathers. This was the most distinctive feature of Barn Owls, and he really did not want to think of it growing singed and sooty. Maybe he was vain but he couldn't help it.

"Pay attention! Soren!" Elvan barked. "You nearly ran into Otulissa."

Thank Glaux she couldn't speak, thought Soren. That was the only good thing about colliering. It was hard to speak with a live coal in one's mouth. So Otulissa was effectively shut up for once.

"All right, rest time. Drop your coals," Elvan announced.

Rest wasn't really rest, however, as the ryb lectured them the entire time. "Tomorrow you shall begin flying with the coals in your beaks. It is not that different, really, from walking. Although you must take care to keep your coal alive and burning."

"Yeah!" Bubo boomed. "Dead coals ain't going to do me

a bit of good, young'uns. No sense flying in here with a great lot of ashes, cold as Glaux knows what."

"Yes," continued Elvan. "We don't want to disappoint Bubo."

"Oh, Glaux forbid that we should disappoint Bubo," Otulissa mumbled.

Soren stole a glance at her. There was pure venom in her eyes. *Why couldn't she just be angry about being in this chaw? What did Bubo have to do with it?* Soren thought. He knew why, of course. Otulissa thought she was too good to have anything to do with Bubo. Neither Bubo nor any of the owls in this chaw had the distinguished background of Otulissa. It was an outrage, as she told Soren forty times a night, that she had not been included in Strix Struma's navigation chaw.

Elvan continued speaking during their break. "And then, of course, after you have had enough nights of weather training we shall find a nice forest fire for you — nothing too big, mind you. Just a nice little beginning fire with a good mix of trees — Ga'Hooles, firs, pine, some soft and hard woods. Not too many ridges or mountains to complicate wind patterns."

"Pardon me," piped up the little Northern Saw-whet Owl, Martin, who had been rescued the same night as Primrose.

"Yes, Martin," Elvan said.

"Well, I don't understand why we need new coals all the time. Once you start a fire going, wouldn't there always be new coals?"

This was some smart little owl, Soren thought. Why hadn't the others thought of this question? Why were new coals from a new fire needed?

Elvan turned to Bubo. "Bubo, as chief smith, would you care to answer that?"

"Sure thing, mate." Then he stepped up to Martin and, towering over him, began to speak. "A very good question. You are right, it is very possible to keep fires going forever and that is fine for some things — things like cooking and warming up a hollow. But for certain tasks, especially certain metalwork in the forge, we need new fresh coals that have been born of sparking trees full of sap. They become the blood of our hottest fires. Then again, we need a variety of coals. Certain coals from certain trees last longer. That's how a fire gets bonk."

"What's bonk?" asked Martin.

"Ah, it's an old smithy term. Hard to explain unless you've been working with the fires for some time. Then you know when you got a bonking good fire going in your forge. You know you got to look for the blue in the flame and then, this is the hardest, a tinge of green around the blue."

Soren was impressed. Being a blacksmith was truly a complicated business. Even though Bubo did not have the title of ryb, Soren thought he must be very smart.

Soon, rest time was over, and they were told to begin marching without their coals to establish the rhythm again.

"I simply can't bear this a minute longer," Otulissa said.

"I think it's going to be great fun when we can fly," said Ruby, a ruddy-colored Short-eared Owl that Soren nearly bumped into.

"How can you say that, Ruby? This is really not the appropriate chaw for you, either, no more than for me. You of all owls, with your family background — you should be in tracking."

"Just because my family nested on the ground doesn't mean I can't try something new."

"But you fly low and slow; that's good for tracking."

"But I've never flown through a forest fire. And I can't wait until weather interpretation — a hurricane! Just imagine flying through that. Life in that ground nest was boring. We were out there in the grasslands — every day just the same. The sound of the wind in the grass just the same, the way the grass moved just the same. Oh, yes. Sometimes it moved slower or faster, depending on the wind. But there was a terrible sameness. I can't believe how lucky I am to be double chawed." Ruby sighed with pleasure.

Soren blinked. He wished he felt this way. He wanted to ask Ruby if she was nervous about Ezylryb, but at the same time he didn't want to admit that he was. Ruby was a very tough little owl. She had been brought in by search-and-rescue shortly after Soren had arrived. She had not fallen from a nest, for indeed to fall out of a ground nest was virtually impossible. But something had scared her so bad when her parents were out hunting, she had actually flown before her primaries were fledged. No one was quite sure what had scared her. She had been found ex-hausted but perched in one of the few trees in the grass-lands, declaring, "They'll never find me here! They'll never believe that an immature Short-eared made it to here!" But no one knew who *they* were. And Ruby never said.

Finally, chaw practice was over. Soren dreaded teatime. If it was like yesterday, Twilight would be bragging about his power dives and reverse spiral twists. Gylfie and Digger would both be talking about how exciting their practices were, and he, Soren, would have nothing to say. Maybe he would skip tea. Just as he was having this thought, Bubo waddled over to him.

"It gets better, Soren. It really does. I know this is tough for you. It wasn't the chaw that you wanted, but it's really an honor — double chawed and all. I think you're the first Barn Owl ever to be. Come on now, lad. Come with me. Take tea in the forge. I got some fresh moles, you can have them raw or smoked — whatever takes your fancy, and Cook made a nice milkberry tart."

So Soren followed Bubo into a cave not far from the Great Ga'Hoole Tree, which served as both Bubo's forge and home. Soren had never been in Bubo's cave before and, once one went deep enough into the cave to escape the heat, it was quite comfortable — all fitted up with mole-skin rugs and a surprising number of books. Soren had never taken Bubo for a bookish sort of owl.

He could not help but think of the dying Barred Owl's cave and wondered if that owl had been a blacksmith. But a blacksmith for what? That owl had lived completely alone in those woods. Somehow Soren didn't feel comfortable talking to Bubo about the Barred Owl because it made him think of "you only wish."

"What's this?" Soren said as he spotted a contraption dangling from the ceiling of the cave. It had bright-colored things swirling about, catching the reflections of the many lit candles. As the bright bits swirled, they cast spots of color all over the cave.

"Ah, me whirlyglass. Plonk helped put it together for me."

"Madame Plonk?" Soren couldn't keep the surprise out of his voice. He had never heard anyone refer to her as simply "Plonk."

"Oh, yeah, Plonk and me go back — way back." He winked his eye. Soren wondered if Bubo was part of Madame Plonk's book about her life and fabulous times. "She's got a special relationship with Mags so she can get me lots of bits of glass." Bubo shoved a cup of milkberry tea over to Soren and a morsel of mole. "You know, when you start flying weather with Ezylryb, he won't let you eat meat cooked. He likes you to eat it raw with the fur on it. Says you can't fly into a blizzard or a hurricane with burnt-up meat in your gut and nothing for your gizzard to grind."

"Oh," said Soren. "But who's Mags?"

"Oh, dear me, ain't you never heard of Trader Mags?" Soren shook his head. "I forget, you only just got here a bit ago, didn't you, and Mags, I guess, she hasn't been here since summer."

Bubo pointed a talon at the whirlyglass. "Those bright pieces came from what was called a window in something called a church."

"Churches!" Soren exclaimed. "I know about them. And that's stained glass from their windows! Barn Owls used to live in churches."

"Certainly did. Some still do, live in churches and barns as well, and even castles."

"Castles — what's a castle?"

"Well, it ain't a church and it ain't a barn, but it's a big old fancy thing made from big stones, towers, walls, one of them things that the Others made."

Soren had heard of the Others but he was never exactly sure what the Others were, except that they definitely were not owls, or birds, or really any other living thing that he had ever seen. And, for that matter, they were no longer living. They were creatures from long, long ago, maybe in the time of the first Glaux. Glaux was the most ancient order of owls from which all other owls descended.

"Castles," Soren said dreamily. "Sounds exciting, beautiful — very grand."

"Oh, grand indeed. But you ask me, no owl, Barn Owl or not, belongs in a church or a barn or a castle. Better life in a tree."

"But you live in a cave."

"That's different."

"I don't see why."

Bubo squinted one eye at Soren as if studying him more closely. "Got a lively mind, don't you, lad?"

"I don't know." Soren shrugged self-consciously.

Then, as if trying to change the direction of the conversation, Bubo said abruptly, "Don't you want to know about glass?" Soren nodded again. "Well," continued Bubo, "the churches and castles, they have these windows made of glass and they colored the glass."

"Oh, I read about that in a book in the library."

"Yes, they made it all pretty. Well, Mags the trader, she knows where there are a lot of broken-down old churches with smashed-up windows. Leave it to a magpie to find such bits, but that's their nature and she knows Plonkie."

Plonkie! Soren thought, *They must have been close!*

"Plonkie has a weakness for all these colored bits and things. So Mags always brings a bagful with her here when she comes to trade. Plonk thought this place needed brightening up" — Bubo gestured around the cave with his talons — "so she made me this whirlyglass. Plonk has a number of them in her apartments — as she call her place — ridiculous name, if you ask me."

It did brighten it up, but Soren couldn't help but ask another question. "Don't you miss living in a tree? I mean, it's not like you were born a Burrowing Owl used to living in holes. Don't you miss the sky?"

Soren thought of his own hollow that he shared with Gylfie and Twilight and Digger. There was an opening just the shape of an owl's beak through which they could glimpse the sky. So during the day there was always a pretty slice of blue in their hollow and when they came back from night flights before the dawn rose, it perfectly framed the last of the evening stars. They could feel the wind and hear the stirring of the milkberry vines. Soren did not think he would like living in a cave.

"I warn't born a Burrowing Owl, that's the truth. I be a Great Horned, and it ain't customary for any Great Horned to go about life in a cave. But you see, I be a smith. It's in my gizzard, this feeling for the metals." He gestured toward his bookshelf that indeed had many books about metals and forging. "And we smiths, no matter if we're Great Grays or Great Horneds or Snowies or Spotted Owls, get these special feelings in the old gizzard, you know. We fly, yes, we love the sky, but we is drawn to the earth as well — not like the Burrowing Owls, not the same thing at all. It be a strange and most peculiar force. It's as if all these years working with the iron, we get a bit of the magnet in us, you know. Like them special metals, you know, iron. It's got what we call a field. Well, you'll be learning this in metals class, in higher magnetics, where all the unseeable parts are lined up. It makes this force that draws you — same thing with me — I get drawn to the very earth from which them little flecks of iron come from."

"Flecks!" Soren nearly screamed. Flecks were part of Soren's worst memories from St. Aggie's.

"What's a matter, boy? You gotta yarp? Go right ahead. We ain't formal around here."

"At St. Aggie's, they made us pick apart pellets for bones and things and then something they called 'flecks.' Only first-degree pickers could pick for flecks."

"You don't say?" Bubo blinked his eyes.

"But Gylfie and I never knew what flecks were. And, of course, we could never ask. But we did know they were kept in the library."

"Odd place to keep iron."

"Is that what flecks are — iron?"

"Yes, in their smallest bits, but better if you can find a nice big hunk of iron ore, just like if you can find a nice hunk of silver or gold in a creek. The metals chaw brought me back a very handsome piece of gold the other day. Wouldn't you know Plonk spotted me with it practically as soon as they lit down and was all over me to make something for her. 'Course Boron and Barran will have a thing or two to say 'bout that. Silver, gold, that is all kept for the whole tree and not for one vain old Snowy with a taste for the glitter." He made the soft churring sound of laughter. "Speaking of which, Plonk's going to start singing good light any minute. You better fly on up to your hollow. A lot to do tomorrow. Elvan thinks you'll be ready to fly with the coals. Now you pay attention, son. Don't go smacking into Otulissa like you nearly did in practice." Then he squinted at Soren. "You know, not everyone is chosen to be double chawed like you. Boron and Barran must think you got something special. And Ezylryb, too."

"But why me? I don't get it. I'm not that special."

"Oh, but you are. You had the mark on you."

"The mark on me? What are you talking about?"

"Ezylryb spotted it. None of the rest of us could see it, of course. He got something special with that squinted eye of his. You'd been messing about with coals — hadn't you, lad? Ain't nothing to be ashamed of. Good Glaux, no! Flew with one, maybe?" Bubo cocked his head and looked quizzically at Soren.

"I did, but I washed off the smudge."

"Ah, but you still be marked. Only none else can see it, except Ezylryb. He's a tough one, Ezylryb. And smart! Smartest owl in the whole place. He wouldn't just choose any old owl. He wanted you, mark or no mark. So you be all you can be, Soren."

Be all you can be. What exactly did that mean? Especially when he wasn't even sure what he wanted to be, except not in a double chaw with Otulissa and have Ezylryb as his ryb. Soren kept thinking of Bubo's words long after Madame Plonk's song had ended, and Twilight and Gylfie and Digger were asleep. Or at least he thought so. But just then he heard the slightly raspy voice of Digger curling through the milky light that slipped in through the opening of their hollow.

"Soren, are you all right?"

"Yeah, why?"

"I'm just worried about you. I mean, you've been so quiet since the tapping, and you didn't come to tea, and all."

"Well, don't worry, Digger, it's not your problem."

"But it is."

"No, it's not, Digger. You worry too much. You just need to worry about yourself. Not me. That's not your job."

"It's not a job, Soren," Digger said with a slight edge in his voice. "It is what I am."

"Now what do you mean by that?"

"Well, you might think I'm only a Burrowing Owl, you know, perfect for tracking with my long strong legs, but I am more than just this bunch of feathers and bare legs. I can't explain it. I just feel things. And right now I am feeling very sorry, very bad for you."

Soren blinked. He thought about what Digger had just said. It made him think of his conversation with Bubo, who had, in a sense, said the same thing. When he asked

383

Bubo why he lived in a cave, he said that he was not simply a Great Horned Owl. In other words, Bubo, like Digger, was not just a bunch of feathers on a pair of legs, weak or strong, with a pair of wings. He was something more, and it was this that had drawn him to a cave in the earth to live, closer to the metals he knew and worked with. Maybe this was what Bubo had meant when he told Soren to be all he could be. Maybe it had something to do with an owl's true nature that went beyond his or her species as a Barn Owl or a Burrowing Owl. Soren's head swirled with these confusing thoughts.

Then Digger asked a truly astounding question. "Soren, what do you think it means to be an owl?"

"I don't know. I mean, I'm not sure what you mean."

"I'm not sure, either," Digger said. "But it's just as if it is so easy to describe us. You know, there are so many things that we have that are different from other birds, but do you really think that is the meaning of being an owl? Just because our heads can spin nearly all the way around, that we can see what other birds cannot at night, that we fly slow and silent — is it just these differences that make us owls?"

"Digger, why do you ask these questions? They're impossible to answer."

"Maybe that's why I ask them — because they are impossible to answer. It's kind of exciting. It means that there can be unexpected truths and meanings to why we are what we are. You see — that is why I know I am much more than strong legs and weak wings. And you are, too, Soren — you are more than your lovely white face and your sharp ears that can hear anything and your strange black eyes."

Digger was a curious owl. There was certainly no doubt about it. Soren looked out the opening into the last of the morning as it began to blare into the lightness of midday. If, indeed, what Digger said was true — that there were unexpected truths and meanings to be found, Soren wondered what that might mean for him. He looked at his friends sleeping peacefully now: Twilight, huge, a luminous silvery gray in the morning light; Gylfie, like a little dusty smudge not much longer than one of Twilight's talons; and Digger, his peculiar, featherless legs, long and sinewy, his stubby tail, and his rather flattish head.

Soren remembered when, in anticipation of going to the Great Ga'Hoole Tree, he and Gylfie imagined it as just the opposite of St. Aggie's, but it was really much more. And maybe he could become more, too. The beak-shaped opening in the hollow flared white in the noonday sun as Soren finally fell asleep.

CHAPTER SIXTEEN
The Voices in the Roots

P sst ... pssst," something hissed in Soren's ear.

"Gylfie, what are you doing up at this hour? It's broad daylight. Are you yoicks?"

"Not at all." Soren could see that Gylfie was practically hopping up and down with excitement. "Soren, there's a very important meeting going on in the parliament hollow."

"So?"

"Soren, I think they are talking about the Barred Owl and" — Gylfie gulped and shut her eyes tight — "and ... and ..." Gylfie was seldom at a loss for words. "The 'you only wish.'"

Soren was suddenly fully awake. "You're kidding."

"I wouldn't kid about something like this, Soren, and you know it."

"How do you know this? I mean, how did you find out? Were you in the meeting?"

Gylfie blinked and looked down at her tiny talons in

embarrassment. "Look, I know it's not nice to eavesdrop, but I couldn't sleep and you know how Cook always says come down to the kitchen if we can't sleep and she'll make us a nice cup of milkberry tea. So I went down, and on my way back I just thought I'd take a different route, so I followed one of those deep inner passageways that is very winding and pretty narrow, and it actually started to go down instead of up toward the sleeping hollows. There's a spot where something happens to the timber of the Great Ga'Hoole Tree. It is very thin, and I could hear voices, and then I found this perfect slot that is just Elf Owl size."

"Do they have one just Barn Owl size?" Soren interrupted.

"Maybe. There's an even better one my size higher up, but I would need a perch."

"At your service, Gylf!" Twilight was suddenly awake. "What a team we'll make. On the shoulders of giants, the little Elf will bring back the word!"

"Twilight, puhleeze!" Soren said.

"Why not? Makes perfect sense."

"Well, I might not be a giant like you, but I can hear better than any of you. I'm going, too. So count me in," said Soren.

"Me, too." Digger was stretching his legs and seemed at least half awake.

"Do you even know what we're talking about?" Gylfie turned to the Burrowing Owl.

"No, but we're a band, remember? Nobody gets left out. Fill me in on the way to whatever we're doing."

And so the band of four, as quietly as possible, moved out of their hollow with Gylfie in the lead. They left by the sky opening and flew a quarter way down the tree, where they entered a very small opening that Gylfie had discovered, which twisted and turned, pitched and curled through the huge trunk of the tree, until they had wound around to the back side of the Parliament hollow and found themselves actually slightly beneath that hollow, in the root structure of the tree. It was not that the walls were thin, Soren soon realized. It was rather that the roots of the Great Ga'Hoole Tree were transmitting the sounds.

Gylfie hopped on Twilight's shoulders and Soren pressed one ear to a root, as did Digger.

"And so you say, Bubo, that no trace of the dear Barred Owl was found? Our noble servant perished in the region of The Beaks?"

The four eavesdropping owls blinked and suppressed gasps of astonishment. It had to be the same owl. It just had to. Soren pressed his ear closer.

"Not rightly sure if he exactly perished, Boron. I mean he mightn't be dead. He might just be captured."

"By St. Aggie's patrols or . . ." Now all four owls strained to hear, but they could not make out what Boron had said. Indeed, it seemed as if there was a little hole in the conversation, as if a word had dropped out, perhaps a word too awful to say. Soren wasn't sure. But he felt a chill run through him.

"Either way it's a bad piece of work." It was Ezylryb's voice. Soren could tell.

"We done lost one of our best slipgizzles and a darned fine smith as well, one of the best of the rogues." Bubo was speaking again.

What is a slipgizzle? Digger mouthed the words. Soren shrugged. He had never heard the word before. He might have heard the word "rogue" but he wasn't sure what that meant, either.

"Without a reliable slipgizzle," now Barran was speaking, "it's going to make it very difficult to get any information about their activities in The Beaks."

"It was a very strategic spot where he set up his forge."

So that was it! thought Soren. That cave that, as Digger had said, not only held the spirit of the Barred Owl within its walls, sooty and scorched by countless fires, but also was his forge. He was a blacksmith, like Bubo. But he was also something else — a slipgizzle. Gradually, the four owls began to understand that a slipgizzle was some sort of owl who listened hard and found out things.

"That old Barred had ears like a Barn Owl," Boron was saying. "We got more information from him than three other slipgizzles put together. And, as you said, my dear, his forge in The Beaks was ideally situated near the four points area where Ambala, The Beaks, Kuneer, and Tyto almost touch. Couldn't be better. Flew egg guard in Tyto, I hear. Trained up a bunch of young ones to go into Ambala when they were having the worst of their problems. . . . Oh, my. Well, to the immediate business. We must not lose a moment in shoring up the four points region. We're going to need to cultivate a new slipgizzle, of course, but in the meantime we'll have to send out some egg patrols and a small reconnaissance team. Nothing too big. Don't want to attract undue attention. I don't need to tell you how dangerous it will be with the recent reports we've been getting. A lot of groundwork and, as you know, bobcats are numerous there."

"I'll go!" a voice said. Soren blinked. It was that old boring Ga'Hoology ryb.

"Count me in," said Bubo.

390

"And me." It was the voice of another owl that Soren didn't recognize.

"I think that's enough," Boron spoke in a low voice. "Bubo, you sure about going?"

"'Course I'm sure, sir. He was a smith."

"Yes, Bubo, I know that, but you are our only smith. If we lose you . . . well, where would we be?"

"I ain't going to get lost, sir. Ain't going to get captured. Ain't going to get eaten by a bobcat. You need me on this mission. I can see what happened in that cave. It takes a smith's eye and a smith's nose to figure something like this out. He couldn't have just vanished into thin air, and I don't believe the Barred could have been captured by St. Aggie's or them others. But there'll be clues."

Them others? It was so maddening, Soren thought. Who were they? Who exactly was the "you only wish" Barred Owl?

"Well," continued Boron, "that taken care of, I think the time has now come to honor our brother the Barred Owl, who had no name and elected never to live with us on this island in the middle of the sea, never to be embraced by the lovely ancient limbs of our Great Ga'Hoole Tree, but served as nobly in his own peculiar way as any Knight of Ga'Hoole. Let us raise a flagon of milkberry mead and think gentle thoughts of this brave and noble owl who made safer the hollows and nestlings of so many other owls in the Kingdoms of Ambala, Kuneer, and Tyto. Slipgizzle beyond compare, artisan of metals, courageous defender against the growing tides of evil, a Glaux-blessed owl. Hear! Hear!"

And with that, the parliament of owls was adjourned. An immense fluttering swelled up as they left. Soren, Gylfie, Twilight, and Digger looked at one another with tears in their eyes.

"And to think," Digger said, "that we are the ones who found him."

"But that's just the problem," said Gylfie. "What do we do now? Tell Boron and Barran that?"

"Then they'll know we were eavesdropping," Twilight said.

"Precisely," Gylfie replied.

Soren began to speak slowly, "I think we shouldn't say anything, at least not now. Nothing we will say will change their plans. They still need to send in a reconnaissance team or whatever they call it and find a new slipgizzle. Our knowing that the Barred Owl is dead and telling them really doesn't change anything."

"I think Soren's right," Gylfie spoke. "You know, eavesdropping like this . . . well . . . I have a feeling Boron would really be mad."

"Definitely," said Twilight.

So the four owls wound their way back to their hollow and slept until First Black.

CHAPTER SEVENTEEN
Weather Chaw

A sliver of wet ice hit Soren's face and woke him up abruptly. Outside the hollow, the wind shrieked and a gale raged.

"Great Glaux, it's a mess out there," Twilight muttered.

"It's cold, too," said Gylfie, her tiny body shivering.

"Hop under here," Twilight said, and spread one of his enormous wings so that it touched the other side of the hollow and knocked Digger from his bed.

"Twilight!" Digger complained. "Watch it with that wing."

"Gylf is cold."

"I sure hope they will serve something hot for breakfast," Gylfie said through her clattering beak.

"Me, too," said Twilight.

The owls got up and crept from their hollow out onto a madly shaking branch and took off for the dining hollow. There was acorn porridge and steaming cups of milkberry tea, roasted tree slugs and braised mice. But as Soren

394

headed for his place at Mrs. Plithiver's, a voice scratched the air.

"Over here, boy. Weather chaw eats it raw with the hair on." It was the unmistakable voice of Ezylryb.

"What?" Soren beaked the word in disbelief.

"You mean you haven't heard?" Otulissa was suddenly beside him.

"Heard what?" Soren said, not sure if he really wanted to know.

"We're having our first weather interpretation chaw tonight."

"You have to be kidding, Otulissa. We aren't going out in this gale."

"Oh, but we are," she said. "And I think it's outrageous. I'm going to have a word with Strix Struma. I'll go right up to Barran if I have to. This is reckless. This is endangering our lives."

"Oh, hush up, dearie. Sit down and eat your mouse — and all the hair, mind you, and that goes for every one of you." It was the fat old blind snake named Octavia, who had served as the weather chaw table for years. Unlike the other blind snakes whose scales were colors varying from rose to pink to a deep coral, Octavia was a pale greenish-blue. Soren sat next to Martin, the smart little Northern Saw-whet who had asked the question in colliering practice about the need for fresh coals. Indeed, Soren realized suddenly that there was more room at the table than he was accustomed to and as he looked about he knew it was because all of the young owls in the weather chaw seemed to have diminished in size. Their feathers were pulled in tightly, indications that the owls were very nervous about their first weather flight. When relaxed, an owl's plumage is loose and fluffy. When angered, owls can puff up their feathers until they appear much, much larger. But now it was as if they had all become suddenly slim. The tension hovered in the air.

Ezylryb fixed the young owls in the amber light of his squinted eye. "Eat up, maties . . . every single little hair. You've forgotten what raw meat tastes like with the fur, as you call it. Poot here is my first mate. He'll tell you what it's like to fly with no ballast in your gizzard."

"I remember that time before I had acquired the taste for hair and thought I could go through that hurricane. Last time I ever tried that. Nearly got caught in the rim of the eye, I did. Now, you don't want to do that, young'uns." Poot was a Boreal Owl like Soren and Gylfie's old friend Grimble.

"What happens if you get caught in the rim of the eye of a hurricane?" asked Rudy.

"Oh, you spin around till you're dead. Just around and

around and around. Awful nasty way to go. Usually get your wings torn off in the process," said Poot.

"Now, don't go scaring them, Poot," Octavia said and gave a ripple so that all their plates clattered a bit. "And please, young'uns, don't try that trick of slipping the fur under the table. Remember, I *am* the table and it itches something fierce."

It was not even dark yet, but the weather chaw owls were already on the takeoff limb. It was all they could do to hang on as the gale lashed about them and the limb bucked in the turbulent wind. Shards of ice flew through the air.

"We take off upwind, naturally." Although Soren was not sure in this gale which way upwind even was. "We're going to fly straight out over the Sea of Hoolemere. Try to find the main part of the gale." Ezylryb spoke in short snappish sentences. "Now listen up. Here's what you need to know about a gale, or any storm, really — except for hurricanes — they be a little different with their eyes and all. But what you got in a gale, or storm, is you got your gutter. That's what we call the main trough where the wind runs its punch through. It's at the center. It not be like the eye in a hurricane. Not nearly so dangerous. Then on either side of the gutter you've got the scuppers. That's where the edge of the winds from the gutters spills over. Then at the very outside edge of the scuppers you got your swillages — more about them later. I fly point. Poot flies what we call upwind scupper. You just follow behind. Do what you're told. Any questions?"

Otulissa raised her talon. "Ezylryb, sir, with all due respect, I have to say that I am surprised that we are going out before it is completely dark. Isn't there a very real danger that in this light we could be mobbed by crows?"

Ezylryb began to laugh and then said, "With all due respect, Otulissa, no one else is yoicks enough to be out on a day like this!"

Soren couldn't help but laugh. But how could he be laughing when he was scared to death? Then again, how could he have been bored in colliering chaw when he was also scared? If this was being all one could be, as Bubo had told him, he certainly had a lot of confusing feelings.

And then, suddenly, with an enormous scream, the old Whiskered Screech Owl spread his wings and lifted into the ice-spun twilight.

They flew straight out over the Sea of Hoolemere. The storm was so fierce and the torrents of sleeting rain so thick they could barely see the water, but they did hear the crashing waves. Otulissa was flying near Soren.

"I have never heard of a ryb who used such poor judgment. This is so irresponsible. I am going to have to speak with Boron and Barran. I cannot believe that they would approve of this."

Soren, meanwhile, could not believe that Otulissa could fly through this mess and still keep talking. It took all of his concentration just to fly. The winds seemed to come from every direction. They were constantly buffeted by confused drafts. Martin, the little Saw-whet, was a tumbling blur ahead of him. He had been instructed, as the smallest, to begin flying in Ezylryb's wake for better control.

One minute the owls might be buoyed up several hundred feet and the next they might fly into a dead fall, a kind of hole in the wind, and drop. And, of course, there was the ice and rain. Constantly, Soren was having to use the transparent eyelid, the third eyelid that all owls have, to clear out the debris. Great Glaux, he hoped his third lid didn't simply wear out under these conditions. No wonder Ezylryb squinted. A lifetime of flying into this stuff would be enough to shred any owl's eyelid.

"Oh, for Glaux's sake," Otulissa hissed.

"What now?" Soren said, trying to anticipate the next dead fall, almost hoping for it, to get away from Otulissa.

"He is speaking with seagulls!"

"So?"

"So? How can you say 'so,' Soren? I know you come from a very fine family. I can see that you have been well brought up. You must know that seagulls are the absolute worst kind of bird. They are, pardon the coarseness of my language, the scum of the avian world. Trashy, loud. You want nothing to do with them. And look, there he is talking — laughing with them."

"Maybe he's getting weather information from them," Soren said.

"Oh, now that's a thought," Otulissa said and was quiet for several seconds, an amazing occurrence in and of itself. "I think I'll fly up and ask him."

"Don't bother him, Otulissa."

"No, you heard him say if we had any questions we should ask." So off she flew.

"Pardon me, Ezylryb. I am most curious to know why you were — how shall I put it — consorting with seagulls? I thought perhaps it was to gain weather information."

"Seagulls? Oh, no, darlin'. They are the dumbest birds on earth and the laziest."

"Well, then why would you even consort with them?"

"I wasn't consorting. I was telling dirty jokes."

"What?" Otulissa gasped.

"Yes, they love wet poop jokes even though they are the wettest of all poopers. 'Oh, tell us another one Ezyl,' they always say! And, I must admit, I get a few from them. But the blasted birds are so dumb, half the time they can't remember the punch lines. Very frustrating."

"Well, I never!"

"The jokes were really funny, Otulissa," Martin, the Northern Saw-whet, piped up.

"Now, don't go getting your feathers in a twist, darlin'. You just mind your own business. Get back into position. We're getting near the gutter now. And this is when the fun begins."

"Hoooh-hah!" Poot let out an enormous, raucous hoot. "Here we go, mates. Climbing the baggywrinkles and then straight into the gutter. Follow us!" The baggy-wrinkles were the shredded air currents that lay between the scuppers and the gutter. A power thrust was required to get over them. Soren banked and followed the veteran owl, Poot. Martin was in between the two. The tiny owl would get a boost from Poot's speed, as a vacuum would be created, through which he could be sucked up and over the baggywrinkles right into the gutter. Ruby was just ahead of him. She let escape a small joyous hoot. And then, suddenly, Soren knew why. Here, at the center of the gale, in the gutter, the winds all seemed to flow like one great turbulent river. And if one let one's wings sweep slightly forward, just as Ruby was doing, and angled the tail — well, it was a wonderful sensation, a cross between soaring and gliding — no effort at all. And in the gutter, the ice shards seemed to melt away.

"Oh, tickle me hollow bones. Ain't this the life!" It was Ezylryb, who had dropped back from the point position and now flew between Soren and Otulissa. He yarped a pellet into the river of wind that flowed about them. "Now follow me to the edge of the scuppers, maties, and I'll show you the hurly-burly. And then we'll climb the baggywrinkles and dump right into the scuppers for the ride of your life."

"What is he talking about?" huffed Otulissa. "He should have given us a vocabulary list. He's very disorganized as a teacher."

Why would a vocabulary list matter? Soren thought. What was the use of a word if one could not feel the action in his gizzard? And right now Soren's gizzard was in a fantastic quiver of excitement. This was flying as he had never known it.

"Here we go!" cried Ezylryb. "Now I want to see you punch the wind and then we pop the scuppers and it's tail over talons."

"Oh, my heavens!" Otulissa shrieked and Soren gasped

as he saw the distinctive three-taloned foot of Ezylryb scratch the moon-smudged sky. He was flying on his back! Then right side up and in the scuppers.

Suddenly, Soren saw a red blur as Ruby did a talons-over-tail somersault and popped the scuppers to join him. "Oh, come on!" she cried. "There's nothing to it."

"Nothing to it. Who's ever heard of an owl flying upside down? I think there's something most unsavory about it!" Otulissa gasped. "It's reckless, unsafe — yes, unsavory, unsafe, un-owl."

Oh, shut up! Soren thought and punched the wind just as Ezylryb said, and in a flash he was arcing up toward the sky that spun with dark clouds and was splattered with sheets of icy rain, and then he was right side up in the scuppers next to Ruby.

"Push forward a bit with your talons and keep angling your tail. It gives you a lot of control and you can ride the waves," Ezylryb called back.

Finally, Otulissa arrived, sputtering with rage and talking about a report that she was going to make about "this outrageous activity."

"Oh, shut your beak!" Poot screeched at her. And then they skidded and spun, doing what was called the hurly-burly. In the scuppers, Ezylryb began to squawk a raucous ditty into the teeth of the gale.

We are the owls of the weather chaw.
We take it blistering,
We take it all.
Roiling boiling gusts,
We're the owls with the guts.
For blizzards our gizzards
Do tremble with joy.
An ice storm, a gale, how we love blinding hail.
We fly forward and backward,
Upside down and flat.
Do we flinch? Do we wail?
Do we skitter or scutter?
No, we yarp one more pellet
And fly straight for the gutter!
Do we screech? Do we scream?
Do we gurgle? Take pause?
Not on your life!
For we are the best
Of the best of the chaws!

CHAPTER EIGHTEEN
Mrs. Plithiver's Dilemma

F lying upside down!" Primrose gasped. "How do you do that? It's impossible."

"It's not as hard as you think," Soren said excitedly. "It really doesn't take that much skill. It's kind of like when you first start to fly. You have to just sort of believe you can do it."

"But upside down?" Gylfie said.

"Do you think a big burly Gray like me could do it?" Twilight said.

"Sure, if the conditions are right. See, that's the problem — you can't try it until you're in the gutter of a gale."

"Gutter of a gale?" Twilight said. "You telling me a gale has a gutter? Now, I've seen a lot but . . ." It was hard for Twilight to admit that anyone had seen or experienced something he had not.

Gylfie and Soren looked at each other and blinked in amazement. Twilight did brag, but he did not have that obnoxious sense of superiority that Otulissa had. Still, he was constantly getting reprimanded in his chaw practices for challenging the rybs. Sometimes he could be annoying but, in spite of this, he was a "good soul," as Mrs. P. would put it. There was never an owl more fiercely loyal than Twilight. As Digger often said, "He makes the best friend and the worst enemy."

"You might not have seen the gutter of a gale," Gylfie said, trying to restrain the peevish note in her voice. "I know you've seen a lot, Twilight, but it is possible that you have not penetrated a gale in the same manner Soren did, under the instruction of Ezylryb."

"Oh, I've flown into the teeth of many a gale, Gylf. I might have been in the gutter and not known I was there. That I admit. Soren here, talking about all this structure of a gale business — just words, you know. No offense, mind you, Soren. But you can fly through something and not know what it's called."

"Yes, I think you're right. Otulissa was making a big fuss about how Ezylryb should have given us a vocabulary list before we took off last night."

"Oh, honestly," Primrose muttered, "was there ever a duller owl?"

"Well, I am going to the library because that's part of our assignment now — to read up on the structure of gales and blizzards and hurricanes. But I'm glad we flew it first. I think it will have more meaning. We're supposed to have a test soon."

"A flying test or a book test?" Gylfie asked.

"Book test. I promised to help Ruby. She's a fantastic flier but she has a hard time with book things — reading and writing."

"Believe me, as long as she can fly that's what counts." Twilight nodded.

"The grand old sage of the Orphan School of Tough Learning!" Gylfie muttered.

Mrs. Plithiver gave a slight flinch as she often did when she heard an unkind remark at her tea table. It was then that Soren realized that Mrs. Plithiver had barely said a word during the entire teatime. This was most unusual, especially since he had come back so excited from weather chaw. Normally, she would have been thrilled over Soren's enthusiasm. He hoped nothing was the matter. If there was time before good light, after he went to the library, he would go visit her.

Soren flew up to the library humming happily the last verse of the weather chaw song. *How quickly life changes*, he thought. It was only yesterday that he had returned from walking around with a live coal in his beak, thinking that life could not be much worse — unless, of course, he was in St. Aggie's picking pellets in the pelletorium. And now he was a member of the best of the best of the chaws.

When he entered the library he saw Ezylryb in his usual spot with a pile of dried caterpillars. He trotted up to him. "Hello, Ezylryb. It was a wonderful chaw. Do you think there's any chance of another gale coming through soon — or maybe a tornado? Poot says tornadoes are fantastic to fly."

But Ezylryb barely looked up from his book and growled in that unfriendly way he had. Soren took a step back. He was confused. How could Ezylryb be so different now than he had been when they were flying? During weather chaw, Ezylryb had been loud and boisterous and cracking wet poop jokes and singing raucously, and now he was just Ezylryb, a distant, gruff old scholar with his beak buried in a book. "Better study for your test. And Ruby over there needs some help. Flies like a dream but can't spell worth a pellet."

Soren backed away and then turned to Ruby, who was hunched over the book *Weather Systems and Their Structure: How to Fly Them, Analyze Them, and Survive Them,* by Ezekiel Ezylryb.

"This is sooo hard, Soren! I'll never pass the test."

"Oh, come on, Ruby. You'll do fine. Anyone who flies like you can't flunk a test."

"But it's all these words. I feel flight in my gizzard, but, you know, I can't feel words in my gizzard, except maybe when Madame Plonk sings."

Soren blinked. What Ruby said he thought was probably quite true. "Look, Ruby, I don't think you should try and feel words in your gizzard. You just have to learn a little bit of what they mean in your head — just for the test. Come on, I'll help you. Let's see the book."

Soren took a look. There were a lot of pictures, drawings of storms and hurricanes and blizzards. Soren flipped through the pages with his talon. "Let's start right here with a gale, because that is what we know."

"But what in Glaux's name is a pyte?" Ruby said.

From the corner of the room came a voice. "A pyte is a unit of measurement roughly the wingspan of a Whiskered Screech like meself. It is used for measuring the different structures of a weather system such as gutters, scuppers, et cetera."

"What's et cetera?" whispered Ruby.

"I don't think that's an important word," Soren said. "Now we know what a pyte is, and that's what counts."

Ruby wasn't what Soren would call dumb, but she certainly had terrible handwriting and difficulty with large words. "Finning in the sw —" She read the heading at the top of one page.

"Finning in the swillages," Soren said.

"What is that?" Ruby asked.

"Ruby, you did it. You were the only one who could do it. Don't you remember? You climbed the baggywrinkles out of the scuppers and flew right on the upper edge, twitching your tail. It was very advanced."

"Oh, you mean like this?" And Ruby did a perfect re-creation of what she had done that night.

"Yes, that's it. And it says here that the swillages are measured in tailspans of the individual owl. So if you feel the breeze on either side of your tail at one time you know that it is one tailspan wide."

"Oh, I'll never remember all this! The words, the numbers, it's too much."

"Yes, you will, Ruby."

Otulissa had just come into the library and was pulling out another book on weather interpretation.

"Did you get your chaw changed, Otulissa?" Soren whispered, for he knew she had applied directly to Barran.

Otulissa blinked. Large tears were forming in her eyes. "No! I'm stuck and I can't fly nearly as well as either of you. I'll probably get killed."

For the first time, Soren felt really sorry for Otulissa. Just then a dried caterpillar dropped into the book she had opened.

"You'll do fine, child. Spotted Owls have an amazing talent for sensing pressure changes. Of course, it does make them fussy and hard to live with. I suggest you read that book over there — *Atmospheric Pressures and Turbulations: An Interpreter's Guide*. It was written by Strix Emerilla, a renowned weathertrix of the last century. But I always want a Spotted Owl in my chaw, even if they continually beak off." Ezylryb, with his odd three-taloned walk, hobbled out of the library.

Confound that owl, Soren thought. *He is as impenetrable as any weather system.* Here, he had hardly spoken to Soren and now seemed to go out of his way to chat it up with Otulissa.

"A Strix wrote this?" Otulissa said as she opened the book. "Oh, my goodness, it could be a relative. And, of course, you know, to become a weathertrix requires the most highly refined sensitivities of all. No wonder a Strix would become one. With our ancient lineage, I would imagine these skills have been honed to perfection through the ages."

Oh, Glaux, did this owl ever shut up? Soren decided to go visit Mrs. P. before good light.

"Well, I don't know. I just don't know. I don't think I'm sure about anything, really." Soren stopped just outside the small hollow that Mrs. P. shared with the two other nest snakes. It was the sadness in Mrs. P.'s voice that really stopped him. Mrs. P. never sounded this way. She was always so positive and full of hope. He listened for a few moments.

"The harp guild is the most prestigious and I think it is my destiny to become a member," the other snake was saying. "You know, the way the owls feel things in their gizzards. Now I know that we don't have gizzards, but even so."

"Mercy! The very idea." Mrs. P. sounded genuinely shocked by the suggestion. She spoke sharply now. "I think it is very presumptuous of us to ever think of ourselves as anything like these noble owls. We are not of their station." Now she was sounding like herself again. Mrs. P. did not have feelings of inferiority. She felt she was the best nest-maid snake ever, but she would never presume, as she said, to think she shared anything with the members of the finest class of birds. Her duty in life was to serve them, and to serve them well was a noble task.

"But Mrs. P.," the snake continued, "you must have some preference for a guild."

"Oh, it is more than a preference. When we went for our tour of the guilds, I knew immediately that the harp was for me. As I slipped through the strings from one note to another, climbing the scales, leaping octaves, the vibrations never left me. And the very best part was to try to — oh, how shall I explain — weave the music into Madame Plonk's voice. So that together the sound of the harp and the sound of Madame Plonk's voice made something so large and splendid."

Soren blinked. Mrs. P., he thought, had something much better than a gizzard.

"Must be off myself," the other nest snake said cheerily. "I'm just going around to drop in on Octavia, bring her a few well-seasoned milkberries. She does love them so and, as you know, she does keep the nest for Madame Plonk. Never can hurt, can it? Ta-ta!" And she slithered out of the hollow.

Soren wedged himself into a corner where he wouldn't be seen. But he heard Mrs. P. muttering after the other snake was out of earshot. "To presume to have a gizzard and then go slithering off to Octavia, humming tunes and besieging her with milkberries. Well, I never!"

Soren decided to skip visiting Mrs. P. He knew what he must do. He must "drop by" Madame Plonk's, and he must tell her that here was a very special snake, a snake that had something even finer than a gizzard, a snake of the highest — what was that word Mrs. P. was always using? — "Sensibilities, artistic sensibilities."

CHAPTER NINETEEN
A Visit to Madame Plonk

You see, Madame Plonk, I know that perhaps this is not proper — me coming to you this way." Soren could hardly keep his mind on what he was saying, as he had never in his life seen a hollow like this one. The air spun with colored light from the whirlyglasses that hung from the ceiling and sometimes jutted out from the walls, suspended on twigs jammed into cracks. There were several openings through which light poured. There were pieces of cloth embroidered with beautiful designs and one little niche spilled over with strands of luminous beads. Indeed, the hollow seemed to swirl with color. And in the middle of all this color there was a dazzling whiteness — Madame Plonk.

Soren gulped and tried to keep his eyes from straying from that whiteness. "But I just know that Mrs. P. is rather shy and would never dare."

"Mrs. P.?" Madame Plonk broke in. "I don't believe I know this snake."

"She came with me, ma'am. She's my family's old nest-maid snake."

"Oh, and you were saying that she wants to be in the harp guild?"

"Yes, ma'am." Soren thought he sounded so stupid. *Who cares?* he thought. He was here for Mrs. P. She wanted this so much. Then it was as if Madame Plonk nearly took his next thought directly out of his head.

"But wanting is one thing. One cannot merely want."

"Yes, yes, just because you want something doesn't mean it should always happen."

Madame Plonk blinked and nodded. "Very wise, young'un. But tell me now — why do you think she, this Mrs. P. as you call her, wants it?"

An idea suddenly popped into Soren's head. "You know," he began thoughtfully, "some snakes might want it just because it is thought of as the most important guild, one for snakes who have served in nests of very old, distinguished families. But I don't think that is why Mrs. P. wants it."

"No?" Madame Plonk seemed surprised.

Soren had a dreadful feeling that he had said something wrong. He took a deep breath. There was no backing out of it now. "No, I don't think she gives two pellets about that kind of thing."

Madame Plonk blinked.

She's laughing at me, Soren thought. But he continued. "I think she wants to be a member of this guild not because it is the most important but because it is the most artistic."

Madame Plonk gave a little gasp. "That's very interesting. Now what do you mean by artistic, young'un?"

Oh, dear, Soren thought. It was as if his gizzard had just dropped out of him. He had no idea what he meant by artistic. But he knew that what he had said was right in some way.

Madame Plonk waited.

Soren continued. "When Mrs. P. spoke about music she said how when she visited the great harp, she tried to weave the notes not just through the strings of the harp but into your voice. So that together the sound of the harp and the sound of your voice made something that she called splendid and grand. Well, I think that is what it means to be an artist."

There was silence in the apartments. And then Madame Plonk sighed deeply and reached for a hankie made by the lacemakers' guild. She blew her beak and dabbed her eyes. "You are most unusual for a Barn Owl." Soren did not know if that was good or bad. "Now I think you must go. It is almost time for Evensong. So, go along. I hear you're doing quite well in weather chaw." Soren was about to ask how she knew about weather chaw but then remembered that Octavia took care of both Madame Plonk's and Ezylryb's nests. "Now fly along."

"Yes, yes, thank you for your time, Madame Plonk," Soren said, backing out of the hollow.

"Octavia!" Madame Plonk called as soon as Soren had left. "Octavia, come in here immediately."

The fat old nest snake slithered in from a branch where she had hung herself just outside the apartment.

"Did you hear that, Octavia?"

"Yes, ma'am. I think we got ourselves a G-flat!"

CHAPTER TWENTY

Fire!

Ezylryb perched on a limb at the very top of the Great Ga'Hoole Tree and squinted into the blueness of the early summer day. He had been perched here for the last two days almost continuously with Poot by his side. They were studying the cloud behavior on the far side of Hoolemere.

"Bring the chaw up," he ordered tersely. "There's enough for them to observe."

"What! What!" Soren yawned sleepily as Poot shook him awake. "It's the middle of the day, Poot. We're supposed to be sleeping."

"Not now, young'un. Important lesson, top of the tree. Cap wants you there now. Quick-o!"

What could it be? Soren thought. Poot only called Ezylryb "Cap" when they were on a flight mission. But there wasn't any bad weather. It was a calm, perfectly clear day. It was the time of the golden rain, when the strands of

Ga'Hoole berries that hung from the limbs turned a rich yellow.

By the time Soren got to the top limb, the others had assembled — albeit sleepily. Martin was yawning into the morning sun, but Otulissa was alert and full of questions and already peppering the air with her observations of cloud formations. Ruby yarped her morning pellet and looked to Soren as if she was so sleepy she might pitch forward off the limb. Just at that moment, Bubo and Elvan arrived. This was the first time Soren had seen Bubo for a while. Presumably, he had been on the reconnaissance mission to The Beaks, and, thankfully, returned safely, as had the others.

"Put a mouse in it, Otulissa," Bubo growled and delivered a field mouse headfirst into the talkative owl's beak.

"Thank you, Bubo," Ezylryb said in a low growl and blinked.

"Now, anyone know why we are here?" Ezylryb turned to the owls of the weather chaw. Otulissa's talon immediately shot up even though she could not yet talk with her beak stuffed full of mouse. Soren looked around. This was the first time the three rybs, although Bubo was not officially a ryb, had ever been together with the weather chaw. It was obvious: The days of practicing with Bubo's coals from the forge were over. They were now going into a forest fire. A silence fell upon the young owls. They pulled in their feathers tight to their sides. The only sound was Otulissa gulping the last of the mouse. Then, in barely a whisper, her voice shaking with fear, she said, "But I just ate. How shall I ever fly on such a full stomach?"

"Don't worry," Ezylryb said. "We're not flying yet. Not until later. But I want you up here today because you're going to see how fire changes things — the wind, the clouds. You can see these changes even from here. You see, young'uns, there is a fire burning over there across Hoolemere. A great fire." He bobbed out on the branch toward the water. "So later, we shall cross Hoolemere. Then we'll fetch up on some high cliffs on the other side that are perfect for a closer look. We shall camp there for a day or two and then we shall fly in."

For the rest of the morning, they observed the unique behavior of the clouds on the far side of Hoolemere. The young owls of the weather chaw were used to odd words such as baggywrinkles and scuppers and gutters. But now there were even stranger words as the rybs discussed "pressure differential," "thermal inversions," and "convective columns."

By mid-afternoon, they were dismissed to take a short

nap. They would be awakened at tween time, that time between the last drop of sun and the first shadows of twilight, and then take off across Hoolemere.

"Are you nervous, Ruby?" Soren said as they made their way back from the top limbs for their naps.

"I'd be a fool not to be," replied the rusty-feathered owl.

"But you fly so well."

"Not to mention," Martin added, "that both of you are about twice as big as me."

"What are you most scared of?" Soren asked.

"That thing they call crowning," Ruby said quickly. "When the fire leaps from treetop to treetop. I can't imagine what it does to the air. I mean, flying through it must be almost impossible. You could never even half guess where the dead falls might be."

"Technically, the fire does that" — Otulissa had caught up with them — "because the fire climbs what is called, according to the literature, a fuel ladder."

"Yes, and think of me," Martin now spoke. "I am on the ground, supposedly looking for the smallest embers. One of these crowning things happens, and at my weight I get sucked straight up the fuel ladder."

"We all have to spend time on the ground, not just

you," Soren said. "It could happen to any of us. You don't have to be little." Martin cocked his head and blinked. He did not look convinced.

Although they had yet to be in an actual forest fire, each member of the chaw had a type of coal or ember they were in charge of gathering. Ruby, being the best flier, would seek airborne embers that were dispersed to the highest parts of the thermal draft columns. Soren and Otulissa were assigned a midpoint position on various sides of the convection column and little Martin was on the ground. But, indeed, they would all have to do a certain amount of groundwork.

Soren could not help but think about how different this flight across Hoolemere was from the time he had crossed the sea to the Great Ga'Hoole Tree nearly six months before. He remembered how the blizzard had raged, how the entire world had turned a swirling white, and the sky and water had melted into one indistinguishable mass. Today, the air was clear, the sea below calm with barely a white cap to ruffle the blueness. Seagulls dipped in the last rays of the setting sun. The silvery glint of a fish leaping to escape a larger fish sometimes flashed above the water's surface. Yet as they drew closer to the opposite shore, the air did seem different. And although Soren, like other owls, did not have the keenest sense of smell, the air seemed tinged with an acrid odor.

They landed on the ridge of some high cliffs. Ezylryb was already pointing with his three-taloned foot to some clouds just beyond the ridge. "We call them Ga'Hoole clouds. You know why?"

Otulissa's talon shot up. "Because they are the shape of the seeds found in the Ga'Hoole fruits."

"Right-o, missy," Ezylryb said.

Martin gave a little sigh. "She never stops, does she?"

It was clear that Martin was very nervous. More nervous than the others. Soren felt bad for him. He was the smallest owl in the chaw. It had to be scary. "Don't worry, Martin. You're going to be all right."

"Soren, that's kind of you, but do you realize that I am the first Saw-whet to ever be in the colliering chaw?"

"They must think you're special, Martin," Soren said.

"But what if I'm not?" Martin said, a squeak of desperation creeping into his voice.

Ezylryb continued speaking about the Ga'Hoole clouds. "The reason their tops are curved like that is because — well, you tell me."

Once again, Otulissa's talon shot up. "It's simple weather physics. I was reading about it in Emerilla's, the renowned weathertrix's book — she's a Spotted Owl, I might add." Otulissa cast her eyes downward in what Soren thought was an outrageously phony show of modesty.

"Just get to the point, darlin'," Ezylryb barked.

"Oh, yes, of course. It is because the winds atop the cloud are blowing much faster than the winds below."

Soren felt Martin begin to tremble. "I might become one of those burning airborne embers that Ruby grabs on the fly," he said in a voice drenched with fear.

"All right now, we camp here and we wait. We wait until the fire is safe for penetration and retrieval. Elvan and Bubo shall take over the mission at that point, directing you to the richest coal and ember beds. I shall remain here and watch the weather and fly in for periodic reports. You do as you're told and no one will get hurt. Ruby and Poot fly top layer. Elvan with Otulissa will be mid-layer. Below them is Soren, who covers Martin on the ground. Bubo and I will be ready if anyone needs help. You are to keep your eye out for your mate."

It was close to midnight when Ezylryb announced that they would be taking off for the next ridge. He had already flown several reconnaissance flights with Poot. He now arrived back on the ridge.

"There's a possible temperature inversion at the east end of the valley. We're not sending any owl down there.

Temperature inversions trap smoke, and then do you know what can happen when the smoke starts to rise?" Soren thought that it must mean that the temperature might change, but again, and most annoyingly, Otulissa's talon shot up. "Shut your beak, Otulissa," Ezylryb snapped. "I feel that Soren might have the answer despite not being as deeply familiar as you are with Strix Emerilla."

How does he feel that I have the answer? Is this like being marked — Ezylryb seeing things in me that others can't? But Soren did feel that he knew the answer. So he proceeded tentatively. "I think that it means that when the smoke rises there could be a change in the air." Ezylryb looked straight at him. The light from his yellow eyes did not burn now but seemed to illuminate Soren's entire brain. Soren felt surer, more confident, but mostly he could easily envision the invisible air. "The air would rise and turn and circulate upward and when this happens, I think the fire will burn harder, more fiercely."

"Exactly!" boomed Ezylryb. "And how do you know this, lad?"

"I see it in my mind. I can imagine it. I feel something, I think in my gizzard, about the movement of air and heat and . . ."

"Yes, thank you, lad." Ezylryb turned to the other owls of the chaw. "There are many ways to learn — through books, through practice, and through gizzuition. They are all good ways, but few of us have gizzuition."

"But what is gizzuition?" Otulissa asked warily.

Ezylryb began to speak but kept his gaze on Soren. "It is a kind of thinking beyond the normal reasoning processes by which one immediately apprehends the truth, perceives and understands reality. It cannot really be taught, but it can be developed by being extremely attentive and sensitive to the natural world."

Soren blinked. *I AM something in this old owl's eyes. I am almost as smart as Otulissa, and Ezylryb believes in me!*

It was now time to move to a ridge closer to the fire. The chaw lifted into the air, each owl flying close to its buddy. They were not halfway to the next ridge when they saw the thick smoke, almost white in the night, rolling up, and then the tongues of flame dancing against the night. Ezylryb began a steeply banking turn. The others followed. Bubo and Poot arrived shortly with fresh voles and mice in their talons, some still squirming.

"Eat light, eat all the hair!" Ezylryb barked.

"I wonder why he always calls it hair?" Martin said quietly.

"They say he comes from a distant place called the

land of the Great North Waters and they have odd ways of speaking," Ruby said.

"But hair? What's hair?" Martin persisted.

"Well, there's fur and there's feathers — I think it's something in between," Ruby said. "Do you want me to ask Otulissa?"

"No!" Soren and Martin both groaned.

Less than an hour had passed when Bubo flew down from his higher perch. "Prepare to fly."

The owls stood on the thin granite lip of the ridge, their talons hooked over the edge. They spread their wings, and Bubo gave the command. "FIRE!" They lifted off — first Bubo and Elvan, then Ruby and Poot, next Otulissa, Soren, and Martin, and last, as a rear guard, Ezylryb.

They had not flown very far before they felt the heat on their faces. They had anticipated the heat but not the noise. A monster roar raged in their ears. Soren had never heard anything like it. Bubo and Elvan had prepared them for everything but this noise. They knew about the heat. They knew about the violent updrafts, the so-called cool spots, and the dead falls. They even knew about the most dreaded trick fire could pull — fire blinking. This happened when the fire, raging with all its deadly beauty, actually transfixed an owl so that it could not fly. It went yeep and, with its wings locking, the owl lost its instincts to fly and suddenly plummeted to the ground. Or if the owl was already on the ground and the fire began to spread rapidly toward it, the owl simply could not lift off, for its wings hung still and motionless like dead things by its side. But no one had told him about the noise.

"You'll get used to it." Elvan had flown up just over Soren and Martin. "It's always a shock at first. There is no way to describe it." He had to shout over the roar of the fire. Below, a sheet of flame lay flat against a hillside. The thermal drafts came up like slabs of rock. Martin and Soren were sucked up at least twenty feet but as they passed the hill they felt a terrific coolness and they dropped another thirty feet. Soren realized that it was only cool compared to the heat they had just flown through. Bubo now circled back. He had been flying far out in front. "Good ember beds ahead. Perfect for all of you."

So this was it, Soren thought. This was when they became true colliers. Just then, like a shooting star, something red whizzed by.

"Beautiful catch, Ruby," shouted Poot.

"What a natural that Short-eared Owl is!" Elvan gasped in amazement.

Ruby began to wing off toward the coal buckets that Bubo had set up on the ridge. The small buckets made in his forge, with bits of kindling in the bottom already lit, would keep the coals hot.

"All right, Martin going in!" Elvan called out the command. The little owl began a tight spiraling plunge to earth. "Cover him, Soren."

Soren would fly cover until Martin returned with a beakful of cinders. Elvan actually carried the very small cinder pot in his talons. Martin was supposed to not only collect cinders but report back on the larger coals that Soren and Otulissa were to retrieve.

Soren hovered above with a careful eye on the little owl. He was getting used to the noise. Indeed, not only was he getting used to it but within the thunderous roar he could seek out smaller sounds, like the sound of Martin's beating heart, which grew more rapid as he plunged. As Martin's heartbeat quickened, Soren hoped with all his heart, gizzard, and soul that the little Saw-whet Owl would be all right. He could see now that Martin was on the ground.

"Play your position, Otulissa," Elvan rasped. Ruby had just caught another sparking coal.

"But all the good ones go up there. We never get a chance."

"Shut your beak. You want to be sent back to the ridge? You'll have your chance."

But Soren was not paying any attention to them. He must keep his focus on Martin, who was now just a little smudge on the ground. A cloud of smoke temporarily obscured him and Soren flew lower.

There he was! There he was! Good heavens, he was coming up fast!

"He's coming in loaded!" Bubo slid in next to Elvan.

And then he was there. Cinders poured from his small beak. His face was sooty and smudged but his eyes danced with a light as bright as the fire. "I did it! I did it!"

"You certainly did, young'un." Bubo flew up and tousled Martin's head feathers with his talon.

"I can't wait to go back," Martin shouted.

"Hold on there," Elvan said. "First, your report."

"Embers about the size of pellets uphill from where I landed."

"Excellent," Elvan said. Elvan then flew off to confer with Bubo and Ezylryb.

"Soren, there is nothing like it. I can't tell you. As soon

as I got there I just wasn't frightened at all. And I can't describe what it's like to grab the cinders in your beak. It's . . ."

"Intoxicating," Otulissa broke in. "Yes, I read about it. You must be careful, though. Strix Emerilla wrote that some colliers get so drunk on the cinders that they do not heed weather warnings."

"Well, it's very strange the feeling you get when you grab them and then fly with them. It's something," he paused. "Something very powerful."

"Now's the time, Soren. You're going in!" Elvan ordered.

"What about me?" Otulissa wailed.

"Shut your beak, your turn will come," Bubo yelled.

Soren pitched into a spiraling downward twist. He felt himself buffeted by a sudden fierce updraft, but he had gathered enough speed to bore through it. Then he was on the ground. It was a strange landscape. Charred skeletons of trees clawed the night, and then scattered about were the coals like hot glowing rocks. They were told to work quickly but at the same time not to rush. A steady pace is the best pace, Bubo had told them. How had Martin, so little, done it and found cinders perfectly sized for his beak? Great Glaux, how embarrassing it would be, Soren thought, if he could not find embers, if he came back empty-beaked. Bubo and Elvan had tried to emphasize that no one should be embarrassed. Oftentimes in the beginning a young collier did not find a suitable coal. There was no shame in returning empty-beaked. But Soren knew there was.

Suddenly, Soren heard a terrible cracking sound. The flames turned a stand of trees just in front of him into one immense torch. He looked up and saw the crowns of other trees igniting. Crown fire! Ruby's worse fear. But Ruby had been worried about the air above and now here he was below. He began to feel a mighty pull on him. Was he going to be sucked up? The last thing Soren remembered thinking about clearly was himself turning into a feathery ball of embers. A thought raced through his head: *With my luck, I'll be caught by Otulissa. What will it matter? I'll be dead.*

CHAPTER TWENTY-ONE
"A Coal in My Beak!"

I have a coal in my beak! I have a coal in my beak! The words kept running through Soren's head. He was flying in ascending circles, effortlessly. He was not singed. He was not burning, and there was this wonderful glowing thing in his beak that, indeed, seemed to flood his entire being with an extraordinary feeling. It was as if every single one of his hollow bones, every feather shaft brimmed with this feeling of transcendent power. Joy filled him, a joy such as he had never felt since perhaps the first time he had ever flown. But how he got this coal was still a mystery to him. He flew back to the ridge where the buckets were. Martin was beside him.

"You were spectacular, Soren. I was so nervous when I saw that crown fire break and then when we saw you getting sucked up, I nearly went yeep."

"But what happened?" Soren asked. They were to stay on the ridge until the rest of the chaw returned.

"You mean to tell me you don't know?"

"Not exactly."

"You did a reverse loop to escape the pull and as you were coming out of it this coal flew by. Bubo said he never saw a coal of that size go up so high, but you caught it! Caught it on the loop, Soren. I mean it was better flying than anything Ruby has ever done. It was absolutely spectacular."

"Great Glaux, I wish I'd seen it," Soren said.

Martin hooted loudly. "You did it, Soren! You did it!"

Otulissa flew in next with Ruby and Poot. She had a full beak and dumped the coals into the bucket. "I got one! I got one!" And then she stopped and looked up, genuinely modest now. "But, Soren, it is nothing compared to what you did."

"Well, thank you, Otulissa . . . er . . . uh . . . That is very kind of you."

Otulissa bobbed her head and actually said nothing for once. Martin blinked at Soren as if to say, "I wonder how long that will last?"

Soren looked about for Ezylryb. He wondered if Ezylryb had seen him. Just then, the Whiskered Screech alighted with a bucket. He barely looked at Soren but busied himself shifting some of the coals into the new bucket.

Oh, no, Soren thought. *Will I ever understand this owl?*

Ezylryb was making his way down the line of buckets now. As he came next to the bucket where Soren had dropped his coal, he turned to look at him. The coal he held in his beak cast an eerie glow on his whiskered face. His amber eyes appeared red. "I hear you did a fair night's work," he mumbled through the coal. Then added, "Magnificent, perhaps." He dropped the coal in the bucket and flew off to confer with Poot.

They began their homeward journey with just an hour to spare before First Light. "Don't worry about crows and mobbing," Elvan said. "They never come near when we're carrying live coals."

It was a beautiful time to fly. The air grew fresher and a light wind now ruffled the water into lacy crests. Even now, with the coals and cinders tame in the buckets, their power seemed to touch them. Fire, of course, was perhaps the most important element that made the Great Ga'Hoole Tree different from any other kingdom of owls. It made them more than a community or a gathering of owls. It made them a fellowship. And if they were to rise each night into the blackness and perform noble deeds, it was perhaps the fire that helped them do this: fire punched up to fierce heats with Bubo's bellows for forging metals into battle claws; fire tamed into candle flames for reading and learning. And here these young owls of the chaw, just barely finished with being owlets themselves, were flying back across the Sea of Hoolemere with this precious element. No wonder they felt powerful. And now, as the sun rose bloodred in the east, Bubo's deep rumble began to ring out across the water. It was the song of the colliers.

> *Give me a hot coal glowing bright red,*
> *Give me an ember sizzling with heat,*
> *These are the jewels made for my beak.*
> *We fly between flames and never get singed*
> *We plunge through the smoke and never cringe.*
> *The secrets of fire, its strange winds, its rages,*
> *We know it all as it rampages*
> *Through forests, through canyons,*
> *Up hillsides and down.*
> *We'll track it.*
> *We'll find it.*
> *Take coals by the pound.*
> *We'll yarp in the heart of the hottest flame*
> *Then bring back its coals and make them tame.*
> *For we are the colliers brave beyond all*
> *We are the owls of the colliering chaw!*

They arrived shortly after daybreak at the Great Ga'Hoole Tree, their faces smudged, their beaks sooty black. But they were welcomed as heroes. The coals were delivered to Bubo's forge and then there was a great banquet.

"Where's Twilight?" Soren said as he sat down with Gylfie at Mrs. Plithiver's table. "And Primrose?" Soren wanted to tell Twilight about the forest fire. Few things impressed Twilight but this might.

"They're both out on a mission and so is Digger. They needed the tracking and search-and-rescue chaws. Something big's going on," Gylfie said.

"What?"

"I'm not sure exactly. Boron is being very quiet about it. But suddenly a lot of owlets need rescuing fast." Just then, he saw Ezylryb huddled with Boron and Strix Struma in a corner of the dining hollow. They looked terribly serious, and he saw Ezylryb nodding quickly every now and then. Poot started to approach the three owls, and he was immediately shooed away.

Because Ezylryb had not taken up his usual position with Elvan at the head of Octavia, the weather and colliering table was empty. Martin and Ruby had joined Soren and Gylfie at Mrs. P.'s, along with Otulissa. "Thank goodness we can now have our vole roasted," Otulissa said. "It seems like forever since we've had anything cooked."

"I would have thought you would have had your fill of things roasting after flying into that fire," Mrs. P. said, and they all laughed. "Now I do have a little announcement to make." The old nest-maid snake spoke softly.

"What is it, Mrs. P.?" Soren asked.

"Well, I have been asked to join the Harp Guild."

"Oh, Mrs. P.!" they all cried.

Perhaps Soren's visit to Madame Plonk had counted for something. He had dared not even hope ever since he had visited her extraordinary apartments that day. Soren couldn't have been happier. Everything, he thought, was really perfect. But as soon as he thought of the word "perfect," he realized no, not quite. And once more that strange melancholy feeling began to creep like a mist over him. He knew what it was immediately this time. Eglantine. What had happened to his dear baby sister? He supposed that if she were alive, and if she had not been captured by St. Aggie's or something worse, she would be flying by now. But who would ever see her? Not his parents. Who knew if they were still alive? Soren grew very quiet. Mrs. P. sensed his sadness.

"Come up later, Soren dear, and sit with me a spell and tell me all about your adventures in the burning forest."

"Sure, Mrs. P.," he said distractedly.

But he didn't. He was simply too tired from the flight, the work at the fire, to do anything but go right to sleep. He was so tired he did not even hear the beautiful voice of Madame Plonk. And underneath the voice that morning there was an especially lovely rippling sound, almost liquid, as Mrs. Plithiver slid with a steady pressure very quickly from the midpoint on a string and stretched for the next octave, all the way to G-flat. It was a virtuoso move and Madame Plonk knew that she had made the right decision. This Mrs. P. had a maestro's touch to match her own magnificent voice.

But, of course, Soren slept through it all, dreaming perhaps of his little sister, but perhaps he was even too tired for dreams.

CHAPTER TWENTY-TWO

Owlets Down!

While Soren slept, in a distant woods across the Sea of Hoolemere, Twilight swooped through the gathering gloom at the end of the day. He and Primrose and Digger worked together. Digger, of course, as part of the tracking chaw, did the groundwork, looking for telltale pellets, a fluff of down, or, sometimes, a wounded or dead owlet. Primrose, who was in the search-and-rescue chaw along with Twilight, flew all levels as an outrider and kept a sharp lookout for enemies. Twilight did most of the heavy work of lifting the owlets and when possible restoring them to their nests.

This particular mission had started as what Barran described as routine. But it quickly became something much more complicated. In the first reconnaissance wave, a number of owlets had been reported on the ground, but they did not seem to be near their nests. At first the rescuers thought these owls, stunned and cold, simply had forgotten where their nests were, which trees they had fallen from. But then it became apparent that in the nearby trees there were no hollows, no possible nests for these young owls. So where had they come from? Had they been snatched by St. Aggie's patrols and then, in flight, somehow mutinied and escaped the talons of their captors, falling to the ground? But why would St. Aggie's patrols not retrieve them? It was all quite mystifying. The other thing that was peculiar was that they were all Barn Owls, not just *Tyto alba* like Soren, but Masked Owls and Grass Owls and Sooty Owls, all belonging to the Barn Owl family.

Twilight divided his attention between Digger below and Primrose, who was flying over him. He had retracted his battle claws, because there did not seem to be any St. Aggie's agents around and it was necessary to pull them in when picking up a fallen owlet, so as not to hurt it. Another Great Gray was wearing his battle claws fully extended and circling in case of ambush. They traded off. This was how the search-and-rescue chaw operated — in pairs, with one owl flying in full battle suit while the other was prepared to pick up an owlet in distress. When one was found, it was taken to a gathering spot in a large hollow presided over by one of Barran's assistants, who could administer medical attention before flying the owls back to the Great Ga'Hoole Tree. When there were enough owlets gathered, they set off. But now there were more than enough. That is why backup had been requested. More of everything was needed. More search-and-rescue workers, more assistants at the gathering spots, more trackers. It was an almost overwhelming situation. Never had they dealt with so many nestless owlets. Where were their parents? Where were their hollows? They seemed to have dropped out of nowhere.

Twilight spotted a Sooty Owl on the ground. This was the most difficult time of the day for owls to spot downed owlets. And Sooties were the most difficult of all owls to spot. Neither black nor white but indeed a smudgy ash color, they seemed to blend in with the twilight. But Twilight himself, with his peculiar gift for seeing at this time, was well suited for the task. Making sure his battle claws were locked back, he began a quick plunge. He hoped the little fellow wasn't dead.

Cautiously he poked it with his beak. He detected a heartbeat. Then gently he scooped it up in his talons. It stirred a bit and tried to lift its head. He thanked Glaux, there was life in this one. There was nothing worse than picking up a dead owlet. Despite their small size, they seemed to be especially heavy, and if their eyes weren't closed and they were dead, it was awful! Barran had not expected that they would encounter any dead owlets on their first mission. She was very upset for the new members of the chaw. "It wasn't supposed to be like this," she kept saying.

"Now you take it easy, little Sooty," Twilight spoke gently to the owlet. "We're going to get you nice and fixed up. Don't you worry. You're in the talons of a champ here!" Twilight couldn't resist a little exhibition of his finer flight maneuvers. Besides, an owlet might find them comforting.

> *Hush little owl,*
> *You're with Twi.*
> *I got the moves to get you by.*
> *Big bad crows.*
> *St. Aggie's scamps*
> *Ain't got nothin to show this champ.*
> *I'll pop a spiral*
> *With a twist,*
> *Do a three-sixty*
> *And scatter mist —*

In the middle of what Twilight considered one of his finest poetry compositions that he had ever made up midair, the little Sooty began to make a sound like a weak whistle.

"My Tyto, my Tyto, why hast thou forsaken us in our purity?"

Twilight looked down at the limp little Sooty in his talons. "What are you talking about? Forsaken? You call this forsaken? Look, I'm not Glaux but you're safe right here in my talons. Safer than you were down on the ground." But the little Sooty just stared at him with vacant dark eyes.

Strix Struma was suddenly on his upwind side. "Don't be upset, Twilight. All these owlets are babbling some kind of nonsense. It's all very weird. This is not like what they did at St. Aggie's with the moon-blinking business, but it's strange. Very strange talk all the time about Tyto. Bubo and Boron are on their way and Ezylryb is coming as well."

"Ezylryb?" Twilight was surprised. Ezylryb never left the Great Ga'Hoole Tree, except for forest fires and weather interpretation. A lot of owlets falling out of nowhere didn't seem to be a weather situation or a forest fire.

"We need all the help we can get and not just for the rescue. Something's going on out here and we must get to the bottom of it." What Strix Struma did not add was that it was for precisely that reason why they needed Ezylryb. Only Ezylryb, with his immense knowledge gleaned from years of reading and his long life of experiences through-out every owl kingdom, might be able to begin to understand what was going on here. Strix Struma was as worried as she had ever been. Was it a plague of some sort? A spell? A bewitchment? She didn't believe in such nonsense. She broke off these thoughts. "Get that Sooty back to the gathering spot and then if you have it in you and feel you could fly one more mission, do so." She sheered off downwind.

"All this talk about purity and Tytos. Never heard such a bunch of babble in my life." It was Elsie, a rather bunchy-looking Barred Owl, who seemed to have more feathers than her small body could manage. The bar designs on her wings had almost faded into a blur. But she was a kindly old bird, who, along with Matron, was in charge of the care and feeding of all the newly arrived young owlets at the Great Ga'Hoole Tree. Never before had the two owls been actually brought out to a gathering station on a search-and-rescue mission, however.

"Over here, Twilight," Matron called. "I have just fluffed up a place. That Sooty will fit in nicely. Elsie dear, spare me a bit more down for this Sooty."

Elsie obliged by plucking out some downy fluff from beneath her primaries. Twilight blinked. It was just as Elsie said. A low babble came in a steady stream from the little owlets, and they were all reciting some kind of poetry, and it made absolutely no sense to Twilight.

One little Grass Owl was now chanting in a thin little voice, "Tytos now forever, so pure, so rare! Yet supreme!" A Masked Owl spoke of a Tyto to whom righteousness belonged and still another was crying out, "Oh, Tyto, who is pureness beyond compare, show thyself . . . Tyto, how long shall the impure triumph?"

"Depressing little ditties, aren't they?" Bubo said as he lighted down next to Twilight.

"What are they talking about?" Twilight said.

"I don't know, but I've heard more cheerful tunes in my day than all this whining about Tytos."

As Twilight and Primrose and Digger took off for their last mission, the ragtag ends of mournful songs seemed to trail out behind them. "My goodness," sighed Primrose. "It's enough to make you long for a nice little wet poop joke." She dropped down to her mid-level surveillance position, and then Digger flew under her. It was well beyond the last of the daylight. It was night. No longer flying on that silver border, Twilight would wait for signals from Primrose or Digger if they found any owlets down. Digger now swooped in close to the ground. In the muddy runoff from a creek, he saw the distinctive markings of a Barn Owl's front talons, the toes exactly equal lengths. He followed the talon marks down the muddy path. Perhaps this one was not injured so badly if it could walk, Digger thought. But where could it have walked? And why? He saw a buff-colored feather in the path ahead. A feather of an almost fully fledged owl, it would seem. So why not fly? And just within that moment, under the low branches of a juniper, he saw a tawny glow in the night and he heard the long, drawn-out hiss, the begging call of a *Tyto alba*. "Coo coo ROOOO! Coo coo ROOOO!"

Digger hooted the signal indicating a downed owlet.

As Digger waited for Twilight to spiral down, the strangest feeling began to steal over him. Twilight settled down next to him.

"What have we got here?" Twilight said.

"Another Barn Owl, but not a Masked or a Sooty or a Grass Owl."

"No," Twilight said in a whisper. "A *Tyto alba*."

"Like Soren," they both said at once. Digger looked at Twilight. He almost didn't dare say it. "Do you think it could be?"

"Remember," Twilight said, "how Soren once told us that his sister had a speckle near her eye. That it looked as if one of those dots from her head feathers had just slipped down to her eye and that it was the same with his mother, that she, too, had a slipped dot?"

"Yes," said Digger slowly.

"Look!"

The two owls brought their beaks close to the little

owl, whose cries had grown weaker and weaker and then stopped. They almost forgot to breathe in their anguish. There was indeed a tiny speckle in the darker feathers on the inside corner of her eye. But if this was Eglantine, was she alive? Was she dead? Was she truly . . . ?

"Eglantine?" they both called softly.

CHAPTER TWENTY-THREE

At Last!

I need some more worms over here, quick!" the nest-maid snake called out.

"The Ga'Hoolology chaw is digging them as fast as they can," another snake called. "Oh, my goodness, what a mess this little Sooty Owl is." The snake nudged the last worm of her supply on the gash in the Sooty's wing. "Poor little fellow. Now stop that babbling, dear. You don't have enough energy." But the owlet kept up a steady singsong about a world of Tyto purity and supremacy.

There had never been such a flurry in the Great Ga'Hoole Tree. The infirmary was brimming with stunned and wounded owls. And no one was spared a moment's rest. The owls of the tree were cutting back and forth between branches, flying in the new arrivals, rushing about getting fresh worms for their wounds, plucking down from their own breasts to make up new beds, bringing cup after cup of milkberry tea. The nest-maid snakes were at the point of complete exhaustion and even Madame

Plonk, who rarely lifted a talon around the tree to do anything, could not bear seeing her harp guild so worn out. So she joined in right beside them, learning how to place worms properly on the open wounds. Soren and Gylfie worked as hard as anyone, either fetching things for the nest-maid snakes or cleaning out new hollows, because the infirmary was too full to accommodate any more. There was barely time to wonder about what had brought this on. But, of course, in the back of their minds was the horrible nagging fear that St. Aggie's was somehow involved, and if not St. Aggie's, perhaps the "you only wish"! Were the poor little owls babbling about the same horror that the murdered Barred Owl had when he gasped the words "you only wish"? But what did it really matter? Owlets were wounded and dying.

For the life of him, Soren could not understand this babble that seemed to pour out of the owlets' ceaselessly clacking beaks. It never seemed as if there was an entire phrase. The words came out disjointed and broken, but always there was something about Tytos, or Barn Owls.

Then overhead, Soren heard the arrival of a new batch of owlets being brought in. There was no quiet flying this day. Owls that once prided themselves on silent flight beat their wings furiously, in their desperate efforts to get the injured owlets to safety.

"SOREN!" The sound of his own name split the warm air. Soren looked up from his task of pecking out worms. It was Twilight who had called down to him and he was flanked by Primrose and Digger. The rest of the search-and-rescue chaw was following.

"Soren, get up here fast as you can," Twilight called again.

Then Digger spiraled down. "This is important. Bring that worm and come on."

"No! No!" another owl said tersely. "All worms must be put into the pile first. Our chaw ryb said so."

"Drop the worm, Soren, and just come." Soren couldn't imagine what could be so important that they needed him so quickly. He followed Digger to a new hollow they had just fixed up to take care of the overflow from the infirmary. Outside the hollow, Gylfie and Primrose perched on a branch. They were very still. Soren got an awful feeling in his gizzard. He hesitated. He really did not want to go into that hollow. Digger gave him a bit of a nudge. Then Gylfie came up on the other side. The shadows from the hollow seemed to draw him in against his will. He blinked. Twilight stood beside a heap of golden feathers splotched with blood.

"So?" Soren said.

Twilight's usually gruff voice became a soft whisper. "So, Soren, is this your sister, Eglantine?"

Soren felt his gizzard drop to his talons. He wobbled but Gylfie was on one side and Digger on the other. He forced himself to look down at the battered little owlet. But she really was hardly an owlet anymore. She was fully fledged and streaked with blood. A red bubble burbled from her beak as she, too, tried to babble.

"No! No! This can't be!" Soren wailed. He felt his legs collapse under him and he crumpled beside her. "Eglantine! Eglantine!"

"Get Mrs. Plithiver, quick!" Gylfie rasped.

Time began to have no meaning for Soren. Was it day? Was it night? How many nights had passed since they had brought in Eglantine? At first, he was numb. He could not do anything. Mrs. Plithiver nursed Eglantine ceaselessly. "Will she live?" That was all Soren could say.

"I'm not sure, dear," Mrs. P. said honestly. "All we can do is try."

Finally, Soren began to help. He tried feeding her a bit of milkberry tea and in a low voice kept saying, "Eglantine, it's me, Soren. It's your brother Soren." But Eglantine, with her eyes half shut, only continued to babble a word or two of the singsong ditties they all sang. She did seem to be getting better, however, stronger. And when her eyes opened fully, Soren grew excited. "Eglantine!" He leaned over her. "Eglantine. It's me. Soren! And Mrs. P. is here, too!" But there was not even a flicker of recognition in her eyes. She merely clacked her beak a couple of times and resumed the babble. Soren sighed.

"Patience, dear. Patience," said Mrs. Plithiver. "All things take time. See how much stronger her voice is."

But Soren did not like what he was hearing. She spoke only of Tytos, of Tytos reigning supreme, seeking vengeance, of Tyto purity, of Tyto superiority, of a world only of Tytos. How would he explain to her that his best friends were an Elf Owl, a Great Gray, and a Burrowing Owl? That these were his very best friends in all the world, that they were a band?

By the next evening, Eglantine was well enough to get up on her talons and take a few steps. Soren led her carefully out on the branch and stood beside her. But he might as well have been standing beside a stump. She did whatever he told her, but there was still no recognition. He brought her into the hollow he shared with Twilight, Digger, and Gylfie to sleep, and Primrose came just before Madame Plonk began her song, to show Eglantine some especially pretty berries she had strung.

"See, Eglantine. Ever since I have been here, I have collected a few berries from each season. So I have white ones from winter and silver from spring and now I've got my golden ones from summer, and I'm making a necklace. I'll make you one, too." But Eglantine did not respond.

"This is worse than being moon blinked," Soren whispered to Gylfie.

Gylfie didn't know what to say. She felt desperately sorry for Soren. She knew that Soren had missed Eglantine so fiercely. But to have her back like this was almost worse than not having her back at all. Gylfie, of course, would never dare say such a thing to Soren. Just then Otulissa peeked her head in.

"May I come in?"

"Sure," Soren said.

"Look, I've been in the library all this time working on Tyto research, to see if there is anything that would explain this — all of them being Tytos and babbling about Tytos, but I somehow got distracted and started looking at a book by a distinguished Spotted Owl that's about owls' brains and feelings and gizzards."

"Great Glaux," Twilight muttered and yarped a pellet out the hollow's opening. "No doubt a relative of yours, Otulissa."

"Well, possibly. There were many distinguished intellects in our ancestry and we do go back so far. Anyhow, in this book it says that your sister might be suffering from something he calls 'gizzlemia.' It is a blankness of the gizzard. It is as if the gizzard is just walled off and nothing can get through, and because of this there is a malfunction in the brain as well."

"Well, that explains so much," Soren said sarcastically. "What in Glaux's name am I supposed to do about it?"

"Well . . . well," Otulissa stammered. "I'm not sure. I just thought you'd like to know what's making her this way. It's not as if she doesn't want to remember you. She just can't help it," Otulissa said feebly. "I . . . I mean . . . I'm sure she loves you still." Soren stared at her with a hard glint. "Oh, dear. None of this is coming out right." Otulissa's eyes welled with tears. "I was just trying to be helpful."

Soren just sighed, turned away, and began to fluff up the bed they had made for Eglantine.

That day, as the darkness leaked away into the morning and the light of morning turned harsh in the glare of noon, in that hot slow time of the day when the silence pressed down despite the babble, Soren felt as lonely as he had ever felt in his life. Lonelier than that first frightening night on the ground when he had been pushed out of the nest by his brother, Kludd, lonelier than when he had been at St. Aggie's, lonelier than when he had almost given up on ever seeing any of his family again. This was the most excruciating loneliness he had ever imagined. Eglantine was here at last, but was she really?

CHAPTER TWENTY-FOUR

Trader Mags

Soren had been looking forward, it seemed forever, to the day that Trader Mags would come with her wares. But now it meant nothing to him. Still, there was certainly a buzz of excitement as they roused themselves at the end of the day in anticipation of the magpie's arrival around twilight. Everyone was excited except for Soren and, of course, the nest-maids, who considered magpies among the worst of the wet poopers, almost as bad as seagulls. He supposed he would go and drag Eglantine around, although he doubted it would mean anything to her. Mags would be showing her wares all evening, so there was no rush.

She was late and no one was more upset than Madame Plonk. From his hollow, Soren could hear her several branches above him on a lookout perch, waiting with other owls. "If that bird was ever on time in her life, I'll eat my harp!" Madame Plonk was fuming. "She has no sense of time. Here it is past twilight, nearly First Black." But suddenly, curling out of the night, came a lovely warbling sound.

"It's the carol!" someone shouted. And a cheer went up. Mags was approaching and her caroling threaded through the night. The warble of magpies was known as a carol and was like no other birdsong in the world. He heard the owls now, swooping down through the branches to the base of the tree where Mags would set up her wares. She came with several assistants, carrying baskets of her latest "collection," as she called her wares.

"Want to go down, Eglantine?" Soren said. Eglantine, of course, said nothing but got up and followed Soren. She had recovered her flight skills almost immediately and the two alighted on the ground together as Mags and her assistants spread out the collection.

There was a festive mood with much chattering and special treats that cook had whipped up. Bubo stomped forward and gave Mags a great hug with his wings that nearly knocked her over. Mags looked nothing like Soren had expected. Her feathers were mostly black and the sleekest, blackest black he had ever seen, but she did have some streaks of white feathers. Her tail was immensely long and, on this moonlit night, her black tail feathers had a greenish gloss. She wore a jaunty bandanna on her head. "More where these came from, my dears!" she squawked.

Soren could have been knocked over by that squawk. How could the same throat that produced that lovely carol be squawking as raucous as a seagull?

"Come on up, don't be shy," Mags said. "Bubbles, Bubbles!" she squawked at a smaller magpie. "Where're them sparklies I got at the whatchamacallit for Madame? You know the ones. And I got you some nice velvet, dear," nodding to Madame Plonk, "ever so squashy. Tassels, tassels anyone? Tie some crystals to them and yeh got yerself a charming windchime. . . . Bubbles! Get them crystals out here on the double! I tell you, Boron, you can't get a good apprentice these days. I mean one would think that to serve Mags the Trader, known from here to Tyto, from Kuneer to Ambala, would be enough incentive, if you catch my drift, but no. How's the missus, now where she be?"

"Away," Boron said cryptically.

The little black eye almost covered by the bandanna gave a quick piercing stare. "Oh," she said. Then muttered to herself as Boron walked away. "I just mind me own business. I don't ask no questions, don't butt my beak in where it ain't wanted."

"Ha!" Bubo laughed. "If that ain't a pile of yarped pellets."

"Oh, scram, Bubo," she replied merrily. "Get out of here

with your yarping pellet talk. Remember, we're not fit to associate with you, we wet poopers."

"Now, Maggie. I ain't no snob and you know it. I never held that against you. I mean, you're different from seagulls, sweet gizzard."

"Don't you go 'sweet gizzarding' me, Bubo. And I'll say we're different from seagulls. About twice as smart and ten times prettier. Not as pretty as Madame Plonk, though, in that gorgeous tapestry piece I found for her." She flew over and began to help Madame Plonk arrange it more artfully on her high white shoulders.

Soren felt Eglantine flinch. "You okay, Eglantine?" She said nothing but he noticed that she had turned toward Madame Plonk, who was admiring herself in a fragment of mirror that Mags had brought.

They had moved on. Walking along, they looked at other simpler cloths that had been spread with a variety of items — a bright pocket watch, several broken saucers with a sign that said "mendable," a strange flower that Soren paused to look at. "It ain't real," the little magpie, Bubbles, said.

"Well, if it isn't real, what is it?" Soren asked.

"It's an unreal flower," Bubbles answered.

"But why have an unreal flower?"

"It ain't never gonna die. Ya see?"

Soren didn't see but moved along. Despite all the merriment, he noticed that Boron and Strix Struma were always huddled together in tense conversation. They seemed, in fact, very apart from the entire festive spirit of the evening.

Soon Soren and Eglantine joined Twilight and Digger and Primrose. Primrose had traded one of her strung milkberry bracelets for a tiny comb. And Digger had traded a very smooth pebble for a shell. "They say it comes from a very faraway ocean and that once a tiny animal lived inside it," he explained.

The moon was beginning to slip away, and Mags had begun to pack up her wares. It would be time for good light, but suddenly Soren noticed that Eglantine was not by his side. He had a terrible moment's panic but then spotted her standing rigidly in front of a cloth covered with fragments of glass and pretty stones. Bubbles was packing up. "She ain't moved an inch," Bubbles said. "Just staring at this stone here, with the sparkles. Ain't really gold, Mags says — just little bits of something she calls isinglass, some calls it mica. But makes a right pretty rock. Kind of sparkly in places and, if you hold it up, light can shine through it a bit. It's kind of like a dusty mirror. Certainly caught your sister's fancy. There be something wrong with her, I s'pose?" she said quietly to Soren. "Here, dear, I'll show you something real pretty we can do with it." She picked up the stone, which was as thin as a blade. "See what it does now." She held it up to the moon as it swept down on the dark horizon. When the light of the moon touched the stone it grew luminous. At that very same moment, the harp could be heard as the guild began their evening practice. No one else noticed, of course, but for one fraction of a second the stone blade shimmered in a swirl of flickering light and sound.

Eglantine began to shake uncontrollably. "The Place! The Place!" Eglantine screamed.

Something started in a dim way to make sense to Soren. He put a talon on his sister's shoulder and spun her around to face him. "Eglantine," he said softly.

His sister blinked. "Soren? Oh, Soren!" she cried as he swept her under his wings.

"I ain't done nothing, Mags, I swear. Nothing." Bubbles was crying and sputtering in near hysterics. "I just held up this here piece of glass we got from that castle over in Ambala and she done gone yoicks."

"Take me to the music, Soren. Take me to the music. Take us all to the music," Eglantine cried.

CHAPTER TWENTY-FIVE
In the Folds of the Night

Soren perched on a slender branch next to Eglantine. He draped one wing over her shoulders. It seemed like a miracle. His sister was back — really back. And now she said they must listen to the harp music. If she had told him to hang upside down and be mobbed by crows, he would have. He had never been happier in his life. The other owlets that had been rescued were now gathering on the limbs outside the concert hollow. Madame Plonk rarely allowed owls to observe harp practice but she made an exception now. Boron came and perched on the other side of Eglantine. They all watched as the nest-maid snakes of the guild gathered at the harp and took their positions. Half of the guild snakes played the higher strings and the other half played the lower strings, and then there were a very few, the most talented harp snakes, that were called sliptweens. The job of the sliptweens was to jump octaves. An octave contained all eight tones of the scale. This harp had six and a half octaves, from C-flat below middle C to the G-flat. G-flat was three and a half octaves above middle C. To find a snake that could do that jump and do it well in a split second, causing the most beautiful liquid sound to pour from the harp, was rare. And it could be exhausting work, depending on the composition.

Mrs. P. was a natural sliptween. And Soren now blinked as he saw a pink streak pass through the strings of the harp and a beautiful sound drifted into the air. It was Mrs. P. Then, in a flash, she was back in her original position, weaving bass notes. It was lovely to watch. Not only was the music magnificent but the snakes themselves, in their varying hues of rosy pinks, wove a continually shifting pattern as they shuttled through the strings of the harp.

They were now playing an old forest cantata. And Madame Plonk's voice blended perfectly with the sounds of the harp.

Soren looked at Eglantine. She had a relaxed, dreamy look in her eyes. All of the rescued owlets seemed different now. There was not one clack of a babbling beak. The owls were silent and happy.

Boron had been watching them all from a higher perch. He was deeply perplexed. Happy, of course, that all the owls they had rescued had stopped their babbling. But mystified as to how it had happened. Beyond Hoole, he sensed that there was a danger lurking that was worse than the owls of St. Aggie's. And why had Ezylryb not returned yet? Barran had come back during the harp practice, but she was surprised that Ezylryb was not yet back. She thought he had a head start on her. "Don't worry, dear. He'll show up."

Soren looked at Boron and Barran. Despite their words, they did seem worried. And Soren himself had a funny feeling in his gizzard. Gylfie suddenly turned to him.

"I think they're worried about Ezylryb."

Soren blinked. "Maybe tomorrow we should go out and take a look."

Twilight and Digger alighted at that moment next to them on the branch.

"Take a look?" Digger asked. "A look for what?"

"Ezylryb," Twilight said. "I heard them talking, too."

There was a sudden pulsing of light in the sky and then a gasp from all the owls as a radiance swept the black night.

"What is it? What is it?"

"Oh, great Glaux, we are blessed!" hooted Barran.

"It is the Aurora Glaucora," Boron sang out.

Soren, Gylfie, Digger, Twilight, and Eglantine all looked at one another. They had no idea what Barran and

Boron were talking about. But the sky seemed rinsed with colors, colors that streamed like banners through the night. Suddenly, Madame Plonk abandoned her perch by the harp and flew out into the brilliance of the night. Still singing, she swept through the long lances of light, her white body reflecting the colors. It was irresistible. Soren remembered that morning months ago when he and Madame Plonk had flown through the rainbow. But the rainbow was pale next to these pulsing banners of light that draped the sky. His worries about Ezylryb grew dimmer as the colors grew brighter. The sky beckoned, the shimmering light drew them. But there was a strangeness to it all. He felt a shudder deep in his gizzard. Behind those banners of throbbing light he knew there was blackness. Ezylryb was still missing, St. Aggie's was still a threat, and now there was the almost unthinkable, the nearly unspeakable "you only wish." Yes, Eglantine was back, but was she really back? Was it the same dear Eglantine? Soren felt as if he could no longer trust. For the world on this night had suddenly become too strange. It was as if everything had been turned inside out and the thing that owls called heaven, glaumora, had come down to Earth and swallowed the night. But this was not quite right, Soren thought. Just at that moment Eglantine swept in beside her brother.

"Isn't it beautiful, Soren? Isn't it just beautiful?"

"Just beautiful," Soren said absently.

But even as he spoke, he felt a strange dread in his gizzard. *Well,* he finally thought, *Eglantine and I are together at last, and we need no colors, for just flying with her at my side is as good as glaumora on Earth. Tomorrow, yes tomorrow, I shall search for Ezylryb.* Soren recalled the amber squint of the old Whiskered Screech's injured eye that indeed sparkled with the glint of deepest knowledge. But tonight . . . Soren and Eglantine tipped their white faces to the tinted sky and flew off into the painted night just as the Golden Talons began to rise.

And yet the talons were no longer golden, just as the sky was no longer black.

THE OWLS
and others
from

GUARDIANS of GA'HOOLE
The Journey

SOREN: Barn Owl, *Tyto alba*, from the kingdom of the Forest of Tyto; snatched when he was three weeks old by St. Aegolius patrols; escaped from St. Aegolius Academy for Orphan Owls

> His family:
> KLUDD: Barn Owl, *Tyto alba*, older brother
> EGLANTINE: Barn Owl, *Tyto alba*, younger sister
> NOCTUS: Barn Owl, *Tyto alba*, father
> MARELLA: Barn Owl, *Tyto alba*, mother
>
> His family's nest-maid:
> MRS. PLITHIVER, blind snake

GYLFIE: Elf Owl, *Micrathene whitneyi*, from the desert kingdom of Kuneer; snatched when she was three weeks old by St. Aegolius patrols; escaped from St. Aegolius Academy for Orphan Owls; Soren's best friend

TWILIGHT: Great Gray Owl, *Strix nebulosa*, free flyer, orphaned within hours of hatching

DIGGER: Burrowing Owl, *Speotyto cunicularius*, from the desert kingdom of Kuneer; lost in desert after attack in which his brother was killed and eaten by owls from St. Aegolius

℥ ℥ ℥

BORON: Snowy Owl, *Nyctea scandiaca*, the king of Hoole

BARRAN: Snowy Owl, *Nyctea scandiaca*, the queen of Hoole

MATRON: Short-eared Owl, *Asio flammeus*, the motherly caretaker at the Great Ga'Hoole Tree

STRIX STRUMA: Spotted Owl, *Strix occidentalis*, the dignified navigation ryb (teacher) at the Great Ga'Hoole Tree

ELVAN: Great Gray Owl, *Strix nebulosa*, the colliering ryb (teacher) at the Great Ga'Hoole Tree

EZYLRYB: Whiskered Screech Owl, *Otus trichopsis*, the wise weather-interpretation ryb (teacher) at the Great Ga'Hoole Tree; Soren's mentor

POOT: Boreal Owl, *Aegolius funerus*, Ezylryb's assistant

BUBO: Great Horned Owl, *Bubo virginianus*, the blacksmith of the Great Ga'Hoole Tree

MADAME PLONK: Snowy Owl, *Nyctea scandiaca*, the elegant singer of the Great Ga'Hoole Tree

OCTAVIA: Madame Plonk's blind nest-maid snake

TRADER MAGS: Magpie, a traveling merchant

/3   /3   /3

OTULISSA: Spotted Owl, *Strix occidentalis*, a student of prestigious lineage at the Great Ga'Hoole Tree

PRIMROSE: Pygmy Owl, *Glaucidium gnoma*, rescued from a forest fire and brought to the Great Ga'Hoole Tree the night of Soren and his friends' arrival

MARTIN: Northern Saw-whet Owl, *Aegolius acadicus*, rescued and brought to the Great Ga'Hoole Tree the same night as Primrose

RUBY: Short-eared Owl, *Asio flammeus*; lost her family under mysterious circumstances and was brought to the Great Ga'Hoole Tree

GUARDIANS
of GA'HOOLE

BOOK THREE
The Rescue

Soon the walls of the castle ruins rose in the dawn mist.

Contents

CHAPTER ONE
Blood Dawn

The tail of the comet slashed the dawn and in the red light of the rising sun, for a brief instant, it seemed as if the comet was bleeding across the sky. Every other owl had already tucked into their hollows in the Great Ga'Hoole Tree for the day's sleep. Every owl, that is, except for Soren, who perched on the highest limb of this tallest Ga'Hoole tree on earth. He scoured the horizon for a sign, any sign of his beloved teacher, Ezylryb.

Ezylryb had disappeared almost two months before. The old Whiskered Screech, indeed the oldest teacher, or "ryb" as they were called, of the great tree had flown out on a mission that late summer night to help rescue owlets from what was now referred to as the Great Downing. Scores of young orphan owlets had mysteriously been found scattered on the ground, some mortally wounded, others stunned and incoherent. None of them had been found anywhere near their nests, but in an open field that for the most part could boast no trees with hollows. It was a complete mystery as to how these young owlets, most of whom could barely fly, had gotten there. It was as if they had simply dropped out of the night sky. And one of those owlets had been Soren's sister, Eglantine.

After Soren himself had been shoved from his nest by his brother, Kludd, nearly a year before, and subsequently captured by the violent and depraved owls of St. Aggie's, he had lost all hope of ever seeing his sister or his parents again. Even after he had escaped St. Aggie's with his best friend Gylfie, a little Elf Owl who had also been captured, he had still dared not to really hope. But then Eglantine had been found by two other dear friends: Twilight, the Great Gray, and Digger, the Burrowing Owl, both of whom had flown out with others on the night of the Great Downing on countless search-and-rescue missions. And Ezylryb, who rarely left the tree except for his responsibilities as leader of the weather interpretation and the colliering chaws, had flown out in an attempt to unravel the strange occurrences of that night. But he had never returned.

It seemed grossly unfair to Soren that once he had finally gotten his sister back, his favorite ryb had vanished. Maybe that was a selfish way to think but he couldn't help it. Soren felt that most of what he knew he had learned from the gruff old Whiskered Screech Owl. Ezylryb was not what anyone would call pretty to look at, with one eye held in a perpetual squint, his left foot mangled to the point of missing one talon, and a low voice that sounded like something between a growl and distant thunder — no, Ezylryb wasn't exactly appealing.

"An acquired taste," Gylfie had said. Well, Soren had certainly acquired the taste.

As a member of both the weather interpretation and the colliering chaws, which flew into forest fires to gather coals for the forge of Bubo the blacksmith, Soren had learned his abilities directly from the master. And though Ezylryb was a stern master, often grouchy and suffering no nonsense, he was, of all the rybs, the most fiercely devoted to his students and his chaw members.

The chaws were the small teams into which the owls were organized. In the chaws, they learned a particular skill that was vital to the survival of not just the owls of Ga'Hoole but to all the kingdoms of owls. Ezylryb led two chaws — weathering and colliering. But for all his gruff ways, he was certainly not above cracking a joke — sometimes very dirty jokes, much to the horror of Otulissa, a Spotted Owl, who was just Soren's age and quite prim and proper and was given to airs. Otulissa was always carrying on about her ancient and distinguished ancestors. One of her favorite words was "appalling." She was constantly be-

ing "appalled" by Ezylryb's "crudeness," his "lack of refine-
ment," his "coarse ways." And Ezylryb was constantly
telling Otulissa to "give it a blow." This was the most impolite way an owl could tell another to shut up. The two
bickered constantly, and yet Otulissa had turned into a
good chaw member and that was all that really counted to
Ezylryb.

But now there was no more bickering. No more crude
jokes. No more climbing the baggywrinkles, flying upside
down in the gutter, punching the wind and popping the
scuppers, doing the hurly burly and all the wonderful maneuvers the owls did when they flew through gales and
storms and even hurricanes in the weather interpretation
chaw. Life seemed flat without Ezylryb, the night less
black, the stars dull, even as this comet, like a great raw
gash in the sky, ripped apart the dawn.

"Some say a comet's an omen." Soren felt the branch he
was perched on quiver. "Octavia!" The fat old nest-maid
snake slithered out onto the branch. "What are you doing
out here?" Soren asked.

"Same thing as you. Looking for Ezylryb." She sighed.
But, of course, Octavia, like all nest-maid snakes, who ti-
died up the hollows of owls and kept them free of vermin,
was blind. In fact, she had no eyes, just two small indentations where eyes should be. But nest-maids were renowned

for their extraordinary sensory skills. They could hear and feel things that other creatures could not. So, if there were wing beats out there, wing beats that had the sound peculiar to those of Ezylryb, she would know. Although owls were silent fliers, each stirred the air with its wings in a unique fashion that only a nest-maid snake could detect. And Octavia, with her musical background and years in the harp guild under Madame Plonk's guidance, was especially keen to all sorts of vibrations.

The harp guild was one of the most prestigious of all the guilds for which the blind nest-maid snakes were chosen to belong. Dear Mrs. Plithiver, who had served in Soren's family's hollow and with whom he had been miraculously reunited, was also a member of this guild. The snakes wove themselves in and out of the harp's strings, playing the accompaniment for Madame Plonk, the beautiful Snowy Owl with the shimmering voice. Octavia had served as a nest-maid for Madame Plonk and Ezylryb. Indeed, she and Ezylryb had arrived at the Great Ga'Hoole Tree together from the land of the North Waters of the Northern Kingdoms years and years ago. She was completely devoted to Ezylryb and, although she had never said much about how she and the old Screech Owl had first met, there were rumors that she had been rescued by Ezylryb and that she, unlike the other snakes, had not been born blind. Something had happened to make her go blind. She certainly did not have the same rosy scales as the other snakes. She was instead a pale greenish blue.

The old snake sighed again.

"I just don't understand," Soren said. "He's too smart to get lost."

Octavia shook her head. "I don't think he's lost, Soren." Soren swung his head around to look at her. *Then what does she think? Does she think he is dead?* Octavia said very little these days. It was almost as if she was afraid to speculate on the fate of her beloved master. The others, Barran and Boron, the monarchs of the great tree, speculated constantly, as did Strix Struma, another revered teacher. But the creature who knew Ezylryb the best and the longest offered no such speculations, no ideas, and yet Soren felt she did know something that truly scared her. Something so horrible as to be unspeakable. Thus, her seemingly impenetrable silences. Soren felt this about Octavia, he felt it in his gizzard where all owls sensed their strongest feelings and experienced their most powerful intuitions. Could he share this with someone? Who? Otulissa? Never. Twilight? Not Twilight. He was too action-oriented. Maybe Gylfie, his best friend, but Gylfie was too practical. She liked definite evidence, and was a stickler for words. Soren could imagine Gylfie pushing if he said that he felt Octavia knew something: *What do you mean by "know"?*

"You better get along, young'un," Octavia said. "Time for you to sleep. I can feel the sun. The dawn's getting old."

"Can you feel the comet, too?" Soren asked suddenly.

"Ooh." It was more like a soft groan or a whispering exhalation. "I don't know." But she did know. Soren knew it. She felt it, and it worried her. He shouldn't have asked, and yet he could not stop himself from asking more. "Do you believe it really is an omen like some say?"

"Who is some?" she asked sharply. "I haven't heard anyone in the tree nattering on about omens."

"What about you? I heard you just a few minutes ago."

Octavia paused. "Listen, Soren, I'm just a fat old snake from the Northern Kingdoms, the country of the North Waters. We're a naturally suspicious lot. So don't you pay me any heed. Now flutter back down to your hollow."

"Yes, ma'am," Soren replied. It didn't pay to upset a nest-maid snake.

So the young Barn Owl swooped down through the spreading branches of the Great Ga'Hoole Tree to the hollow he shared with his sister, Eglantine, and his best friends, Gylfie, Twilight, and Digger. As he flew, looping through the limbs, he saw the sun rise fierce and bright. As clouds the color of blood crouched on the horizon, a terrible apprehension coursed through Soren's hollow bones and set his gizzard aquiver.

Digger! Why had he never thought of sharing his feelings about Octavia with Digger? Soren blinked as he stepped into the dim light of the hollow and saw the sleeping shapes of his best friends. Digger was a very odd owl in every sense of the word. For starters, he had lived his entire life — until he was orphaned — not in a tree but a burrow. With his long, strong, featherless legs, he had preferred walking to flying when Soren and Gylfie and Twilight first met him. He had planned to walk all the way across the desert in search of his parents until mortal danger intervened and the three owls convinced him otherwise. Nervous and high-strung, Digger worried a lot but, at the same time, this owl was a very deep thinker. He was always asking the strangest questions. Boron said that Digger possessed what he called a "philosophical turn of mind." Soren wasn't sure what that meant exactly. He only knew that if he said to Digger, "I think Octavia might know something about Ezylryb," Digger, unlike Gylfie, would go deeper. He would not be just a stickler for words or, like Twilight, say, "Well, what are you going to do about it?"

Soren wished he could wake Digger up right now and

share his thoughts. But he didn't want to risk waking the others. No, he would just have to wait until they all rose at First Black.

And so Soren squashed himself into the corner bed of soft moss and down. He stole a glance at Digger before he drifted off. Digger, unlike the others, did not sleep standing or sometimes perched, but in a curious posture that more or less could be described as a squat supported by his short stubby tail with his legs splayed out to the sides. *Good Glaux, that owl even sleeps odd.* That was Soren's last thought before he drifted off to sleep.

CHAPTER TWO

Flecks in the Night!

The dawn bled into night, flaying the darkness, turning the black red, and Soren, with Digger by his side, flew through it.

"Strange isn't it, Soren, how even at night the comet makes this color?"

"I know. And look at those sparks from the tail just below the moon. Great Glaux, even the moon is beginning to look red." Digger's voice was quavery with worry.

"I told you about Octavia. How she thinks it's an omen, or at least I think she thinks it is, even though she won't really admit it."

"Why won't she admit it?" Digger asked.

"I think she's sensitive about coming from the great North Waters. She says everyone there is very superstitious, but I don't know, I guess she just thinks the owls here will laugh at her or something. I'm not sure."

Suddenly, Soren was experiencing a tight, uncomfortable feeling as he flew. He had never felt uncomfortable flying, even when he was diving into the fringes of forest fires to gather coals on colliering missions. But, indeed, he could almost feel the sparks from that comet's tail. It was as if they were hot sizzling points pinging off his wings, singeing his flight feathers as the infernos of burning forests never had. He carved a great downward arc in the night to try to escape it. Was he becoming like Octavia? Could he actually feel the comet? Impossible! The comet was hundreds of thousands, millions of leagues away. Now, suddenly, those sparks were turning to glints, sparkling silvery-gray glints. "Flecks! Flecks! Flecks!" he screeched.

"Wake up, Soren! Wake up!" The huge Great Gray Owl, Twilight, was shaking him. Eglantine had flown to a perch above him and was quaking with fear at the sight of her brother writhing and screaming in his sleep. And Gylfie the Elf Owl was flying in tight little loops above him, beating the air as best she could to bring down cool drafts that might jar him from sleep and this terrible dream. Digger blinked and said, "Flecks? You mean the ones you had to pick at St. Aggie's?"

Just at that moment, Mrs. Plithiver slithered into the hollow. "Soren, dear."

"Mrs. P.," Soren gulped. He was fully awake now. "Great Glaux, did I wake you up with my screaming?"

"No, dear, but I just had a feeling that you were having some terrible dream. You know how we blind snakes feel things."

"Can you feel the comet, Mrs. Plithiver?"

Mrs. P. squirmed a bit then arranged herself into a neat coil. "Well, I can't really say. But it is true that since the comet arrived a lot of us nest-maid snakes have been feeling — oh, how shall I describe it — a kind of tightness in our scales. But whether it's the comet or winter coming on I don't know for sure."

Soren sighed and remembered the feeling in his dream. "Does it ever feel like hot little sparks pinging off you?"

"No, no. I wouldn't describe it that way. But, then again, I'm a snake and you're a Barn Owl."

"And why . . ." Soren hesitated. "Why is the sky bleeding?" Soren felt a shiver go through the hollow as he spoke the words.

"It's not bleeding, silly." A Spotted Owl stuck her head into the hollow. It was Otulissa. "It's merely a red tinge and it's caused by a moisture bank encountering random gases. I read all about it in Strix Miralda's book, she's a sister of the renowned weathertrix —"

"Strix Emerilla," Gylfie chimed in.

"Yes. How did you know, Gylfie?"

"Because every other word out of your mouth is a quote from Strix Emerilla."

"Well, I won't apologize. You know I think we are distantly related, although she lived centuries ago. Emerilla's sister, Miralda, was a specialist in spectography and atmospheric gases."

"Hot air," Twilight snarled. *Glaux! She frinks me off,* Twilight thought. But he did not say aloud the rather rude word for "supremely irritated."

"It's more than hot air, Twilight."

"But you aren't, Otulissa," retorted the Great Gray.

"Now, young'uns, stop your bickering," Mrs. P. said. "Soren here has had a frightfully bad dream. And I for one feel that it is not a good idea to push bad dreams away. If you feel like talking about your bad dream, Soren, please go right ahead."

But Soren really didn't feel like talking about it that much. And he had decided definitely not to tell Digger of his feelings about Octavia. His head was in too much of a muddle to be able to explain anything. There was a tense silence. But then Digger spoke up. "Soren, why 'flecks'? What made you scream out, 'flecks'?" Soren felt Gylfie give a shudder. And even Otulissa remained silent. When Soren and Gylfie had been captives at St. Aggie's they had been forced to work in the pelletorium picking apart owl

489

pellets. Owls have a unique system for digesting their food and ridding themselves of the waste materials. All of the fur and bone and feathers of their prey are separated into small packets called pellets in their second stomach, that amazingly sensitive organ of owls, the gizzard. When all the materials were packed up, owls yarped the pellets through their beaks. In the pelletorium at St. Aggie's, they had been required to pick out the various materials like bone and feather and some mysterious element that was referred to as flecks. They never knew what flecks were exactly but they were highly prized by the brutal leaders of St. Aggie's.

"I'm not sure why. I think those sparks that come off the comet's tail somehow glinted like the flecks that we picked out of the pellets."

"Hmm," was all Digger said.

"Now look, it's almost breaklight time. Why don't you sit at my table, Soren? It'll be comfy, and I'm going to ask Matron for a nice bit of roasted vole for you."

"No can do, Mrs. P.," Otulissa said in a chipper voice.

If Mrs. P. had had eyes she would have rolled them, but instead she swung her head in an exaggerated arc and coiled up a little tighter. "What is this 'no-can-do' talk? For a supposedly educated and refined owl" — she emphasized the word refined — "I consider it a sloppy and somewhat coarse manner of speaking, Otulissa."

"There's a tropical depression that's swimming our way with the last bits of a late hurricane. The weather chaw is going out. We have to eat at the weather chaw table and . . ."

"Eat meat raw," Soren said dejectedly.

Good Glaux, raw vole on top of a bad dream and eating it literally on top of Octavia! For such were the customs of the weather and colliering chaws.

The nest-maid snakes served as tables for all the owls. They slithered into the dining halls bearing tiny Ga'Hoole nut cups of milkberry tea and whatever meat or bugs that were being served up. The chaws always ate together on the evenings of important missions. And if one was in the weather or colliering chaw, it was required that they eat their meat raw with the fur on it. Of course, Soren, like most owls until they had come to the Great Tree, had always eaten his meat raw. He still liked raw meat, but on a nippy evening like this, something warm in the gut was of great comfort. Well, he would at least try to avoid sitting next to Otulissa. Eating raw vole with that Spotted Owl yakking in his ear was enough to give any bird indigestion — or maybe even gas, and not of the random variety.

He would aim to sit between Martin and Ruby, his two best friends in the chaw. Martin was a little Northern Sawwhet, not much bigger than Gylfie, and Ruby was a Short-eared Owl.

"Glaux almighty!" Soren muttered as he approached the table of Octavia. The place between Martin and Ruby was taken by one of the new owlets who had been rescued in the Great Downing. He was a little Lesser Sooty called Silver. The name fit for he was, like all the Sooty Owls, black, but his underparts were silvery white. Sooties were all part of the same family of Barn Owls as Soren, the Tyto species, but a different group within that species — Soren being a Tyto alba and Silver a Tyto multipunctata. Still, in the whole scheme of things, they were considered "cousins." And they shared the heart-shaped face common to all Barn Owls. Silver, much smaller than Soren, now swiveled and tipped his head back.

"You shouldn't take the name of Glaux in vain, Soren." Silver spoke in a voice that was somewhere between a squeak and a shriek.

Soren blinked. "Why ever not?" Everyone said "Glaux" all the time.

"Glaux was the first Tyto. It's disrespectful to our species, to our maker."

The first Tyto, Soren thought. *What's he talking about?*

Glaux was the most ancient order of owls from which all other owls descended. Glaux was the first owl, and no one knew if it was a Tyto, let alone male or female or whatever. It didn't really matter. Apparently, Soren was not the only one confused.

"Glaux is Glaux no matter what you call him, her, whatever," said Poot. Poot was the first mate of the weather chaw but now, in the absence of Ezylryb, served as captain.

Silver blinked. "Really?"

"Yes, really," said Otulissa. "The first owl from whom we are all descended."

"I thought just Barn Owls — owls like Soren and me."

"No, *all of us*," Otulissa repeated. "No matter what kind of feather pattern, no matter what color eyes we have — yellow, amber, black, like yours — all of us are descended from Great Glaux." Otulissa could be surprising. For Otulissa to say the words "all of us" was somewhat remarkable for an owl who could be impossibly snooty and stuck-up.

It was a bit peculiar that all of the owls that had been rescued in the Great Downing had been some kind of Barn Owl. They were either Greater or Lesser Sooties like Silver, or Grass Owls, or Masked Owls. But despite the different names and slightly different coloration, they all had the distinctive heart-shaped faces that marked them as belonging to the family of Tytos, or Barn Owls. Like Silver, they had all arrived with some very strange notions and behaviors. Even the most seriously wounded owls when they were rescued had babbled nearly unintelligible fragments, but they were entranced with music. As soon as they heard Madame Plonk and the harp guild, their strange babbling had stopped.

The young owlets were getting better every day as they spent more and more time with normal owls. Of course, the owls of Ga'Hoole were not quite *normal*. When Soren was very young, his parents would tell him and Kludd and Eglantine stories. They were once-upon-a-time stories. The kind that you might wish were true but somehow don't quite believe could be. One of his and Eglantine's favorites began, "Once upon a very long time ago, in the time of Glaux, there was an order of knightly owls, from a kingdom called Ga'Hoole, who would rise each night into the blackness and perform noble deeds. They spoke no words but true ones. Their purpose was to right all wrongs, to make strong the weak, mend the broken, vanquish the proud, and make powerless those who abused the frail. With hearts sublime they would take flight ..."

But it *was* true! And when he and Twilight and Gylfie and Digger had finally found the Great Ga'Hoole Tree on an island in the middle of the Sea of Hoolemere, Soren found that in order to fulfill this noble purpose, one needed to learn all sorts of things that many owls never learn. They learned how to read and do mathematics and, with their entry into a chaw, they learned the special skills of navigation, weather interpretation, the science of metals. This kind of learning was called the "deep knowledge" and they were taught by the "rybs." The word "ryb" itself meant deep knowledge.

Tonight, the weather chaw would fly and, for Silver and another young Masked Owl named Nut Beam, it would be their first flight with the chaw. They had not been assigned yet, or "tapped" as it was called, to the weather chaw. They were not even junior members yet. They were only going on a very minor training flight to see if possibly they might be suitable. Before his disappearance, Ezylryb seemed to be able to tell with one glance if an owl might work in the chaw. But now with him gone, Boron and Barran felt it was best for the young new owlets to be tried out for this particular chaw, which required highly refined skills.

"Are we really going to fly into a hurricane tonight?" Silver asked.

"Just a mild tropical storm," Poot answered. "Nice little depression due south of here kicking up some slop in the bight and beyond."

"When do we get to fly into a tornado?" Silver asked.

Poot blinked in disbelief. "You yoicks, young'un? You don't want to fly into a tornado. You want your wings torn off? Only owl I ever seen who got through a tornado alive with his wings came out plumb naked."

Now it was Soren's turn to blink. "Plumb naked? What do you mean?"

"Not a feather left on him. Not even a tuft of down."

Octavia gave a shiver, and their cups of milkberry tea shook. "Don't scare the young'uns, Poot."

"Look, Octavia, if they ask me I tell them."

Ruby, a deep, ruddy-colored Short-eared Owl, who was the best flier in the chaw, blinked. "How'd he fly with no feathers?"

"Not well, dearie. Not well, not well at all," Poot replied.

CHAPTER THREE
What a Blow!

"Meatballs! Good and juicy." Poot swiveled his head and flung off a glob of weed, dead minnows, and assorted slop from the Sea of Hoolemere that had landed between his ear tufts.

"Storm residue. He has a very coarse way of speaking," Otulissa murmured primly to Nut Beam and Silver. She was flying between the two young owlets, and Soren was in their wake making sure that they didn't go into a bounce spiral caused by sudden updrafts, which could be dangerous.

"See? That's what you get," Poot was saying. "You don't have to go swimming to feel the water below getting warmer do you? You can feel it now, can't you?"

Soren could feel warm wet gusts coming off the waves that crashed below. It was odd, for although they were on the brink of winter, the Sea of Hoolemere in this region of the bight and beyond held the summer heat longer than any other. "That's what causes a hurricane, young'uns, when the cooler air meets up with warm water. Now, I've sent Ruby out to the edges of this mess to reconnoiter wind speeds and such."

Poot paused and looked back at his chaw members. "All right now — a little in-flight quiz."

"Oh, goody," Otulissa said. "I just love pop quizzes." Soren gave her a withering look despite the remnants of a meatball that were splattered around the rims of his eyes.

Poot continued, "Now, Martin. Which way does the wind spiral in a hurricane?"

"Oh, I know! I know!" Otulissa started waving her wings excitedly.

"Shut your beak, Otulissa," Poot snapped. "I asked Martin."

But then Nut Beam piped up, "My grandma did a special kind of dive called the spiral."

"My grandpa had a kind of twisty talon like a spiral," Silver said loudly.

"Great Glaux." Soren sighed. He had forgotten how young owlets could be. It was clear that Poot did not know how to deal with such young ones. But Otulissa interrupted what was about to turn into a free-for-all bragging match about grandparents.

"Silver, Nut Beam," she said sharply, and flew out in front of the two little owls. "Attention. All eyes on my tail, please. Now does anybody here have anything to say that is not about their grandparents, parents, or any other relatives or spirals?" There was silence. Then Silver waggled his wings. Otulissa sighed. "I feel a wing waggle from behind." She flipped her head back. "What is it, Silver?"

"My great-grandma was named for a cloud, too. Her name was Alto Cumulus."

"Thank you for that information," Otulissa said curtly. "Now may we proceed? Martin, will you please answer the question?"

"The wind spirals inward and this way." The little Northern Saw-whet spun his head almost completely around in a counterclockwise motion.

"Very good, considering you've never flown in a hurricane," Poot replied. None of them had, as yet, except for Poot.

"We might not have flown in one yet but we've read all about them, Poot," Otulissa said. "Strix Emerilla devotes three chapters to hurricanes in her book, *Atmospheric Pressures and Turbulations: An Interpreter's Guide.*"

"The most boring book in the world," Martin muttered as he flew up on Soren's starboard wing.

"I've read every word of it," Otulissa said.

"Now, next question," Poot continued. "And all you older owls shut your beaks. Which is your port wing and which is your starboard?"

There was silence. "All right. Wiggle the one you think is port." Nut Beam and Silver hesitated a bit, stole a look at each other, and then both waggled their right wing.

"Wrong!" Poot said. "Now, you two have to remember the difference. Because when I say strike off to port, or angle starboard, you're going to fly off in the wrong direction if you don't know."

Soren remembered that this was difficult for him to learn when he first started flying in the weather chaw. It took Ruby, the best flier, forever to learn port from starboard, but they all did — finally.

"All right, now," Poot said. "I'm going out for a short reconnaissance in the opposite direction of Ruby. I want to cover everything. Soren and Martin, you're in charge here. Keep flying in this direction. I'll be back soon."

Poot had not been gone long when a definite whiff seemed to wash over the small band of owls.

"I think I smell gulls nearby." Otulissa turned her beak upwind. "Oh, Great Glaux, here they come. The stench is appalling," Otulissa muttered. "Those seagulls! Scum of the avian world."

"Are they really that bad?" Nut Beam asked.

"You can smell them, can't you? And they're wet poopers on top of it all!"

"Wet poopers!" Silver and Nut Beam said at once.

"I've never met a wet pooper. I can't imagine," Nut Beam said.

"Well then, don't try," Otulissa snapped testily.

"It's hard to believe that they never yarp pellets at all," Nut Beam continued to muse.

"My sister actually had a friend who was a wet pooper, but they wouldn't let her bring him home. I think he was a warbler," Silver announced.

"Oh, Glaux, here we go again," said Martin.

"I think maybe I've met one once," said Nut Beam.

"Well, it's not something to be proud of. It's disgusting," Otulissa replied.

"You're starting to sound like a nest-maid snake, Otulissa," said Soren, and laughed. Nest-maid snakes were notoriously disdainful of all birds except owls because of what they considered their inferior and less noble digestive systems due to their inability to yarp pellets. All of their waste was splatted out from the other end, which nest-maids considered vile and disgusting.

"They give us a lot of good information about weather, Otulissa," Soren said.

"You mean a lot of dirty jokes. You can find good information in books."

Poot was soon back with the seagulls in his wake.

"What's the report?" Martin asked.

"Storm surge moderate," Poot said, "but building. The gulls say the leading edge of this thing is at least fifty leagues off to the southeast."

"Yeah, but I got news for you." At that moment, Ruby skidded in on a tumultuous draft and a mess of flying spume. She was accompanied by two gulls. It was as if she had come out of nowhere. And suddenly Soren felt an immense pull on his downwind wings. "You've been talking to the wrong gulls. It's not just a storm with a leading edge. It's a hurricane with an eye!"

Hurricane! Soren thought. *Impossible. How has this happened so quickly?* No one except Poot had ever flown a hurricane — and these young owlets! What ever would happen to them?

"It's still far off," Ruby continued. "But it's moving faster than you think and building stronger. And we're very near a rain band. And then it's the eye wall!"

"Eye wall! We've got to alter course," Poot exclaimed. "Which way, Ruby?"

"Port, I mean starboard!"

"The eye wall!" Soren and Martin both gasped. The eye wall of a hurricane was worse than the eye. It was a wall of thunderstorms that was preceded by the rain bands that delivered violent swirling updrafts that could extend hundreds of leagues from this wall.

"You can't see the band from here because of the clouds."

Oh, Glaux, thought Soren. *Don't let these young owlets go off on their stories of grandparents being named for clouds.*

"I think that right now we might actually be between two rain bands," Ruby continued.

And then it was as if they all were sucked up into a swirling shaft. *This IS a hurricane!* Soren thought. He saw Martin go spinning by in a tawny blur. "Martin!" he screamed. He heard a sickening gasp and in the blur saw the little beak of the Saw-whet open in a wheeze as Martin tried to gulp air. He must have been in one of the terrible airless vacuums that Soren had heard about. Then Martin vanished, and Soren had to fight with all of his might to stay back up, belly down, and flying. He could not believe how difficult this was. He had flown through blazing forests harvesting live coals, battling the enormous fire winds and strange contortions of air that the heat made, but this was terrible!

"Strike off to port, south by southeast. We're going to run down. Rudder starboard with tail feathers! Extend lulus." The lulus were small feathers just at the bend of an owl's wing, which could help smooth the airflow. Poot was now calling out a string of instructions. "Downwind rudder, hold two points to skyward with port wing. Come on, chaw! You can do it! Primary feathers screw down. Level off now. Forward thrust!" Poot was flying magnificently, especially considering that under the lee of his wings he had tucked the two young owlets Nut Beam and Silver for protection.

But where was Martin? Martin was the smallest owl in the chaw. *Concentrate! Concentrate!* Soren told himself. *You're a dead bird if you think about anything but flying. Dead bird! Dead bird! Wings torn off!* All the horrible stories he had heard about hurricanes came back to Soren. And although owls talked about the deadly eye of the hurricane, he knew there was something worse, really — the rim of that eye. And if the eye was fifty leagues away — well, the rim could be much closer. Soren's own two eyes opened wide in terror and his third eyelid, the transparent one that swept across this eyeball, had to work hard to clear the debris, the slop, being flung in it from all directions. But he paid no heed to the slop. In his eye was the image of little Martin vanishing in a split second and being sucked directly into that rim. The eye of a hurricane was calm, but caught in the rim, a bird could spin around and around, its wings torn off by the second spin and most likely gasping for air until it died.

The air started to smooth out and the clammy warmth that had welled up from below subsided as a cooler layer of air floated up from the turbulent waters. But it had begun to pour hard. A driving rain pushed by the winds slanted in at a steep angle. The sea below seemed to smoke from the force of the rain.

"Form up, chaw! SOFP," Poot commanded. They all assumed the positions of their Standard Operational Flight Pattern. Soren swiveled his head to look for Martin off his starboard wing. There was a little blank space where the Northern Saw-whet usually flew. He tipped his head up to where Ruby flew and saw the rusty fluff of her underbelly. She looked down and shook her head sadly. Soren thought he saw a tear well up in her eye, but it could have been some juice from a leftover meatball.

"Roll call!" Poot now barked. "Beak off, chaw!"

"Ruby here!" snapped the rust-colored Short-eared Owl.

"Otulissa here!"

"Soren here!"

Then there was nothing — silence, or perhaps it was more like a small gulp from the position that Martin had always flown.

"Absence noted. Continue," Poot said.

Absence noted? Continue? Was that it? Soren gasped. But before he could protest there was that piercing little voice, "Silver here."

"Nut Beam here! But I'm feeling nauseous."

"WHERE IS MARTIN, FOR GLAUX'S SAKE!" Soren shrieked in rage.

"Owl down," Poot said, "Search-and-rescue commence."

Then there was a muffled, slightly gagging sound and a terrific stench. At first, Soren thought Nut Beam had thrown up. But then out of the smoking Sea of Hoolemere, a seagull rose and in its beak was a wet little form.

"Martin here!" gasped the little owl. He hung limply in the beak of the seagull.

CHAPTER FOUR

The Spirit Woods

I'm not sure if it was the impact on the water or the stench that got me, but I'm still feeling a bit dizzy. I have to say, however, that seagull stench is now my favorite fragrance." Martin turned and nodded at Smatt, the seagull who had rescued him.

"Aw, it warn't nothin.'" The seagull ducked his head modestly.

When he had first vanished, Martin had been sucked straight up, but it was a narrow funnel of warm air and almost immediately it had swirled into a bank of cold air that created a downdraft, and Martin had plunged into the sea. Smatt, who had been navigating between these funnels of warm and cold air, plunged in after him and grabbed him in his beak as he might have grabbed a fish — although Martin was considerably smaller than any fish that seagulls normally ate.

They had lighted down now on the mainland, in a wooded area on a peninsula that fingered out into the sea.

It seemed, for the moment, calm. Although Soren, as he glanced around, found the forest quite strange. All the trees were white-barked and not one had a single leaf. Indeed, although it was night, this forest had a kind of luminance that made the moon pale by comparison.

"I would guess," said Otulissa as she studied the sky, "that we are between rain bands here." For some reason this rankled Soren. It sounded to him as if Otulissa was trying to sum up the weather situation the way Ezylryb would have, being the most knowledgeable owl of all about weather. Poot, who had succeeded him as chaw captain, really had very little knowledge in comparison, but he was a great flier. Now it seemed as if Otulissa had become the self-appointed weather expert.

Poot looked around uneasily. "That, or a spirit woods."

A chill ran through them all. "A spirit woods?" Martin said softly. "I've heard of them."

"Yeah, you've heard of them. You don't necessarily want to spend the night in them," Poot replied.

"I don't know, Poot," Ruby spoke in a nervous low voice, "whether we've got much choice. I mean that hurricane's still going. I've seen the worst of it. It's not something you want to mess with."

"Well, folks." Smatt began to lift his wings. A fetid smell wafted toward them. "I think I'll be clearing out now." The seagull looked apprehensively at Poot. In a flash he had lifted off and vanished.

"What are we gonna do, Poot?" Silver asked, a slight tremor in his voice.

"Not much choice, as Ruby said. Just hope we don't disturb any scrooms."

"Scrooms!" Nut Beam and Silver wailed.

"Well, I don't believe in them," Martin said and stomped his small talons into the moss-covered ground. Then, as if to prove it, he lifted off and began to search for a tree to light down in.

"You mind what tree you choose. You don't want to disturb a scroom," Poot called after him. But Soren thought that maybe after having been sucked up in a rain band, then dropped into the sea, a scroom was nothing to Martin.

Scrooms were disembodied spirits of owls who had died and had not quite made it all the way to glaumora, which was the special owl heaven where the souls of owls went. Nut Beam and Silver, however, had begun to cry uncontrollably.

"Pull yourselves together, both of you," Otulissa exploded angrily. "There's no such thing as scrooms. An atmospheric disturbance. False light. That's all. Strix Emerilla has written about it in a very erudite book entitled, *Spectroscopic Anomalies: Shifts in Shape and Light.*"

"Yes, there are scrooms!" the two owlets hooted back shrilly.

"My grandma said so," Nut Beam said defiantly and stomped a small talon on the moss.

"I've heard enough about your grandmas," Otulissa snapped. "Poot, how long do we have to stay here?"

"Until the hurricane blows through. Can't take these young'uns" — he nodded toward Silver and Nut Beam — "out in this. Too inexperienced."

"You're making us stay here — with scrooms?" Nut Beam protested. And as if on cue, Silver started to wail again.

Ruby flew up and then lighted directly in front of the two owlets. She looked almost twice her size as her rust-colored feathers had puffed up in the manner of owls who are extremely angry. In the pale eerie white of the forest, Ruby looked like a ball of red-hot embers. "I'm fed up with all your whining. I don't give a pile of racdrops if there're scrooms here. I'm hungry. I'm tired. I want a nice fat rat or vole. I'll take squirrel if I have to. Then I want to go to sleep. And you two better shut your beaks because I'll make your life more miserable than scrooms ever could!" The other owls looked at Ruby with astonishment.

"I think we need to organize a hunting party," Otulissa said.

"Yes, yes, immediately," Poot said. He began to flutter about the group. "Now, there's no telling what one can find in such a woods."

It was obvious to Soren, Ruby, and Martin that Otulissa had embarrassed Poot, who might be a terrific flier but not a natural leader. They felt the absence of Ezylryb more than ever.

But then, Poot seemed to be jarred into action. He swelled up with authority and tried his best to sound like a leader. "Soren," Poot said, "you and Ruby can cover the northeast quadrant of this woods. You fly it hard now, young'uns. We got some hungry beaks here. Martin and Otulissa can cover the southwest one. I'll stay here with the young'uns."

"Ha!" Ruby gave a harsh sound and ascended through the branches. "I think Poot's scared of scrooms. That's why he sent us out. You scared, Soren?" They had gained some altitude now, and the strange mist that floated through the white trees below seemed to evaporate.

"Sort of," Soren said.

"Well, at least you're honest. But what do you mean by 'sort of'?"

"I think the idea of a scroom is not so much scary as sad. I mean scrooms are supposed to be spirits that didn't quite make it to glaumora. That's kind of sad."

"I guess so," Ruby said.

Guess so? Soren blinked at Ruby. He thought it was terribly sad, but Ruby wasn't the deepest owl. She was a fantastic flier and a great chaw mate and lots of fun but, although she felt things in her gizzard like all owls, she was not given to reflecting deeply. But now she surprised him. "How come they don't make it to glaumora?"

"I'm not sure. Mrs. P. said that it was because they might have unfinished business on earth."

"Mrs. Plithiver? How would she know? She's a snake."

"I sometimes think that Mrs. P. knows more about owls than owls do." Soren cocked his head suddenly. "Sssh." Ruby shut her beak immediately. She, like all other owls, had great respect for the extraordinary hearing abilities of Barn Owls. "Ground squirrel below."

There were actually three in all. And Ruby, who was incredibly fast with her talons, managed to get two in one single slicing swipe. They were more successful than Martin and Otulissa, who had only come back with two very small mice.

"Hunter's share," Poot said, nodding to the four of them. It was customary that the owls who did the hunting got first choice of the catch. Soren chose a thigh from his ground squirrel. It was rather scrawny, and it wasn't the most flavorful ground squirrel he had ever eaten. Maybe a spirit wood wasn't the best place for a ground squirrel to get plump and juicy. Then Soren had a creepy thought. Maybe they fed on scrooms or perhaps scrooms fed on them — spirit food. His gizzard hardly had to work to pack in those bones and fur.

By the time they had finished eating, the night was thinning into day. Although with the mist that seemed to wrap itself through the branches of the white-barked trees, Soren thought that it seemed like twilight in these woods.

"I think," Poot announced, "it's time for us to turn in. Not for a full day's sleep, mind you. We'll leave before First Black. No fear of crows around here." He slid his neck about in a slow twist as if scanning the wood.

"No. Just scrooms," Nut Beam said.

"Nut Beam, shut your beak," Martin screeched fiercely.

"Now, now, Martin! Don't like that tone, lad," Poot said, trying to sound very —

Very what? wondered Soren. *Like Ezylryb? Never like the Captain.*

"Well, I've been doing some thinking," Poot went on to say. "And I think that this being a spirit woods as some calls 'em, I think it's best that we keep to the ground for sleeping, no perching in them trees." He swiveled his head around in a slow sweeping movement, as if he were almost trying to push back the bone-white trees that surrounded them.

A hush fell upon the group. Soren thought he could hear the beat of their hearts quicken. *This scroom stuff must really be serious*, he said to himself. Even Ruby looked a little nervous. For an owl to sleep on the ground was almost unheard of, unless, of course, it was a Burrowing Owl who lived in the desert, like Digger. There were dangers on the ground. Predators — like raccoons.

"I know what you be thinking," Poot continued nervously and seemed to avoid looking them in the eye as Ezylryb would have. "I know you're thinking that for an owl to ground sleep ain't natural. But these ain't natural woods. And it's said that these trees might really belong to the scrooms. You never know which one a scroom might light down in and it's best to leave the trees be. I'm older than you young'uns. Got more experience. And I'd be daft not to tell you that my gizzard is giving me some mighty twinges."

"Mine, too!" said Silver.

"Probably has a gizzard the size of a pea," Martin whispered.

"Now don'cha go worry too much. We just got to be vigi-ful," Poot continued.

"You mean 'vigilant'?" Otulissa said.

"Don't smart beak me, lassie. We's gonna set up a

watch. I'll take the first one with Martin. Otulissa and Ruby you take the next. And Soren you take the last. You have to do it alone, but it be the shortest one, lad. So nothin' to fear."

Nothing to fear? Then why doesn't he take it? Soren thought, but he knew that the one thing a chaw owl never did was question a command. All of the owls turned their heads toward Soren.

Martin stepped forward. "I'll stay up with you, Soren."

Soren blinked at the little Northern Saw-whet. "No, no — that's very kind of you, Martin, but you'll be tired. You must already be tired. I mean you've fallen into the sea. Don't worry, Martin. I'll be fine."

"No, Soren, I mean it."

"No, I'll be fine," Soren said firmly.

The truth was that during that first watch they were all too nervous to sleep and the ground was a terrible place to even try to sleep to begin with. But as the dark faded and the white of the trees melted into the lightness of the morning, they did grow sleepier and sleepier. The owls' heads began to droop lower and lower until they were resting on their breasts or on their backs, as it was the habit of very young owls to twist their heads around and rest them just between their shoulders.

"Your watch, Soren," Ruby said.

His eyes blinked open. He lifted his head.

"Don't worry. There is nothing out here. Not a raccoon, not a scroom, not a scroom of a raccoon." Otulissa churred softly, which was the sound that owls made when they laughed.

Soren walked over to the watch mound that was in a small clearing. He spread his wings and, in one brief upstroke, rose to settle on the top of the mound. The fog in the forest had thickened again. A soft breeze swirled through the woods, stirring and spinning the mist into fluffy shapes. Some of the mist clouds were long and skinny, others puffy. Soren thought of the silly jabber of the young owlets when they had been flying earlier, before encountering the hurricane. The owlets were sort of cute, he guessed, in their own annoying little way. It was hard to believe, however, that he had ever been that young. He had barely known his parents before he had been snatched, and he had never known his grandparents. There had been no time. He blinked his eyes at the mist that was now whirling into new shapes. It was strange how one could start to read this ground mist like clouds, find pictures in them — a raccoon, a deer bounding over a tree stump, a fish leaping from a river. Soren had tried sometimes to make up stories about cloud pictures when he was flying. The vapors just ahead of him had clumped together into one large shapeless mass, but now they seemed to be pulling apart again into two clumps. There was something vaguely familiar about the shapes that these clumps were becoming. What was it? A lovely downy bundle that looked so soft and warm. Something seemed to call to him and yet there was no sound. How could that be?

Soren grew very still. Something was happening. He was not frightened. No, not frightened at all. But sad, yes, deeply and terribly sad. He felt himself drawn to these two shapes. They were fluffy and their heads were cocked in such a familiar way as if they were listening to him. And they *were* calling to him, and they were saying things but there were no sounds. It was as if the voices were sealed inside his head. Just then, he felt himself step out of his body. He felt his wings spread. He was lifting, and yet he was still there on the mound. He could see his talons planted on the mossy top with the tangle of ivy. But, at the same time, he could see something moving out of him. It was him — but not him. It was his shape, pale and misty and swirling like the other shapes. The thing that was him but not him was lifting, rising, and spreading its wings in flight to perch in the big white tree at the edge of the clearing where the two other misty figures perched.

False light?

No, not false light, Soren.

Scrooms?

If you must.

Mum? Da?

The mist seemed to shiver and glint like moonlight scattered on water.

He floated over the mound but when he looked back he saw his own figure still standing there. He extended a talon but it was transparent! And then he lighted down on the branch. In that instant, Soren realized he felt in a strange way complete. It was as if there had been a hole in his gizzard and now it had been filled and closed. He reached out with his talon to touch his mum but it simply passed through her.

Am I dying? Am I becoming a scroom?

No, dearest. No one had called him "dearest" like that since he had been snatched.

Soren cocked his head and tried to look at his parents, but the mist was continually shifting, sliding, and recomposing itself into their shapes. They were recognizable but yet it was not images he was seeing. It was more like a foggy shadow. Still, he knew without a doubt it was them.

But why, why after all this time were they here, seeking him out?

Unfinished business? Is that what it is?

We think so. It was the voice of his father in his head.

You don't know?

Not exactly, dear. We're never sure. We know something isn't right. We have feelings, but no real answers to these feelings.

Are you trying to warn me of something?

Yes, yes. But the hard part is we don't know what it is we should warn you about.

Soren wondered if they knew about Kludd. He wanted to tell them how Kludd had pushed him from the nest, but he couldn't. Something stopped in his brain. Words began to tumble out of his mouth, and now he could actually hear those words. He was telling them about Kludd, but his mum and da were unmoved. They were not hearing anything of what he was saying. And there was a blankness now in his head. This was all very weird. When he could hear his own voice, the words in the normal way, his parents could not. Their only way of speaking to one another was this silent language that seemed to exist only in their heads. And yet Soren could not form the ideas in his head to tell them about Kludd, and they could not tell him about the danger.

Metal! Beware Metal Beak! The words exploded in

Soren's head. It was the voice of his father but it seemed to have taken all his energy to do this. His father was dissolving before his eyes. His mother as well. The mists that had been their shapes were swirling, seeping away. Soren reached out with his talons to hold them. "Don't go! Don't go. Don't leave me! Come back."

"What's you yelling about, lad? Wake us all up, will you?" Soren was suddenly on the ground, and Poot was standing in front of him, blinking. How had he gotten on the ground? He had been in that tree a second ago but he had no memory of flying down from it. And there was no mist now. None at all.

"I'm sorry, Poot. I flew up into that tree there. I thought I saw something." Soren nodded.

"No, you didn't," Poot said. "I woke a few minutes ago. You were standing right here on the mound. Perfectly alert — being a good lookout. Believe me, I would have had your tail feathers if you hadn't been."

"I was right here?" Soren was incredulous.

"Course you were, young'un," Poot said and looked at him curiously as if he'd gone yoicks. "Right here you were. I would have noticed you up in the tree, believe me."

Had it just been a dream? Soren thought. *But it felt so real. I heard Mum's and Da's voices in my head. It* was *real.*

"Time we be takin' off." Poot looked at the sky that was

turning a dusky purple. Pink clouds sliding against it. "Wind's going our way," Poot remarked, after studying the clouds for a minute. "We'll catch a westerly and come in on a nice reach." A reach was easy flying with the wind being not on the beak or on the tail feathers directly, but a little aft of the wing, giving a nice steady boost to their flight. The others were beginning to stir from their daytime slumbers.

"Form up!" Poot commanded. It was to be a ground start, which was a bit harder than taking off from a branch. But they did it nonetheless. Soren and Martin were the last to rise in flight. They ascended in tight spiraling circles and were soon clear of the spirit woods.

When Soren looked back, he saw the mist gathering again. Like silky scarves, it began to wind through the trees. He strained his eyes to find those two familiar shapes. Just one more glimpse, that's all he wanted. One more glimpse. But the mist lay thick and shapeless over the white forest. Had Soren been able to see through it, however, he might have spotted a feather, just like one of his, but nearly transparent, drifting lazily down from the branch of a tree in the spirit woods.

CHAPTER FIVE

Bubo's Forge

Soren had been back for two days. But he had said nothing of his strange experience in the spirit woods to anyone, not even his closest friends, his friends in the "band" — Gylfie, Digger, Twilight, himself, and now, since her rescue, his sister, Eglantine. But every day when he fell to sleep he dreamed of the scrooms of his parents. Had it been a dream in the spirit woods as well, just a dream? And the words *Metal Beak*, those two words seemed to almost clang in his brain and send ominous quivers to his gizzard. The words took on a life of their own and grew more dreadful with each passing hour.

"Something's spooking you, Soren, I just know it," Digger said as they were sitting in the library one evening after navigation practice.

"No, nothing at all," Soren said quickly. Soren had been reading a really good book, but he was distracted and had read the same sentence about five times. Leave it to Digger to pick up on the worries that haunted him day and night.

"Nothing at all, Soren?" Digger blinked and looked at him closely. The fluffy white brow tufts that framed his deep yellow eyes waggled a bit.

Soren looked back at Digger. *Should I tell him about the scrooms — about Metal Beak? The best thing is to be honest, yet ...*

"Digger, something is bothering me, but I can't tell you just now. Do you understand?"

Digger blinked again. "Of course, Soren. When you're ready to tell, I'll listen," the Burrowing Owl said softly. "No need to say anything until you're ready."

"Thank you, Digger, thank you so much."

So the Barn Owl got up, closed the book he was reading, and went to put it on the shelf. The shelf was next to the table where Ezylryb always sat absorbed in his studies, munching on his little pile of dried caterpillars. The library wasn't the same without the old Screech Owl. Nothing seemed the same without him. Soren slid the book back into its place on the shelf. As he turned to leave, a book on metals caught his eye. Metals! Why hadn't he thought of this before? He must go to see Bubo, the blacksmith. He must immediately go to Bubo's forge. Soren might not be ready to tell Digger, but he was ready to tell Bubo — not all of it, but part of it — the part about Metal Beak.

He flew out of the Great Ga'Hoole Tree, spiraled down

toward its base, and then swept low across the ground to a nearby cave. This was Bubo's forge. The forge was just outside the entry of the cave and the rock had blackened over the years from Bubo's fires. It was to this forge that Soren and the other members of the colliering chaw brought the live coals that fed the fires, which smelted the metals used for everything from pots and pans to battle claws and shields for the great tree. If anyone knew about metal beaks, or whatever it was that the scrooms had spoken of in the whispery voices that still swirled in Soren's head, it would be Bubo. The fire had been dampened down, however, and there was no sign of Bubo. Perhaps he was inside.

Although Bubo was not a Burrowing Owl, who always made their nests in the ground, he preferred living in a cave to a tree. As he had once explained to Soren, blacksmiths like himself, no matter if they were Great Horned Owls, Snowies, Spotted, or Great Grays, were drawn to the earth where, indeed, the metals lodged.

Soren now stepped into the shadow of the overhanging rock ledge of the cave's opening. Deep inside, he could see the glints of the whirlyglasses that Bubo had strung up. These contraptions were made from bits of colored glass and when light crept into the cave and struck the glass, reflections spun through the air and bounced off the walls in swirling dapples of color. There was no moonlight tonight, though. It was the time of the dwenking when the moon disappeared to barely a sliver.

"Bubo!" Soren called. He waited. "Bubo!"

"That you, Soren?" A large shadowy bundle of feathers started to melt out of the darkness of the cave. Great Horned Owls like Bubo were large, but Bubo himself was unusually large and towered over Soren. His two ear tufts, which grew straight up over each eye, were exceedingly bushy, giving him a slightly threatening demeanor. But Soren knew that beneath the gruffness there was no owl who had a gentler heart than Bubo. Although, like most Great Horned Owls, his feathers were basically the dull somber grays, browns, and blacks, they had been shot through with bright red and hot yellow like the hottest of fires — the ones said to have "bonk." Bonk was the word that blacksmiths like Bubo used to describe the strongest and most energetic fires. Such fires have special hues and colors unlike ordinary ones. Bubo also could be said to have bonking colorful plumage. It was as if he had been clothed in the flames of his own forge instead of just the usual drab feathers of his species. "What brings you here, lad?"

"Metal Beak," Soren blurted without preamble.

"Metal Beak!" Bubo gasped. "What'cha know about him, laddie?"

"Him?" Soren blinked. "It's a him?" Until that moment, Soren thought that the scrooms of his parents had been referring to a thing — something that struck dread in him, like flecks. Yes, he had suspected flecks because it was Bubo himself who had first explained to him that the flecks they had been forced to pick at St. Aggie's were a kind of special metal with what he had called "magnetic properties." He had said that when all the tiny unseeable parts, the flecks in these metals were lined up, it created a force that was called magnetic. Now Soren didn't know what to think. He was relieved that Metal Beak had nothing to do with flecks. But why was Bubo so agitated? The big, flaming Horned Owl was almost hopping out of his feathers.

"You stay clear of him. You ain't to go tangling with that owl, Soren."

"Metal Beak is an owl?"

"Oh, yeah."

"What kind?"

"No one is for sure what kind he be. A bad kind, that's all I can tell you."

Soren was confused. "How can you not be sure about what kind he is?"

"Because he wears a metal beak and a metal mask over most his face."

"Why's that?"

"Wouldn't really know," Bubo said as if he didn't really want to discuss it. "Some say he flies noisy like a Pygmy Owl, but he ain't no pygmy size, I'll tell you that. Well, maybe Barn Owl but bigger, much bigger, but not as big as a Great Gray. Some swear he's got ear tufts like a Great Horned, yours truly here. Others say no. But there's one thing they all agree on."

"What's that?"

Bubo's voice dropped. "He's the most brutal owl in all the kingdoms of owls. He's the most vicious owl on earth."

Soren swore that he felt his gizzard drop to his talons. When Soren and his band had been on their journey to the Great Ga'Hoole Tree, they had come across a dying Barred Owl. To Soren and his mates it looked like a murder by St. Aggie's top lieutenants.

"Was it St. Aggie's?" Glyfie had asked. And the dying Barred Owl had responded with his last breath. "I wish it had been St. Aggie's. It was something far worse. Believe me — St. Aggie's — Oh! You only wish!"

Soren, Gylfie, Twilight, and Digger could not imagine anything worse, anything more brutal than St. Aggie's. But the Barred Owl had told them differently. There *was* something far worse. It was nameless and now possibly faceless, but so frightened were the four owls that they had begun to refer to this monster or possibly monsters as the "you only wish." The few times they had begun to ask about this evil thing, the owls of the Ga'Hoole Tree, the rybs, had deftly turned the conversation to something else. But now Bubo was telling him of this brutal owl known as Metal Beak.

Bubo would never turn away from a young owl's question. That simply wasn't his style. So Soren did not feel reluctant to press him. "You know, Bubo, how Gylfie, Digger, Twilight, and I found that dying Barred Owl in The Beaks?"

"Yes, I heard tell of that and the bobcat that you four young'uns managed to kill right stylishly, I'd say. Dropped a coal in his eye, direct hit from how far up was it?"

"Oh, I'm not sure, Bubo. But tell me this — do you think that the Barred Owl might have been done in by this Metal Beak?"

"Very possible! Possible, indeed. Maybe even probable, which, as you know if you study your arithmetic, can happen more often than possible. In other words, probable is more possible than possible."

"Yes, yes, of course." Bubo could go off in this way, and it could be very difficult to get him back on track. "I see what you mean. But why would it be very possible, or maybe even probable, that this Metal Beak killed the Barred Owl?"

"Well, the Barred Owl were a rogue smith, warn't he." But it really wasn't a question. Soren wasn't quite sure if he understood Bubo's meaning. It was as if Bubo was saying that if an owl was a rogue smith, this sometimes could happen.

"Yes," said Soren hesitantly. "But . . ."

"But what?"

"Well, Bubo, I am not sure exactly what a rogue smith is."

"Don't know what a rogue smith is, don't you?"

Soren shook his head and looked down at his talons.

"Nothing to be ashamed about, lad. A rogue smith is a blacksmith just like me. But he ain't attached to any kingdom. I mean, we here at the Ga'Hoole Tree be the only ones who know how to use fire in all different ways, like for cooking, and the light for the candles for reading and, of course, for tools, like battle claws, and pots and pans and cauldrons. But these rogue smiths, they know about forging some and they mostly make battle claws. Weapons, you know."

"But who do they make them for?"

"Anyone who comes along. They don't ask no questions about the who, but seems like they get plenty of information one way or the other. They have to deal with rogue colliers. Get a lot from them."

"Rogue colliers? You mean colliers like me and Otulissa and Martin and Ruby?"

"Yep, but no chaw. You get it? They just go it alone."

"Alone into forest fires?"

Bubo nodded. "But it's the smiths who really get all the good information. This Barred was a slipgizzle."

"Yes," Soren replied.

"Now, you know what a slipgizzle is, don't you?"

"Uh . . . kind of a secret agent owl?"

"That's it, basically. Keeps their eyes and ears open for any news, then reports back to us. But they never stay long when they come. They likes living wild. I think I recall this Barred Owl coming in here once a while back. A rough-trade sort of bird. Didn't like his meat cooked, no sirree. Said candlelight, smell of wax wobbled his gizzard."

"Are there any other rogue smiths?" Soren asked. An idea was forming in his head.

"Oh, yes — a few. There's a Snowy Owl over near the border between The Barrens and Silverveil."

"Do you know his name?" Soren asked.

"His? What makes you think it's a 'his'?"

"Hers?" Soren asked tentatively. Bubo nodded. "I've never heard of a female blacksmith."

"Well, now you have." Bubo batted his talon on one of the whirlyglasses and the colors seemed to ignite as they were caught in the light of a candle dappling the walls of the cave.

"What's her name?" Soren asked.

"Don't know. Most of them rogue smiths keep their names to themselves. They're an odd sort, I'm telling you." Then he looked narrowly at Soren and fixed him in his amber gaze. "Rogues are unpredictable and not only that, they are often visited by bad sorts. After all, they make weapons. So, Soren, don't you be getting ideas."

But that was just exactly what Soren was doing: getting an idea!

CHAPTER SIX

Eglantine's Dilemma

"Beware of Metal Beak.' It was the scrooms who told me." Soren was in the hollow with Twilight, Gylfie, Digger, and Eglantine.

"But did they actually say it out loud?" Gylfie hopped up close to Soren and looked straight up.

"Well, no — not exactly. Scrooms don't speak out loud."

"Then how do you know," Eglantine asked in a broken voice, "that it was them, the scrooms of Mum and Da? Because if it was, that means they are dead, doesn't it, Soren?" Tears began to leak out of his sister's coal-black eyes.

"It does, Eglantine, and there is nothing we can do about that," said Soren.

"Dead is dead," Twilight said in his usual blunt way. Gylfie turned and kicked him in his talons.

"What did you do that for, Gylfie?"

"Twilight, she has just found out for sure that her parents are dead. You could be a little more sensitive!"

"But it's the truth, isn't it?" Twilight said, slightly abashed by Gylfie's reprimand.

"It is, and it isn't," Soren said. "You asked me how I heard them, how I could be sure. I can't explain exactly. It was them. I felt their spirits, and their words were not out-loud words but seemed to form in my brain. First, they would come like fog or mist, and then they would gather into a shape that had meaning, a picture. But I felt so close to them. I knew it was them."

Digger now spoke. "But why do you say that it is and it isn't true that they are dead, Soren?"

"Mrs. Plithiver told me that one reason the scrooms of owls do not go to glaumora is because they have unfinished business on earth. I think Mum and Da's unfinished business was to warn me about Metal Beak. We must find this Metal Beak, and I think that the best way is to go to the rogue smith of Silverveil."

"But we can't, Soren," Eglantine said in an almost whiny voice. "I have navigation and Ga'Hoolology, and they really get mad at us new owls if we skip class. Especially the Ga'Hoolology ryb. She says that these are the most important days for the tree."

Ga'Hoolology was the study and care of the great tree, which not only gave habitat to the owls of Ga'Hoole but nourishment through its nuts and berries. Indeed, there was hardly a part of the tree that was not used in some way.

"Yes, but the berry harvest is coming up," Soren said.

"So?" said Eglantine.

"It's a big festival." Gylfie turned to Eglantine. "There are no chaw practices or classes for three days. We all have to help with the harvest and then on the third night, there's a big banquet that goes on every night for another three or four at least, to celebrate. They say the rybs always get very tipsy on the milkberry wine. It'll be the easiest time to fly off with no one noticing."

"Oh," said Eglantine. She sounded slightly deflated as if some last hope had vanished for her. "So when does this festival start?"

"Five days," Digger said.

"Five days!" Eglantine sounded panicked.

"Yes," said Soren. "But we shouldn't plan to leave until after the banquet is really going. The banquets don't begin for another eight days."

"Yes, yes," everyone agreed. They began making plans immediately. Should it just be the five of them or should they include others like Martin and Ruby? Soren felt it might be a good idea because colliers knew the ways of smiths and other colliers and, quite honestly, Soren realized he did not want to take on the entire burden with this rogue smith. She might prove difficult. He wondered to himself if Eglantine was really strong enough to go yet. She still seemed frail to him — even though it had been almost two months since her rescue — not just physically frail, but frail in the gizzard. Then again, would her feelings be hurt if she were left behind?

"What about Otulissa?" Gylfie asked.

There was a resounding "No!"

"She can't keep her beak shut," said Twilight.

"Right," said Digger. "She'll be hooting about it all over the tree."

"I can come, can't I, Soren?" Eglantine asked in a small tremulous voice.

"Do you feel strong enough?"

"Of course I do!"

Soren didn't have the heart to say no.

Then another thought suddenly occurred to him. "You know, all this time I have been thinking that this Metal Beak, whoever he is, might be the one who killed the Barred Owl. Do you suppose that —"

It was as if the three owls, Twilight, Digger, and Gylfie, all read Soren's mind. "Ezylryb," they all gasped.

"Exactly. Do you think Metal Beak could have something to do with Ezylryb's disappearance?" The owls began whispering in excited voices.

"We must work out our strategy," Gylfie said.

"We better go to the library and look at maps of Silverveil," Digger added.

"Well, Bubo said the rogue smith was on the border between Silverveil and The Barrens. So doesn't that mean it could be in either place?" Soren asked.

"But they call her the rogue smith of Silverveil," Gylfie said. "So most likely she is closer to Silverveil."

There were countless details to work out. Should they "borrow" battle claws from the armory? No, they would be found out immediately even if the older owls were tipsy. Could they leave any earlier? What weather was coming in? If it was a south wind and they were flying south by southeast, it could slow them down. Amid all this jabber there was one little pocket of silence. And that was when Eglantine retreated to her own corner of the hollow and tried to weep as silently as possible in the fluffy nest of down. But it wasn't her mum's down. It didn't smell anything like her mum, and there was too much moss in it. But she couldn't let Soren see her crying. She had just told him that she was strong enough to fly with them to Silverveil. She wanted to be included so much. They mustn't think she was a baby. Well, there was only one place to go when she was feeling this bad — to Mrs. Plithiver. She hoped Mrs. P.'s hollow mates — two other nest-maid snakes — wouldn't be there. It would be all over the tree if they saw her crying. Nest-maids were notorious gossips.

"There, there, dear." Mrs. Plithiver had coiled up and was stretching as far as possible to stroke Eglantine's wing. "It can't be that bad."

"But it is, Mrs. P. You don't understand."

"No, I don't. Why don't you start at the beginning?"

So Eglantine told the old nest-maid snake about what Soren had seen in the spirit forest, about the scrooms of their parents, and how Twilight had said "dead is dead." But Soren had said "not exactly" and the part about Metal Beak and the unfinished business. "See, Mrs. P., I know this is wrong but if the business gets finished, Mum and Da will go to glaumora, and then I'll never see them again."

Mrs. Plithiver was silent for a long time. If she had had eyes they might have wept. Finally, she spoke. "It's not wrong, Eglantine, to want to see your parents again, but the real question is would you be happy if you saw them — or their scrooms — and they were very, very sad and worried about you?"

Eglantine blinked. She hadn't thought of that.

"Was Soren happy?" Mrs. P. continued. "Did he say anything about being so happy and glad to have seen them?"

Now that Eglantine thought about it, Soren hadn't seemed at all happy since he had returned from the spirit woods. He seemed completely dragged down by something. And Mrs. Plithiver, as if seeing directly into Eglantine's brain, said, "It's the scrooms. Scrooms with unfinished business, although they seem only to be made of mist and vapor, can be a terrible weight on the living. I noticed it as soon as Soren returned."

"You did?" Eglantine blinked in astonishment. Mrs. P. nodded her rose-colored head, and her eye dents seemed to flinch. "How?" Eglantine asked.

"I've told you, Eglantine, that although we are blind, nest-maid snakes have very finely tuned sensibilities. We pick up on these things, especially if it concerns family members, and I worked for your family for so long — well, I just know when any one of you is out of sorts. But, Eglantine, the main thing is that you must rid yourself of this notion that to see your parents just one more time, to meet their scrooms, would make you feel happy. It won't, my dear, believe me."

"It's hard." Eglantine paused.

"I know, I know. But you know, dear, you must think about the good times you had with your parents, the happy times."

"Like when Da would tell us the stories of the order of

the guardian owls of Ga'Hoole before we went to sleep. 'Knights' he called them."

"Yes, dear, I listened to his stories, too. He had a lovely sonorous voice, especially for a Barn Owl."

"But Mrs. P., Da thought that the stories were just legends. He didn't know they were true and that now Soren and I are here and someday we, too, shall be Guardians of Ga'Hoole. If Mum and Da only knew." Eglantine sighed deeply.

"But I think they do, dear. That's just the point. Why else would their scrooms have tried to warn Soren? They might have had unfinished business, but they knew that you and Soren and Twilight and Digger and Gylfie could finish the business, for you are almost Guardians of Ga'Hoole, are you not?"

"Well, they are. But not me — yet."

"Oh, yet!" Mrs. Plithiver swung her head as if to wipe away the word. "In your gizzard, I know you feel it. And that you are."

"Really, Mrs. Plithiver?"

"Really, Eglantine."

Eglantine returned to the hollow feeling much better. Indeed, she was almost excited about their adventure.

CHAPTER SEVEN
The Harvest Festival

At the Great Ga'Hoole Tree, there were four seasons, beginning in winter with the time of the white rain, then spring, which was known as the time of the silver rain, followed in the summer by the golden rain, and finally the autumn, which was known as the season of the copper rose. The seasons were thus called because of the vines of milkberries that cascaded from every branch of the great tree. The delicious berries of the vines made up a major part of the owls' nonmeat diet. From the ripened berries they brewed their tea, and made stews and cakes, loaves of fragrant bread, and soup. The dried berries were used for highly nutritious snacks, and as a source of instant energy as well as flavoring for other dishes.

Right now, at the time of the copper rose, was when the berries were the ripest and the plumpest for picking. During this time, the owls forsook their usual schedule and even shortened their daytime sleep so they could harvest the strands. The Ga'Hoolology ryb, a Burrowing Owl known as Dewlap, supervised the harvest. For the past week, they had all been on shifts under her command, cutting lengths of the berry vines just the right way.

"Remember, young'uns," Dewlap trilled as they flew with the strands of vines in their beaks. "No cutting below the third nodule. We must leave something so the vine shall sprout again come the time of the silver rain."

Soren and his friend Primrose, a Pygmy Owl, who had been rescued the night that Soren had arrived at the Great Ga'Hoole Tree, were flying together with a vine between them.

"She is such a bore," sighed Primrose. "Aren't you thankful that none of us got the Ga'Hoolology chaw?"

"Yes, just going to Dewlap's classes is bad enough. I was really worried that Eglantine might get the chaw."

"Never!" Primrose said. "She's perfect for search-and-rescue with her fine hearing skills. She's a natural for the chaw, I would say."

Soren, of course, could not help but wonder about their own mission to the border between Silverveil and The Barrens, which, if all went according to plan, would begin tonight just after the last of the vines had been cut.

Just then a cheer began to rise, and with the first strains of the harp, a song rang out. It was a solemn song, the "Harvest Hymn," led by Madame Plonk and Dewlap.

Dearest tree we give our thanks
for your blessings through the years.
Vines heavy with sweet berries
nourish us and quench our fears.

And in times of summer droughts,
searing heat or winters cold,
from your bounty freely given
we grow strong and we grow bold.

Let us always tend with care
your bark, your roots, your vines so fair —

And then, suddenly, a raucous song blasted out, led by Bubo.

Drink, drink to old Ga'Hoole —
boola boola boola boole!
Come along, mates, and give a tipple —
how that wine makes gizzards ripple!

Just as the song swelled with Bubo's voice leading, Otulissa swept up beside Soren and Primrose. "I can't believe Madame Plonk. She's sashaying about with a rose in her beak and wiggling her tail feathers in a most unseemly fashion. And Dewlap had hardly finished with the hymn before that coarse old owl began his vulgar song. Simply appalling."

Soren thought if he heard Otulissa say the word "appalling" one more time he might crack her on the head. Then that Spotted Owl would really see spots. But he didn't. Instead, he just turned to her and blinked. "Give it a blow, Otulissa. It's a festival for Glaux's sake. We can't be singing hymns the whole time."

"I agree," said Primrose. "Who wants a festival to be all serious? I'm hoping to pick up a few wet-poop jokes."

"Why, I never!" Otulissa said, genuinely shocked. "You know, Primrose, that wet-poop jokes are strictly forbidden at mealtimes."

"But they say all the grown-ups get very tipsy and start making them themselves."

"Well, I'm sure Strix Struma won't." Strix Struma, an elderly Spotted Owl who taught navigation, was one of the most esteemed owls of the tree. She was elegant. She was fierce. And she was revered, especially by Otulissa, who absolutely worshiped the old Spotted Owl. It was difficult, in fact, thinking of Strix Struma doing anything the least bit vulgar. The young Spotted Owl flew off in a huff toward the entrance of the Great Hollow.

As they passed through, two owls helped to part the

moss curtains as they had on the night when Soren, Gylfie, Twilight, and Digger had first arrived nearly a year before. Now, however, the Great Hollow was festooned with strands of milkberry vines that seemed almost to glow in the reflected light of hundreds of candles. The festivities had already begun and owls were swooping in flight to the music of the harp. The great grass harp stood on a balcony and was played by the nest-maid snakes who belonged to the harp guild. Their pink forms glistened as they wove themselves through the strings of the harp. Soren scanned the strings for Mrs. P., who was a sliptween. Only the most talented of the snakes were sliptweens, for they were required to jump octaves. Mrs. P. usually hung around G-flat. Ah, he spotted her!

Just then, Otulissa swept by wing to wing with Strix Struma doing a kind of stately waltz that owls called the Glaucana. Then Bubo lurched by in a jig with Madame Plonk herself. They were butting flight feathers and laughing uproariously.

"Already had a tipple, I would say." Gylfie slid into flight next to Soren. Soren was dying to say, *Yes, and we better not.* For tonight was the night that they would steal away to find the rogue smith, but not until everyone else was in their cups. Their Ga'Hoole nuts cups contained the milkberry wine or even the more strongly brewed berry mead.

Soren could not really say this in front of Primrose for she had not been included in this adventure. And he must be careful around Martin and Ruby as well. They had decided that it should only be their original band and Eglantine who went on this mission to Silverveil. But, in truth, Soren was having serious doubts about Eglantine.

The plan for getting away was fairly simple. At a certain point well into the evening, the dancing would move outside among the branches. It would be easier to slip away then. They planned to go, if possible, one by one and meet at the cliffs on the far side of the island. Owls very seldom went to that side of the island, for it lengthened any journey across the Sea of Hoolemere. But the wind this evening was light and favorable so it might not lengthen their crossing by too much.

The evening, however, seemed to drag on and on. Owls were getting tipsy, but would the dancing ever spill over to the outside? Otulissa had come up and insisted on a dance with Soren. He didn't even like to dance. He felt awkward and stupid. It wasn't like flying at all, even though it was done in the air. Now Otulissa had taken it on herself to instruct him in this silly dance called the Glauc-glauc.

"Look, Soren, it's not that hard. It's one two, glauc-glauc-glauc. Then backward one two, glauc-glauc-glauc." Otulissa was batting her eyes and shaking her tail feathers.

Great Glaux, was she flirting with him? Suddenly, he had an idea. If she was flirting with him he might as well use it to his advantage.

"You know, Otulissa, I think I could do this better if we were outside."

"Oh, that's an idea!"

Now, hopefully others would follow.

Twilight was doing the Glauc-glauc with another Great Gray, and Soren caught his eye. Twilight, always a quick study, steered his partner outside, following Soren.

Others began to fly out of the Great Hollow and weave their way through the branches in the Glauc-glauc dance. Now Eglantine was coming with another Spotted Owl. *Perfect!* Soren thought. He knew that Otulissa had a crush on the particular Spotted Owl whom Eglantine now had as her dance partner. He came from a lineage as ancient and distinguished as Otulissa's own. Soren managed to glauc-glauc-glauc across the air and through some branches to where the Spotted Owl and Eglantine were dancing.

"May I cut in and have a dance with my own sister?"

When Otulissa saw with whom she was about to be partnered, she nearly swooned midair.

Soren danced Eglantine off toward Gylfie and Digger, who were dancing with each other. Digger had a lot of smooth moves for being such a great walker, as all Burrowing Owls were. He combined these with flight maneuvers in a unique way.

"Watch this, Soren. I do the Glauc-glauc with a four-four beat. It's incredible. It's like the Glauc-glauc squared. Ready, Gylf?"

"Ready, Diggy!" *Diggy!* This was too much. Had they all been drinking?

"Listen!" Soren said sharply. "I think it'll be time to go soon. Everyone's pretty much in their cups from the look of it."

"I'll say," said Twilight, flying up to them without his partner. "Madame Plonk has passed out."

"Passed out!" The others gasped.

"Oh, I've got to see this," said Gylfie. Before Soren could stop her the others had followed.

Sure enough, just inside the Great Hollow in a niche in one of the galleries there was a huge pile of white feathers. Octavia, who served as nest-maid to both Madame Plonk and Ezylryb, was slithering along the gallery toward her, muttering about how Madame couldn't hold her berry wine, and it was always this way. But just at that moment, there came a roar from outside and then, "Aaah!"

"The comet!" someone cried. And its red light seemed to flare for a brief moment and spill into the hollow, casting a fiery glow over everything. Madame Plonk's feathers shimmered red and just in that same instant, Octavia, who had been nursing Madame Plonk, swung her head toward Soren. The old blind snake seemed to look right through him.

Does she know? Does she know what we are planning and that this might be connected with Ezylryb? A shiver ran through Soren.

"All right, it's time," he whispered to the others. "I'll leave first, then Eglantine, then Gylfie, next Digger, and last Twilight. See you at the cliffs!"

With that, Soren swept from the Great Hollow, but the entire time until the moss curtains parted, he felt the eyeless gaze of Octavia boring into him. Outside, the night seemed tinged with red. The moon, still newing, was just a sliver slipping over the horizon. In the light of the comet it looked like a battle claw dipped in blood.

CHAPTER EIGHT

Into a Night Stained Red

Where's Eglantine?" Soren said in a taut voice. "She was supposed to leave right after me." All the other owls had arrived at the cliff except Eglantine. "Do you think she got frightened?" Soren asked.

"Maybe she got caught," Gylfie offered.

"Oh, Glaux — I hope not." Soren sighed. He wondered how long they should wait.

"I hear something!" Digger said suddenly.

Owls were unusually silent fliers, all owls, that is, except for certain ones like Pygmy and Elf Owls who did not have the soft fringes called plummels at the leading edges of their flight feathers. The wing beats that Digger heard were the unmistakable sound of Primrose. Soren knew it in an instant, for he had flown behind her many a time in navigation class. What in the name of Glaux was Primrose doing here?

Eglantine, along with Primrose, slid onto the cliff and

perched beside Soren. "I know what you're going to say, Soren," she blurted out breathlessly.

But he said it anyway. "Primrose, what are you doing here?"

The Pygmy Owl shyly looked down at her talons. "I wanted to come, Soren. You helped me when I came to the great tree. You stayed with me all that first night, the night I lost my parents, my hollow, my tree, and the eggs." Primrose's parents had gone off to help out in some borderland skirmishes. They thought that she and the eggs would be safe, but a forest fire had broken out in their absence. Primrose had been rescued by owls from Ga'Hoole. But she had never seen her parents again. The truth, however, was that Primrose was from Silverveil, and Soren sensed that she wanted to go back to see if perhaps she could find her parents. This could be a distraction from their mission.

"Primrose." Soren fixed the little owl in the shine of his dark eyes.

"I know what you're going to say, Soren."

Everyone seemed to know what he was going to say, Soren thought, so why did he bother even saying it?

"I am not going to look for my parents. They are dead. I know it."

"How do you know it?" Gylfie asked.

"Do you remember the night after Trader Mags came

last summer?" Soren would never forget that night, for it was the first night that Eglantine had really been back to her old self after being rescued. It had been a beautiful summer night and then, as if in celebration of his sister's return, the sky had blossomed with colors — colors like he had never seen before. It was the night of the Aurora Glaucora, and all of the owls had flown in and out of the colors that throbbed and billowed in the sky.

"Of course, I remember that night." It was a night to remember for several reasons, one of the least happy was because on that night it had been confirmed that Ezylryb had disappeared. But in the ecstasy of the shifting colors of the sky, Soren had actually willed himself not to think about his favorite teacher.

"Well, I remember it, too, because that was the night that I saw the scrooms of my parents," Primrose said.

"What?" They all gasped.

"You saw your parents' scrooms?" Gylfie asked and there seemed to be an ache embedded deep in her voice. For although she knew that Soren had returned much saddened by his encounter with his parents' scrooms, there was something in Gylfie, just as there had been in Eglantine, that longed for one last glimpse.

"Yes," replied Primrose. "I saw them that night as we were flying through the colors of the Aurora Glaucora."

"Did they have unfinished business here on earth?" Soren asked, wondering to himself just how much unfinished scroom business they could manage on one mission.

"Not really." She paused. "Well, I suppose you could say that I was their last piece of unfinished business. They wanted me to know that during the forest fire, they knew that I had tried my best to save the eggs. They just said that there was nothing to forgive. They were proud of me. That was their unfinished business — to let me know that they were proud of me." There was a deep silence in the night as Primrose started to explain. "You see, Soren, my encounter was not at all like yours. I didn't really get to talk with my parents in that strange wordless way that you described to Eglantine."

Soren looked sharply at his sister. *Why had she gone and told Primrose all this?*

"It was much different."

"How?" Soren said, genuinely perplexed.

"You see, my parents were in glaumora."

"What?" Soren said in disbelief. "How do you know that?"

"I saw them there. They saw me. They were happy. They knew I had done my best for the eggs that never hatched. They weren't angry. They knew that I was in a good place. A place they had never quite believed in, but they now know is real. And I suddenly became so happy. It was like a river of happiness and peace flowing between us out there, in the Aurora Glaucora." Primrose's voice was barely a whisper now.

"A river of happiness," Soren said softly. No words about Metal Beak — no words at all, just happiness. He tried to imagine his parents and a river of happiness flowing between them and himself and Eglantine. Then he jerked himself back from such reveries. What he had to say next was going to be very difficult. He was going to have to refuse to have Primrose and Eglantine on this mission.

"Primrose, there will be a time when we will need you and Eglantine." He paused.

"What?" Eglantine was stunned. "You're not taking me? You promised," she whined.

"Eglantine, you are not ready. You proved this tonight by blabbing to Primrose." He then spun his head toward Primrose. "Primrose, you are certainly ready but it was our decision that the fewer the better on this mission. The less chance that we'll be missed if it is just us."

"I understand, Soren. Don't apologize."

"But what about me?" Eglantine whined again. "I'm your sister."

"Yes, and someday you will be stronger, stronger in wing and stronger in gizzard. And we shall need you, and you shall be included."

Eglantine's wings drooped by her side. Her black eyes seemed to swim with the reflected light of stars.

"We must prepare to go now," Soren said.

"Good luck," Primrose said in a full strong voice. "Be careful."

"Yes, be careful, Soren," Eglantine said softly.

"Eglantine, don't be mad. A promise is a promise. When you're ready we'll both know it."

"I could never be mad at you, Soren. Never."

"I know," he replied softly.

Soren now looked to the south. The wake of the comet was still visible. But it made for a strange light in the sky, a light that could be deceiving. He would have Twilight, whose vision for marginal conditions like these was renowned, fly in the point position. "Ready for takeoff! Twilight, fly point, Gylfie, port side. I'll fly starboard, Digger, fly tail."

They lifted off into the strangely colored night. Why was the night stained red? When he had first seen the comet a few weeks before, it had appeared red because it was dawn and the sun was just rising, but now it was night and there was no rising sun. It gave Soren the shivers to think about it and the more he did, the more the sky looked not simply rusty, but like blood. And there was another curious phenomenon. The wind was a light head wind and should have slowed them down. But, indeed, it was the reverse. It seemed as if the comet had cleared a path, created a vacuum through which they passed easily. It was as if they were being pulled instead. He was supposed to be the leader of this band. But where was he leading them, and what were they being pulled toward? Suddenly, the night seemed ominous to Soren. He felt something cold and quivering deep in his gizzard.

CHAPTER NINE
The Rogue Smith of Silverveil

Dawn was breaking. They had been flying over Silverveil for what seemed like hours, scouring the landscape below for any sign of smoke. It was the smoke that had led them to the cave of the dying Barred Owl so many months before.

"Do you think we'll ever find him?" Soren called across from his starboard position.

"Her," Gylfie said. "It's a *her*."

"Oh, sorry, I just can't get used to a female as a blacksmith."

"Well, get used to it," Gylfie said somewhat testily.

"Rotate positions," Soren called out. "Let's look for a rest spot. Crows will be up soon. We don't want a mobbing." Soren, Gylfie, Twilight, and Digger had been mobbed once before on their way to the Great Ga'Hoole Tree. It was not an experience they wished to repeat. Digger had been seriously injured. Owls flying in the daytime are not safe, except perhaps over water. Crows have a system for alerting other crows to the owls' presence and can come upon them in a swarm, often pecking out their eyes, stabbing them from beneath, and making their wings collapse. In the night, it is quite the reverse. Then it is the owls who can mob the crows. Just as Soren was about to take over the point position, Twilight spotted a big fir tree below, perfect for fetching up for a day's sleep.

"Fir tree below!"

Soren's gizzard gave a small twitch. It was a fir tree just like the one in which he and Eglantine had been hatched and had spent a brief childhood with their parents. There were countless little ceremonies, rites of passage, that marked the development of a young owl. And because of his snatching and whatever it was that had happened to Eglantine when she had fallen from the nest or perhaps been pushed by Kludd, the two young owls had missed many of these. Whenever Soren mentioned this in front of the others, they all seemed quite sympathetic, except for Twilight. Twilight had been orphaned at such a young age that he had no nest memories and prided himself on having actually skipped such folderol ceremonies, as he referred to them. Not the most modest of owls, he bragged about having learned it all on his own in what he called the Orphan School of Tough Learning, which, frankly, became quite a bore to the others.

The fragrance of the fir needles filled Soren with a great sense of longing. He yearned for his parents, not the scrooms, but his real, live parents.

Soren could not let himself give in to these feelings. "Before we take a snooze, we have to plan." Action, Soren always felt, was the best remedy for sad feelings. "I've been thinking that when we met the Barred Owl, he was not just on a border, he was really on a point where the corners of four borders touched, those of Kuneer, Ambala, The Beaks, and Tyto."

"A convergence point," Gylfie offered.

"Yes, I think we should look for such a point of convergence. Gylfie, you're the navigator. You've studied the map. Which way should we head?"

"Well, for a convergence we need to head toward the point where Silverveil, the Shadow Forest, and The Barrens meet," Gylfie said. "Tonight, when the constellation of the Great Glaux rises, we have to fly two degrees off its westerly wing, just between that and the claw of the Little Raccoon."

"All right, everyone get a good rest. We'll leave at First Black," Soren said.

Three hours after First Black they had still seen nothing. They had been in the region of the convergence for two hours. Soren told himself he could not get discouraged. He was the leader of this band. If the owls sensed he was discouraged, then their spirits, too, would begin to fall. They could not fail. Too much was at stake.

Digger flew up to Soren. "Permission for low-level surveillance, Soren."

"What for?"

"Tracking, Soren. I'm used to low-level flight for finding downed owls and anything else on the ground. Look at me. We blend in with everything, desert sand and fallen leaves in autumn. And I can fly slow, really slow, noisy but slow. And," he paused, "I can walk!"

"All right, but I expect you back within the quarter hour."

"Yes, Captain."

Captain! He wanted to cry out, *Don't call me Captain. Only Ezylryb can be called Captain.*

Soren watched as Digger went into a plunging dive.

As he neared the ground, Digger began a slow survey, first for any sign of caves, or scattered coals that might indicate the presence of a rogue smith. When he found no caves, he wondered if a blacksmith would ever build a fire in a clearing. Possibly. Then, of course, there was the fact that this blacksmith was a Snowy Owl. Pure white. She should certainly show up on a night like this. With the moon far from full and still just newing, the night was very black. Perfect for seeing white.

The quarter of an hour was running out. Digger became more determined than ever, more intense in his search. Scanning by rotating his head as he had been taught to do in tracking, he dodged bushes, tree trunks, rocks, and other ground obstacles just in the nick of time. He sensed them almost before he got to them. But he hadn't sensed the large black mound ahead. Neither rock nor shrub nor trunk, the mound suddenly sprung to life.

"Watch where you're going, idiot!"

Digger's gizzard froze.

"Racdrops!" Another scream from the mound. Digger felt something soft and then there was a small blizzard of sooty particles. He tumbled head over talons and this smothering cloud seemed to follow him. They were rolling down a small incline.

"Glaux almighty! You splat-brained idiot!" A scathing rant rang out. Digger had never heard such a stream of swears. The vilest curses scalded the night air and rained down on his ears. Bubo was no match. "Great stinkin' Glaux, I might have known — a Burrowing Owl with most likely a small burrow where your brain should be. What happened? Did it fall out?"

"I beg your racdrop pardon! You wretched piece of wet poop." Digger drew himself up to his full height. He surprised himself with his own swearing.

"Wet poop! I'll splat you."

This isn't working, Digger suddenly thought. He could not stand here trading insults with this sooty black thing. "Truce," he said. The creature stopped and stood still. "Who are you? What are you?" Digger asked.

"A bird, you darned fool."

"A bird?"

"An owl. A Snowy at that."

"Snowy!" Digger gasped and nearly laughed out loud. "You are the blackest Snowy I have ever seen."

"What did you expect? I'm a blacksmith, idiot!"

It was music to Digger's ears. "A blacksmith," he said, his voice drenched in awe and relief. "The rogue smith of Silverveil?" Digger asked softly.

"What business is that of yours? You want battle claws? I rarely make them for Burrowing Owls. They're lousy fliers. It's a waste."

Digger swallowed his anger at this insult. "No, no, Bubo told us about you."

"Bubo!" the owl suddenly exploded. "You're from Ga'Hoole? Bubo sent you here?"

"Not exactly,"

"What does that mean?" The Snowy narrowed her eyes until they were two yellow slits.

"Uh . . . I better go get my friends," Digger stammered and quickly took off.

CHAPTER TEN

The Story of the Rogue Smith

Soren blinked as he and the three other owls lighted down. Digger had not been kidding when he had said that this was the blackest Snowy he had ever seen.

"So what brings you here, young'uns? I take it that you're not here on a sanctioned visit."

Gylfie was the only one who knew what the word "sanctioned" meant. So she answered, "No, this is not an official visit. As a matter of fact —"

The black Snowy finished her thought. "Sneaked away, didya? A little escapade, I imagine? Dreams of glory? Huh?"

Soren fluffed up his feathers in a bristle of annoyance. "It is not an escapade. It is a mission, and we do not dream of glory. We hope for peace, for we have been warned."

"Warned of what?" the smith said with a slight note of disdain.

This owl frinks me off! Soren took a deep breath. "Metal Beak."

A tremor went through the black Snowy and little puffs of coal dust sifted down from her feathers. "What'-cha doin' messin' with that creep for? He ain't around these parts. And I'll have you know, I don't sell to him. Not on your life. Not on my life. Course that's a risk in itself, not selling to him."

"What do you know about him?" Gylfie asked.

"Very little. I steer clear of him and his gang. And I advise you to as well."

"Gang?" Soren said.

"Yeah, gang. Don't know how many."

"Is he part of St. Aggie's?" Gylfie asked.

"You only wish," the black Snowy said. And with these words, Soren, Twilight, Gylfie, and Digger froze in terror. For, in fact, these were the very same words spoken by the dying Barred Owl, his last words when Gylfie had asked him if it was St. Aggie's that had mortally wounded him. For these four owls to imagine anything worse than St. Aggie's was terrifying. Now, however, it seemed that the "you only wish" could be tied to Metal Beak. And there was not just one of them but possibly many.

"Did you know about the murder of the Barred Owl of The Beaks?" Twilight asked.

"I heard a thing or two about it. I don't go poking into things that ain't my business. Not my way." Soren remembered what Bubo had said about rogue smiths never attaching themselves to any kingdom.

"Where's your forge?" Gylfie asked looking around.

"Not here."

This is one tough owl, thought Soren. *Almost like she's not used to talking.* But then Digger had said she could swear like nobody's business. Used words that he had never even heard Bubo use. That was something — an owl who could out-curse Bubo. Although the owl hadn't said that much, there was something oddly familiar in her tone. Soren couldn't place it, however.

"Well, may I be so bold as to ask where your forge is? " Gylfie persisted. *Good for you, Gylf.* This was one of the advantages of being small, Soren thought. No one ever expected you to be bold or aggressive.

"Yonder!" The smith turned her head and indicated somewhere behind her shoulder.

"Might we see it?" Gylfie took a tiny step forward. The black Snowy towered over her, looked down and blinked.

"Why?"

"Because we're interested. We've never seen a rogue smith's forge before."

The Snowy paused as if to consider if this was an adequate reason. "It ain't fancy like Bubo's."

"That doesn't matter," Twilight said. "Do we look

fancy?" Twilight puffed himself up. The inverted curves of white feathers that swept from his brow framed his eyes and beak and made his fierce glare even fiercer. He looked anything but fancy.

The black Snowy turned to Gylfie. "You're small to be out here with this bunch of hooligans."

"We're not hooligans, ma'am," Gylfie replied.

"Why'd you call me that?" The smith glared at Gylfie but the Elf Owl stood her ground firmly and met the blazing yellow gaze.

Uh-oh, thought Soren. *This bird does not like being called ma'am.* Soren remembered what Bubo had said about the rogue smiths being loners. How had Bubo put it? *They likes living wild.* Being called ma'am — or sir, for that matter, if it were a male — would prick their gizzards.

"We aren't hooligans. We are a band. Soren here is like a brother to me. We escaped from St. Aggie's together. Shortly after we escaped, we met up with Twilight and Digger. Soon we shall have our Guardian ceremony and become true Guardians of Ga'Hoole." Gylfie turned and swept her wing toward the three other owls who seemed almost spellbound by her words. "And I called you 'ma'am' because underneath all that coal dust, I know there is a beautiful Snowy. As beautiful as the most beautiful Snowy of the great tree, Madame Plonk."

At that, the smith seemed to choke and then tears began to leak from her eyes. *That's it!* That's who the smith reminded Soren of. The tone of her voice, it was the same melodic sound, the same *pling* that he heard in Madame Plonk's voice each night when she sang the "Night Is Done" song.

"How did you guess I was Brunwella's sister?"

"You mean Madame Plonk? Is that her name?" Soren asked.

"Yes. Come, follow me to the forge, young'uns. I'll tell you the story. I have some fresh voles. Mind you, I don't roast them here like you do in the Great Tree."

"Don't worry," Soren said. "I fly weather and colliering with Ezylryb — or did — and we always have to take our meat raw."

"Oh, yes. I heard about Ezylryb. No sign of him yet?"

"No," said Soren sadly as they flew the short distance to the forge.

"Dear old fellow. We go back, way back."

Soren wondered what the Snowy meant by that? Well, perhaps they would soon find out.

"What is this?" Digger asked as the band lighted down in the stone ruins. There were two-and-a-half walls of ancient stone that had been neatly stacked upon one another. Old vines crawled over them and in the center was the pit where the smith had her fire. On one of the walls, a new set of battle claws and a helm hung. Soren could see that the work was very fine, every bit as good as Bubo's.

"It used to be a walled garden. At least, that's what I think. Maybe part of a castle."

"The Others?" Soren asked.

"Oh, you know about the Others do you?" the smith asked.

"Just a little, from the books in the library when I was reading about castles and churches and barns. Being a Barn Owl, it interested me. I just know that they were creatures from long, long ago, and they weren't owls or birds or like any other animals we've ever seen."

"That they warn't. Did you know that not only did they not have wings or feathers, but that they had two long sticks for legs that were just for walking."

"That's all?" Digger said. This, of course, interested him, being a Burrowing Owl who walked as well as he flew. But he certainly preferred having the option to do either one. "How did they get along?"

"Not that well, apparently. They're gone now. In addition to no feathers, they didn't have fur."

"Well, no wonder they didn't last," Twilight snorted.

"Rocks, they had rocks," the Snowy said.

"Rocks? What can you do with a rock?" Twilight muttered.

"Plenty," the Snowy replied. "They built with them — castles, walled gardens."

"Why would anyone want to wall in a garden?" Digger asked, thinking of the lovely gardens that were planted around the Great Ga'Hoole Tree that seemed to meet up in a seamless way with the ferns and wildflowers of the forest.

"Don't ask me," the Snowy said.

The Snowy had begun to lay out some freshly killed voles and a couple of ground squirrels.

She chuckled to herself as if she had discovered something terribly amusing and a light drift of coal dust sprinkled down on her face.

"So it's hard for you all to believe that I am the famous Madame Plonk's sister, eh?"

"To put it mildly," Gylfie replied.

"She's a good soul but she's very different from me. We were born, my sister and I, deep in the Northern Kingdoms, far beyond the Ice Narrows, on the eastern coast of the Everwinter Sea. Some say that is where Snowy Owls originated. But there were others up there. Your teacher Ezylryb came from an island near where I was born. And he's a Screech Owl. Anyhow, there was always a lot of fighting up in those parts. Warring clans. The fiercest warriors came out of the region of the Everwinter Sea. My father and my mother being two of them. But despite their war-like ways, my parents were artists, and for generations the line of Plonk singers were renowned. For thousands of years in every community, in every kingdom, there has been a Plonk singer. But the singer for the Great Ga'Hoole Tree is an inherited position and it is given to only one Snowy in each generation — the one considered the finest. Well, that was my sister, Brunwella. I could have lived with that, but what I couldn't live with was my step-mother.

"After my mum was killed in the Battle of the Ice Talons — the last battle in the War of the Ice Claws — my da found a new mate, a horrible old Snowy. She treated me like seagull splat. And, of course, fussed over my sister be-cause my sister was going to be the singer for the great tree. I had to leave. Even Brunwella saw that it was impos-sible for me to continue in the hollow. My father, however, was besotted with this female. She could do no wrong. I wasn't sure where to go. For some reason, I felt it was im-portant for me not only to get as far away as possible from my family but to take up a whole new line of work. My voice wasn't bad. But not nearly as good as that of most Plonks which, of course, meant it was a lot better than anyone else's. But I wanted no part of it. And I wasn't as lovely-looking as my sister. I was given to gray scale, which made for unsightly splotches where the feathers fell off. As a matter of fact, my stepmother used to call me 'Splotch.'"

"How mean!" Gylfie said. "What is your real name?"

Will she say what it is? Soren thought. He looked at her closely.

"My true name?"

"Yes," Gylfie said in a barely audible voice. It was as if she sensed she had ventured into forbidden territory.

"That is for me to know, and only me."

But what about your sister? Soren thought. *Doesn't she know your true name? And what is the difference between a true name and a real name? Is there a difference?*

"So, as I was saying, I was looking for something new and different. I really wanted to separate myself from the Plonks. My sister had been good to me, but my father seemed not to care. I really had no one else to turn to. So I just left. I flew about in the Northern Kingdoms for a year or more, and then I came upon Octavia. You know Octavia, don't you?"

"Of course," they all cried.

"She's Ezylryb's and your sister's nest-maid snake," said Soren.

"Oh, she's working for my sister now, is she? Well, she's a good old soul. I, of course, met her before she was blind."

The owls all gasped in disbelief.

"You mean," said Gylfie, "she wasn't born blind?"

"I had heard a rumor that she had not been born blind, but I really didn't believe it. I thought all nest-maid snakes were born blind," Soren said.

"They are — except for Octavia. Haven't you noticed that she's not rosy-scaled like the others?"

Soren had noticed and wondered about Octavia's pale greenish-blue scales.

"But that's a whole other story. It was Octavia who told me about a rogue smith on the island of Dark Fowl, a desolate place that is lashed constantly by ice storms and gales, rocky, not a tree, not a blade of grass. But this smith was supposed to be one of the most superb blacksmiths on earth. So I went there. I wanted to learn how to make battle claws. I wanted to avenge my mother's death. I had a dream of making battle claws that would slice to shreds the clan that had killed my mum. I had the fire in my gizzard as they say. Smithing came naturally to me, more natural than singing, I'll tell you." She sighed and seemed to reflect happily for a moment. "And I did kill my stepmum with some magnificent claws I made."

"You killed your stepmother?" Twilight had swollen up

with excitement. Never having even known his own parents he had no romantic notions in general about them, and an evil stepmother set his gizzard to boiling. Then the Great Gray looked down at his talons in what Soren thought was a pathetic display of shyness — for shy was the last thing that Twilight was. "I don't want you to think I'm a violent sort of bird."

"Ha!" the other three owls laughed.

"Well, I'm not!" Twilight said stubbornly and blinked at his mates.

However, any one of them could see the Great Gray could hardly contain himself.

"But how'd you do it? Quick slice to the gullet? How? Talon to talon? Stab with the beak to the nether down?"

"I don't care about how," Soren interrupted. "But why? I mean, I know she was bad, but that bad?"

"She betrayed my father. Turned out she was a slipgizzle for the other clan. Had planned to marry him from the start — as soon as they got rid of Mum."

"How did you learn this?" Digger asked.

"I had my ways. Working for a master rogue smith you find out a lot of things. All sorts come to you by the by."

Digger looked at the coal-dusted Snowy carefully. "Did Octavia have something do with this? Or maybe —" But the blacksmith cut him off.

Cut Digger off too quickly, Soren observed. Then the rogue smith of Silverveil seemed to clam up. Oh, she was very hospitable, giving them the best parts of the voles and making sure that they had comfortable perches for the day.

Soren did have one more question for her but something kept him from asking it. He wondered, however, if the rogue smith of Silverveil thought that Metal Beak was in any way connected with Ezylryb's disappearance. Soren wrestled with his question all through their daytime sleep and finally, just before First Black when he noticed that the Snowy was stirring, he decided he just had to ask.

He flew down to where the blacksmith was taking some coals from a niche in the wall to build up her forging fire.

"I knew you'd come and ask," the Snowy Owl said. Soren blinked. "You want to know if Metal Beak had something to do with Ezylryb."

"Yes. How did you know?"

"Never mind that," she snapped. "The fact is I'm not sure, but Ezylryb, well, how to explain? Ezylryb has a past. He is a legend. He does have enemies."

"Enemies?" This was unbelievable to Soren. Ezylryb never went into battle. This was a well-known fact at the great tree. He might be gruff, but he was the most nonviolent owl imaginable. How could such an owl have ene-mies? He didn't even own battle claws. In fact, he once said he despised them. Thought the owl kingdoms were be-coming much too dependent on them. "Give them books, give them tasty milkberry tarts, teach them to cook, teach them the ways of Ga'Hoole," he had said to the owl parlia-ment, "and every cantankerous owl will be on our side." *Ezylryb violent! It's absurd.*

"One last question," Soren said.

"Yes?"

"Why do they call that owl Metal Beak?"

"He got half his face torn off in a battle. A rogue smith had to make him a mask and a new beak."

Soren felt as if he might be sick.

CHAPTER ELEVEN

Flint Mops

I t's the part about Octavia not being born blind that absolutely blows my gizzard," Gylfie was saying.

"It's the enemies thing for me," Digger said. "It's unbelievable that the rogue smith told Soren that Ezylryb has enemies, and that's why Metal Beak might be connected to his disappearance."

"I know," Soren said, "that's what gets me, too."

They had returned to the great tree. No one seemed to have missed them and now, in their hollow, Gylfie, Twilight, Soren, and Digger were reviewing and telling Eglantine all they had learned from the rogue smith of Silverveil. They really weren't sure if they had learned that much. They were, in truth, still quite mystified. Were they any closer to Metal Beak? Was there any chance of them actually being able to do something about the scrooms' warning?

"Tell me about the rogue smith's forge again?" This was about the fourth time Eglantine had asked. For some reason, she was fascinated by their description of this place. So Soren began once more to describe how the stones were stacked in walls, walls that the Snowy thought might have enclosed a garden.

"Did she say anything else?"

Twilight sighed as if he was extremely bored with this conversation, but Soren felt that answering Eglantine's interminable questions was the least he could do for his little sister after making her stay back at the tree.

"What do you mean by anything else?"

"Did she say what it might have been other than a garden?"

"Well, now that I remember she actually did say that it could have been a walled garden that was part of a castle."

"A castle!" Eglantine's eyes blinked.

"You know, one of those things that the Others built."

"Yes, I know. . . ." Eglantine responded in a tremulous voice.

She suddenly seemed very agitated. "What's wrong, Eglantine?" Soren asked.

"I'm not sure. It's just that the way you described those stones, those walls remind me of something."

Soren suddenly remembered that when Eglantine was still in her state of shock after her rescue and could not even recognize him, her own brother, that it was a colorful piece of isinglass, or mica, as it was also called, that had jolted Eglantine out of her numbed state. Mags, the magpie trader who sometimes came to the tree with her odd bits scavenged from various journeys, had brought the fragment. When someone had held the isinglass up to the moon, the thin, nearly translucent piece of stone had shimmered and, suddenly, Eglantine had started shaking and screaming, "The Place! The Place!" But no one could ever figure out quite what place she was talking about, and until now Soren hadn't really thought about it that much. At the time, he hadn't thought it really mattered. After all, his sister had recognized him and had quickly come around to her old self. But now, Soren wondered why his description of these walls reminded her of something. He hadn't the slightest idea. He sent Gylfie down for some milkberry tea, thinking that it might calm Eglantine enough for her to get to sleep. He hated to see his sister so distraught.

But it was Gylfie, returning with a small flask of milkberry tea in her talons, who was truly distraught.

"We've been discovered!"

"What?" Soren almost shrieked. "What are you talking about?"

"I didn't tell, I swear!" Eglantine spoke in a desperate whisper.

"Of course you didn't. I trust you, Eglantine. I know you'd never tell." Eglantine seemed to almost melt, not just in relief but with the simple knowledge of her brother's trust in her. She had felt she was just about useless, good for nothing of importance. But that Soren trusted her meant everything.

At that very moment, Primrose flew into their hollow. "It wasn't Eglantine, and it wasn't me."

"Otulissa!" Twilight hissed.

"No, not Otulissa. Dewlap."

"Dewlap!" They all gasped. Dewlap was the Burrowing Owl who was head of the Ga'Hoolology chaw, generally thought to be the most boring chaw in the entire tree. It was devoted to understanding the physiology and natural processes of the great tree where they lived, which sustained their lives. And even if you were not in a particular chaw, you were still required to take classes in that subject.

"Oh, racdrops!" Twilight slapped the air with his feathers, causing a hearty gust to sweep through the hollow. "Dewlap gave me a flint mop for acting up in class the other day. I completely forgot." Twilight was always getting into trouble in Ga'Hoolology. It was easy as it was so boring. In fact, the other owls lived for Twilight's antics during that class. He was the only source of relief from boredom. "I was supposed to go help her bury pellets at tween time."

Tween time was the time between the last drop of sun and the first shadows of the evening.

"Well, she started snooping around and found all of you gone," Primrose said.

"Do they know where we were?" Soren asked.

Gylfie shrugged. "I don't know. But the four of us are to report immediately to Boron and Barran." Gylfie paused. "In the parliament."

"Oh, Glaux! In front of everyone?" Digger said. There were in all eleven owls who made up the governing body of the Great Ga'Hoole Tree known as the parliament. They decided to which chaws the new owls, after a period of general training and education, would be assigned. They planned the precise dates on which the milkberries would be harvested. They were in charge of all missions of diplomacy, war, and, most important, support to owls or groups of owls in need. They supervised all the many ceremonies and festivals of the great tree and settled all arguments. They also decided on appropriate "flint mops," as they were called, since there was no real word for "punish" or "punishment" in the language of the owls of Ga'Hoole. Owls were never struck, hit, bitten, locked up, or given less food. They did not even believe in taking away privileges such as attending parties or festivities or banquets. What they did believe in was the flint mop. Flint stone was the most valuable tool the owls of Ga'Hoole had. It was with their flint stones that they ignited their fires. The word flint had, over the years, become a synonym for anything of great value. To say something was flinty or had flint meant it had real worth. Therefore to be a flint mopper was to be someone who scorned the value of something. And if you scorned the value of something, you were required to pay back what you had taken away. Thus, the term for the payback came to be known as a "flint mop" as well. A flint mop was as close as owls came to the word punishment. And the flint mop in Twilight's case was helping Dewlap, the Ga'Hoolology ryb, bury pellets which nourished the roots of the tree.

"So we have to go to the parliament right now?" Soren asked.

"Right now." Gylfie nodded. "And I don't think we should be late."

"Enter!" It was the loud resonant hoot of Boron through the bark doors of the parliament hollow. This hollow was one of the few that had actual doors, for the business of the parliament was often top secret. Although Twilight, Soren, Gylfie, and Digger had, in fact, discovered a place deep within the tangled roots of the tree where something strange happened to the timber of the trunk just above and the voices of the parliament owls could be heard. Sometimes the four owls listened in. Had this been found out it might be considered worse than what they had done now. Although Soren was still not sure what they had done that was so bad. Yes, they had gone away during the harvest festival — but was that really all that bad? It was bad if it had been found out where they had gone perhaps, but the only one who could really be considered a flint mopper was Twilight, who had completely forgotten to do his flint mop.

Only three owls of the parliament were perched on the white birch branch that had been bent into a half circle. There was Boron, his mate, Barran, and Dewlap. He supposed he should be relieved that there were just three and not the entire parliament. And, insofar that the only other owl present besides the monarchs was Dewlap, this might mean that indeed the worst error was Twilight's forgetting his flint mop.

"Young'uns," Barran began. "It was brought to our attention by the good ryb Dewlap that Twilight was absent from his flint-mopping tasks of burying pellets, which nourishes our great tree. Upon further investigation, it was found out that all four of you, the entire 'band' as you are known, had left the tree on the night of the festivities. So not only was Twilight unavailable for flint mopping but the rest of you could not participate in the sorting and grading of milkberries, as is customary after the harvest festivities, not to mention the award ceremonies, which follow the sorting, for those who have distinugished themselves at the harvest through their diligence."

Sorting, grading awards? Soren had never heard about all this. He stole a look at Gylfie who appeared equally bewildered.

Then Barran, as if reading their minds, continued, "Yes, young'uns, there are things you do not yet know about — practices and ceremonies that we have here at the Great Ga'Hoole Tree. For example, Soren, it was while you were gone that we had a First-Meat-on-Bones ceremony for your sister, Eglantine, and other young'uns from the Great Downing who had missed that owl stone event." An owl stone event was one that was considered of great significance in the development of a young owl. The First-Meat-on-Bones ceremony was one of the most important of all the ceremonies that marked a young owl's passage through life from hatchling to fully fledged flier to adept hunter. Boron and Barran felt that even though owls like Eglantine had long been eating Meat on Bones because they had been orphaned early on and missed this ceremony with their parents, it was still important to have these moments recognized. "Better late than never," Barran always said.

"I missed Eglantine's Meat-on-Bones!" A sob seemed to swell in Soren's gizzard. "Why . . . why . . ." he stammered.

"Why didn't she tell you about it?" Barran asked. Then she proceeded to answer her own question. "Because isn't it always a surprise when your parents come home with that first whole vole or ground squirrel and say 'Beak up! Down the gullet!'? No more of their stripping out the bones like when you were a baby. So why shouldn't it be a surprise here?"

Soren merely blinked. Tears filled his eyes, and the big old Snowy blurred like a cloud. "But she didn't even tell me about it when I got back."

"Eglantine is a sensitive young owl. I'm sure she knew that you would have felt awful for missing her First-Meat-on-Bones ceremony, and the last thing your sister would want is for you to feel bad. She loves you too much, Soren."

Soren's wings hung limply by his side. He felt positively horrible.

"Now, young'uns," Boron had begun to speak for the first time since saying enter.

Oh, Glaux. He's going to ask us where we've been, Soren thought.

"You were off looking for Ezylryb, I'd wager?" Soren nodded. "Well, that's to be expected."

Dewlap suddenly swelled up in a puff of indignation. "I beg to differ, Boron, but duty is what is expected."

"Oh, you're right. You're right, of course." But Soren sensed that Boron did not think that the boring Burrowing Owl was *exactly* right. Maybe they'd get off with just a light flint mop but, more important, maybe Boron would not ask them where they had been.

"Where have you been?" squawked Dewlap.

"It doesn't really matter where," Boron spoke now. "What matters is that in going away, the band missed the sorting and grading of the milkberries. Soren missed his sister's First-Meat-on-Bones ceremony, and Twilight missed his flint mop for you. Thus, the tree suffered as a whole."

"I would say," Dewlap's voice thundered, "it's payback time! The four of you are on pellet-burying detail for the next three days, twice a day."

As they flew back to their hollow from the parliament, Soren muttered under his breath to the others, "We can't complain.... We can't complain.... We got off light."

"Light? You call having to bury pellets a 'light' flint mop?" Twilight hissed.

"Look," Gylfie said, "it was because you forgot your

flint mop that we were discovered in the first place. So just shut your beak."

"You know," Digger was saying, "in spite of my being a Burrowing Owl and Dewlap being a Burrowing Owl, I feel I have nothing in common with that old hoot."

"How could you?" Gylfie asked. "She is so boring."

"And mean," Soren added.

The others blinked. They had never thought of Dewlap as mean, just boring. So had Soren until Dewlap had squawked, and he had seen a weird greenish glimmer in her yellow eyes that seemed to mask a stingy gizzard. Soren's mother had always told him that it was a stingy and envious gizzard that made owls mean. His mother had said that envy and stinginess were the worst faults an owl could have. Her words came back to him: *There is never any call for envy or stinginess in owls, Soren. We have the sky, we have the great forests and the trees. We are the most beautiful fliers on earth. Why would we envy any other bird or animal?*

CHAPTER TWELVE

Rusty Claws

By the time the four owls had returned to their hollow, Eglantine had fallen sound asleep. And soon the rest were also sleeping. Eglantine was twitching nervously in her sleep. She had seemed upset ever since they had told her about the walled garden of the forge.

Soren couldn't think about any of that now. There was still this dreadful unfinished business of Metal Beak and the "you only wish." A horrid image if there ever was one — a half-faceless owl flying around slaughtering creatures. Then again, there was just getting through the flint mop for Dewlap. Gylfie stirred and Soren saw that she was awake, too.

"Gylfie, why do you think Boron and Barran didn't ask us where we had been?"

"They knew that it had something to do with Ezylryb. They know how you feel about him. They didn't have to know exactly where you went."

"You know," Soren said slowly, "I have the feeling that

in some way Octavia might be important to all that stuff the rogue smith of Silverveil told us."

"How?" Gylfie asked in her usual practical way. "What's the link?"

"I feel it in my gizzard," Soren continued, thinking aloud, "that she somehow is connected to Ezylryb's past when perhaps he was a different kind of owl."

"Different?" Gylfie asked.

"Remember how the Snowy told us that she met Octavia before she was blind?" Gylfie nodded. "And it was Octavia who told her about the Dark Fowl Island where the master blacksmith nested. There's a connection there, a link with Ezylryb. Did Ezylryb know her then, too, before she was blind? And the rogue smith said they came here together years and years ago. She was blind then, but what was she really before that? What did she do for Ezylryb? How does a snake know about a forge on an island that makes battle claws?"

"What are you suggesting we do, Soren?" Gylfie asked.

He turned and looked at his best friend in all the world, the little Elf Owl with whom he had already endured so much. Could he ask her to do this? He knew it would shock her. He took a deep breath and then told her what he wanted to do. "I am suggesting that we get into Ezylryb's hollow when Octavia is not around."

Gylfie gasped so loud that she almost woke Twilight. "Soren, I can't believe it. That's trespassing, snooping, spying, and Ezylryb is your favorite teacher. It's so . . . so . . ."

"Scummy," Soren offered.

"Well, yes," Gylfie nodded. "I was going to say unethical. But yeah, 'scummy' just about sums it up. Soren, you surprise me. I mean, that's really asking for a flint mop."

"Who cares about flint mopping? This is life or death. If we can discover something that would help us find and save Ezylryb, it can't be scummy, unflecktual."

"Unflecktual!" Gylfie whispered hoarsely. "Flecks, Soren? Do you think this is connected with flecks?"

Soren blinked. He had meant to say that word Gylfie had used — unethical. But it had come out wrong. Still it was just a slip of the beak. But was it connected with the flecks in some way? There was a web being spun here. He could feel them all being reeled in, and at the center of the web sat a spider with a Metal Beak.

"I have to go," Soren said.

"I won't let you go without me," Gylfie said.

"It should only be the two of us."

"No," Digger suddenly spoke up.

"You awake?" Gylfie asked.

"I just woke up. Listen, I want to be in on this. You'll need a lookout. I'll stand guard. What are you two going to do if Octavia slithers in? I could distract her long enough for you to get out. Ezylryb does have a few sky ports in his hollow, doesn't he?" Sky ports were the openings directly to the outside of the tree from which the owls could fly from their hollows. There were smaller holes called trunk ports which the nest-maids usually came through.

"Of course," Soren replied.

So it was set. They would go the next day just after tween time and their flint mop for Dewlap, during harp practice. Octavia, as a member of the harp guild, would be attending.

"Gylfie! My dear, that hole is simply not deep enough." Dewlap came up to the Elf Owl. "Here, let me demonstrate. And don't use that excuse of being an Elf Owl and your beak being too tiny. One of my best chaw members ever was an Elf Owl. She dug exquisite holes."

"Doesn't she ever sleep?" Digger said under his breath at tween time as the four owls poked holes with their beaks in the soil to bury the pellets.

When the first chords of the harp rang out, they all breathed a sigh of relief. Their flint mop was done for now. And the investigation of Ezylryb's hollow could begin. The other owls were still sleeping, for during these first days following the harvest festival, the owls tended to rouse themselves later. Soren, Gylfie, and Digger made their way to Ezylryb's hollow. Located in one of the highest parts of the tree, the hollow was the only one facing the northwest, the direction of the cold prevailing wind that most owls did not fancy. But, of course, Ezylryb was not most owls. And perhaps he liked facing the direction of the Northern Kingdoms from which he had come.

As soon as they entered the hollow, Digger took up his lookout position at the trunk port. He tried to take in as much as he could of the old teacher's quarters, which appeared to have hundreds of books and maps, but Soren and Gylfie hurried him along to his watch post.

"Where do we begin?" Soren asked, looking at all the piles of papers, charts, maps, and infinite numbers of gizmos that Ezylryb had to help him interpret weather patterns. There was a vial of sand that he often hung outside his hollow, which registered the moisture in the air. There was another vial of quicksilver to gauge atmospheric pressure changes. There were at least twenty wind indicators. Ezylryb was always experimenting with new wind indicators that used feathers sometimes plucked from his own body, but it was usually a molted one from some very young owl who had just shed its baby down.

"It would be easier to know where to begin if we knew exactly what we were looking for," Gylfie replied, lighting down on a dangerously tilting stack of books.

Soren just sighed. There was something so sad about the hollow. In the month or so before the Great Downing, Ezylryb had taken to inviting members of the weather chaw to his hollow to share tea. The old ryb would talk about his latest weather theories or inventions for interpreting weather. But now the coals in his grate were cold. The plates of his favorite snack food, dried caterpillars, went untouched and a fine layer of dust had settled on all the books.

Soren knew that off of this main parlor of Ezylryb's hollow there was a smaller one where he slept. Gylfie had already flown into it. So Soren followed her. "Anything here?"

"Practically nothing," Gylfie replied.

In definite contrast to the parlor, the sleeping hollow was sparsely furnished to the point of austerity. There was a bed, a mixture of down with generous portions of Ga'Hoolian moss known for its fleecy quality. By the bed stood a small table with a slender volume of poems atop another large leather-bound volume. Soren peered at the book.

"What's the book?" Gylfie asked.

"Something called *Sonnets of the Northern Kingdoms,* by Lyze of Kiel."

"Whoop-de-doo," Gylfie said. "Sounds exciting, doesn't it?"

"Well, you know Ezylryb. Everyone says he is the best scholar here. He likes all this weird obscure stuff. It's not all just weather science with him."

"What's the other book?" Gylfie asked.

Soren moved the poetry volume. "I can hardly read the title, this book is so ancient." The leather had crackled into fine lines and the gold leaf in which the title had been written had nearly flaked away. But underneath was the faint impression of an outline of the embossed letters. Soren, looking hard at the letters, spoke slowly. "*Sagas of the North Kingdoms: The History of the War of the Ice Claws* by Lyze of Kiel."

"Talented fellow, I guess," Gylfie said. "I mean, sonnets and war history." Gylfie was talking as she flitted here and there in the almost bare chamber. "What's this?" she said suddenly.

"What's what?" Soren asked. "Oh, it looks like a perch. Must be for his exercises or something."

"No, I don't think so." And at the moment Gylfie lighted down on the perch, it fell from the wall. The Elf Owl tumbled through the air and landed lightly on her small talons. "Some perch! Can't even hold an Elf Owl like me."

Soren blinked in dismay. That was weird. Where the perch had been was a hole. Soren flew up to the hole and then, using fast, scooping motions of his wings and by angling his tail, he managed to tread the air in order to hover. *Glaux! I wish I were a hummingbird!* he thought. Hovering in a tight space for a bird of Soren's size was no easy matter. "Gylfie, get over here and hover. You're smaller. You can do this better than I can. Peek into that hole. I see something."

"You do?" Gylfie had flown up as Soren backed off. Now Gylfie hovered and then suddenly poked her beak in and within a fraction of a second came back with a string clutched in it. It was a long string and it was firmly attached to something in the hole.

"Pull it!" said Soren.

Gylfie gave a little tug. "I can't, you're stronger."

So Soren came up and gave a yank. There was a creak and suddenly a door, previously invisible, opened. The owls blinked at each other. There was no need to ask if they should or should not go in. Their minds were instantly made up. Soren entered first. It was dark but, of course, darkness never bothered an owl. They could actually see better in the dark. They made their way through a very narrow corridor. Flying through it was almost impossible even for an Elf Owl. Soon, however, the corridor widened and they found themselves standing in another hollow, about the same size as Ezylryb's sleeping quarters.

A secret chamber, thought Soren. Then both owls blinked in astonishment.

"Soren, do you see what I see?"

"I certainly do!"

Hanging on the wall in front of them was a pair of ancient, rusted battle claws. *Yes, a secret chamber for hiding secrets.* Soren now thought of his last conversation with the rogue smith of Silverveil. The words came back to him: *Ezylryb has a past. He is a legend. He does have enemies.*

How shocked Soren had been. How unbelievable it was to him that the most nonviolent owl on earth could ever have an enemy. Ezylryb, the owl who had the greatest contempt for battle claws!

"Well, will you look at these claws! Holy Glaux!" Gylfie had flown up close to them. "Makes my gizzard wilt to even be this close. Soren you won't believe this. These suckers are deadly. They've got jagged edges. Glaux almighty. Come up here and look at them."

"No!" Soren said. He couldn't stand the thought of his teacher — his hero — wearing those. Killing. He himself had killed before. He had helped kill the bobcat in the forest of The Beaks, and he had helped kill the top lieutenants of St. Aggie's, Jatt and Jutt, when the two Long-Eared cousins had attacked them in the Desert of Kuneer. But this was different somehow. This was like being a professional killer. Yes. What had they called those owls he had heard about — Hireclaws? They hired out to anyone to fight and kill. That was the only reason that an owl would have his own set of claws. All the claws in the Great Tree were kept in the armory. There weren't many rules at Ga'Hoole, but it was strictly forbidden to keep arms in your hollow.

But Soren was drawn to them nonetheless. Slowly, he flew in short hops toward the claws on the wall. "Well, they're rusty," Gylfie said, looking nervously at her friend. She knew how much Soren admired Ezylryb. She knew this must be difficult for him. Hireclaws were the lowest of the low.

"Because they're rusty, I don't think he uses them much. Maybe not for years and years, Soren."

"Maybe," Soren said weakly. He peered more closely at the claws. There was something familiar about them. Something in the way the claws curved in such an exact likeness to the way an owl's talons curved and were angled. *The fit must be perfect,* Soren thought. Then it burst upon him.

"Gylfie," he turned suddenly to the Elf Owl, "these claws were made by the rogue smith of Silverveil."

"No, young'uns," the two owls whirled around. Slithering into the chamber was Octavia. "Not the smith of Silverveil, but her master from Dark Fowl Island in the Everwinter Sea. They were made for Lyze of Kiel, poet, warrior, and writer of sagas."

"Lyze of Kiel," Soren whispered the words. They rang in his ears. The letters rearranged themselves in his mind's eye. Their true meaning turned in the deepest part of his gizzard.

The old blind snake seemed to sense all this. "Yes, Soren. You're getting the picture, aren't you?"

"Huh?" Gylfie said.

"Lyze of Kiel, Gylfie. Rearrange some of letters and it spells Ezyl."

CHAPTER THIRTEEN

Octavia Speaks

Yes, my dear, the 'ryb' was added after we arrived here and the owls knew that the greatest of scholars and warriors had come to the Great Ga'Hoole Tree." She paused. "You know him as Ezylryb."

At that moment, Digger entered the secret chamber. He was frantic. "I called and called trying to warn you. I tried everything to distract her. I'm really sorry."

Octavia swung her head toward the Burrowing Owl. "Don't worry. For a long time I have felt that Soren was up to something. Since that first night of the harvest festivities. I would have found out sooner or later."

Soren remembered now how Octavia had slithered out onto the gallery to help Madame Plonk, who had passed out from the milkberry wine. Everyone else had been distracted by the comet's appearance. It was the perfect distraction, camouflage for their leaving. But just as Soren was sweeping from the Great Hollow, he had felt the gaze of the sightless snake boring into him. She did have extraordinary powers, even if she had not been born blind.

"You won't tell anybody, will you, Octavia?" There was almost a pleading tone in Soren's voice.

"No. What good would that do? It wouldn't help get Ezylryb back."

"Do you think that his disappearance has something to do with his past — with someone who wants to get even?"

Octavia coiled up and extended her head directly toward Soren. He had that same feeling again as if her gaze were penetrating his deepest thoughts. "Who told you that?"

"The rogue smith."

"Of Silverveil?" Octavia lifted her head slightly. "Yes, I might have known. She's quite different from her sister, isn't she?" It was useless asking this snake how she knew anything — she just seemed to know.

But how come she doesn't know where Ezylryb is? Soren asked himself.

Now Octavia picked up her feather duster and began whisking the film of dust off a stack of books on a desk near the claws. Gylfie gave a little sneeze. "Allergies, don't worry. Go ahead, Octavia."

"The place is a mess, isn't it? It's hard for me to come in here and tidy up. Too many memories."

"Of course," Soren said softly, but he had a feeling that Octavia was about to recount some of those memories, and perhaps moving about, keeping busy with this simple task of dusting, would loosen her forked tongue.

"You see, young'uns," Octavia began as she neatened a stack of papers and continued dusting Ezylryb's desk. "Ezylryb and I go way back, back to the time when he was known as Lyze, the almost legendary warrior of the War of the Ice Claws."

The three young owls hardly dared to breathe as the chubby old snake began her tale.

"This War of the Ice Claws was the longest in history. It was well into its second century by the time Lyze was hatched. He was groomed, trained, raised to be a warrior, as were all the young owls from the Stormfast Island in the Bay of Kiel in the Everwinter Sea. His father, his mother, his grandparents, his great- and great-great-grandparents all were superb soldiers. Every single one of them had been a commander of an air artillery division. They were learned, too. Knew how to fight with their minds, not just with their talons. But it was soon apparent, as soon as Lyze first fledged and took to the wing, that this was one extraordinary young Whiskered Screech Owl. More brilliant than any of his siblings, which was later to cause trouble in the nest. He soon became the youngest commander of an air artillery division and shortly thereafter began in earnest to train colliers.

"Now you are probably wondering where I came in. Well, on the island of Stormfast there were, of course, nest-maid snakes. They were blind. But there was another breed of snake called Kielians, and they were not blind. They didn't have rosy scales, but the blue-green ones like my own. I am a Kielian snake. We are known for our industry and wit. More muscular than the blind snakes and extremely supple."

Octavia paused for a moment. "This isn't all fat, you know!" She twisted her head about and patted her body with it. "Lots of muscle there. In any case, we could get into places that were unreachable to blind snakes and, because of our musculature, we could actually dig holes, be it on the ground or in a tree. Yes, our fangs were as effective as a woodpecker's beak."

The three owls froze as two long fangs shot from her mouth.

"Scary, aren't they?" She paused to give the owls another good look, then continued with her story. "It was Lyze who first thought of using us in battle. Lyze and I were about the same age. My parents knew his parents, but there really wasn't much mingling between snakes and owls in general on Stormfast. You have to understand that creatures who live in the Everwinter Sea and along its coast aren't really sociable types. They stick to themselves. It's such a harsh environment that it, well, does not lend itself to — how should I put it? — frivolity. Except for yours truly here.

"I was a problem snake. A problem as a young'un, and it only grew worse as I grew older. I loved fooling about, having fun, getting into trouble. I don't mind telling you I was a terrible flirt in those days. It seems the whole industry thing for which our species was known had just passed me by. I can remember my mum saying once that if she didn't know better, she'd think she and Pa were raising a chipmunk. Chipmunks are silly, incredibly irresponsible, frivolous creatures. I was driving my parents to distraction by the time I was a teenager. It was just around that time that Lyze came up with the idea to train Kielian snakes for battle. One day when Lyze was flying over the rocky crag where my parents had their nest, one of the few sunny days and I was out sunning myself, doing nothing, and my mum was ranting at me. Lyze heard her from above. He had just had the idea for a stealth force of Kielian snakes. He lighted down and said to my mum, 'Give her to me, ma'am, and she'll never have another lazy day in her life. I'll turn her into a crack soldier.' I, of course, was horrified by the idea. But before I knew what had happened, Mum and Pa had nodded their consent, and I was in Lyze's talons being flown off to a training camp. The only compensation was that there were some handsome male Kielians. But my goodness, after a day's training I wasn't fit for anything but sleep.

"Well, you might not believe it, but I turned into a pretty fair soldier for the stealth force. I think it was Lyze who made me, to tell you the truth. That owl could inspire anybody."

Soren felt a twinge in his gizzard. *How true it is,* he thought, and remembered his times flying with Ezylryb through forest fires, gales, and the worst of storms.

"Lyze took a mate shortly after I came into training. In a sense, that was when his troubles with his brother really began. His brother, a seemingly quiet, gentle owl named Ifghar, had fancied Lyze's mate, but she did not fancy him. The War of the Ice Claws was getting fiercer. The league of Kiel, for it was the islands of the Bay of Kiel and the coast that had gathered into an alliance, was being beaten back by the league of the Ice Talons farther to the east. The King of the Ice Talons region was a brutal old Snowy who really wanted dominion over the entire Northern Kingdoms. It was at about that time that I was promoted to the most elite of the stealth-force units. This unit, called Glauxspeed, was in Lyze's division, of which he was the commander in chief. I served him directly.

"Lyze and his mate, Lil, made a beautiful couple in battle. It was as if they did not even have to speak. Their gizzards were so in tune, so harmonious, that they instantly knew what the other was thinking. Together, they were a fearsome team. Their timing, their precision, couldn't be matched. They were the anathema of the enemy. Everyone knew if the war was going to be won it would be because of Lyze and Lil."

"So what happened?" Digger asked. "Was the war won?"

Octavia sighed deeply and put down her duster. "No, Ifghar became a turnfeather, betrayed them, betrayed his brother, his family, the entire Kielian league. So jealous was he that, by this point, he went to the other side and swore he could break up the team. His only condition was that Lil be given to him as a mate."

"Oh, no!" all three owls said at once.

"I found out about the plan but it was too late. They were already on the wing, set to attack a recon unit on an island in the Bay of Fangs. I usually flew aboard a heavy old Barred Owl. He was a terrific flier, fast and silent, but he wasn't available. They got me a Spotted Owl instead but she didn't have the speed. I got there just in time to see the ambush led by Ifghar. It was all going according to his evil plan, except for one thing — Lil was mortally wounded. Ifghar went berserk, and Lyze . . . well, Lyze went yeep."

"Yeep!" Soren was stunned. When birds went yeep due to some enormous fright, some gizzard-chilling terror, their wings folded under and they plummeted to earth. "It was lucky that a bald eagle was flying over just then. The eagle took a plunge and caught Lyze just before he would have hit the water. But he caught him by a talon, severely injuring it. Still, it would have been worse if he had fallen into the sea. He would have drowned. Owls can't swim worth racdrops. The injured talon never healed properly. It was causing him a great deal of pain. So he finally bit it off himself."

"Bit off his own talon?" Soren said in dismay.

"Believe me, after the first pain he began feeling much better." She stopped talking.

Digger sensed that there was still more to tell. He stepped forward. "Is there something else?"

"Yes, it was in that battle — the Battle of the Ice Talons, it was later named — that I was blinded. I was so distracted with Lyze going yeep that I didn't see the fierce old Great Gray Owl coming up on the windward flank. I had coiled up to my tallest height and was frantically yelling at

Lyze to break the yeep spell. The Great Gray swept by and in two seconds plucked out my eyes. That was the end of my military career. And it turned out to be the end of Lyze's as well. He never picked up a pair of battle claws again." She paused. "Not to fight, at least." She nodded at the ones on the wall. "These old rusty ones are the ones he wore in that battle. I convinced him to retrieve them so they wouldn't fall into enemy talons."

"So what did you do?"

"Well, Lyze and I had become quite fond of each other by this time. He said that he was finished with war and had decided to retreat to a small island far from the Ice Claw Wars, which was in the Bitter Sea. There was a retreat there, an order of Glauxian brothers who were devoted only to study. They had a great library. So that is where we went for a good long time. Nobody asked any questions. Lyze read and read and read. And began his history, the one you saw on the history of the War of the Ice Claws. He also began his serious study of weather at the retreat. It was there I learned how to be a nest-maid snake and tend to his hollow and the hollows of many of the other brothers."

"Where did Madame Plonk's sister come into all this?" Gylfie asked.

"Oh, a year or so before the great tragedy, she had left her family's hollow, desperate to escape because of her stepmother. Her life was utterly miserable. Music was not for her. There was something about her that Lyze and his mate, Lil, took a fancy to. I think they liked her toughness, and she seemed extraordinarily skillful with her talons. So Lyze gave her an introduction to the rogue smith on the island of Dark Fowl."

"When did you decide to come to the great tree?"

"It was actually one of the Glauxian brothers' ideas. He felt that Lyze had so much knowledge that it was a shame for it to be all locked up in a retreat. There were no young ones at the retreat. He felt that Lyze could be a natural teacher. So he advised him to go to the Great Ga'Hoole Tree where there were always young owls to teach. And Lyze said he would but he would never ever train an owl to fight. He would never ever touch a pair of battle claws again. So we came here. I swore an oath of peace, as well." Octavia paused for several long seconds. "But you know, now I think it is time to break it. I'll do anything to rescue my beloved master."

CHAPTER FOURTEEN
Eglantine's Dream

There was stunned silence when Octavia finished her extraordinary tale. It was almost too much to absorb. Soren, Digger, and Gylfie made their way back to their hollow. It was past First Black, and Twilight and Eglantine had overslept. They were just now getting ready for evening chaw practice.

"Where have you been?" Twilight asked suspiciously.

"No time to explain now," Gylfie replied.

"We'll tell you all about it later," Soren said and turned to look at Eglantine. She looked a bit peaked. Her usually lustrous black eyes seemed dull. "You all right, Eglantine?" he asked.

"I didn't sleep that well. Bad dreams I think, but I can't remember them really."

The five owls left for their various classes. All the owls were required to attend all classes, even if they were not a member of that particular chaw. Tonight, however, they were all quite distracted and in navigation; Soren nearly crashed into Primrose.

"Soren, attention please!" Strix Struma hooted. "Too much harvest celebration, I think!" And she made a clicking sound with her beak.

In the dining hollow, near dawn after classes ended, Soren, Gylfie, Digger, Twilight, Primrose, and Eglantine gathered at Mrs. P.'s table.

"I'll stretch myself out longer," Mrs. Plithiver said, "if you'd like to invite some friends over."

"Oh, that's all right, Mrs. Plithiver," Gylfie replied. "We're fine just the six of us."

But they weren't really fine. Gylfie, Soren, and Digger were very quiet. Eglantine was twitchy; Twilight sensed that he had missed out on something important, and so did Primrose, for that matter. Soren thought it might have been better if they had invited a few other owls over, even Otulissa. A nonstop talker like Otulissa would have made it easier. Their breaklight, as this meal was often called, was delicious with Ga'Hoole nut porridge and milkberry syrup poured over it from the new harvest. Toasted mice and caterpillars dipped in a sweet juice made from the plump berries. No one, however, seemed especially hungry. In fact, they were ready to turn in by the time the first rays of the sun slid over the horizon. But first, of course, they had to go and bury pellets for Dewlap. There was only one more day and then they would have completed their flint mop. It couldn't come quickly enough.

Soon they were all asleep in the hollow. But Soren, even in his sleep, could sense his sister's restlessness as she fluttered in some storm-tossed sea of dreams. Then toward noon when the sun was reaching its highest point, a terrible shrill scream split the air of the hollow. A small tornado of downy feathers swirled up from the dreaming Eglantine.

Soren was immediately by her side. "It's just a bad dream, Eglantine, a bad dream. You're here at the tree safe in the hollow with me and Twilight and Digger and Gylfie. You're perfectly safe."

Eglantine put her talon out to touch Soren as if to make sure he was real and this was not a dream. "Soren," she spoke in a quavering voice. "I knew those stone walls that you described, where the rogue smith had her forge, reminded me of something."

"Yes?" Soren said slowly.

"Remember the isinglass when Trader Mags came last summer? When I saw that, it reminded me of something, too. It was after that, that I came out of my, my . . ."

"Condition," Gylfie added slowly.

"Yes, Gylfie. It was after that, that I recognized Soren again. Well, in this dream, I dreamed of stone, and it has helped me remember more."

"Remember what?" Soren said in a whisper. All the owls waited tensely.

"I know where they kept us now, kept all of us from the Great Downing."

"Where?" Soren was now in a fever. For months, Boron and Barran had tried to figure out the mystery of the Great Downing. Where had the owls been before? Why they had been dropped in an open field far from any hollows or nests? The owls themselves were so confused and stunned, they could give no clues as to the answers to any of their questions. In fact, for the first several days, the only words they uttered in their strange little singsongy voices were weird chants about the purity of Tytos. The owls rescued in the Great Downing had all been some sort of Barn Owl, and the formal name for the family of Barn Owls was Tytonidae, or Tytos for short. Even when they finally were rested and brought back to health, not one of them could recall what had happened to them.

Eglantine opened her beak slightly as if she were about to speak then shut her eyes tightly. There was a long pause. "You see, it comes in patches. When I saw that thin sliver of colored stone last summer — the isinglass — and the moonlight through it, and I heard the harp tuning up, I remembered how much they hated music."

"They? Who is they?" Twilight leaned forward, towering over Eglantine.

"Well, they were Barn Owls like us for the most part — some Sooties and some Grass Owls, a few Masked ones."

"Yes," Soren said slowly. "Now try and tell us more, Eglantine."

"Well, they hated music. Music was forbidden."

"Why was that?"

"I'm not sure, but for some reason we all craved music. They said we weren't working out."

"What did they mean by that?" Gylfie asked.

"I don't know." Eglantine cocked her head quickly in one direction and then the other, in the way young owls often did when they were confused or disturbed.

"Do you remember anything about the place you were in or how you got there?" Soren pressed.

"Not really."

"Was it a forest? " Digger asked.

"No. "

"Was it a deep stone pit?" said Gylfie, remembering the

bleak stone prison of St. Aggie's that spread itself through rock gulches and canyons with nary a tree or a blade of grass.

"There was stone. Most definitely there was stone like the stones of the rogue smith's forge in Silverveil, all carefully carved and stacked into walls." Eglantine blinked, and blinked again as if trying to see an image, an image dim and faded and steeped in shadows.

Soren suddenly had an idea. Last summer, Eglantine had started to shake, to have her fit, and then she remembered who she was when she had seen the fragment of the isinglass on Trader Mags' cloth. Just seeing the sliver of isinglass had jolted her out of her stunned state. And then all the owls from the Downing started clamoring to hear the music, for, indeed, Madame Plonk had just started harp practice. The owls of the Great Downing had been frantic to get to the music. And it did seem to restore them.

"Gylfie." Soren turned to the little Elf Owl. "Don't you have some isinglass from Trader Mags?"

"Yes, I was going to string it into a whirlyglass, but I haven't had the time. It's almost all strung but just not hung together yet."

"May I have a piece for a minute?" Soren asked.

"Certainly," Gylfie replied.

Just as Soren was picking up a string with sparkling pieces of the mica stone, the noonday sun flared into the hollow. Eglantine turned and gasped and her eyes fastened on the bits of glass that Soren held. Slowly, the colored spots of light dappled the air and the dancing colors spread across her brother's pure white face. "You look just like the stained glass windows in the castle," Eglantine said softly.

"A castle!" the other four owls exclaimed.

"Yes," Eglantine said. "When we first got there, we thought it was so beautiful, even though it was in ruins with many of the walls down and just parts of others standing, but we soon learned." Eglantine was talking now in a dreamy voice as if she were in some kind of a trance. "It was beautiful but there was ugliness, too. They called themselves the Pure Ones and, at first, they seemed kind. They wanted to teach us to worship Tytos because they said we were the purest of the pure of all the owls, and that is why we spoke the praising songs. But it wasn't at all the way that Mum and Da used to read to us, Soren. No, not at all. I mean, you remember how Mum would try to hum a little tune and almost sing. We could not do that. They wanted nothing to do with music. They thought music was like poison." It reminded Soren of St. Aggie's, where questions were thought to be poison and the worst punishments were reserved for those who asked questions.

"But it was the one they called the High Tyto," Eglantine continued, "he was the worst. He never said much. But he was so frightening. He wore a kind of mask, and they said his beak had been torn off in a battle." Then Eglantine realized what she had just said and fell into a faint.

"Metal Beak!" they all whispered in terror.

Gylfie immediately began flying over Eglantine, wafting drafts of air down upon her face to revive her. Twilight also tried, but his wings churned the air so violently that Eglantine was practically lifted off the floor of the hollow.

Eglantine's eyes blinked open. "My goodness, I fainted, didn't I?" Then she looked up at Soren as she staggered to her feet.

"Take it easy now, little one," Twilight said. "You've just had a bad fright."

"No, no I'm fine. I'm really fine. I feel so much better. But just imagine — I came face-to-face with Metal Beak. It's all coming back to me now. He was the one who hated music the most. He thought it was impure. In fact, he thought any owl who was not a Tyto alba was a little less than completely pure. He made the Sooties and the

Masked Owls and the Grass Owls do all the worst jobs. Oh, and yes, before we could become true members of the Way of Purity, we had to sleep in stone crypts with the bones of the old Tytos that they called the Purest Ones."

"The Purest Ones?" Soren said, perplexed.

Gylfie had remained very quiet, but when she heard about the little owls being put in the stone crypts, she began to speak. "I think that they did to Eglantine with stone what the owls of St. Aggie's did to us with the full moon." Gylfie was referring to the horrendous moon-blinking process during which the young owlets at St. Aggie's were forced to sleep with their heads directly exposed to the scalding light of the moon. It disturbed their gizzards in a profound way and seemed to destroy their will, along with any of the individual characteristics that made up an owl's personality.

Gylfie continued, "Only instead of being moon blinked, they were stone stunned. I think I've heard of it. In the Desert of Kuneer, there are a series of deep, blind canyons — a maze really — and if one gets lost in them, the stone can affect the brain. If the owls come back, they are a bit odd, you know, weird in the head." But there was something else that Gylfie felt in her gizzard but did not mention. She was almost sure that the bones in those crypts were not the bones of owls, but of the Others. The thought, however, was too chilling, too sickeningly terrifying to even mention.

Soren's eyes fastened on Eglantine's wing where she had suffered her most severe wound from the Great Downing. The feathers had grown back, but patchily. He felt swollen with anger at this vile owl Metal Beak. "I can't believe how he hurt you, Eglantine. It makes me want to kill him. No wonder Mum's and Da's scrooms warned me."

"But you don't understand, Soren. It wasn't the Tyto owls of the castle that did this to my wing. Oh, they did plenty. Feelings in my gizzard are just really coming back now, but it was the other owls, the ones who raided the castle and snatched us. That is really how I and all the rest of us got hurt. They nearly got away with us but the owls from the castle, the High Tyto and the Pure Ones, followed. There was this huge battle as they tried to snatch us back, and I dropped. So did a lot of us because something came along and scared them all. I was surprised that I survived the fall. But then I was worried that I would be snatched again. That is why I dragged myself to hide under that bush where Digger and Twilight found me."

"Were the owls who snatched you, Barn Owls as well?" Gylfie asked.

"Oh, no. All sorts. There was a raggedy-looking Great Horned, and she had a huge bare patch on her wing that made her fly all funny."

"Skench!" Gylfie and Soren both blurted out at once. Skench, whose cruelty knew no bounds, the Ablah General of St. Aegolius Academy for Orphaned Owls had just such a patch on her wing.

"So they were from St. Aggie's!" Soren said.

It had all come back so clearly to Eglantine that now she could hardly stop talking. But meanwhile, one thought prevailed in Soren's mind. Were they actually any closer to finding Ezylryb? Could Eglantine remember where this castle was with its odd rituals that celebrated the purity of Barn Owls in such an awful way? Was Ezylryb there, or had he simply gotten lost? Had he been stone stunned? Or was he dead?

CHAPTER FIFTEEN
The Chaw of Chaws

In times of trouble, however, there can come a certain closeness, a kind of coziness of spirit. It was never so true as in the hollow of Soren and his mates, Gylfie, Twilight, Digger, and now Eglantine. The stories that Eglantine told held a peculiar fascination for the owls in the hollow. Finally, it was Digger who asked, "Eglantine, can you remember what the ground was like around the castle? I mean, was it like Silverveil or The Beaks?"

"I've never been to The Beaks, but how do you mean, Digger?"

"Well, were there tall trees, or was it scrubby with short bushy plants? Was it hard-packed earth, bare, or maybe sandy like a desert?"

"Oh, none of those, I think. I can't remember exactly, for they hardly ever let us out. Although from the broken walls, I could catch a glimpse. They didn't permit us to fly up high. I think there was grass, though. And they used to speak of a meadow. But I don't think there were big trees or trees with leaves, because I can remember when I was just hatched, the hollow in our fir tree — remember, Soren, how you could hear the wind through the leaves of the nearby trees? No, we only heard the wind whistling around the stone corners of the castle."

"Well, that's helpful," Digger said thoughtfully.

"Why?" asked Gylfie.

"I was just thinking, that's all." There was a tense silence in the hollow.

But Soren was thinking, too. Of course, Digger would be interested in the ground. Digger knew the ground — what kind of plants grew there, the feeling of every kind of soil. He had become one of the best in the tracking chaw. In fact, when Soren gazed around he realized that within this hollow were the best of the best of each chaw.

"Eglantine," Soren asked, "do you remember how long you had been flying before you were dropped?"

"Not long, I think." There was another pause.

"Eglantine, do you think that there is any way you might be able to lead us back to the castle? You see, I am thinking that it's been more than two months since Ezyl-ryb disappeared. Endless search parties have been sent out but so far nothing. In fact, Boron just assumed that was what we were doing when we went to Silverveil. Indirectly it was, but really we went to find out more about Metal Beak. Now, what's to stop us from trying to find Ezylryb? Between us . . ." Soren stopped and looked around. "We could put together a pretty good chaw."

"What are you talking about, Soren?" Gylfie asked.

"Gylfie, you are the best navigator Strix Struma has ever taught. I heard her telling that to Barran. Digger, you can track like no one else, and Twilight you can fight" — Soren's voice dropped off — "if that's necessary." Twilight swelled in anticipation. "Don't you see?" Soren continued. "We have the makings here of a great chaw — the best of the best of the chaws."

"Let me get this straight," Gylfie said. The little Elf Owl stepped right up to Soren and stood directly under his beak. "Are you proposing that we should undertake this search for Ezylryb on our own? No rybs, no grown-up owls?"

"That's exactly what he's proposing, Gylfie," Twilight boomed. "For Glaux's sake, we went to Silverveil on our own. Found the rogue smith. She gave us our first real clue, in a sense, about Metal Beak." Twilight paused and nodded deferentially to Soren. "Well, after the scrooms of your mum and da that is."

"Well, if that is the case . . ." Gylfie's voice fell to a whisper. Soren was nervous. If he didn't have Gylfie's support, he couldn't do it. "If that is the case, Soren, you must be our leader."

All of the owls in the hollow nodded their heads in agreement. Soren was stunned. He didn't know what to say. Finally, he spoke. "I thought the plan up, that is true. But the plan would be nothing without each one of you. Your faith in me has stirred my gizzard. I shall do my best for you."

"Soren!" Otulissa suddenly flew into the hollow. "I want to come, too." The meddlesome Spotted Owl had been perched on a branch just outside the hollow. Otulissa's yellow eyes were dim with tears. "Ezylryb made me believe in myself and not just my . . . my . . ." It was the first time Otulissa had ever been at a loss for words. "You know how I was before I joined the chaw. Ezylryb made me believe I could do things because I was just me, and not just because I was a Spotted Owl. I hate that thing that you were talking about before."

"What thing?" Soren asked.

"That stuff about purity, that one kind of owl is more pure or better than another. The most ancient order of owls, the owls that all of us are descended from — whether we are Barn Owls, Snowies, Spotted, or what- ever — those first owls were all called Glaux. And every owl celebrates the spirit of Glaux. My mum told me that, and it is true. For indeed with that ancient order began a special kind of bird. As owls, we owe our uniqueness, our ability to fly silently, to see through the darkness of the night, to spin our heads almost all the way around to those first owls. And you know from navigation that we call our grandest constellation that shines through every season the Great Glaux. But for those owls that Eglantine talked about, that was not enough. They want to destroy all the others."

They were all dismayed by Otulissa's gracious speech. Soren thought that she must have been eavesdropping more than once to have learned all this. She almost started to blubber now with tears and chokes. It was the most un-Otulissa moment any of them had ever witnessed. "I feel so strongly about this. You know me, I'm not an emotional kind of owl but this . . . this . . . I . . . I can't explain, but you must let me be a part of this."

"Of course," Soren said. Otulissa was very smart and beyond being smart, she of all of them possessed the most sensitivity to atmospheric pressure changes. She had proved herself invaluable to the weather chaw.

And this would be the best of the best of the chaws! Indeed, it would be the chaw of chaws!

CHAPTER SIXTEEN

The Empty Shrine

They had picked an evening to leave when there were no classes and no chaw practices, but still they were careful to leave the tree in twos or threes near First Black and then once again take off from the cliffs where they would not be spotted. And they all, even the smallest, wore battle claws. They had filched them from the armory in the forge. Bubo happened to be gone so it was not a problem. Twilight had gone early in the morning of their flight and taken them from the forge and placed them in the crags of the cliffs.

Soren had insisted that they practice with the claws, for none of them had flown that often with them. Eglantine had never flown "clawed," as the expression went.

"You need a lot of tail ruddering, Eglantine. See, you don't have the same balance as before," Soren called out as he watched his sister fly in a wobbly line out from the cliffs.

"She'll get it," Twilight said.

But Soren wasn't sure. Eglantine still seemed so fragile to him. Was she ready for this? She was the only one who would be able to recognize the ruined castle where she had been imprisoned. But then suddenly her flight seemed to even out.

"That's it! That's it!" Soren cheered her on, her wings set and balanced on a smooth horizontal plane. "Phew!" Soren blew through his beak in relief. Still, it disturbed him that he was in fact doing just the opposite of what Ezylryb had sworn never to do again. Soren was not only picking up battle claws but arming a young innocent owl with them, as well. Then he thought of Octavia and the words she had spoken to them in the very chamber where Ezylryb's old claws hung rusted but not forgotten. *I swore an oath of peace, as well. But you know, now I think it is time to break it. I'll do anything to rescue my beloved master.*

The time had come, Soren realized. If there was any chance of rescuing Ezylryb they must do it now before winter set in. There was no choice. The first blizzard could happen any day now and by then it might be too late. Soren ordered Eglantine back to the cliff. Then he stood before the chaw and spoke in a quiet but strong voice that did not waver as he gave the order. "Flight positions. Get ready to fly. Lift!"

And six owls rose into the night.

The plan was to first fly back to the place where Eglantine had been found in the Forest Kingdom of Ambala. They would then somehow try, with Eglantine's help, to find their way to the castle ruins and hopefully to Ezylryb. As they flew, Soren wondered that if they were successful in reaching the castle, and if Ezylryb was there, how would they actually rescue him? Perhaps he shouldn't think so far in advance. When they got there, maybe a plan would come to him. The first task was to get there — to this awful place where young owls were forced to sleep in crypts with bones of these so-called Purest Ones, whatever that really meant.

Twilight was flying point at the moment and Digger flying below, for they were the ones who knew the territory where Eglantine had been found. "We are in Ambala and approaching the area of the Great Downing," Twilight called down to Digger. Digger immediately went into a ground dive. Gylfie began to hover over him.

Twilight turned to Soren and nodded. This was the place. Soren looked up and found the Star That Never Moves.

"Gylfie, take a sighting of our position between Never Moves and the first head star of the Great Glaux constellation."

When Gylfie had their position fixed, they all began to spiral down, except Twilight. Twilight continued to hover above — alert for any other owls in the region. Then, with Digger and the others, they would try to work backward from the spot where Eglantine had been found and reconstruct a path to the castle ruins.

They lighted down in the dry creek bed. "Well, the tracks are gone by now as I expected," Digger said. "But I do remember where I first picked them up."

"Let's start with the actual bush where you first found her, Digger."

With long strides, the Burrowing Owl was there in no time. The others followed.

"Oh, my!" said Eglantine. "This is surely the place. I wouldn't forget it. It seemed as if I spent forever here."

"Now, Eglantine," Digger said, "fly along this creek bed and try to remember where you were dropped."

They had flown less than a minute. "Do you think it was here?" Digger asked. For this was where he had picked up her tracks.

"No, I think it was farther. It was pretty wet."

They flew a few more minutes. "Here! Here!" Eglantine

suddenly said. She lighted down. There was a very small, gurgling stream of water, no more than a few inches deep. "I remember that rock!" She lifted a talon and pointed. "I remember thinking, 'Lucky I didn't fall on that.'"

"Good! Good!" said Soren. "Prepare to fly! We'll make at least three circles overhead and, Eglantine, you try and sense which direction you came from."

"Oh, I don't know, Soren. That's going to be hard. I was so scared, and there was so much commotion. I mean, it was a battle up there."

"Just do your best, Eglantine. That's all you can do. If we have to, we'll fly out in every direction from this spot — Gylfie, you're navigator, so keep track of our position."

Eglantine couldn't remember, and they did begin the slow process of flying out in all directions.

The night is not simply black to an owl. There are layers of blackness of different densities. Sometimes the black is thick, a gooey black unleavened by starlight or the moon, and sometimes the black is thin — still black, but an almost transparent sort of blackness. It all has to do with the shine and the set of the moon above, of the constellations rising or vanishing, and the features of the earth below — whether the land is clad in forests or barren and hard with rock. Just as Twilight was an expert at seeing through the very deceptive grays of twilight and dawn, so Soren was skillful in "reading the black" of the full night.

"Thin-to-coarse black," he called out as they flew over a sparsely wooded area. Then, half an hour later as they flew in another direction, "Water black turning to crunchy."

"No!" said Eglantine, "I know that we never flew over water."

The owls banked steeply and went back to their starting positions. As they settled down on the limbs of a tree, Gylfie suddenly had a brilliant thought. "If these owls just wanted Barn Owls, and mostly Tyto albas, at that, doesn't it make sense that their castle might be located either in Tyto or very near one of its boundaries? More specifically, the boundary it shares with Ambala, which is very small."

So they headed in the direction of the Ambala-Tyto boundary. Soren asked Otulissa to fly out as a scout. It was not long before she came back with the report of a meadow. "Upwind and to the west, but I spotted a forest fire just a little bit north of west. I would say two points off the second head star of the Great Glaux. I don't think we need to worry with the wind in this direction."

"Good work, Otulissa," Soren said.

* * *

Soon the walls of the castle ruins rose in the dawn mist. Only one tower had remained complete. The rest had crumbled down, so they stood only slightly higher than the castle walls. A peaceful haze rolled over the meadow below.

"We'd better fetch up in that small grove of trees," Soren said. "I have a feeling there might be crows around."

From their perches in an alder, the six owls had a good view of the castle. It must have been lovely in its time, Soren imagined, and even in its ruined state, two stained glass windows could be seen in the still-standing east wall. An embroidery of ivy and moss crept over the stone.

"It seems different," Eglantine said after several minutes.

"How?" asked Soren

"Well, it seems very still."

"But it's almost full morning. They are all probably asleep."

"I know, but at full morning the guard usually changes. That's why I said we had to get here just before dawn — exactly at twixt time. The tower has no view toward the east and, at twixt time, the guard changes so we are really safe. But I would be able to see the changing of the guard, for the old guard usually circles the tower one time upon leaving."

"I haven't seen any owls circling," said Twilight.

"And the hunters usually went out to catch a few meadow voles. It's a good time just after twixt time for catching them," Eglantine added.

They waited a good while longer. Finally, Eglantine sighed. "I think something is very odd. It is just too still. Look — see that deer going up to the east wall? That would never happen if the owls were there. . . . But I wouldn't want to be wrong. I mean, I wouldn't want us to go in there and then be attacked."

Soren had been thinking the same thing. He had an idea. "Gylfie, do you think you could fly through that meadow grass without getting tangled up and have a closer look?"

She gave him a shocked look. "Of course. Look, Soren, with all due respect, I might be a noisy flier compared to some but I can thread my way through that grass like a nest-maid through harp strings." Elf and Pygmy Owls, although quite small, were considered noisy fliers for they lacked the soft fringe feathers known as plummels that swallowed the sound of their wings passing through the air.

"Good. I was never doubting your abilities, really. Now, why don't you go up and take a look? But be careful. Come back at the first sign of any danger."

Gylfie was off before they could wish her well.

"Great Glaux," Otulissa sighed. "Look at her go. She might be noisy but look, the grass is hardly moving where she flies through."

Gylfie was back in less than a quarter of an hour. "It's empty. Completely empty."

"No sign, I take it, of Ezylryb?" Soren asked.

"Not that I could see."

"Well, we better have a look for ourselves, then." Soren paused a moment and gazed toward the castle. "All right. We'd all better go together in a tight formation in case of crows. At the first sign of crows, we'll all pack in tight. There are six of us. I can't believe they'd mob us."

A thrush whistled softly in a gallery as the owls lighted down within the cool shadows of the highest wall of the castle ruins. There were things in this place that Soren had never seen before, things that were not of the forest or the meadows or the deserts or the canyons. An immense gilded — but rotting — thing that Eglantine called a throne, where she said the High Tyto perched. There were stumps of broken stone columns with grooves carved in them. "What is that?" asked Soren, pointing with his talon to a high stone perch with stone ledges leading up to it.

"Well," said Eglantine hesitantly, "it was from there that the High Tyto often spoke to us when he was not perched on the throne."

"The High Tyto?" Soren asked. "You mean Metal Beak?"

"Yes. Sometimes they called him 'His Pureness,' but never Metal Beak."

"Great Glaux, it makes me want to yarp!" Twilight snarled. "This purity stuff sounds deadly."

Soren thought that perhaps Twilight didn't realize how true his words really were.

"But I know no one is here," Eglantine continued. "Because of that thrush in the gallery. No one was ever allowed up there."

Eglantine stood quietly peering one way and then the other. It was hard for her to believe that she was back here, but back now with her dear brother, which was even stranger.

She sometimes wondered about Kludd. But she had a bad feeling about him. She had a feeling that he might have had something to do with her fall, as he had with Soren's. She was never absolutely sure. By the time she fell, he was flying about all over, even when he was supposed to be in the nest with her when their parents were out hunting. He made her swear that she would never tell that he'd left her. One night, he came back with blood all over him. She had no idea where he had been, but when their parents came back he told a lie. He said that a fox had been scuttling around at the bottom of the fir tree, and he thought he could get it. Their father was furious. "You could have gotten yourself killed, Kludd."

"Well, it was just a small fox. I wanted to do something nice for you and Mum."

It was a complete lie.

"What's this?" Gylfie said. She was perched in a wooden niche.

Eglantine gulped. "The shrine. That's what they called it, but it's empty!"

Gylfie cocked her head to one side then the other. Then she flipped it back so her beak almost touched the feathers between her shoulders. "It sure is!"

"And they're gone!"

"What's gone?" Soren asked. It was clear that Eglantine was very agitated.

"The Sacred Flecks of the Shrine Most Pure."

"Flecks!" Soren and Gylfie gasped in horror. Flecks — like the ones at St. Aggie's!

CHAPTER SEVENTEEN
A Muddled Owl

In a large spruce tree, the old Whiskered Screech Owl wrapped his seven talons tightly around a slender branch. His head was so muddled it was all he could do to concentrate enough to stay on the limb. He was completely disoriented and had been since he had flown across the small river at the edge of the Kingdom of Tyto. He could have sworn he was flying north, but then none of the stars seemed to line up properly. The Golden Talons, so beautiful this time of year, appeared to him upside down in the sky. And when he thought he was banking for an easterly turn, instead of flying into the glimmer of a rising sun at dawn, he was flying into the darkness of the west. He had known he might be going yoicks when for a trace of a second he thought, well, maybe the sun does rise in the west. And then he realized he had been flying around in circles for days. Finally exhausted, he had settled on the branch of a spruce, so confused he could hardly hunt. Luckily, the food supply seemed plentiful or he would have starved. But summer had passed into autumn and soon autumn would be chased away by the first bitter winds of winter. He would starve, he supposed. *One can never plan these things*, he thought. He had always imagined he would get snuffed into a hurricane's eye and spin around until he died or be sucked up by a rogue tornado wind — the kind they called a torque demon — that tore across the landscape and could pull up not just one tree or two but an entire forest. There was even a story that one torque demon had sucked up a raging forest fire and dumped it on another forest, igniting it as well. Ezylryb snorted. *A fitting end for an old weather owl like me.*

Every day, and he was not even sure how many days had passed now, but with each day he grew more and more confused. Soon, he imagined he would be too confused to even hunt in the very small area that he was able to manage now. So this was what it had all come to. This was to be his death. He shivered as a cool autumn breeze with more than a hint of winter in it ruffled his feathers. He tried to be philosophical about it. He had, indeed, led a grand life — full of adventure, books, and young owls to teach — scholar, sports owl, lover of a dirty joke or two. There had been danger, yes, and heartbreak. He closed his eyes and a tear squeezed out as he thought of his dear Lil. But he had tried to serve well. He hoped, nobly. *Now*, he thought, *in the deep winter of my life, I am on the brink of another winter, my last.*

Ezylryb tried to imagine what he would miss the most. Perhaps the peace of the dawn, the moment of twixt time that hung like a sparkling jewel between the gray of the night and the pink of a new morning. The young'uns — yes, undoubtedly, the young owls whom, throughout the years, he had brought into his chaw and taught to be fair navigators through any weather. Weather, he did like weather. He supposed that was what he did not like about this particular end. It wasn't a torque demon, and it wasn't the eye of a hurricane. It was in fact rather humiliating to die teetering and confused in a forest that he had thought he knew so well.

CHAPTER EIGHTEEN
A Nightmare Revisited

That horrid old St. Aggie's song began to worm its way into Soren's and Gylfie's brains.

> *We shall dissect every pellet with glee.*
> *Perhaps we shall find a rodent's knee.*
> *And never will we tire*
> *in the sacred task that we conspire.*
> *Nor do our work less than perfectly*
> *and those bright flecks at the core,*
> *which make our hearts soar,*
> *shall always remain a mystery . . .*

This was the song that Soren and Gylfie had been forced to sing as they worked in the pelletorium of St. Aggie's. Now it began to roar silently in their heads as they stood in the ruins of the castle and looked up at the empty shrine. Eglantine's dreadful words, "the sacred flecks," still rang in their ears.

"The flecks!" Soren and Gylfie both exclaimed again and stared at each other. The other owls were silent. Finally, the mystery of the flecks, which they had never unraveled, had begun to reveal itself. The image of Skench storming into the library in full battle regalia came back to them in all its terror. They had been just about to fly out of the library, the highest point in the stone maze of St. Aggie's, which offered the best escape route, and Skench, twice their size, advanced toward them, battle claws extended, a fearsome, horrific figure. And then suddenly, for no explainable reason, she slammed into the wall, drawn by some incredible force, and was rendered helpless. Thus, they had escaped. Now Soren remembered one of his very first conversations with Bubo as to why the blacksmith was "drawn to live in a cave." Bubo's words came back to him: *It be a strange and most peculiar force. It's as if all these years working with the iron, we get a bit of the magnet in us. Like them special metals — you know, iron. It's got what we call a "field." Well, you'll be learning this in metals class, in higher magnetics, where all the unseeable parts are lined up. It makes this force that draws you — same thing with me — I get drawn to the very earth from which them little flecks of iron come from.*

Now, finally, Soren realized what the force was.

"The flecks were stored in that wall in the library," Gylfie said.

"Yes, and Skench was wearing metal. There was a strange interaction. But she was so stupid, she didn't know," Soren replied.

"It's simple," said Otulissa.

"Simple?" Digger asked.

"It's higher magnetics. The second volume of Strix Emerilla focuses on disturbances and abnormalities in the earth's magnetic fields. The St. Aggie's owls might not have known what they were doing with flecks but, believe me, these owls of the castle know exactly what they are doing." Otulissa paused dramatically.

What are they doing? The question hung silently in the air.

"Should I go on?" Otulissa asked. She was clearly relishing her superior knowledge.

"Oh, for Glaux's sake, yes!" roared Twilight, seeming to swell to twice his size.

So Otulissa explained how an owl's brain could become muddled to the point of complete directional confusion so that it would be impossible for him to navigate. She was talking on and on, becoming increasingly technical, when Soren finally interrupted. "Eglantine, how many sacred flecks were there?"

"Three golden bags full."

"How big were the bags?"

She thought a moment. "Oh, about the size of" — she hesitated — "an owl's head, say, a Great Gray." She looked at Twilight.

"But how, if the sacred flecks were kept in this shrine, as you call it, how did the owls here protect themselves against the disturbances?"

"Especially Metal Beak," Gylfie added. Soren hadn't thought of this, but why wouldn't Metal Beak slam right into the bags in the same way Skench had in the library?

"I don't know," Eglantine said. "But we never felt anything." She hesitated again. "But maybe we did. When they forced us to sleep in the crypts. Sometimes I felt a strange buzzing in my head, and I would get very confused."

"Aha!" Otulissa exclaimed. She had flown up to the shrine and was investigating the doors that shuttered it closed. "Just as I suspected." She tapped her beak on the lining of the doors. "Mu!"

"Mu?" All the owls said at once.

"Mu metal — magnetically very soft. Surround a magnetic object with it, and it blocks the field. That's what protected you, Eglantine."

"Except when I was put into the crypt."

"And that is what protected Metal Beak," Gylfie said. "His mask and beak must be made of mu metal."

"Precisely," Otulissa nodded sagely.

Soren had said nothing. He was listening and thinking. "There were three bags, Eglantine, right?"

Eglantine nodded.

"But now they are gone." Soren turned toward Otulissa. "Otulissa, what would happen if you set up these three bags of flecks at certain points?"

Otulissa began to tremble, then in a barely audible whisper, she spoke. "There would be a Devil's Triangle."

"So the mu metal protects one from the magnetic disruption. But is there anything that can actually destroy the flecks, the magnetism itself forever?"

Otulissa nodded solemnly. "Fire!"

"Fire . . . mu . . . fire, fire!" Soren spread his wings and rose in flight. He swept from one corner of the castle ruins to another. It was the owl manner of pacing. To fly, to move, helped him to think. Gylfie soon lifted into flight. How often during their long imprisonment at St. Aggie's had the two of them plotted and planned together? Soren felt the comfort of Gylfie's presence as the Elf Owl fell into flight beside him. The other owls were very still except for the smooth turnings of their heads as they followed the two owls' flight with their eyes. Several minutes later, Gylfie and Soren lighted down.

"Is there any way we can get that mu off the doors of the shrine?"

"That shouldn't be hard, especially if it's soft metal," Twilight said, and flew toward the niche. Then with a force that would have torn a fox in half, he ripped off the metal.

"Good!" Soren said. "Now we must leave our battle claws behind and fly out to find that forest fire that Gylfie spotted earlier. Twilight, seeing as we have no coal-carrying buckets, could you somehow bend one of those sheets of mu metal into something like a bucket?"

"Sure thing, Soren."

Thus, a plan had been devised by Soren and Gylfie with the mu metal to protect and shield them. Since the bags were missing, it might be very easy for the owls to accidentally find themselves smack in the middle of a Devil's Triangle. As an ultimate precaution, they intended to first fly to the forest fire and collect burning coals. And, if they did fly upon the bags of sacred flecks, they could, with the coals harvested from the forest fire, destroy the flecks' power. If this triangle existed, they must destroy it. It would be a hazard to all bird life — owls, eagles, seagulls — yes, even crows — as much as they loathed that latter species. Something like this simply could not exist in nature. Otulissa thought that because she was indeed so sensitive to changes in atmospheric pressure she might be able to sense the perimeter of the triangle. So it was decided that Otulissa would fly in the point position.

They had been in the castle a long time. The light was seeping out of the day. Soon it would be First Black. The owls perched on the jagged edges of the north wall of the church and watched the smudge of smoke from an immense forest fire roll up to meet the coming darkness of the night. Gylfie stood beside Soren, hardly reaching his breast feathers. Six owls they were, Soren thought as he slid his head around to look at them. Six strong, quick-witted owls about to fulfill a destiny. They had indeed become a band of owls who would rise into the blackness and embark on the last part of a dangerous quest — to find the lost, to mend the broken, to make the world a better place, and to make each owl the best he or she could be. Soren knew that he was in fact the leader of the best of the best. And so he vowed that no matter how difficult this was, he would do all in his power to not only rescue Ezylryb, but to bring each one of these owls home safe to the Great Ga'Hoole Tree.

CHAPTER NINETEEN
Into the Devil's Triangle

It was, of course, Soren and Otulissa who, as trained colliers, would plunge into the forest fire to retrieve the coals. They had found a high rock ledge downwind of the forest fire that offered them the best point of observation. All the owls were massed on the ledge and listened carefully as Soren began to speak.

"Now, you understand that it is only myself and Otulissa who will go into the fire."

Twilight, Digger, Gylfie, and Eglantine nodded gravely. There would be no argument, not even from Twilight. They all knew that only these two owls had been trained in this very dangerous work that demanded skills far beyond the ordinary. From breathing and flying, to the beak work of seizing a live coal, these owls had received the most specialized of instruction of any chaw.

"If there is a problem, an enemy approaching or whatever — yes, come fetch us. I think it should be Gylfie or Eglantine, because Twilight and Digger, being larger, might have to remain to deal with an enemy. If either of you have to come to us, you must fly what we call the fringes of the fire."

"But what if you're not there when we come?"

"One of us will always be flying lookout, watching for the one below who is retrieving coals on the ground."

How he now wished that Ruby was here. The Short-eared Owl, being the best flier of them all, was particularly skilled in catching airborne embers. There would really be no one to fill that spot tonight. And how he missed Martin, who often performed the wide coal reconnaissance surveys that gave information as to the size and location of various rich ember beds. In addition to that, Martin was very good at finding glowworms. A glowworm was a particular kind of coal that was especially valued by Bubo for his forge. No one had the slightest idea why it was called a glowworm, but there were extra points for those who found them.

"Otulissa?" Soren said.

"Yes, Soren?"

Glaux, he hoped she didn't give him trouble. "Otulissa, you and I shall make alternating dives once we find an entry point, a good shoot. The rest of you must stay with the mu bucket once we find a place to stash it." It did not look exactly like a bucket but rather a shallow pan. It might be hard keeping the coals in it, but if they flew steady, he felt they could work with it. "Now, the good news is that we don't have to harvest nearly as many coals as we normally do. Remember, we don't need coals for a forge, but just for these three bags of flecks."

For the first time, Soren realized he had not cringed as he usually did when he said or heard the word "flecks." Perhaps this was because he was beginning to understand flecks. Yes, they had power, but at the same time, their power was not absolute. He and the band could damage this power and possibly destroy it. Soren realized suddenly that with this small bit of knowledge he had acquired in the last few hours, he knew a great deal more than the brutal owls of St. Aggie's. Whether he knew as much or more as the Pure Ones, as Eglantine had called them, and this horrendous owl called Metal Beak, remained to be seen.

A few minutes later, Soren and Otulissa were shredding the fringes of the forest fire. Shredding was a flight maneuver in which they darted in and out of what they called the dead places at the edge of the fire to find which points would be the best to actually dive in from. This was now Soren's job. Usually Elvan, the co-ryb of colliering, along with Ezylryb led the shred. But Ezylryb had insisted on Soren flying directly behind Elvan enough times that

Soren thought he could do it now. Often they had to make as many as twenty shreds before they found a point of entry. They had made four shreds so far. Now, on this fifth one, Soren felt "a shoot," or a good passageway open up.

"I think this might be it," he said to Otulissa. They made one more pass at the shoot. "All right, let's find a place nearby to stash this mu bucket and then get to work."

When they had found the place for the bucket, Soren and Otulissa left the other owls to guard it and flew toward the fire. Its roar was deafening as it gobbled the trees below. Soren fervently hoped that Eglantine would not have to come to warn them of anything. For an owl not accustomed to flying in forest fires, it was the roar rather than the heat that was often the most intimidating. And now Soren gave the command.

"DIVE!" Otulissa went into a dizzying spiral plunge. Soren kept his eye glued to her as her spots blurred. How often had he done this, flown surveillance not for Otulissa but his chaw partner, Martin? He remembered so well the first time. He had been frightened for Martin but frightened for himself as well. They had imagined every kind of horror that a forest fire could serve up. The rogue winds, the crowning when the fire in an unbridled rage would leap from treetop to treetop, creating fuel ladders that sucked up everything in their deadly heat — including owls on the wing. Yet, nothing really had scared him as much as that hurricane that had caused Martin to plummet into the sea.

Soren kept his eyes on Otulissa below as he recalled all this. He saw the Spotted Owl rising now on a stack of heated updrafts. She whirled in next to Soren, her once-creamy white spots dark with soot. A glowworm sparkled in her beak as she flew to where the mu bucket had been stashed. Now it was Soren's turn. Down he plunged. The coal beds were rich and the size of the sizzling nuggets, although smallish, burned hot. He managed to harvest two at once and flew directly back to the mu bucket.

It only took four more rounds each for Soren and Otulissa to gather enough coals. Well before midnight they turned back to the ledge where the other owls awaited them by the bucket.

Soren and Eglantine carried the mu bucket between them now with dozens of glowing coals. Twilight, being the largest and strongest of the owls, carried in his talons the piece of the mu metal, which had not been turned into a bucket, as a shield against the flecks if they should encounter any of the missing bags. Otulissa was still flying the point position.

Gylfie, the tiniest owl, flew a few feet from the ground

for close surveillance. And Digger would do what he did better than any owl — walk.

It was Otulissa's hunch that by either being very small or, indeed, walking like Digger, these two owls might be able to pass under the destructive flecks' magnetic field, if the flecks were placed high in trees. The plan was that if they found the bags of flecks they would burn them, thus destroying what Otulissa called the "magnetic alignment." It was definitely higher magnetics, and Soren was awfully glad that Otulissa had done the reading. But then again, they could do all of this and still not find any signs of Ezylryb, who might be dead for all they knew. But Soren could not even think of that, and he could not allow the other owls to think of it, either. They were on a rescue mission. Rescue was to save living creatures. And Soren had a very strong sense that somehow Ezylryb's disappearance was linked to Metal Beak. *Gizzuition*, Ezylryb had once called this sense. It was a way of knowing, a kind of thinking. Ezylryb's words came back to him: *a kind of thinking beyond the normal reasoning processes by which one immediately apprehends the truth, perceives and understands reality.* And he had said that Soren had it, that Soren possessed this strange way of knowing. How it had thrilled Soren when Ezylryb had said this, said in essence that he was special — a special owl.

* * *

"Mu shield!" Otulissa banked sharply and flew back. "I felt it. I definitely felt it."

Soren quickly commanded Gylfie and Digger, who flew and walked beneath them to proceed slowly and with great caution. Now it was Twilight who flew in the point position, holding the sheet of mu metal by his talons like a shield. The other owls flew in behind him. Every few seconds, Otulissa would tip her head out and expose herself directly to the magnetic force. If she peeked her head out to the port side of the shield, and came back blinking and looking confused, they knew they were heading in the direction of one of the bags of flecks, and they would destroy it! It seemed to them now that before they could find Ezylryb they must commit themselves to destroying the three bags of flecks that could threaten all owls' and other birds' flight and navigation abilities. If Otulissa peeked out to the starboard side and felt no change, they knew they were off course from the flecks. Gylfie and Digger flew or walked below completely undisturbed as Otulissa had thought they would.

It took them a while to navigate toward the first bag, and it was actually Digger who spotted it from the ground and called up, "Alder tree ahead. Object wedged between limb and trunk."

Protecting themselves with the shield, they flew to the

tree. Their timing was precise. Twilight passed the shield to Soren who had given the coal bucket to Eglantine. He then reached out with one talon and gave a quick push to the bag, which fell to the ground. Immediately, the effect could be seen on Gylfie and Digger. Digger began to stagger, and Gylfie simply lighted down. Her wings, in a yeep state, hung at her sides as both owls felt the strange buzz in their heads. Soren dipped his beak into the bucket and dropped the coals on the bag with perfect accuracy. There was a flare as the bag caught fire. After several minutes, Otulissa peeked out from behind the shield. "It's a miracle!" Otulissa said and stepped out from behind the shield. The magnetic force at this point had been completely destroyed. Digger and Gylfie, looking fully alert once more, picked themselves up. Digger began to walk straight again, and immediately headed toward the burning clump. He kicked up some dirt with his talons to put out the fire.

"Don't put it all out. We might need some more coals," Soren said. He retrieved some of the brightest coals from the fire, and Otulissa scooped up some cinders. The other owls watched amazed.

"How do they do it?" Digger whispered.

When the owls had the coals and were sure that the remains of the fire were safely smothered, they lifted off into flight.

They had destroyed one bag, but that was only one point of the triangle. The second point would be the hardest to discover, for it could be anywhere radiating out from this first point. They didn't know if this particular triangle was pointing east, west, north, or south. They flew almost an hour in various directions before Otulissa began to sense a disturbance. Then everything happened quickly.

"Oak!" Gylfie called up. From her low-flying position, she sensed that the disturbance that she was feeling came from the large tree dead ahead.

This time the bag of flecks was stuffed into a hollow, and because the hollow was slightly damp, they were able to burn the bag right inside, thus containing the fire and not setting the entire tree ablaze. Digger flew up with talons, grasping clots of wet mud to extinguish the flames. Now, once again, they lifted into flight to find the third and final point in the Devil's Triangle.

Ezylryb blinked as he perched on the limb of the spruce. Had he been dreaming or was what he felt real? It seemed to him that the buzz was dissipating and with it a fog of sorts was lifting from inside his head. He slowly spread his wings and swung his head to look in every direction. He almost felt as if he might be able to fly again with purpose and direction and not become muddled. Something was different. Perhaps he might try at least getting to another nearby tree. He should be able to do this without too much confusion. After all, he had been able to catch small prey that wandered directly beneath his tree. *Keep it simple*, he told himself. *Just keep your eye on that poplar over there. Focus on one branch. Lift off, then two wing beats and you're there. Concentrate. Meditate, the way the Glauxian brothers taught you so many years ago.*

Ezylryb was just about to lift off when he heard something flying noisily low to the ground.

"Ezylryb!" Gylfie cried out. "It's Ezylryb!"

He must be dreaming. It was the little Elf Owl, Soren's best friend. Then, overhead, he heard the unmistakable whistling sound of an owl with a coal in its beak. He sniffed the air. *The chaw is here!*

From a very high tree outside the triangle, an unusually large Barn Owl with a metal beak and mask covering half his face looked on in dismay as the owls burned the last bag of flecks and the snare was destroyed.

"Did you know, Your Pureness, that fire could do this to the sacred flecks?"

"Shut your beak." The High Tyto was tempted to rake

the vile owl with his talons, but with his other troops off in Kuneer, he needed all of his owls right now. There were six from the Great Ga'Hoole Tree, but there were ten of the Pure Ones. It was the Great Gray that would be their hardest foe. Now, of course, they had seven with the old one. But the old one was weak. He was weak but he was smart. And how close they had come to making him theirs. If they had only found a new castle, a fort, anything that the Others had left behind that could serve as their headquarters, they could have lured the Whiskered Screech there. As it was, they had had to stash him here and mind that enough game came his way so he wouldn't starve. He would do them no good dead. How valuable his knowledge would have been. With the old one, they would have not only dominated the Southern Kingdoms but the Northern ones as well, for that was where the old Screech came from — the land of the great North Waters, the land of the legendary warriors. And it was the old Screech who had probably taught them the trick with the fire. This owl had to be theirs. Throughout all the kingdoms of owls, this one — the one they called Ezylryb — or sometimes Lyze, was the most renowned. It was said that he possessed powers and knowledge that were unimaginable. The Pure Ones needed him. He might not be a Tyto but they needed him nonetheless. And they would get him. And once they got him they would crypt him and then they would truly possess him.

"Your Pureness, the Great Gray looks fierce. He might be a problem."

"A problem?" the High Tyto said slowly in a voice that frightened the Sooty Owl who had just spoken. "Has it escaped your notice, Wortmore, that these owls wear no battle claws?"

"That's right, sir. Never thought of that." Wortmore's voice quivered.

"Prepare to attack!"

Nine owls, all with heart-shaped faces, some dusky, some pure white, and one with a metal mask, unlocked the talons of their battle claws.

CHAPTER TWENTY

Attack!

Ezylryb stood with the two members of his chaw and the others in a circle on the ground as they watched the bag burn. As the last of the flecks glowed with an almost white heat, there was a feeling of great release. The chains that had bound the triangle had been broken and then it was as if the links of those chains had simply melted into the thin air of the night.

Soren was still reeling with disbelief. They had never in their wildest dreams expected to find Ezylryb smack in the middle of the Devil's Triangle.

"We should be able to get home by morning, before first light, I think," Soren finally said. He could barely speak, he was so filled with joy at the sight of his old ryb. Soren was just about to say that Digger could go on and bury this fire, that there was no need for coals, when suddenly the night ripped with the shrill screeches of owls.

"It's an attack!" Twilight cried and rose up huge, his talons extended. Soren saw there were ten owls, all with battle claws. And one with a metal beak was flying directly for Twilight. Twilight dodged in the nick of time. All Soren could think was, *We have no battle claws. We are only six, seven if you count Ezylryb. They'll rip us to shreds!* They would never survive.

Then, amazingly, ducking and dodging every parry from the oncoming Metal Beak, Twilight began one of his battle taunts.

> *You think those metal claws scare me.*
> *I'll clack my beak till you see three!*

The attacking owl almost stopped mid-flight. He was completely startled by this strange chant.

> *Your gizzard's soft as a worm*
> *I'm going to make you*
> *squirm, squirm squirm. . . .*

Twilight was filling the air with his hoarse, raucous rage. He was everywhere at once. He grabbed the mu shield they had been carrying and raised it just in time to catch a high blow from one of Metal Beak's claws. The battle claw raked through the soft metal of the shield but Twilight was protected nonetheless. The Great Gray Owl advanced. Soren, in the meantime, was dodging the battle claws of an angry-looking Sooty. But he was not sure how long he could keep this up. He could only dodge and fight defensively. He had nothing to attack with. Suddenly, a fiery spitting sound zinged through the forest. Had the red come come sizzling down to earth? Soren opened his eyes wide in sheer amazement. It was not the comet. It was Ruby with a burning coal in her mouth. *How did she find us?* And, unbelievably, Martin, his chaw buddy was close behind with a beakful of burning twigs. The odds were getting better. The sides more even with nine owls including Ezylryb from Ga'Hoole and ten followers of Metal Beak.

Ruby had ignited a branch of spruce and was flying with it in her talons, sweeping the air around her. There were still coals burning. Soren and Digger looked at each other and quickly grabbed whatever they could. They would attack. They could fight offensively and perhaps rout these owls. Otulissa joined in. In an instant, the air was whizzing with firebrands as the owls of the colliering chaw flew through the forest night. Gylfie and Eglantine kept the supply of firebrands coming as they dipped twigs and limbs into the coals. Soon, however, Gylfie and Eglantine discovered that they were not too small or too inexperienced to carry the slenderest of flaming striplings through the night to singe the underbellies of the enemy owls.

Deft and precise, the counterattack had begun in earnest. And all the time, Twilight's singsong gibes and jeers rang out through the forest, a jangling, blaring scornful taunt that distracted and struck fear into the Metal Beak's troops.

We got the fire, we got the punch,
we're gonna make you yarp your lunch.
One two three four five,
you're gonna wonder if you're alive.
Six seven eight nine ten,
you're as stupid as a big ole hen.
I can count forever and a day,
and maybe you better start to pray.

You call yourself pure,
the best owls in sight.
Well, you stink to high heaven,
and you ain't so bright.
You're stuck up as can be
and your gizzards can't handle milkberry tea.
You're no better than gull splat,
and even though you fly,
you're lower than a rat.

At that last verse, one of the Sooties was driven to such distraction that he flew straight into a burning branch that Ruby was holding. "Great Glaux!" the Short-eared Owl muttered. "I didn't have to even attack. He came right to me." The smell of singed feathers swirled in the air. Another one, who had been poked with a branch that had been ignited by a glowworm, flew off screaming.

But Metal Beak, undaunted, was advancing on Twilight in a rage that was deadly, his battle claws extended and glaring in the light of the flames. Ruby quickly slid in on Twilight's exposed flank, with her burning branch, and joined the battle against this large, horrifying owl. Soren and Otulissa advanced with flaming branches, slashing them like fiery swords at the other owls. One owl in Metal Beak's group went yeep and plunged to the ground. Immediately, Martin dropped a beakful of cinders on his flight feathers.

"I aimed for the eye," he breathlessly told Gylfie. "But I'm not nearly as good a marksman as Soren was with that bobcat."

"On your tail, Martin, watch it." A Sooty with claws extended raked out toward Martin's tail. With no thought of her personal safety, Gylfie dove into the heap of burning feathers of the owl who had gone yeep and came up with a wad in her mouth, trying to hold it just as she had seen the colliers hold the coals. Hurtling herself toward the owl that had attacked Martin, she spiraled upward and ignited his belly feathers. There was a terrific yowl and then the Sooty turned into an airborne burning missile on a wild trajectory. "Dodge! Eglantine!" Eglantine went into a lateral spiral, leaving a clear track for the missile that smashed headfirst into the trunk of a tree. The owl's battle claws had dropped off on the way. Soren swooped down and retrieved one. Otulissa the other.

"Together we might make a pair and do some damage!" Otulissa shouted to Soren.

"Twilight needs help! Get a burning branch." Eglantine flew up with a freshly ignited branch for Soren.

Otulissa had fearlessly flown ahead. *I've never flown with such big battle claws. Twilight should have these*, the thought raced through her head, but some instinct took over. She darted up and behind the huge owl, then plunged with the claws locked in the downward position and gave him a terrific blow. Metal Beak staggered mid-flight. He hadn't seen it coming, and now Soren flew up in a flanking maneuver and shoved the slender, burning stripling branch under the mask. He shoved harder and a great piece of the mask lifted and fell to the ground.

Soren blinked. He felt his heart stop, his gizzard turn to stone.

"Kludd!" The name boiled up from Soren's throat. His own brother now flew at him, his claws raised ready to rake out Soren's eyes.

"Surprise, little brother!" Soren dodged. His gizzard felt suddenly as if it was falling right out of him. Going yeep! Was he going yeep?

"He means to kill you, Soren!" It was Gylfie crying out, which brought him back to his senses. He dove for the still-burning branch. There was a thicker one beside it. He picked up that one instead and then, like a volcano spewing live embers that blistered the air, Soren rose to do battle with his brother. Extending his talons, one foot with the battle claw, the other with the fiery branch, he advanced on Kludd, who lurched forward in a feinting maneuver and then dove. Soren felt the air stir beneath him. Two seconds before, Kludd's battle claws would have raked his belly. Soren pivoted and flew straight up, an incredibly difficult maneuver but one that he executed perfectly. Kludd spun upward after him. But Soren could sense him before he saw him on his tail. Soren slowed his flight abruptly and plunged. Kludd overshot him, cursing all the while. Making a steeply banking turn to come back,

Kludd shouted down to Soren who was thirty feet or more below, "I'll get you!"

This was the hardest part. Soren had to hover — hover and not bolt and not go yeep! *Let him come, let him come. Steady, steady. Now!* Soren roared up underneath Kludd, holding the burning branch straight up. The embers landed on what little bit was left of the metal mask.

There was a deep grunt, followed by a quaking, horrendous scream. Then Ruby, Soren, and Twilight backed off and watched in a kind of hypnotic horror as the metal that had covered half the owl's face began to melt into a molten mass and spread across the entire face. Metal Beak's wings started to fold.

He's going yeep! Soren thought breathlessly. But then he blinked with disbelief as the owl, finding some extraordinary reserve of energy, raised his wings, twisted his head around, and opened the melting beak. "Death to the Impure. Long live Tytos supreme! Death to Soren! Turnfeather of the Pure, the true owls! Death to Soren!" The entire night seemed to sizzle with the words and then the enraged owl simply flew off into the night. Four owls were dead on the ground, the rest followed their leader, the Pure One with his beak still glowing red.

Suddenly, it was quiet. A singed feather drifted lazily

on a small night breeze. Soren perched on a branch. *My own brother. My very own brother is Metal Beak, and he wants to kill me. Kill me.* The forest, the world around him, seemed to dissolve. Soren felt as if he were alone in some weird space that was neither earth nor sky.

"Soren," Gylfie flew up and perched on the branch beside him. "Soren, you're going to be all right. Soren, he's crazy. It's what your mum's and da's scrooms were warning you about." Soren turned to the little Elf Owl. His eyes welled up with tears.

"But, Gylfie, there is still unfinished business on earth. He still lives. My parents' scrooms must still be far from glaumora."

"They're a little closer, Soren. They must be. They must be so proud of you. Look at what you have done."

Soren looked to a nearby branch on the same tree. All of his owls were safe, and there was Ezylryb perched on a lower branch with tears in his eyes as he looked at the young owls who had saved his life. But Soren was still seized by the terrible and overwhelming thoughts of Kludd. What Kludd had done to him and Eglantine, and what he, Soren, had done to Kludd. It was all simply too horrific to dwell on. So he turned his thoughts to something else — his best friend in the world, Gylfie. And she had just said that perhaps the scrooms of his parents were a little closer to glaumora. *Maybe, maybe,* he thought.

Soren looked down at Gylfie. How did she always know the right thing to say at the right time? But what about her own parents? Did she ever wonder if they were alive or dead? If they were scrooms between earth and glaumora?

"Gylfie," Soren said hesitantly. "Do you ever wonder about your parents?"

"Of course, Soren. But I think they're dead."

"But what if they aren't?"

"What do you mean?"

Soren was silent for a minute. He couldn't say what he really meant, for it was simply too selfish. If they were alive, it would mean that Gylfie would return to the Desert of Kuneer to live with them, and Soren didn't know if he could stand to lose the little Elf Owl.

"Oh, nothing," Soren answered and tried to make his voice sound light.

"Maybe someday we'll go to Kuneer and see. There's a spirit desert there, you know. If their scrooms are still around for unfinished business, that's where they would be."

"Yes, yes, I suppose so," Soren said quietly.

CHAPTER TWENTY-ONE

Good Light

Octavia slithered out on a limb of the great tree and scanned the sky. The night had grown thin, the black threadbare like a worn garment through which the first dim streaks of the morning would soon begin to glimmer. She had sensed that Soren and his little band would do something after she had discovered them in the secret chamber. Although she had not been born blind, she had grown to possess those extraordinary instincts and sensations of the other blind snakes. And now as Octavia slithered farther out onto the branch, she did sense something flying toward the tree. She coiled up and swung her head about. Something from far away was coming! Something was stirring the air. The vibrations seemed to ripple across her scales. Then she heard the lookout cry. "Owls two points north of east! Great Glaux! It's Ezylryb flying point! He's back! He's back!"

Tears began to stream from Octavia's sightless eyes. "He's coming back! He's coming back!" she whispered.

The Great Ga'Hoole tree began to shake with the sound of cheering owls. From every hollow, owls flew out — Snowies and Spotted Owls, Horned Owls and Great Grays, Elf and Pygmy Owls — to perch on the thousands of branches and cheer the return of the best of the best of the chaws and the greatest ryb of the great tree — Ezylryb.

As night faded into day, as Soren, Gylfie, Twilight, Eglantine, and Digger nestled into the down of their hollow, the clear music of the harp's strings began to slip through the branches of the great old tree. The voice of Madame Plonk so lovely, so eerily beautiful, as beautiful as the most distant stars, rose in the pale light. Soren heard the soft breathing of Eglantine beside him. He knew in a hollow high above theirs, Ezylryb was probably munching a caterpillar and perhaps, by the light of the fire in his grate, reading an old book. From the opening in their hollow, Soren could see the constellation of the Little Raccoon, its hind paw scratching the late autumn sky before it slipped off into another night in another world on another side of the earth. Madame Plonk's voice shimmered through the tree. Then he heard the loveliest liquid sound pour from the harp. It seemed to wrap them all in its music. He, of course, didn't know it but Octavia, old and fat as she was, had just jumped three octaves for the first time in years. She was so happy that she felt like a slim young thing again. She could almost see the notes as they floated out into the last darkness of the old night to touch the dawn.

"Good light," Soren said softly, and he said it seven times, for each of the owls he had led on their quest to mend a world that had been broken and to rescue a teacher who was loved.

"Good light," he said again. They were, however, all sound asleep.

In a hollow high up on the northwest side of the Great Ga'Hoole Tree, an old Whiskered Screech sat down at his writing table for the first time in months. He winced as he plucked a feather from his starboard wing. It always seemed that he grew his best quills on his starboard side for some reason. He then took out a new piece of his best writing parchment, dipped the quill into an inkwell, and began to write.

In a forest dark and tangled,
smoke and fiery sparks did spangle
the trees, the sky, the moon on high —
it seemed as if Glaux did sigh.

A Barn Owl with a metal face,
bellowed of his mighty race.
The chaw of chaws, did they cower
in what might be their final hour?
With their branches burning bright,
they tore into this evil night.
The flames danced across the mask —
a demon owl from Soren's past!

Nine others flanked him,
dark eyes so grim,
claws gleaming in the air,
set to rip, to stab, to tear.
So in that dark and tangled night,
the chaw of chaws rose to fight,
with talons bloodied, feathers singed.
A battle won — a war begins!

Ezylryb sighed deeply and put down his quill as the glare of the morning seeped into his hollow.

THE OWLS
and others
from

GUARDIANS *of* GA'HOOLE
The Rescue

SOREN: Barn Owl, *Tyto alba*, from the kingdom of the Forest of Tyto; snatched when he was three weeks old by St. Aegolius patrols; escaped from St. Aegolius Academy for Orphaned Owls

His family:
KLUDD: Barn Owl, *Tyto alba*, older brother
EGLANTINE: Barn Owl, *Tyto alba*, younger sister
NOCTUS: Barn Owl, *Tyto alba*, father
MARELLA: Barn Owl, *Tyto alba*, mother

His family's nest-maid:
MRS. PLITHIVER, blind snake

GYLFIE: Elf Owl, *Micrathene whitneyi*, from the desert kingdom of Kuneer; snatched when she was almost three weeks old by St. Aegolius patrols; escaped from St. Aegolius Academy for Orphaned Owls; Soren's best friend

TWILIGHT: Great Gray Owl, *Strix nebulosa*, free flier, orphaned within hours of hatching

DIGGER: Burrowing Owl, *Speotyto cunicularius*, from the desert kingdom of Kuneer; lost in the desert after an attack in which his brother was killed and eaten by owls from St. Aegolius

🪶 🪶 🪶

BORON: Snowy Owl, *Nyctea scandiaca*, the King of Hoole

BARRAN: Snowy Owl, *Nyctea scandiaca*, the Queen of Hoole

STRIX STRUMA: Spotted Owl, *Strix occidentalis*, the dignified navigation ryb (teacher) at the Great Ga'Hoole Tree

EZYLRYB: Whiskered Screech Owl, *Otus trichopsis*, the wise weather-interpretation and colliering ryb (teacher) at the Great Ga'Hoole Tree; Soren's mentor

POOT: Boreal Owl, *Aegolius funereus*, Ezylryb's assistant

MADAME PLONK: Snowy Owl, *Nyctea scandiaca,* the elegant singer of the Great Ga'Hoole Tree

OCTAVIA: Blind nest-maid snake for Madame Plonk and Ezylryb

DEWLAP: Burrowing Owl, *Speotyto cunicularius,* the Ga'Hoolology ryb at the Great Ga'Hoole Tree

BUBO: Great Horned Owl, *Bubo virginianus,* the blacksmith of the Great Ga'Hoole Tree

TRADER MAGS: Magpie, a traveling merchant

ß   ß   ß

OTULISSA: Spotted Owl, *Strix occidentalis,* a student of prestigious lineage at the Great Ga'Hoole Tree

PRIMROSE: Pygmy Owl, *Glaucidium californicum,* rescued from a forest fire and brought to the Great Ga'Hoole Tree the night of Soren's and his friends' arrival

MARTIN: Northern Saw-whet Owl, *Aegolius acadicus,* rescued and brought to the Great Ga'Hoole Tree the same night as Primrose; in Ezylryb's chaw with Soren

RUBY: Short-eared Owl, *Asio flammeus,* lost her family under mysterious circumstances and was brought. to the Great Ga'Hoole Tree; in Ezylryb's chaw with Soren

SILVER: Lesser Sooty Owl, *Tyto multipunctata,* brought to the Great Ga'Hoole Tree after being rescued in the Great Downing

NUT BEAM: Masked Owl, *Tyto novaehollandia,* brought to the Great Ga'Hoole Tree after being rescued in the Great Downing

☙ ☙ ☙

THE ROGUE SMITH OF SILVERVEIL: Snowy Owl, *Nyctea scandiaca,* a blacksmith not attached to any kingdom in the owl world

Kathryn Lasky has had a long fascination with owls. Several years ago, she began doing extensive research about these birds and their behaviors. She thought that she would someday write a nonfiction book about owls illustrated with photographs by her husband, Christopher Knight. She realized, though, that this would indeed be difficult since owls are shy, nocturnal creatures. So she decided to write a fantasy about a world of owls. Even though it is an imaginary world in which owls can speak, think, and dream, she wanted to include as much of their natural history as she could.

Kathryn Lasky has written many books, both fiction and nonfiction, including *Sugaring Time*, for which she won a Newbery Honor. Among her fiction books are *The Night Journey*, a winner of the National Jewish Book Award, and *Beyond the Burning Time*, an ALA Best Book for Young Adults, as well as the Daughters of the Sea and Wolves of the Beyond series. She has also received the Boston Globe-Horn Book Award and the Washington Post Children's Book Guild Award for her contribution to nonfiction.

Lasky and her husband live in Cambridge, Massachusetts.

A peek at
THE GUARDIANS *of* GA'HOOLE
Book Four: *The Siege*

The Brown Fish Owl looked up and blinked. The red comet had passed by for the last time nearly three months before. What could this glowing point in the sky be? It was hurtling toward the lake at an alarming speed. Great Glaux, it was screeching the most horrid, foulest oaths imaginable!

The Brown Fish Owl stepped farther out on the sycamore branch that extended over the lake. If this were not a Fish Owl, it would need rescuing. Most species of owls, save for Fish Owls and Eagle Owls, were completely helpless in the water. The Brown Fish Owl began to spread his wings and was ready to flap them quickly for a power takeoff. Within the sliver of a second before he heard the splash, he was off.

There was a sizzling sound as Kludd hit the water, and then there were wisps of steam. Simon, the Brown Fish Owl, had never seen anything like this — an owl glowing like a coal from a forest fire, plunging into the pond. Was it a collier owl? But colliers would know better. Remarkable as it seemed, a collier owl could do its work without ever getting burned. The Brown Fish Owl grabbed the mysterious owl with his talons just in time. But his gizzard went cold as he saw the owl's face — a mangled deformity of molten metal and feathers. What was this?

Well, better not worry now. At least it was alive, and as a pilgrim owl of the Glauxian Brothers of the Northern Kingdoms, Simon's duty was not to question, nor convert, nor preach, but simply to help, give solace, peace, and love. This owl seemed sorely in need of all. And this was precisely why the brothers took seasons away from their retreat and study; to go out into the world and fulfill their sacred obligation. The Brother Superior often said, "To study too much in retreat can become an inexcusable indulgence. It behooves us to share what we have learned, to practice in administering to others what we have gathered from our experience with books."

This was Pilgrim Simon's first season of pilgrimming

and this seemed to be his first big challenge. The burned owl would need tending. No doubt about it. Restoring fallen owlets to nests, making peace between warring factions of crows — the Glauxian Brothers were among the few owls who could speak sense to crows — all that was nothing compared to this. It would take all of Simon's medicinal and herbal knowledge to fix up this poor owl.

"Easy there, easy there, fellow," Simon spoke in a low soothing voice as he helped the wounded owl into the hollow of the sycamore. "We're going to fix you up just fine." This was when Simon could have used a nest-maid snake or two. What a luxury they had been back at the retreat in the Northern Kingdoms. But here the pilgrims were charged to live simply. To avail themselves of the blind snakes that tended so many owls' nests, keeping them free of vermin, was not deemed appropriate for the pilgrim owls who were dedicated to service. They had been instructed to live as sparely as possible. Simon would have to go out and dig the medicinal worms himself. Leeches were the best for healing these kinds of wounds, and being a Fish Owl, he was fairly adept at leech gathering.

As soon as Simon had Kludd arranged in the hollow on a soft bed made of down plucked from his own breast and a combination of mosses, he set out to gather the leeches. As he flew to a corner of the lake that was rich with leeches, he reflected on how this owl, which might be a Barn Owl, had fought when he had tried to preen him. This was very odd. He had never known an owl who had resisted being preened. This owl's feathers were a dirty, tangled mess. That he could have flown at all was amazing. Smooth flight depended on smooth feathers. On every flight feather there were tiny almost invisible hooks, or barbules, that locked together to produce an even surface over which the air could glide. This owl's barbules had become unhooked in the worst way. They needed to be lined up and smoothed out again. But when Simon had first tried, the owl had pulled away. Odd, very odd.

Simon returned in a short while with a beakful of leeches and began placing them around the curled edges of the strange metal mask that had melted over most of the owl's face. He didn't dare try to remove it. Upon closer examination, Simon was sure that this was a Barn Owl, an exceptionally large one at that. With patches of soaked moss, he squeezed drops of water into the owl's beak. Occasionally, the owl's eyes would flutter open, but he was clearly delirious. In this state he spewed a nearly constant stream of curses laced with tirades of vengeance and death addressed to some creature he called Soren.

Day and night Simon treated the strange Barn Owl, changing the leeches, squeezing drops of water beneath the twisted piece of metal that was where a beak must once have been. The owl's agitation calmed; the rancorous curses fewer — most thankfully, for the Brothers of Glaux were a gentle order who eschewed fighting. For two days the Barn Owl had slept long uninterrupted stretches, and now on the third day, his eyes blinked open. Simon could tell that he was fully conscious at last. But the first words out of that metallic beak shocked the pilgrim Brown Fish Owl almost as much as the curses had. "You are not a Pure One."

A Pure One? What in the name of Glaux is this owl talking about? "Forgive me, but I am afraid I do not understand what you are talking about," said Simon.

Kludd blinked. *He should be afraid.* "Never mind. I suppose I must thank you."

"Oh, don't suppose anything. You need not thank me. I am a pilgrim. I am merely doing my Glauxian duty."

"Duty to what?"

"Duty to our species."

"You are not of my species!" Kludd barked with a ferocity that shocked the Fish Owl. "I am a Barn Owl, Tyto alba. You are" — Kludd seemed to sniff — "judging from your stink, a Fish Owl — not my species."

"Well, I was speaking generally, of course. My Glauxian duty extends to all owlkind."

Kludd responded with a low, growlish hoot and shut his eyes.

"I'll leave you now," said Simon.

"If you're going hunting, I would prefer red meat to fish — vole, to be precise."

"Yes, yes. I'll do my best. I'm sure you'll be feeling better as soon as I get you some meat."

Kludd glared at the Brown Fish Owl. *You can be sure of nothing with me. Glaux, what an ugly owl — flattish head, muddled color, not quite brown, not quite gray or white. Miserable little ear tufts. It doesn't get much uglier than a Brown Fish Owl, that's for sure.*

Kludd, however, thought he had heard of these pilgrim-type owls. Might as well learn a bit more. "So you say you're a pilgrim. Where are you from?"

Simon was delighted that the Barn Owl was taking any notice at all. "The Northern Kingdoms."

This interested Kludd. He had heard of the Northern Kingdoms. That was where the ancient and brilliant owl Ezylryb, whom he had almost captured, had come from. It was because of Ezylryb that he had nearly died in this last battle. "I thought the Northern Kingdoms were known for their warriors, not pilgrims."

"Owls of the Northern Kingdoms are very fierce, but

one can be fierce in love and in peace as well as in hatred and in battle."

Glaux, this owl frinked him off. Made him want to yarp a dozen pellets right in his ugly face. "I see," Kludd said. But of course he didn't see at all. Still, sometimes diplomacy was necessary. And this was what Kludd considered a diplomatic response to an owl that made his gizzard turn green.

"Well, why don't you fly off and get me some good red meat, nice and furry, good bones — my gizzard needs something to grind." *And I need time to think.*

The Northern Kingdoms! The mere mention of them by the disgusting Brown Fish Owl had set Kludd's mind ablaze. He had to plan carefully now. The capture of the old Whiskered Screech Ezylryb had failed miserably. Of course, one hardly could have called it a great scheme. No, the great scheme had been to build a force large enough to lay siege to St. Aegolius Academy for Orphaned Owls, better known as St. Aggie's. The academy had been snatching owlets for years and training them to mine flecks, among other things. With flecks, one could create weapons of unbelievable power. Not simply weapons that killed, but weapons that could warp the minds of owls. St. Aggie's had the largest known supply of flecks. But the owls of St. Aggie's didn't know what to do with them. Still, ignorant as they were, they had found the stronghold of the Pure Ones in the castle ruins and tried to make off with the owlets that Kludd and scores of Tytos had captured. The Pure Ones, of course, fought back to recover what was, in their minds, rightfully theirs. This resulted in the Great Downing. Scores of baby owls dropped while the two powerful and lawless forces battled it out. And it was the Great Downing that had alerted the owl world — in particular, those noble owls, known as the Guardians of Ga'Hoole, who rose in the darkness of the night from the Great Ga'Hoole Tree — that there was something out there more fearful than St. Aggie's.

Before the Great Downing, the organization of the Pure Ones had been secret, and this state afforded them valuable time and opportunity to build their forces and develop their strategies. The Great Downing had brought the Ga'Hoolian owls out in full force. And, most significantly, it had brought out the legendary warrior from the Northern Kingdoms, known there as Lyze of Kiel and now in the Southern Kingdoms as Ezylryb. But it was not Lyze of Kiel the warrior who had interested Kludd. It was Ezylryb the scholar. It was said that this owl had the deepest knowledge of everything — from weather, to fire, to the very elements of life and the earth. And this owl best understood the lurking powers of the flecks.

So when the Pure Ones had lost the owlets, their source for new owl power, Kludd had abruptly decided to change tactics. The capture of one owl like Ezylryb would be worth more than one hundred baby owls. The only way he could think of capturing the old one was through a Devil's Triangle. By placing three bags of flecks in three different trees to form a triangle, Kludd had laid a trap that had ensnared the old Whiskered Screech by causing massive disruptions to his powers of navigation. The flecks set up a magnetic field. That this field had been broken was not only unexpected, but disastrous. And it had been broken. Other owls had come to Ezylryb's rescue. They had snapped the power of this field as if it had been no more than a brittle twig. Higher magnetics! Ezylryb knew these dark sciences. And that was why Kludd had wanted him.

There had been a fierce battle with the owls who had come to rescue Ezylryb. Much to Kludd's horror, one of them had been his own baby brother, Soren, whom he had pushed out of the family's nest when Soren was an owlet too young to fly. At the time, Kludd thought that he had been delivering up his younger brother to the Grand Tyto Most Pure, for that had been the requirement — to sacrifice a family member and thus assure one's own admission to the highest ranks of the Pure Ones. But something had gone wrong. St. Aggie's had shown up and taken his brother. Now this very brother had nearly killed him. And not only had the Pure Ones had their new recruits stolen from them, not only had they lost Ezylryb, but their stronghold had been discovered. They needed to find a new place to roost, a headquarters from which to plan their war for supremacy.

Well, no need to think about all that now. There were other more important matters — like higher magnetics. *All this time,* Kludd thought, *I have dreamed of flecks, of controlling the owl universe and making it pure. I have dreamed of conquering St. Aggie's, with its great reservoirs of flecks and its thousands of owls to mine them. And then I dreamed of capturing Ezylryb. But now I know what I must do. I must lay siege to the great tree on the Island of Hoole, in the middle of the Sea of Hoolemere. Yes, the Great Ga'Hoole Tree must be ours, with its secrets of fire and magnetics, with its warriors and its scholars, it must be ours. I shall bide my time. I shall gain my strength. I shall find my scattered army and then we shall rise — rise a thousand times more powerful than we ever were, against the Guardians of Ga'Hoole.*

"A nice plump vole for you, sir. Strong bones and plenty of fur. Its winter pelt is fully grown. That should set your gizzard grinding just fine." The Brown Fish Owl pilgrim had just returned.

Yes, and so will you, pilgrim. For Kludd had decided that upon regaining his strength, he would kill this owl immediately. His own survival must remain a secret for some time if all his plans were to work. Yes, by tomorrow with the vole's bones like grist in his gizzard, he would be ready to kill the stinking Brown Fish Owl. Kludd, like the best of killers, was patient.

DELVE INTO THE UNSUNG HISTORIES OF THE
GREAT GA'HOOLE TREE AND ITS HEROES!

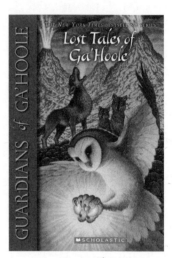

A Guide Book
to the Great Tree

Lost Tales of
Ga'Hoole

Out past the reach
of the Ga'Hoole Tree,
where survival is the
only law, live the
Wolves of the Beyond.

New from Kathryn Lasky

WOLVES OF THE BEYOND

the harsh wilderness beyond
Ga'Hoole, a wolf mother hides in
fear. Her newborn pup has a twisted
paw. The mother knows the rigid
rules of her kind. The pack cannot
have weakness. Her pup must be
abandoned—condemned to die. But
the pup, Faolan, does the unthinkable.
He survives. This is his story—the story
of a wolf pup who rises up to change
forever the Wolves of the Beyond.

www.scholastic.com

WOLVES

With the blizzard blowing so ferociously it was difficult to discern what time of day or night it was. The entire world had dissolved into an impenetrable whiteness. But Faolan made his way back to the den. He was shocked to find it empty. Had Thunderheart gone deeper into the tunnels when the blizzard started? He explored briefly but he knew her scent, and there was no sign of her. He began to pace. He tried to imagine what might have happened to her or where she could have gone. He had picked up no scent on his own journey back to the den. It seemed as if she had simply vanished. *She wouldn't have left me. . . . No, never. She would never just leave me.* The very thought sent a tremor through Faolan until the hackles on his neck and every guard hair on his back stood straight up. It reminded him of something,

something that had happened long, long ago that he couldn't quite remember. She would come back, he reasoned. She had to!

He waited all that night and into the next day. He paid no heed to the grumbles of his empty stomach. Food meant nothing to him. There was only one thing he wanted: Thunderheart. The den was too quiet. The beat of her enormous heart, even in its slow winter rhythms, was gone. He could not live without the sound. It was all he knew, all he had ever known. He stepped out of the den into the rage of the blizzard and began howling. Howling for the great grizzly. Howling for all he had ever known and loved.

Then as he howled, an odd tremor rose through the depths of the snow, from the frozen land beneath it, from the very center of the earth. The tremblings were like faint quivers, but Faolan pressed his splayed front paw deep and these tremulous shakings became quite distinct. And then more incredibly powerful. For a moment, it felt as if the entire snowfield had shifted under his paws, and in the distance, he saw the frozen waterfall crack and suddenly gush to life.

But in that second he thought of death. And he knew with an overpowering certainty that something terrible was happening to his beloved Thunderheart.